HOT <u>AND</u>
BOTHERED

HOT AND BOTHERED

•

Lori Foster

Laura Bradley

Gayle Callen

Victoria Marquez

St. Martin's Paperbacks

For information address St. Martin's Press, 175 Fifth Avenue, New York, NY 10010.

ISBN: 0-312-97968-1
EAN: 80312-97968-3

Printed in the United States of America

St. Martin's Paperbacks edition / July 2001

St. Martin's Paperbacks are published by St. Martin's Press, 175 Fifth Avenue, New York, NY 10010.

10 9 8 7 6

CONTENTS

LURING LUCY

·

Lori Foster

To Kay Johnson, a very respected friend who's also a wonderful mother, a giving person who's loads of fun— and a reader besides! Thanks, Kay!

CHAPTER 1

Sweltering air, humid and thick, tugged at his hair and blew over his bared skin as he accelerated the car to seventy-five. He'd left the top of his Mustang down, knowing he'd need the exposure to the hot wind and the faded blue sky to counteract his increasingly volatile mood.

The sun was a broiling white ball, reflecting off the hoods and windshields of passing vehicles, making the blacktop waver and swim from the heat. There wasn't a cloud in sight along the endless stretch of I-75, promising nothing but more scorching heat. But the heat of the day was nothing compared to the fire pulsing under his skin, demanding release. Anger. Urgency. *Lust.*

Bram Giles gritted his teeth, and his knuckles turned white as his fingers curled and clenched around the steering wheel. He thought of how the night would end, how he'd make it end, and the turbulent thoughts made his lust expand. No matter what, he wouldn't let her run from him tonight. He'd been too patient too long and now she had some harebrained idea of indulging in a summer fling. *With someone else.*

Bram took the exit from the highway on squealing tires and turned left, heading toward the lake community and the woman who had driven him crazy for more years than any man should suffer. By the time he'd realized what she was up to, when that carnal look in her eyes and the way she'd held her lithe little body had finally registered, she'd already gotten a two-hour head start on him. It had taken Bram another frustration-filled hour to throw together some clothes, rearrange his schedule and his plans, and get on the road.

That one hour had felt like a lifetime.

Was she flirting even now, trying to pick up the first

boater who went by? Had she met someone in town on her way to the lake? Maybe she'd even brought someone along with her, guaranteeing her success.

Whoever it was would be swiftly booted out.

Bram's foot pressed harder on the gas, speeding the car along until he hit the narrower gravel road that led to her summer house. She hadn't been to that house in four years, not since she'd caught her husband, David, there with another woman. Bram's stomach tightened with pain.

David was an idiot, now a dead idiot.

Jesus, Bram still missed him; they'd been best friends who were also like brothers.

But more than that, more than anything else in the world, he wanted David's widow. Bram had always wanted her. He had taught himself to live with the clawing desire, to push his needs deep down into his soul so no one else would ever know. But now she was free and obviously over her grief. Now she was ready.

Tonight he would have her.

The winding turns on the old country road forced Bram to slow the Mustang, but it did nothing to slow his thoughts. Sweat trickled down the middle of his chest and stuck his hair to the back of his neck. Was she eyeballing some guy right now? Was she making plans? Handing out come-ons?

Bram wiped the sweat from his brow and cursed. Once he got to the summer house, he'd jump into the crisply cold water of the lake to cool off—*after* he'd set Lucy straight on how things were going to be between them from now on.

She wouldn't like it.

He wasn't giving her a choice.

By the time Bram slipped the Mustang into the sloping drive cut out of the side of the hill behind the house, he almost had himself under control. The road was the highest point on her property, with the land dropping downward toward the lake and the house built in between. The house faced the lake with patio doors and a long, wide deck, while the back butted into the hill, surrounded by mature trees. It was because of the higher vantage point of the road that Bram saw her immediately.

His temper kicked into overdrive at the same time that his lust nearly consumed him.

Lust always rose to the surface when he got near Lucy. As he looked her over from top to toes, Bram cursed softly under his breath. At thirty-nine, Lucy was one sexy-as-sin woman, all lush curves and mature angles. Never before had he seen her put those assets on display.

Today, she was most definitely flaunting her wares. *For another man.*

He drew a deep breath and concentrated on not being a brute, on *not* storming down the hill and terrorizing both Lucy and the guy ogling her by letting his temper loose. It wasn't easy, not with her looking like that.

A sexy little pair of cutoffs, unlike the longer, more staid walking shorts she generally favored at home, hugged her rounded ass like a lover and left a long length of lightly tanned thighs exposed to the casual viewer. Her silky dark hair hung loose to her shoulders, playfully teased by a soft hot breeze, and her bare feet nestled in the thick summer grass.

Worse that that—or better, depending on your point of view—she had on a cream-colored halter top that left her back bare and had the young worker she spoke with fidgeting with lecherous interest. The worker kept looking at her chest, and Bram had the horrible suspicion that her nipples could be seen through the soft material.

A haze of red clouded Bram's vision and he slammed his car door hard, deliberately alerting them to his presence. Both Lucy and the worker, unaware of him until that moment, turned to look up the hill. Lucy shaded her eyes with a slim hand, but the worker took two steps back, obviously seeing the fury on Bram's face despite the mirrored sunglasses still covering his eyes.

Good.

If the guy had any sense at all he'd have already abandoned the mower and headed for his service truck.

Lucy started up the hill, her brow pulled into a worried frown. Bram saw that her nipples were, in fact, puckered against the material and quite noticeable. Every muscle in his body tensed in reaction.

"Bram? What's wrong?" Then with a touch of panic: "Did something happen to the kids? Are they all right?"

Her anxiety smote him hard. Damn, he hadn't meant to scare her; she was a mother first and foremost—which was one of the most appealing things about her. Ignoring the nervous worker as he headed straight toward Lucy, Bram rumbled, "The kids are fine, Lucy. They're at Marcy's."

Her gaze skipped over him, from his athletic shoes up his bare legs to his wrinkled shorts to his sweat-dampened T-shirt with the sleeves cut off. "But I thought you were taking them camping."

Bram had thought that was the plan, too. As an honorary uncle to David and Lucy's two teenage children and as David's best friend, he'd filled the bill of doting uncle rather nicely. The kids loved him, and he loved them—just like they were his own. They'd willingly agreed to accept Marcy as the provider for the next week when he'd told them something vitally important had come up. At fourteen and sixteen, they didn't need a babysitter, but Lucy insisted that an adult be available in case of an emergency.

Bram took his responsibilities to the kids seriously and had made certain they were settled securely before he'd been able to leave.

He hadn't told Karyn or Kent why he had to renege on their camping trip, but he could tell by the look on Marcy's face that she understood. She was Lucy's best friend, the only one who hadn't gossiped about her during the divorce and the horrible scenes that David had caused. Oh yeah, Marcy knew that Bram wanted Lucy. The woman wasn't blind.

Not that Bram minded. Soon everyone in Lucy's

neighborhood and his own would know that he was staking a claim, and to hell with any gossip that might ensue.

Lucy glanced nervously at the worker as Bram descended on them. She was confused by his appearance and probably disheartened to have her illicit tryst interrupted. The little darling had been on the make, and she'd apparently already picked out a conquest.

Bram wanted to take the younger man apart but couldn't really blame him for his interest. He knew any male in his midtwenties, which this guy looked to be, was likely to have been interested. He couldn't go around destroying every guy who looked at her, especially if she started issuing invitations. What he had to do was give Lucy a new target for her erotic curiosity. *Himself.*

Bram didn't slow in his pace and stalked right up to Lucy until he stood mere inches in front of her. Her long dark lashes left feathery shadows on her smooth sun-kissed cheeks, and her full mouth was parted slightly. Her eyes, so clear and bright a blue they put the sky to shame, watched him warily.

Bram could detect the subtle salty scent of her warmed skin and hair. A very light sheen of perspiration glowed on her upper chest and in the cleavage she had clearly on display. Her honey-colored shoulders glowed, too, as did her supple thighs.

Bram felt his own flesh heating with sweat, and it had a lot more to do with the proximity of his woman than it did with the unrelenting sun.

"Bram?" Her voice emerged as a breathless whisper, uncertain, a tiny bit frightened. And, if he didn't miss his guess, tinged with sudden awareness of him as a man. "Why are you here? What's going on?"

Showing his teeth in what Bram hoped looked more like a grin than a warning, he growled, "Because I missed you, of course." Then taking her totally by surprise he caught her arms above her elbows, lifted her to her toes— and kissed her the way he'd been wanting to kiss her for a very long time.

Her parted lips gave him the advantage, letting his tongue slip in deep to taste the sweet hot recesses of her mouth and move lazily along her own tongue. Lust boiled inside him, savage and hungry—and it was just a kiss.

Bram could only imagine how intense it would feel when it was his cock sliding into her tender body, when her legs wrapped tight around his waist and he could fill his hands with her breasts, her luscious ass. He nearly groaned with the thought, imagining her hot and wet, thinking how tight she'd be after four long years of abstinence. . . . His testicles tightened and he did groan, low and raw.

Lucy was obviously stunned by his primal display, but the worker got the message loud and clear—just as Bram had intended.

Lucy held her breath, amazed and embarrassed. She felt caught in a whirlwind, naked and on display, and she didn't understand.

Bram was a friend, practically a member of the family. He'd never touched her sexually before, but wow—he was touching her now!

Ignoring Bram's kiss was out of the question. It wasn't the first time he'd ever kissed her, but the others had all been brotherly pecks and in laughing friendship. Never like this. Never so . . . carnal.

This was a kiss of possession, a kiss of incredible passion. She'd never experienced anything like it, even through fifteen years of marriage, and her heart did two wild flips before settling into a frantic rhythm of panic, excitement, and, amazingly enough, response.

Lucy flattened one hand on Bram's chest, wanting to push him away but using it for balance instead. The damp cotton of his shirt did nothing to shield his hot masculine flesh. He felt blistering hot and wonderfully solid against her palm. She realized he was coiled tightly, his muscles iron-hard and straining, his heartbeat thumping in a fast gallop that mirrored her own.

The young worker whom she'd specifically hired because he'd flirted with her cleared his throat loudly. Bram ignored him, which left her no option but to do the same.

All too aware of the heat of Bram's mouth, his delicious taste, and the overwhelming strength in his muscled body, Lucy tried to protest. All that emerged was a small sound, barely audible, a mere whimper that could have been interpreted any number of ways.

Abruptly Bram released her. Her lips felt swollen and wet, her body both tight and too soft. She would have fallen down the hill and tumbled into the lake if Bram hadn't reached back out for her, throwing one bare, heavily muscled arm around her shoulders and literally anchoring her to his side. Caught in the cage of his body, Lucy felt small and defenseless, and strangely enough, that feeling stirred others, rousing emotions she hadn't dealt with in far too long. Female to male, soft to hard.

The idea of flirting with a stranger had titillated her senses. Bram's kiss had gone far beyond that. She felt as if she'd been torched.

Her brain may have turned to mush, but her body was working on full alert.

Lucy shook her head, attempting to regain control so she could figure out just what it was Bram was doing. Why had he kissed her? Did he think to somehow warn off the worker by intimating a nonexistent involvement? To protect her virtue?

Ha. Bram couldn't know that she wanted the indiscriminate fling. She wanted to *feel* again, to be alive as a woman, as a sexual being—and then she'd sell the summer house and get over the past, burying all the hurt once and for all.

The worker looked at her nervously, as if asking for instructions. The difference between Bram and the young man she'd hired was like the difference between an impressive oak and a new sapling. The younger man was rangy with muscles, lean and toned. But Bram was solid and thick with layered muscle, large and in his prime.

Overwhelming. He exuded sheer masculinity and iron will.

Lucy wanted to fan her face, still reeling from that kiss. She used to wonder what it'd be like to be kissed by the infamous Bram Giles. Shortly into her marriage, when David had lost interest with teasing and nuzzling and foreplay, she'd thought of all she knew of Bram, how the women sang his praises and his own testament—by word and deed—to loving sex and females. She'd always thought that sex with Bram would be something almost too delicious to bear.

Now she knew what it was like to have his mouth, and she doubted she'd ever sleep peacefully again. His kiss alone had been more sexual than anything she'd experienced in half a decade.

What did that kiss mean?

Bram turned his head toward her, but with his reflective sunglasses on she couldn't even begin to read his expression. A little embarrassed, she hoped he didn't see her reaction, that he wouldn't know his tactic to warn off other men in a half-baked plan to protect her had actually turned her on. He was so cavalier about sex and intimacy, accepting it as a natural, healthy part of his life. After her marriage, he probably assumed she was, too.

He'd have been far from the mark on that one.

Lucy held her breath until Bram again looked away. With his free hand, Bram dug into his pocket, pulled out two twenty-dollar bills, and handed them to the young stud she'd hired to tend her lawn—with hopes for more.

"Get lost," Bram ordered in a low rasp, and the worker, after snatching up the money, fled.

"Bram," she protested, looking around at the yard with only half the work done, "he hadn't finished."

"He was finished, all right." She couldn't see his eyes, but she read his fierce expression all the same.

Lucy lost her temper. Oh, he'd thrown her with that kiss, but she was squarely on her feet now. And he'd just chased off her most promising prospect.

If Bram had some macho notion of looking after her, keeping her *pure*, she'd just have to help him rethink it. For this one week, for one time in her life, she didn't want to be pure. She wanted—*needed*—to feel the burning satisfaction of lust one more time.

"Are you nuts?" Lucy demanded in a warning growl. "Just what the hell do you think you're doing, Bram?"

Bram stared out over the diamond surface of the lake. It shone with twinkling sunlight and the occasional ripples from a fish. During the week, the tourism was thankfully low, leaving the area quiet and serene for those who owned lakefront property. On the weekends, though, it got downright rowdy, boats and water-skiers and Jet Skis everywhere.

For now, Bram thought, watching the worker drive away in a cloud of spewing gravel and dust, he had Lucy all to himself. She could rant and rave as much as she wanted, but there would be no one to hear.

Without bothering to explain his intentions, Bram scooped her up into his arms and headed for the house. His body relished the feel of her, her gentle weight. Damn, it felt good to finally hold her, to have her in his arms where she belonged.

Lucy gasped so hard she choked, and when she was finally able to pull in a wheezing breath he was already on the steps leading to the deck. She smacked him hard on the side of the head. *"What . . . is . . . the . . . matter . . . with . . . you?"*

He kissed her again. He wanted to keep kissing her, everywhere, all over her delectable body, but he knew they'd both end up rolling down the hill if he didn't give appropriate attention to where he stepped. "I have something to explain to you, woman, and it's best done in private just in case there's anyone fishing on the lake who might hear you yelling."

"Why," she asked loudly, "would I *yell*?"

"You're yelling now," he pointed out, thinking he sounded most reasonable.

She started to club him again, so Bram squeezed her tighter. Lucy generally wasn't a violent woman. Of course, she usually wasn't on the make, either. "None of that," Bram told her, trying to contain his satisfaction. "I can't very well explain if you knock me silly."

"You can explain no matter what, starting right now!"

The bare flesh of her soft thighs draped over his hard forearm was a torturous temptation for Bram. He wanted to feel the silky skin of her inner thighs on his jaw, his mouth, his hips as he drove into her.

Her breasts, more bared than not, felt so plump and full against his chest. He thought about pressing his face into her cleavage, tasting her pointed nipples through the cloth until she squirmed.

And her mouth—*hell yes, her mouth.* Set in outraged, mulish lines, it made it hard to concentrate on what he was doing.

The second he stepped across the sprawling deck and through the tinted patio doors, Lucy wiggled free. Bram let her go, but not far. Her feet were barely touching the hardwood floors and she was still against his body, where she belonged, when he said bluntly, "I want you."

Lucy pulled back. Her clear blue eyes were wide, her lips parted. She went alternately pale, then flushed.

The need to kiss her again was a clawing ache.

Bram touched her cheek, needing the contact, but she flinched away. "I want you, Lucy," he said again, harder this time to make sure there was no mistake, no misunderstanding. "I've wanted you for a helluva long time."

She shook her head, either denying him or not believing him.

It didn't matter which to Bram, because neither one was acceptable. He fully intended to have his way. "Yes. And I'll be damned if I'll sit back now and watch you indulge in some sort of prurient idiocy."

Her face went blank with shock, then burned with mortification. "Dear God," she rasped, sounding appalled, "what . . . what are you talking about?"

Bram straightened to his full height. At six feet, four inches tall, he stood a good foot above Lucy. She didn't look the least intimidated.

Bram frowned. "Don't bother to deny it, Lucy. You came here to get laid."

Guilt flashed over her features before she sputtered, "That's utter nonsense."

Leaning down close to her, Bram met her nose-to-nose. "Oh no you don't, sweetheart. In general, I know women too well to be fooled, and specifically, I know you as well as I know myself. The second you told me you were coming to the lake, I knew what you were up to."

She didn't want to believe him. "You can't possibly—"

"The hell I can't. This is where David cheated on you; this is where you want to get even."

Crossing her slender arms around herself, Lucy turned away. "David is dead. I can't *get even*."

"In your mind, you can." Bram stepped up to her back and slipped his own arms over hers. He wanted to comfort her, console her. He wanted her digging her nails into his back as he gave her a mind-blowing orgasm. Hands, mouth, penis, he didn't care how he accomplished it; he just wanted it to happen.

"He ruined your marriage by fooling around here, in the family vacation home. A place where you brought the kids, a place you used to love."

In a small voice, she said, "I still love it."

"You haven't been here since, not in four long years. But now you're here, looking incredibly sexy—"

"What?" She tried to twist to see him, but he held her still.

"—and eyeballing a guy who, if I don't miss my guess, is close to the age of that girl you caught here in bed with David. That sounds like getting even to me."

She gave a self-conscious laugh. "Funny. To me, it sounds like a woman who's desperately horny."

Shaking with the possibility of that, Bram gentled his hold, stroking her arms, bringing his groin in closer to her lush ass. Though he had a damn good guess, he still asked, "How long has it been for you, baby?"

She stiffened, but Bram secured his hold, refusing to let her sidle away.

"Don't be embarrassed with me, Lucy," he urged. "We've known each other too long for that. We're friends." And he wanted them to be lovers. He wanted all of her, every way that he could take her.

"If you're asking how long I've been without a man," she replied stiffly, "it's really none of your business."

Bram rocked her. "I'm guessing it's been over four years. You and David were a little on the rocks even before he blew it." He pressed his mouth to her temple in a reassuring kiss. "Am I right?"

He felt her tremble, heard the shuddering breath she drew in. "Bram, don't."

He ruthlessly ignored the pleading in her tone. It was his damned sympathy, his misplaced understanding, that had led her here today with plans to crawl under another man. He wouldn't make the same mistake again. "Four years, Lucy. A short lifetime to go without letting another man get close."

She yanked herself away from his hold and whirled to face him. "What was I supposed to do, Bram? Pick up a guy in the grocery store? At the school? Being a mother to two kids, the president of the PTA, and already the object of scandal made it just a little bit tough to go looking for sex, didn't it?"

For about the hundredth time Bram wished he'd beaten the hell out of David before he died. "No one has ever blamed you, Lucy."

"Bull!"

"David was responsible for his own actions." Sadness welled inside him, but he shook it off. "He was the only one responsible for his death."

"I guess you never heard the neighbors whispering. They think I'm coldhearted, that during one of David's crying jags I should have taken him back."

Bram shook his head. "He was a partier. And it had come close to happening before that." David had slowly grown out of his marriage and had begun flirting, testing the waters. He'd been on the prowl long before he'd gotten lucky. *Or unlucky,* as Bram saw it, thinking of all he'd lost.

"I know," Lucy whispered. "He ogled women everywhere we went." She cast Bram a narrow-eyed glance. "And he envied you."

Bram gently shook her. He couldn't, wouldn't, let her draw a comparison or blame him in any way. She had no idea of the lengths a man would go when the woman he wanted was married to someone else.

"A man who cheats is a cheater," Bram told her, determined to at least ease any ridiculous guilt she might feel. "If it happened once, there's no guarantee it wouldn't have happened again. You can't blame yourself for not liking the odds."

And, Bram thought savagely, a man who cheated on Lucy didn't deserve a second chance. He'd loved David as a friend, but he'd known all along that David wouldn't make her happy. Too many times, David had told him that he resented the restrictions of marriage.

And time and again, Bram had told him what a lucky bastard he was.

Tiredly, as if she'd rehashed the story too many times, Lucy said, "I kicked him out, he went on a two-year drunken spree, and he died in a damn car wreck because of it. *I blame myself.*"

Bram wanted to shake her again. "Lucy," he said, chastising. "You're too smart for that, honey. And too realistic to think you had control over David. He chose his own way, then regretted it. No one made him cheat; no one made him ignore you or the kids. And no one made him drink too much or drive too fast."

He squeezed her shoulders and said quietly, "I know the past few years have been ugly."

Her blue eyes lifted to his face. "You made it easier.

You've been such a help, with the kids, with everything."

Bram shrugged. "The kids are important to me, you know that. I love being with them."

"And they love being with you."

That hurt, too, because he wished they were his own, not David's. Bram loved them like his own. He shook his head. "It's time for you to get on with your life, Lucy."

She ran a hand through her hair, and her bangs ruffled back into place, a little mussed, a lot sexy. Indicating the summer house, which she'd had freshly cleaned and aired, she said, "That's what I was planning to do."

Bram realized that a hard-on was totally inappropriate to the moment, but he'd long since lost his control around Lucy Vaughn. And now, knowing it was only a matter of time until he could get inside her, his body rioted with need.

He held her gaze and whispered, "Good. Now you can plan on me taking part, too."

CHAPTER 2

The air-conditioning kicked on, activated by the open patio doors. He hadn't felt the heat building inside the house, but then, he was so hot himself, it'd take a lot for the external air to catch up to his body temperature. Lucy made a face and stepped back out to the deck.

Watching her, Bram took two deep breaths, concentrated on relaxing his knotted muscles, then followed her out. She stood at the rail, her hands clasped on it at either side of her waist, staring at the lake. The sunshine made tendrils of her dark hair look almost blue; around her temples, her hair was damp, clinging to her skin. The frayed hem of her shorts teased just below the rounded cheeks of her sweet behind, making his fingers twitch with the need to touch her. He'd always thought Lucy had a world-class ass, not skinny and narrow, like so many of the women he knew, but full and soft. He could spend hours just cuddling that bottom, kissing and stroking.

Through the years and two pregnancies, she'd picked up weight in her bottom and in her legs. He'd heard her laughingly complain about it and always reassured her that she had nothing to worry about. Lucy had never known how serious he was.

To him, she was so sexy it hurt just to look at her.

She was rightfully confused now, Bram knew, but he didn't know how to make things clearer to her except to be brutally honest and up-front.

He slid the glass door closed.

"You were his friend," she said, not looking at him but knowing he'd followed her out. "His best friend."

Bram replied quietly, "I loved David like a brother. That doesn't make what he did right."

"He told me once that . . ." Her voice broke and she

hesitated, then cleared her throat. "He told me you felt sorry for him."

Bram went to her side and leaned back on the railing. He could see her face but made a point of not looking directly at her. Though he knew David had probably slanted that sentiment, making it sound like he blamed Lucy, Bram admitted, "I did."

She jerked as if he'd struck her, then gave a humorless laugh. "Well, you weren't alone. Everyone felt sorry for him. But what about me? I was the one who caught him in bed with that woman. Do you have any idea how that made me feel?"

"Yes." Bram knew damn good and well exactly how she'd felt. He'd watched her closely every time he'd seen her after that, and he'd read the strain, the embarrassment and hurt, on her delicate features. It had made him sick with the need to retaliate in her defense. But he hadn't. He'd done his damnedest to stay impartial in case the marriage had succeeded. He'd loved them both too much to get in their way.

But the marriage had crumbled anyway. By the time David had realized all he was throwing away, there'd been no helping him. Thank God the car crash that had taken him hadn't involved anyone else.

Bram had grieved and suffered guilt and helped Lucy and the kids in every way he could.

And now it was finally his turn.

"You felt defeated," Bram told her. "You were betrayed and lied to, and it hurt. You gave up on your marriage and you threw him out. That took guts, Lucy. And I was so damn proud of you."

When she looked at him, not understanding, Bram added, "I felt sorry for David because the dumb son of a bitch had given up the best thing he was likely ever to find in this world, all for a quick fuck with a woman not worth the effort."

Lucy trembled, her eyes direct on his face. "You knew her?"

Softly, intently, he said, "I knew she wasn't you."

She turned away again and paced the length of the patio, stopping at a new perch a good distance away from him. Bram smiled. He had her on the run, but here, at the isolated summer house, she could only go so far. And never out of his reach.

"What are you really doing here, Bram?"

His heart raced as he stared at her slender back, bared by the halter top. His muscles tightened in anticipation and his cock felt full to bursting. "I'm here," he murmured quietly, honestly, "because you want sex, and I'm damn well going to be the only man to give it to you."

He saw her shoulders stiffen the tiniest bit, her back expand as she drew in a sharp breath. She didn't face him when she asked, "Why?"

"Why what?"

"Why would you want to . . ." Lucy gestured with her right hand, but there were no words to accompany her thoughts.

"Why would I want to make love to you?" He stepped toward her, slowly, letting her feel his approach, letting her awareness of him grow to a razor-sharp edge. Sweat trickled down his temples from the suffocating heat. His heart pounded, sounding loud in his ears.

He came close enough that the heat of his body mingled with the heat of the sun to envelop her, to wrap her up in his scent. "Why do I want you naked and under me?" he growled. "Why do I want to be the man to give you what you haven't had in four impossibly long years?"

"Yes." Her hands curled into fists, tighter and tighter. She jerked around toward him and shouted, "Yes and *yes!*"

The look on her face was haunted. Hungry.

"Lucy—" He couldn't tell her yet what was in his heart. He had to get her past the emotional restrictions of being with a man who had been her husband's best friend. He knew Lucy; she'd automatically rebel against the idea, finding it too intimate, too complicated. She'd rather have an indiscriminate fling with a stranger than risk the emotional complications of making love with a man she'd known for a very long time.

"Why, Bram? You can have any woman you want. You *have* every woman you want."

"I haven't had you, so that's obviously not true."

Her chest heaved, but she ignored his interruption. "They're all young and sexy with flat stomachs and enormous boobs and legs to their chins. They're not tired thirty-nine-year-old divorced mothers—"

"Officially, you're not divorced," he pointed out, just to stall her tirade. Voices carried on the lake, and though Bram doubted there was anyone around to hear, he didn't want Lucy to be embarrassed later. "David died before the divorce was final, remember."

"*Widowed,* then! They're not like me."

"Thank God," he said with heartfelt sincerity. The dissimilarities from the women he usually dated were what made Lucy so special.

"The women you gravitate to are twenty-year-olds who fawn all over you and screw you all night and every day—"

Bram laughed. He didn't mean to, but the humor struck him and he just couldn't hold it back. She sounded almost jealous—which thrilled him. And she looked appalled that anyone would want sex that much, which made his chest swell with tenderness.

But he'd show her. Before the week was out, Lucy would learn to love sex as much as he did.

"I'm forty-one, Lucy. Round-the-clock sex is for the young studs, not for me." And with a grin: "Though once at night and a coupla times during the day with you would be a pretty nice balance."

Apparently grinning was the wrong thing to do.

Big tears clouded her eyes and she started to stalk away. Contrite, Bram pulled off his sunglasses and followed her. He almost got squashed in the sliding door when she went to shove it shut this time—hoping, he knew, to close him out.

He figured he'd been closed out too long already.

"Are we going to keep marching in and out?" he asked, trying to tease her into a better mood. He didn't want this to be a battle. He wanted to gently seduce her as she deserved. At least, he hoped to start it that way. Ending it with a hard ride would suit him just fine.

Lucy headed down the short hallway of the one-floor house for the bedroom. "I'm going to go to the lake. You're going to leave."

He followed her straight into the room. "Not on your life, babe. Not with you still planning to—"

"Get out, Bram." Her voice shook audibly and she looked none too certain of her position. She pointed to the door, trying to be forceful. Bram merely crossed his arms over his chest and leaned back against the wall.

"Why?" he asked. "So you can call that young worker back?"

Her chin lifted defiantly. "Maybe."

Jealousy stabbed at him, but he resisted it. She was vulnerable now, doing things she'd never done before. Turning forty did strange things to women, so he could just imagine where her head was with her birthday not too far around the corner. Before the week was over, Lucy wouldn't have a single doubt that she was an incredibly desirable, sexy woman. He'd prove it to her in a hundred different ways.

Damn, he was looking forward to it.

"Is he your type, hon? Midtwenties? Too dumb to really know how to pleasure a woman?"

She looked briefly shocked at his bluntness. "Maybe he would surprise me."

His smile hurt, but Bram managed it. "I don't think so." He tilted his head. "Where'd you find him anyway?"

"Not that it's any of your business, but I met him in town when I stopped to pick up some groceries. He agreed to . . . work on the lawn."

"Oh, he'd have worked all right. But it wasn't the lawn he had on his mind and you know it."

"Is that so?" She looked pleased with the idea, making Bram almost smile again.

"Any red-blooded male with good-enough vision to see is going to want you, Lucy. You're a hottie."

She scowled at him. "That's a weak line for a man with your reputation, Bram."

"Always go with the truth, I say." Deliberately he looked her over from her head to her curled toes; then whistled low. "I can't believe you're unaware of the way you turn heads." *Mine especially,* he wanted to add but didn't.

"I'm not the least surprised, though," Bram told her, seeing that she was hungry for the compliments she should have been getting all along, "that the first guy you smiled at jumped at the chance to try his luck. Hell, at that age males are more testosterone than anything else and a sexy woman is an impossible temptation."

Lucy looked both complimented and annoyed.

"But he doesn't know you the way I do, Lucy," Bram told her, dropping his tone and watching her closely. "He doesn't know what you've been through and what you're after, what you deserve. He'd grope you real quick, have your shorts off in a flash, and two minutes later he'd be walking away, anxious to go brag to his buddies about the eager woman on the hill."

"Shut up, Bram."

"Is that what you want? A reputation with all the guys who're looking for a good time but no commitment?"

Her face was closed, but she shrugged. "It doesn't matter. I'm selling the place anyway."

That surprised Bram and made him wonder if her decision was financial or emotional. Either way, he didn't like it. "Reputations have a strange way of following a person."

She crossed her arms. "I notice a reputation hasn't done you any harm."

"No? Then why are you arguing with me so much now? Why don't we just get our clothes off and I can start helping you enjoy the week?"

Her gaze inadvertently skimmed his body, catching on his groin before she forced her attention back to his face. Her cheeks warmed with color; her eyes darkened. *She wasn't embarrassed.*

"I have no idea," she said a little breathlessly, "what's gotten into you, Bram. Are you trying to shock me?"

"I'm trying to be honest." Bram narrowed his eyes, all humor evaporated. "If you want to get laid, babe, fine. Come and get it. But it'll be with me and only with me."

She licked her lips and her eyes searched his. "I'm too old to play games, Bram."

"I can teach you new games." He stared at her mouth, fascinated with the way she kept chewing her bottom lip, which told him she was nervous. "They're best played in the buff."

Her chin lifted. "I'm also too smart to think you need to chase after me just to have sex, not when you have a string of women at home sitting by the phone. What are you really up to?"

She didn't believe him? Bram shrugged, catching and holding her gaze. "I don't want any other woman. I want you. Naked. Under me or over me, or whatever way you'd like. But I want inside you real bad and I want you to be holding me tight and I damn well want to hear you come."

Her composure wavered, her mouth opening in a small *o* for just a second. Then she regathered her wits. One of the sexiest things about Lucy was her backbone. She had gotten through a lot of strife in her life, and she'd not only landed on her feet; she'd raised two terrific kids besides.

As if for battle, she stood with her thighs locked, her feet braced apart. And she sounded deliberately suspicious. "Since when, Bram? Let me see; wasn't it just a few weeks ago that you were boffing Dede what's-her-name from your gym? Kent came home all bug-eyed with adolescent lust and overflowing with awe for his 'Uncle Bram's' prowess. I got to hear the blow-by-blow dimensions of the woman's body in a leotard. According to Kent, you personally showed her how to use every single piece of gym equipment."

Bram lifted one brow. So Kent had tattled, huh? He'd box that rascal's ears when next he saw him. Then another thought occurred and Bram half-wondered if his touted—and surely exaggerated—exploits had anything to do with Lucy's sudden determination to get frisky. Maybe he had inspired her.

"It was nothing."

She scoffed, adding with disdain, "And here I'd stupidly thought that, as the owner of the gym, you left chores like personal instruction to your employees."

"I never slept with Dede."

"Yeah, right. And I've never touched up the gray in my hair."

Bram bit back a smile. Lucy had started getting silver streaks in her gorgeous inky hair when she was only thirty-five. Now, at thirty-nine, they had all been covered over. Forcing himself to be as somber as the accusation warranted, he said, "Don't get confused here, babe. I'm not David. I've never lied to you and I never will."

That threw her for a moment, and then she rallied once again. "So now you're claiming to be a monk?"

"Far from that." Bram weighed his next words carefully. "I have no doubt that through fifteen years of marriage David caved in to the temptation to talk about me now and then?"

Bram waited, wanting to know how much she knew of him, dying to figure out if her curiosity had ever been as extreme as his own. He hoped she'd asked about him. He prayed that she'd fantasized a time or two, because God and his own conscience knew he'd dreamed about her far too often.

Lucy shrugged. "Yeah, so?"

Satisfaction settled into his bones. "So you already

know I'm about as far from a monk as a man can get. I like women. I love sex." He leaned toward her and reiterated, "But I didn't sleep with Dede."

"You're telling me Kent made it all up?"

"Of course not. I can't imagine Kent outright lying to you like that. But he probably only told you what he saw, which was a little flirting. And the truth is, I considered sleeping with her. You wanna know why?"

"Let me guess? A double-D bra size?"

She was such a prickly little cat today, Bram noted with amusement. Never before had they been at odds. From the time she and David had started to date, they'd all three gotten along. Lucy had often treated him like a brother, so he'd done the honorable thing and kept his wicked thoughts to himself. He'd loved David, and by association he'd learned to love Lucy. There was nothing wrong with that.

It was the lust, and more, that had made him feel guilty.

But he was done with guilt. He hadn't played a hand in their marital problems, and no one, before his current confession to Lucy, knew that he'd been obsessed with her. Lucy wasn't guilty of wrongdoing, and neither was he.

From here on out, he was going after what he wanted. And that meant he was going after Lucy.

Pushing himself away from the wall, Bram closed the distance between them. Lifting his right hand, he stroked her silky dark hair. It was baby fine and arrow straight and he loved it. "Her hair is almost as sleek as yours."

Lucy caught her breath.

"And her eyes—" He looked at Lucy's face, then tilted up her chin so she had to meet his gaze. "She has blue eyes, Lucy, that when I tried real hard reminded me of you."

Lucy shook under his intense regard. "So," she whispered, "the double Ds had nothing to do with it, huh?"

Bram took a step away from her. If he hadn't, he'd

have kissed her again, and with the bed right behind her, things might have gotten out of hand. She was already prepared to bolt, so pushing her wasn't a good idea. "Let me be clear about something here, Lucy. When I get alone in my bed at night and decide I can't take it anymore, it's not Dede's body I think about." He stared at her hard, saw the way her pupils dilated, and admitted gruffly, "It's yours."

Lucy looked frozen and enthralled. "Good God. You're not telling me that you . . . ?"

"Yeah, so what?" Bram figured he was far too old to be embarrassed over his body and the things he felt, the needs he dealt with. "We've already established that I'm not a monk. And at the moment, no other woman is appealing to me. I want *you*, Lucy. I've been wanting you since before David died." He didn't have to tell her yet that he'd always wanted her. That might be a bit too much.

For the first time since he'd arrived, she appeared to be softening. Wryly Bram wondered if she felt sorry for him because he'd admitted to flying solo. The amusing thought brought with it another, and his pulse raced.

Softly he asked, "What about you?"

Wariness returned to her gaze. "What about me?"

"It's been a long time since you filed for divorce. You haven't dated one single time since then." It sometimes made Bram break out in a sweat thinking about a woman like Lucy, a woman so alive and so filled with love, going to her bed all alone every night.

"Don't you get lonely, Lucy? Doesn't your body burn sometimes, wanting the touch of a man? Wanting relief? To the point where you just can't take it anymore?"

In a tone that matched his own, she whispered, "That's why I'm here." She looked away from him, then back again. "What you said, being alone . . . that's not the same as being with someone."

His heart thundered. "No, it's not. It's a damn poor substitute."

"Things . . . things were bad between David and me for a while before he cheated. But even then, even when I knew I was losing him, it was nice to have a man close sometimes, a warm body in the bed with me at night." She swallowed: then in an attempt to explain, she said, "There's a certain type of comfort in just knowing you're not alone, in feeling the body heat, hearing someone else breathe."

Bram's lungs constricted with fresh pain. Through the years of her marriage, it had been a unique form of hell knowing that David made love to her and Bram would never be allowed to. Now he had a chance and he'd be damned forever before he lost it.

He caught her chin on the edge of his fist. "I want to be the man who touches you now."

She immediately shook her head. "Bram, I can't compare with all those young, beautiful women you date."

"Christ." How could she not know, not understand? David had been a bigger ass than he'd suspected. "You don't have to compare with anyone. You're in an entirely different league."

"The minor league?" she teased, but Bram saw her uncertainty, the misconceptions she had about herself as a woman.

Desperately he tangled his fingers in her hair and drew her up against his chest. "I want you for who you are, Lucy. I've always respected your intelligence and your loyalty. I adore your sense of humor and your sense of responsibility."

"Bram." They'd hugged often over the years, and the way she hugged him now was familiar and sisterly. He hated it. "It's not a woman's sense of humor a man sees when she's naked."

He shuddered with the thought. "Seeing you naked," he growled near her ear, "would likely make me come in my pants."

She laughed. "Bram."

Bram took her hand and carried it to his distended fly.

His breath hissed sharply when her warm palm pressed against him.

"Ever since I realized what you intended to do," he gasped, "I've been hard. Thinking about you wanting another man enrages me, and still I'm hard. Knowing you would plan this week rather than come to me makes me want to howl—*and still I'm hard*. Sex with other women is a hollow thing, babe, even worse than jacking off, because I want *you*."

"How . . ." Her fingers didn't leave him and, in fact, curled around him tentatively instead. She was getting used to the idea, Bram decided, and he wanted to roar with his triumph. "How did you know what I was going to do?"

Bram hesitated. The closeness of talking with her like this, touching her like this, had always been no more than a dream. The reality was so much sweeter, so much sharper, that Bram didn't want to run the risk of destroying it. But he had promised her that he wouldn't lie to her, and so he wouldn't.

He kissed the top of her head and said, "Unless you want me to take you now—and I don't think you're quite ready for that yet—we'd better stop what we're doing."

He heard her swallow. "I'm not. Ready, that is." She looked up at him. Her fingers were still curled securely around him through the jean material of his shorts, and he felt them tighten the tiniest bit. "You're . . ." She stopped, took two deep breaths. "Well, you're *huge*."

Women had been commenting on the size of his prick since he was eighteen, and he'd always wallowed in the praise. Now all that mattered was that Lucy was intrigued. If his size helped to interest her, then Bram was doubly thankful for what he'd been given.

His hands gently stroking her shoulders, he said, "I would never hurt you, Lucy."

Her breath came in small pants now. Small *excited* pants. "I don't know about that. I mean, it's been a while for me. A long while—you were right about that." Idly she slid her palm up and down his length, measuring his dimensions again, making Bram lock his jaw with the pleasure of it.

Feeling nearly hollow with desire, Bram growled, "I'd be careful with you, baby. We'd go real slow and I'd make you so wet first, so hungry for it, sliding in will only be pleasure. I swear."

Lucy shuddered, and her hand stroked him one more time, nearly devastating him, before she pulled away. Her eyes were huge, filled with conditional trust. She would try, he realized, but she wasn't making any promises.

For a long moment, Bram simply concentrated on breathing, on not losing control. He could hardly win her over with devastating sex if he came in his shorts from a simple fondling.

When he felt able, he took her hand and led her from the bedroom. "Here's what we'll do." His voice was abrasive and deep, unsteady. "A swim—because I badly need a dousing of ice water—then a fast boat ride just to distract us. While we're on the lake, I'll explain things to you. We can . . . talk." He pulled her out onto the deck again. The heat and the sun hit them like a wave, sealing in the lust, the hot craving. Still somewhat shaky with need, Bram asked, "Do you need your shoes?"

Lucy, too, was trembling despite the steamy summer afternoon. "No." She looked up at him, her eyes slightly heavy with desire, and Bram had to lock his knees to keep from carrying her back inside. "I want to be totally free this weekend. No shoes, no bra. No laundry or phones or nosy neighbors or gossip."

Her statement sounded like a sensual promise to Bram's sensitized nerve endings. Or maybe he was just so damned horny, anything she said would have exacerbated his lust.

He nodded in agreement and they left the patio to follow the stone path down the hill to the lake. Bees buzzed around their feet, going from one clover blossom to another. Bram watched closely where they stepped, not wanting Lucy to get stung. Somewhere far off a cicada split the air with its noisy call. A black bird took flight.

"Do you have the keys?"

Her voice hushed with lingering uncertainty, Lucy said, "They're still in the boat. Life preservers are in the boathouse."

"You've been out in her already?" She should have only been at the cabin a few hours without him. Bram had cleared his calendar and quickly packed once it had dawned on him what she was up to. But she'd had time to scout out the area for other vacationers, if she'd done so right away.

"No, just started it up to make sure everything was in running order."

Bram stopped at the irregular shoreline before walking onto the long wooden dock where the boat was tied. She'd brought it out of the boathouse and removed the tarp cover.

Greenish lake water lapped at the rock retaining wall along the shore with a gentle splash. Sunlight glittered and sparkled, making it necessary for Bram to replace his sunglasses. The air was thick, the sky so vivid a blue it was nearly blinding.

Before he'd gotten run off, the worker had cut the grass, but he hadn't yet trimmed. Everything smelled fresh and new, scents intensified by the damp air and baking sun, filled with possibilities. Bram kissed Lucy gently on the mouth. "When we get back, I'll finish the yard work. Did you pack anything to grill?"

"I figured I'd eat sandwiches. Grilling seemed like too much trouble."

Bram made a mental note to stop by the one and only grocery store located on the lake. He'd talk with Lucy, feed her, and tonight he'd show her part of what her body could expect to feel with him. Before he was done, she'd crave what he could give her. She'd crave him.

"I'll take care of it. I'm a good cook."

She snorted and headed past him to step off the

wooden dock and into the boat. "You're good at everything you do and you know it."

Bram watched her settle herself onto the white leather
seats. Knowing he was damn near a goner, he took a quick
walk off the end of the dock and into the icy water. His
shirt floated up, leaving his abdomen bare; his athletic
shoes felt heavy on his feet. The water closed around his
head, stinging his heated skin but doing very little to cool
his lust.

He doubted a massage with an ice cube would cool
him down right now, not when he was so close to having
what he most wanted.

Lucy was turned around watching for him when he
resurfaced. He slicked his hair back and smiled at her,
then slapped some water her way. With her own smile,
she ducked back into the boat.

Taking long strokes, Bram swam to the ladder leading
into the boathouse and commandeered two life vests. It
was cooler inside the boathouse, and dark. Cobwebs hung
from every corner, testifying to how long it had been since
anyone had disturbed the boat. Exiting the door leading
to the dock instead of the water this time, Bram walked
around the dock to the sleek inboard. His shoes sloshed
with every step, and his shirt stuck to his torso. Lucy
wasn't looking at him. He tossed the preservers into the
back before joining her up front. She was in the passenger's seat, so he assumed she wanted him to drive.

David had bought the expensive boat not long before
Lucy had walked in on him with another woman. As far
as Bram knew, this was the first time Lucy had been in
the boat since.

Bram deliberately let water drip from him onto her as
he adjusted himself behind the wheel. She had slipped on
dark sunglasses and a floppy white hat that shielded her
face from the sun—and from his view. She had her long
legs stretched out before her, her feet propped on the dash.

Refusing to be ignored, Bram trailed one wet fingertip
up the length of her leg, from her ankle to the outside of

her thigh. She shivered, and a small smile teased the corners of her mouth.

Tonight, he thought, appreciating her body, imagining her naked, she would do more than smile. Tonight she'd be screaming his name.

CHAPTER 3

Lucy eyed Bram through her dark sunglasses and the whip of her hair blowing into her face. She had to hold her hat on with one hand because he drove the boat so fast, but it felt good, the rush of the wind and the sound of the wake behind the boat. There were only a few other boaters out, and so the ride was relatively smooth, with only a few choppy waves here and there.

As usual, she was all too aware of Bram, but now it was different. She'd always seen him as a sexual being, a man who beckoned women with his looks, his masculinity, and his smile and charm. But now she knew first-hand how devastatingly clever his mouth was, how he could kiss a woman into a stupor, and how blunt he was about his sexuality. He had no shame, no modesty.

She had a feeling Bram wouldn't know a thing about insecurity or shyness in the bedroom. His only concern would be giving and receiving pleasure.

Her body tightened with the reality of that, her nipples puckering, her stomach flip-flopping. Oh God, he was incredible, more so than she'd ever even realized.

Owning a small, exclusive gym made it possible for Bram to stay in the best possible shape. Working out was a part of his daily routine, and it showed. He didn't have a single ounce of fat on him anywhere, and his power, his strength, was evident in every line of his tall body.

But who was she kidding? The man had always looked that way, even before he'd bought the gym. Back when she'd first met David, she'd been distracted by Bram's body, and he hadn't been much more than a teenager then, because she and David had married when she was twenty.

Perfection was the only word to describe Bram. And disturbingly enough, the older he got, the better he seemed to look.

At forty-one, he had a wide, hard chest with clearly defined muscles that could make a female of any age hungry. His streaked blond hair, always in a somewhat shaggy, unkempt style, was shades lighter than the dark brown hair on his body. Through Bram's wet, tattered T-shirt she could see the muscles moving and shifting on his chest as he turned the steering wheel on the boat, slicing through a bigger wave. She could also see the sprinkling of hair that spread out over his upper chest and then narrowed to a silky line down his abdomen. Lucy realized she was undressing him mentally and tried to pull herself back.

David's chest had been hairy, too, but he hadn't looked like Bram.

Guilt slammed into her and she looked away, determined to keep her thoughts on something other than Bram's magnificent body.

But as if he'd read her mind, he slowed the boat and pulled his wet shirt off over his head, giving her an earth-shattering view of the object of her distraction. He was tanned darker than she, with shoulders twice as wide and narrow hips barely covered by loose-waisted faded jean cutoffs. Soaked, the waistband of the jean shorts curled out away from his body. Lucy could just see the edge of a pair of dark snug boxers.

It was difficult to breathe with so much hunger swirling inside her.

Lucy watched as Bram lowered one large rough hand to his ridged abdomen and lazily scratched. With the other hand, he steered the boat.

Her tongue stuck to the roof of her mouth.

She wanted to touch his abdomen, too. She wanted to hear that enticing rasp in his voice that told her he was aroused. She wanted to tease his navel with her tongue, do things to him that she'd never been able to do with any other man—including her husband.

Lucy closed her eyes against those thoughts. Imagining letting go with a total stranger whom she'd never have to face again was entirely different from thinking of doing wild, wanton things with Bram. She knew him and knew that he thought of her as a lady. How could she confide in him her darkest secrets, her most forbidden fantasies?

"Now," he said, his voice loud over the rumbling purr of the engine, "are you ready for me to explain?"

She was ready to jump overboard.

Maybe the cold water would help her, though looking at Bram's fly, she saw that it hadn't cooled his ardor one bit. There was a very visible ridge in his shorts, a large, solid ridge that couldn't be mistaken for anything other than what it was.

That thrilled her, even as it confused her. She could hardly warrant that Bram wanted her. But looking at him there wouldn't do a damn thing toward getting her calmed. All the stories she'd heard about him were real; he was very well endowed and supposedly knew how to use what he had. A slow explosion of heat nearly took her breath away.

She didn't know if she could really handle all of him, but she very much wanted to find out. Her body clenched with the need to find out.

"Explain what?" she asked stupidly, her mind still on his big hand and his bared flesh and the clear delineation of his maleness beneath his fly. He said he'd been hard for a while. Well, he was hard still. Her heart could barely keep up with her racing pulse.

Glancing at her quickly, Bram reached out and tucked a tendril of her flying hair behind her ear. "I can hear the excitement in your voice, Lucy." He stroked her cheek and over her bottom lip. "Now—and then."

She couldn't deny the now. She didn't *want* to deny it. Bram was here, and even if she couldn't be totally free with him like she could have been with a stranger, neither could she resist him.

But earlier, when she'd given him permission to take the kids camping and explained that she'd be away for a week, Lucy knew she'd been very discreet. She hadn't admitted a word of her real intent to a single soul. She took her status as mother seriously and would never, by word or deed, deliberately make her children uncomfortable.

Planning a brief fling with a stranger was bound to fit into the "uncomfortable" bracket.

Yet she was so lonely, her body so hungry. She was sick and tired of going to sleep with the need to touch and be touched making her crazy. The only thing she'd been able to come up with was a one-nighter to assuage the fever. She was human; didn't she deserve some gratification, even if it was only sexual?

Bram slowed the boat, steering it easily along the shoreline, staying just far enough out to avoid submerged logs and large rocks that could damage the bottom of the boat. Hanging branches from tall trees dipped into the water's edge, shielding snakes and frogs and turtles. Bright orange tiger lilies, black-eyed Susans, and Queen Anne's lace grew in profuse, wild tangles, enticing hummingbirds to flit about.

Farther out on the lake, a bass jumped, drawn by the hot sunshine.

Using just that one rough fingertip, Bram continued to stroke her face. Lucy shivered. His touch was almost casual, as if he'd decided he had the right to touch her and no one was going to stop him.

"I saw your purpose in the way you spoke, the way you held your body. There was anticipation in every muscle, and a glow in your eyes."

Lucy scoffed at such a notion. "Poetic nonsense, Bram. If sexual intent was that easy to read in a person, I'd have known that David was going to cheat."

Bram withdrew, and for several moments he was silent. "Maybe," he finally said, "I just know you better than you knew David. Maybe I'm more observant where you're concerned."

Lucy stiffened, hearing his words as an insult. David had told her many times that she neglected him. She hoped Bram wasn't saying the same. "How so?"

"I watched you marry David." His voice was so low she could barely hear him. His blond hair, still damp, blew straight back from his forehead. The sun glinted off his mirrored glasses. He hadn't shaved that morning, and a light shadowing of whiskers darkened his lean jawline and upper lip.

He had the most sensual mouth Lucy had ever seen. Beautiful white teeth, a strong chin, high cheekbones. But it was the innate sensuality in his eyes, in his every gesture, that usually had women taking a second and third look.

Right now, there was an expression on Bram's handsome face that made her stomach curl with some unnamed emotion.

"I knew what you felt then, too," he said. "During the wedding, and after. I've always been able to read you." He smiled slightly, turning her muscles to soup, and added, "When you were pregnant, I thought you were the most beautiful woman I'd ever seen."

Lucy remembered his fascination with her then, the questions he'd asked, the awe in his expression the first time she'd convinced him to feel the baby kick. She also remembered how he'd avoided her whenever he could. He hadn't come around nearly as often during her two pregnancies. Not until the end of her second pregnancy, when he'd realized that David couldn't keep up with his work at the office and help her around the house, too. Then suddenly Bram was there, proving himself a true friend by keeping the grass cut, carrying laundry up and down the steps for her. He always came when David got home, and together they'd get the extra chores done. Lucy never saw Bram except when David was there.

Something about that memory nagged at her, but she put the thought from her mind.

"When I was pregnant," she half-teased, but knew it was true, "I was fat."

A grin flickered over his mouth. "Lush."

"What?"

"You weren't fat, babe, you were lush." They neared
the boat docks where vacationers could purchase bait, basic groceries, and other necessities. "I remember thinking
you got sexier the further you went along in your pregnancy. Your breasts were incredible, and your eyes were
so pretty. And after Kent was born and you nursed him
. . . it used to choke me up."

Lucy leaned around to see his face, stunned at what
he'd said. "It didn't."

"Hell yes, it did."

He sounded so sincere, her heart twisted. Without
thinking, she touched him. His thigh was hard and hot
and roughened with hair. She felt the muscles flex, go
rigid. "Why, Bram?"

He expertly steered the boat into the dock where a
worker grabbed the lead line and secured it to a grommet.
Bram just sat there, his hands resting loosely on the steering wheel, his gaze straight ahead. Around them, people
on a pontoon chatted and laughed. Another man sat on
the side of his speedboat, reeling in a ski line.

Bram went so long without answering her, Lucy began
to think he hadn't heard her at all.

Then his hand covered hers on his thigh and he pulled
off his sunglasses. His golden brown eyes blazed with
intensity, with emotion. *And with desire.*

He lifted her hand and kissed her palm, the pads of her
fingers. "I got choked up," he explained against the sensitive skin of her inner wrist, "because I knew I'd never
have what you had. And I thought it was all pretty damn
special."

Lucy blinked hard. She cared about Bram, she always
had. Now, more than ever, she understood why. He wasn't
just a sexier-than-sin, macho ladies' man. He was also a
sensitive man, caring about the kids' needs and attentive
to them all as a family. For the first time she realized how
he might have felt like an outsider.

She stood, smiling slightly, and, using her free hand, ran

her fingers through his fair hair. It was tangled from the hot wind, thick and soft. "Of course you could have those things, Bram. You just have to stop tomcatting around and settle on a single woman."

She meant her tone to be teasing, but instead it sounded gruff. Touching him, even casually now that he'd made his desire known, unsettled her.

Bram hesitated, his lips pressed to her wrist, then he shook his head. "I'm not looking for a new woman these days, Lucy. Right now, all I want is you. And tonight I mean to show you just how much."

The sensual threat nearly made her gasp with anticipation. Her knees trembled, and desperately she locked her legs to stay upright. Lucy watched him leap from the boat, then offer her his hand. She didn't know if she could touch him after he'd said such a thing. She was beginning to realize that this wasn't just a lark for Bram. He wasn't just teasing to make her forget about a fling. He wasn't merely flirting to ease her transition at turning forty. He wasn't just in search of a quick and easy sexual adventure.

He really did want her. Bram Giles, lover in hot demand, bachelor in every sense of the word, wanted her. Not just as a conquest, not just because she was handy and desperate. He wanted *her,* as an individual woman. As a woman he found sexually attractive.

"Give me your hand, Lucy."

She looked at him, saw the implacable command in his eyes, the erotic promise. She felt helpless against him and couldn't resist. She reached out to him. *A sexual fling with Bram Giles.*

Talk about shooting for the moon!

They'd taken no more than five steps up the cement walkway when two women, scantily covered in string bikinis, left the shop and started down the walk toward them. The women looked to be in their late twenties, perfectly toned and perfectly tanned, their hair Barbie doll long and just as blond. One of them carried a six-pack of beer, the other a brown paper bag filled with a variety of chips.

They stopped talking when they saw Bram. Even their body language changed, from casual movement to seductive fluidity. They no longer walked; they swayed.

Trying to be inconspicuous, Lucy released Bram's hand. She knew what was about to happen, what always happened when women caught sight of Bram. They'd flirt and simper and strike up a conversation. She didn't want to be in the middle of it when it happened. At nearly forty, she was feeling every single year of her age and didn't care to stand side by side with model lookalikes.

The problem was, though she released him, Bram held on. And he ignored the women, managing to nod politely while not quite looking at them. He dragged Lucy along reluctantly in his wake, and despite herself she snickered when the women frowned at her. "Now you've confused them."

Bram lifted a brow at her. "Hmm? What was that?"

Stunned, Lucy realized he really hadn't paid any attention to the women. She indicated them with a toss of her head. "You missed your newest fan club."

Bram glanced over his shoulder toward the women, then smiled. "Sorry. I was thinking about something else."

"Really?" She found it a little incredible that he had missed the women's attention altogether.

Bram gave her a crooked smile. "Tonight. I was thinking about tonight and how long I've waited and how damn good I know it's going to be."

Lucy only had time to gasp before they stepped into the small grocery shop and icy cold air blasted them from a struggling window air conditioner. Bram tugged her toward the back aisle where the meat was kept. She moved along like a zombie, caught in a sensual trance.

"Bram." She wrapped her arms around herself, trying to contain her heat. "You really were thinking about me?"

As he examined a package of steaks, Bram said idly, "Yeah. You. Naked." He glanced at her. "I'm obsessed."

Heat flooded over her, counteracting the too-cold artificial air. Lucy quickly looked around, but no one was listening. There were only two other people in the store besides the salesclerk, and they were in the farthest corner contemplating a variety of fishing lures.

"Bram," she chastised, unwilling to even consider what he might think if he saw her totally unclothed. She was almost forty. She'd had two kids. And she had no spare time to invest in working out, as he did.

Bram drew his attention away from the steaks, took in her flustered expression, and grinned. His large hand curled around the nape of her neck, and he drew her close. Against her lips he murmured, "I can't wait to see all of you, honey. I expect it'll take me a good long time to look my fill, so you might as well start preparing for it."

Lucy was going to tell him to hush, but he kissed her. Not a killer kiss like earlier, just a nice, soft pressing of his mouth, so warm, so gentle. She leaned into his chest and returned the kiss, wanting so much more.

Bram stroked her cheek and smiled at her. "Damn, I shouldn't start this here."

"No, you shouldn't," she managed to say with less than realistic conviction.

"The cold made your nipples hard," he informed her in a whisper, and bold as you please, he dragged one knuckle over her left breast, teasing the taut tip.

Lucy's breath caught, the touch was so electric. She felt the sweet, aching pull of desire everywhere, but especially between her thighs. She started to turn away, and Bram caught her shoulder. "No, don't abandon me. I've got a boner and it's just a little noticeable."

She glanced down and then quickly closed her eyes. *Little* was not an apt part of the description.

Bram grinned at her. "I'll stay behind you."

Lucy started to nod, not seeing any other recourse, but he just had to go and breathe real close to her ear, "It's a favorite position of mine anyway."

She turned and stalked away, figuring he could either

follow her or not. If she'd stood there one second longer, the look on her face would have given her away and everyone in the store and out would have known what she had on her mind.

When she reached the counter, Bram's warm breath touched her nape, assuring her he had indeed followed. When she got him home . . .

She drew up short on that thought, uncertain exactly how to proceed. And equally uncertain as to what he'd expect.

Bram reached around her, putting not only the steaks on the countertop but two large baking potatoes and two ears of corn as well. Where he'd snagged them she didn't know, and she wasn't about to ask him. It'd be just her luck that her voice wouldn't work and she'd squeak like a ninny.

Then she *did* squeak, when Bram leaned into her and she felt the full hard length of him against her bottom. He pointed to a T-shirt hanging on the wall and said, "An Extra Large please."

The shirt read: WET AND WILD and included a logo from a popular brand of skis. It was also long enough to cover his fly. Lucy sighed in relief. Out of sight, *not quite out of mind,* but at least she ought to be able to stop staring.

The two women they'd passed on the way in were sitting on the edge of the dock when they walked back out. Lucy knew they were waiting and almost resented them, but when she glanced at Bram she couldn't blame them. She'd have waited for another peek, too.

"A few years ago," Bram whispered to her, keeping her close with one arm around her shoulders while he held the bag with his free hand, "I knew a woman who looked just like the one on the right."

Startled, Lucy asked, "Is that maybe her?"

"No, but the similarity is uncanny."

Feeling a tad snippy, Lucy said, "She was rather memorable, I gather?"

"Yeah, she was." Bram led her around another couple coming up the walk, then again steered them toward the boat. "She'd been coming to the gym for about a month before I said anything to her. As soon as I did speak to her, she told me she and her boyfriend had just broken up and she invited me over."

"And of course you just had to go."

Bram shrugged. "You and the kids had just taken off for vacation. I didn't have anything more exciting to do, so yes, I went."

They had reached the dock, and both of the women turned, smiling at Bram. They didn't seem the least put off that he was with another woman, Lucy noted, and she wanted to push them both into the water for discounting her so completely.

Instead she smiled and said, "Hi."

They ignored her.

Bram ignored them.

It was small consolation to watch their faces fall as Bram gave Lucy all his attention. Exhibiting true gentleman tendencies, he helped her into the boat, then handed her the bag. Before he stepped in himself he untied the rope from the grommet. One of the women asked, "Want me to give you a push?"

Distracted, Bram glanced at her as he sat behind the wheel and said, "No thanks. I've got it." Using one long arm, he pushed the boat out and away from the dock, then started the engine and put it in reverse.

Lucy waited until they were well away from the gas docks to say, "OK, so what was so memorable about her?"

Bram glanced at Lucy. "I'll tell you when we reach the house."

"Tell me now."

"Can't." He shoved at the throttle and the boat leaped forward, the engine roaring. "It's tough to talk over the engine," he yelled.

Lucy turned away from him. She hadn't really wanted to know anyway. Thinking of Bram making love to a woman with a perfect body would only disturb her. She wanted to think about him having sex with her instead.

Unable to resist, she turned to watch him as he steered the boat, cutting through the waves with barely a bounce. Tonight, she thought, she'd get to find out what all the talk was about.

She only hoped Bram wouldn't leave disappointed.

"Are you getting hungry?" Bram asked her, watching her face as they carried the few groceries in to the L-shaped dining and kitchen area.

He saw Lucy's shoulders stiffen just a bit, and she said, "I can eat whenever you're ready."

"But you're not overly hungry now?" Bram kept one eye on her while he put the corn and steaks in the refrigerator. She was aroused, bless her heart, not interested in food, but unwilling to be aggressive enough to initiate things. He'd get her over her shyness soon enough.

Lucy kept busy folding and refolding the grocery bag before finally putting it away in a drawer. She had her back to him, but he didn't need to see her face to know what she was feeling. He felt it too, in spades.

"No," she said, "I'm not very hungry."

"Good." Bram closed the refrigerator and approached her before she could turn. He caged her in by flattening his hands on the counter at either side of her hips. He pressed into her bottom and nuzzled her neck. "That woman I told you was somewhat memorable?"

"Yeah, so? What about her?"

Her disgruntled tone tickled him, and he smiled against the nape of her neck, then whispered, "She wanted me to spank her."

Lucy drew tight, her head lifted to attention. *"What?"*

She sounded just like a schoolmarm, scandalized but at the same time entranced. Bram continued to nuzzle against her. "Yeah, she was a little kinky. Sort of took me by surprise, bringing it up so fast and all. I mean, it'd been our first time together."

"Did you . . . that is . . ." She shifted, and her fingers moved nervously on the countertop in front of her.

"Did I oblige her?"

Lucy nodded.

"I always oblige," he rumbled softly. "When I'm with a woman, I want her to be happy. And I insist she leave satisfied. If a red bottom will do that for her, hey, I can handle it." Keeping the laughter out of his tone was difficult. Lucy was downright rigid with indignation.

Very lightly, he bit her neck, right where her pulse was suddenly rioting. "What about you, sweetheart? You have any kinky fantasies?"

"I don't want to be spanked, if that's what you're asking!"

Bram laughed. "I wasn't that into it myself." He couldn't stop kissing her, touching her. "And I'd never ask you to do anything that made you uncomfortable, so I don't want you worrying about that, all right? But most people have something they like to fantasize about, something a little wicked that turns them on."

"Do you?"

"Absolutely." And most of his fantasies centered around her. "I just want you to know you can tell me anything, ask me anything. OK?"

Again she shifted, those nervous little movements that told him so much. He wanted to squeeze her close, crush her to his heart. Instead he waited.

"Did you date that woman much?"

"A date implies time out somewhere, so no. I had sex with her off and on for about a month." Bram trailed the fingertips of his right hand up her arm to her bare shoulder. He saw goose bumps rise in his path. "Sex is a hollow thing when it's between strangers. For a while, when you're young and stupid, that can seem exciting. It can seem like enough. But the older I get, the more I want . . . more."

Idly, Lucy turned her head to rub her cheek against the back of his hand where it rested on her shoulder. The gesture was tender, loving, and his heart twisted.

"Between David and me," she whispered, "things got really . . . stale. I guess we'd known each other too long, gotten too comfortable. Doing anything risqué or different seemed silly. Whenever I tried spicing things up, I ended up feeling foolish."

Struggling not to curse, Bram said only, "David was the fool."

She shook her head. "I don't know. Everything that went wrong wasn't his fault. I'm to blame, too. I guess we'd just known each other too long to change things from mundane to erotic." She gave a self-conscious laugh and added, "The last few years, before I filed for divorce, David had totally lost interest. Sex was something that happened more out of boredom for him than out of love or lust. He didn't want to cuddle, or hold me, or kiss me. He'd say, *'Are we screwing tonight or what?'* And I . . . I just couldn't."

Talking about her with David was killing Bram on several levels. He hated the thought of her with another man, even her husband, and beyond that, he hated knowing how frustrated she must have been, emotionally and especially physically. She was the very essence of feminine sexuality, but all her innate responses had been stifled rather than encouraged.

By word and movement and look, Lucy was a very sensual woman. She deserved to have all her needs met, in any and every way. He wanted to ignite her basic nature, enflame her body. He wanted everything she had to give a man.

"I think," he breathed into her ear, "that we should work on stage one of this week."

On alert, she asked, "Stage one?"

"Yeah." His heart pounded and his temperature rose. "That's the part where I get to take your shirt off you and kiss your pretty breasts and maybe make you half as nuts as I am."

"Right . . . right now?"

"Hell yes. I don't think I can wait much longer." Bram coasted his fingertips back down her arm, over her abdomen, and lower, to fondle her belly. She was soft, giving, and he wanted to tease her, to drag out the fun. Bram angled his fingers upward and just barely touched the underside of her left breast. "I want to move slowly, for both of us. I've wanted you too long to be able to do everything I want to do to you if I get you completely naked. And you're still a little hesitant about things, aren't you?"

"It feels . . . weird, being with you." She rushed to clarify that, in case he'd misunderstood. "I mean, we've been practically related for a long time."

Bram cupped her breast in his palm and felt her heartbeat quicken. Her nipple was elongated, puckered tight, showing her arousal. "Does this feel familial?" he asked, groaning just a bit with the voluptuousness of the moment. "Christ, Lucy, I've wanted to do this forever."

"Bram . . ." Her head tipped back to his shoulder and she shuddered delicately.

Bram caught her nipple and tugged the tiniest bit, rolling the swollen tip, plucking at it.

"Oh, God." Her back arched, her legs stiffened.

She panted, thrilling Bram with the measure of her response. Softly, wonderingly, he whispered, "You need this almost as much as I do, don't you, baby?" Using his left hand, he again stroked her belly, then lower. The heat of her through her shorts scorched him. The soft, worn denim did nothing to disguise her sex. Bram could feel the swollen, delicate folds and the soft tender flesh between.

He slowed, moving deliberately, carefully. He searched her through the denim while he continued to torment and ply her nipple.

"I want to feel your naked flesh," he groaned, "but I'm so goddamned close to the edge, one touch of you and I'd explode myself."

While he watched, fascinated and intensely proud, Lucy's body flushed with the first wave of a building climax. Her legs trembled and parted more, and Bram accepted her invitation, spurred on by her gasping breaths, the heaving of her chest. "Move with my fingers, sweetheart," he instructed, and when she did, when her hips lifted into his touch, he growled, "That's it."

She reached back and her nails dug into his naked thighs. Bram hissed out his pleasure, knowing she was close and it had been so easy. He released her breast to delve into her halter, shoving it down as he did so. It caught and held beneath the weight of her heavy breasts. Looking over her shoulder, Bram could see her large, darkly flushed nipples, pulled tight with desire.

His vision blurred with heat, his cock flexing in reaction to the sight of her. He had to grit his teeth to hold himself in check, to keep from sitting her on the counter and removing her shorts. He wanted to feel her wetness, wanted to taste her, to know every part of her.

With a harsh groan, he opened his mouth on her throat at the same time that his rough fingertips found and captured the naked, sensitized tips of her breasts. From one to the other, he teased them, pinching just hard enough to take her to the edge, then rolling them softly, gently, soothing her so that the next rough touch would be that much more acute. And all the while his hand between her legs kept up a pressing rhythm, pushing her and pushing her until suddenly she cried out, and the sound was one of the most beautiful he'd ever heard.

His balls tightened in response to the quickening of her flesh and he had to struggle not to come with her. It was a close thing. Though he hadn't made that kind of faux pas since he was a kid, now it was nearly impossible to contain the tide of emotion and sexual sensation brought on by her orgasm.

Lucy held herself back, biting her lip, keeping herself as still as possible while the climax rolled through her. Bram knew it, but for now it was OK; for now he'd let her get away with it. After all, they were in a kitchen and this was their first sexual experience together.

Later, when he had her naked in bed, he'd get her to let loose completely. He wouldn't allow any timidity then.

Lucy gulped for air, slumping against him. Her hands dropped away from his thighs, leaving behind small, stinging half-moons from her nails. Bram continued to lightly stroke her, knowing that she was now ultrasensitive and anything more than the most delicate touch would be too much. But letting her go completely was impossible.

"You're so wet," he whispered, and his voice shook as much as his hands. "I can feel how wet you are even through your shorts."

"Bram."

"Hmmm?" She sounded mortified and amazed, and it amused him. He nuzzled her throat, kissing, tasting her skin. He wanted to drown himself in her.

Her swallow was audible, a sign of nervousness. "I . . . I think I'm a little embarrassed."

"I think you're amazing." He kissed her ear. "And sexy." He hugged her tight, rocking her. "And I want more. A whole lot more." Then: "Why are you embarrassed?"

Very slowly, she straightened up and removed her weight from him; her legs were shaky, but he didn't force the issue. He just stood behind her, there for support if she wanted it.

With trembling hands, she pulled her halter back into place. Bram wanted to protest; he loved looking at her breasts and he wanted her to face him, to let him get his fill of looking. He wanted to see her nipples and kiss them and suck them. He wanted to hear her moan as he drew off her, licking and tasting until she couldn't bear it and neither could he.

For years now he'd imagined what she'd look like, whether her nipples were mauve or pink or brown. Were they large or small? Seeing her breasts had been a fragment of a fantasy, pushing him closer and closer to his ultimate goal.

Lucy shook her head. "I'm standing here," she whispered, "in the middle of the kitchen of all places and half-naked and there you are, fully dressed and—"

Bram smiled at her back. "I can drop my shorts if you want."

She didn't refuse him. Instead she warily turned to face him, and her gaze was all over him, but especially on his crotch. He throbbed beneath her intense scrutiny. She might as well have touched him, her look was so carnal, making him swell even more until he hurt with the need for release.

With a deep breath, she said, "Would you? Really? I mean, it wouldn't embarrass you?"

Bram reached for the snap at his waistband, and she caught his hands. Laughing a little in excitement and disbelief, she said, "I think I need to sit down for this."

Heated excitement coursed through Bram. He could barely draw a deep breath, but he mustered up the strength to catch her hand and drag her from the kitchen.

When he headed for the front room, she balked. "Bram? Aren't we going to the bedroom?"

"Not yet." His voice was a rasp, barely discernible, raw with need. "Let's get through stage two first, and if we both survive that we'll eventually make it to the bedroom before the day is through."

Her own voice low with need, Lucy said, "Stage two?"

Bram reached the leather couch that faced the sliding patio doors and pulled Lucy down into the plush cream-colored cushions with him. He kissed her hungrily, devouring her, and to his immense pleasure, she kissed him back. It wasn't easy, but Bram managed to lift his mouth away from hers. "This," he growled, "is where you make me come. And God knows, honey, I need it."

He needed it so badly, in fact, that his body was already pulsing with the expectation of release, like the first stages of orgasm.

Lucy stared down at his lap, her beautiful blue eyes slumberous, her lips slightly parted and swollen. And with a type of incredible feminine torture, she licked her lips.

Bram groaned. He pulled open the snap to his shorts, now dried stiff from his dip in the lake. Carefully, because he was as hard as he could possibly be, he eased down his zipper and guided her small hand inside. His breath caught and held in his chest, making him dizzy.

"Oh my."

There was so much heightened pleasure in her words, such gentle sensuality in the way her soft hand curled around him, that Bram knew he was a goner right there and then.

CHAPTER 4

Lucy was awed by the size of him. She'd heard stories, of course, but had discounted them as typical male exaggeration. Even after feeling him through his jeans shorts earlier, she hadn't been prepared for the actuality.

Her hand barely circled him, her fingers not quite touching together. Sharp awareness blossomed in her belly, spreading outward until she wasn't sure she could breathe. As a mature woman, she knew size didn't matter. But maturity had nothing to do with fantasies and eroticism. His erect flesh was so hot, throbbing with a life of its own.

Using her thumb, she tested the velvety texture from his hair-roughened testicles, now drawn tight, up to the smooth, broad tip and heard him curse very low.

"Bram?"

His head was pressed back against the couch, his eyes squeezed shut, his jaw locked. He looked like a man in pain or incredible pleasure. The muscles in his arms rippled and bunched as his hands curled into hard fists at his sides. "Squeeze me," he muttered through his teeth, *"hard."*

Fascinated by him, by his totally open response to her touch, she did as he insisted. Never had David looked this turned on, this turbulent. Yet Bram didn't seem to care that he was partially exposed to her, sprawled out on a couch, at her mercy. He literally writhed from her attentions.

When her fingers gripped him tighter, he groaned low, then gave a rough laugh. "Christ, having your hand on me is a dream I never thought would come true."

He gasped brokenly as she slowly stroked down his length, then back up again. He caught her wrist. Molten hot and fiercely direct, his eyes opened and captured hers.

"Like this, baby," he instructed, guiding her hand to the base of his shaft, then all the way back to the very tip until her thumb brushed over the end and he froze from the pleasure of it.

Lucy watched his face, as enthralled with his expressions as she was with his nudity and his instruction. She'd fumbled around with David for years, trying to learn what pleased him, embarrassed when she hadn't succeeded. For Bram, it seemed no matter what she did, he enjoyed it. And he was more than willing to teach her, without hesitation, without reserve. His sheer lack of inhibition was a turn-on.

Though the flexing erection she held was fascinating, she couldn't take her gaze off his face.

"What is it?" he asked, his eyes sensually heavy, his high cheekbones slashed with aroused color. "Tell me, Lucy. Anything you want."

She licked her lips, working up her nerve. But the whole point of coming to the summer house had been to indulge her every fantasy, to rid herself of the social inhibitions caused by being with people she associated with on a daily basis. She would not turn coward now.

She cleared her throat. "Will you . . . will you take off your shirt so I can look at you?"

Without a word he grabbed the hem of the T-shirt in his fists and yanked it over his head. The shirt got tossed to the other side of the couch, then Bram spread his arms out along the back of the couch and affected a relaxed pose. His small brown nipples were erect points visible through his sweat-dampened chest hair. His arms were long, roped with muscle, and tufts of lighter, softer hair shone in his armpits. With his lids lowered and his body rigid, he offered himself up to her.

Lucy didn't want to let go of his erection, so she shifted slightly until she could comfortably hold him in her right hand, and with her left she explored his chest. Having Bram watch her, seeing the pleasure in his eyes, made the whole experience more erotic.

"I want to kiss you again."

Bram smiled. "Any time, any place."

Lucy hooked her left arm around his neck and took his mouth. He didn't control the kiss, but he did gently guide her, tipping his head slightly so that their mouths completely meshed, urging her tongue into his mouth by teasing it with his own. He nibbled on her bottom lip until she did the same to him, then he gave a rough sound of pleasure, like a jungle cat purring.

Incredibly, his penis grew harder, longer, in her fist.

Having access to Bram's body was a sensual feast. His skin felt like heated silk, taut over muscles and bones and sinew. She opened her mouth on his throat and relished the taste of him, the saltiness of his skin. Burrowing lower, she kissed his chest and nuzzled her nose through the soft chest hair, drinking in his scent. When she found his small nipples she licked and felt his reaction in the flex of his body and the way he gasped.

Lifting her head, Lucy asked, "You like that?"

Bram stroked her hair. "Lucy," he said tenderly, smiling. "You have my cock in your hand, your mouth on my body. Of course I like it."

She felt color rush to her cheeks, but she ignored it. "I meant this—" she licked his nipple again—"specifically."

His nostrils flared. "Any place you want to put that sweet little tongue is fine by me, but yeah, I suppose it feels close to the same for me as it does for you."

And before she could recover from that discovery, he asked, "Why don't you lose your top, too?" His gaze darkened. "Then I can return the favor."

Lucy froze at just the thought. She didn't want him looking at her thirty-nine-year-old body with all the flaws that came with age and pregnancy and nursing. He would compare her to the other women he'd been with, and she couldn't bear that.

Refusing to lose control of the situation, she summoned up a teasing note and said, "Oh no you don't.

You told me we'd do stage two, and me being topless isn't part of it."

"You being topless should be part of everything." He caught the hand she had wrapped around his penis and started her stroking again. His voice dropped an octave, husky and warm. "Cooking breakfast, doing laundry . . . pleasuring me. Everything could be enhanced if I could see your breasts."

Lucy laughed at him. "Not yet. Let me concentrate on what I'm doing."

With his unshakable gaze locked on hers, he asked, "Do you want to see me come?"

Intrigued by the prospect, Lucy looked at his erection and saw a drop of fluid beading on the tip. "Yes." She felt her own body growing damp again in gathering excitement. "I've never . . . you know. Watched that before."

"But you're curious?" He gasped as she again smoothed her thumb over the tip, spreading the drop of semen around and around. His legs shifted, his heels pressing into the hardwood floor.

Leaning down, Lucy kissed his lower chest. She took little nibbling pecks down his lightly furred abdomen. "Yes. Very curious." His incredible scent was stronger this close to his sex, and it drew her. His chest heaved and his back arched slightly. "I wanted to do things this week," she admitted, "that I've never done before. I wanted to be as wild, as improper and earthy, as any young liberated woman might be."

"Yeah."

Lucy might have smiled at Bram's nearly incoherent agreement—or was it encouragement? She wasn't sure. But she didn't smile because she, too, was caught up in the carnality of it.

Her inky black hair was spread out over his hard belly, and his erection throbbed and pulsed and Lucy knew that this, at least, was one thing she could do, one desire she could satisfy. Squeezing him a little tighter in warning, she kissed just above where her fingers held him, awed by the velvety texture of his shaft, feeling his pulse beat riot against her lips. She circled the head of his penis with small damp kisses, letting her hair tickle him as she did so. He smelled nice, felt nice, and she flattened her tongue over the head of his penis and tasted him.

Bram nearly shot off the couch.

Suddenly his hands were in her hair, holding her, guiding her back while he murmured words of pleasure, words of need and pleading. Lucy licked him again, and again, until Bram was making incoherent sounds of pleasure, his body vibrating, the air charged around them. She opened her mouth and let him in.

He was so large, it wasn't easy, and it turned her on so much, made her so excited and wild to taste him, to know that he was ready to explode. She couldn't take him very deep, just the head. So she concentrated on working on what she could get into her mouth, using her hands to tease the rest of him.

Bram's fingers tightened suddenly in her hair and he groaned roughly. *"Lucy . . ."*

Her tongue swirled, softly, gently, and then she sucked.

Again, his reaction was immediate. "Stop, Lucy. I can't hold back. Baby, *stop.*"

Instead she struggled to hold onto him, to take as much of him as she could, and as if accepting her decision, Bram stroked her nape, curled his fingers around her head—and he came with a shout that echoed through the summer house and rattled the sliding glass doors.

His hips lifted again and again, his big body trembled and shuddered, and finally after a long time he quieted, only his strenuous breaths reverberating in the air. Lucy lazily licked him, pleased with herself and smiling at the way his body continued to flinch with pleasure.

Bram curled himself around her, hauled her up to his lap, and pressed his face into her shoulder. His arms, his whole body, were still shaking.

Stage two, Lucy thought with a smile, *successfully completed.*

Bram watched Lucy as she sliced into her steak. They were both nearly done eating, and while the food tasted good, looking at Lucy was better. There'd been a comfortable silence between them since that incredible episode on the couch, but a secret little smile kept playing around her sexy mouth. She liked it that she'd made him lose control.

Hell, he liked it, too.

Now he wanted more. He wanted her naked. He wanted her to offer herself to him in the same way he'd given her free reign of his body.

He still could barely believe what she'd done. It wasn't the first blow job he'd ever gotten, but it was by far the most emotionally devastating. Having Lucy's mouth on him guaranteed to reside at the top of his list of most erotic and satisfying encounters ever.

"Worked up an appetite, didn't you?"

With her mouth full, she looked at him and promptly choked. Bram reached across the table and patted her on the back until the wheezing turned into laughter. She looked so damn proud of herself that he couldn't stop smiling, either.

A rose blush colored her cheeks, enhanced by the early-evening sunlight filtering through the trees to the deck. This time of day, the deck was more shaded than otherwise, making it comfortable to eat outside. An occasional boater went past, laughter from the vacationers drifting up the hillside, mingling with the chirping birds and the droning insects.

At first, Bram hadn't wanted to leave the couch. With his legs like rubber and his heart still pounding, he wasn't sure he was even able to leave the couch. And he'd been more than willing to move right into stage three—once he'd regained his strength.

But she'd slipped away from his hold, giving him no alternative but to follow her.

The yard work was now done and he'd brought down

his few bags from the car, unpacking them into the same dresser Lucy had used. Whether or not she'd noticed the significance of that, Bram wasn't sure. But she hadn't said anything about it, so neither had he.

While she put fresh linens on the bed, he'd gone for another swim. At the moment, he felt lazy and relaxed and warm with satisfaction.

Lust was just below the surface, waiting for a look, a smile, from her that told him she was ready to go on to the next step. And even if she didn't make a gesture, in a few more hours the sun would set, and he'd already told her what he planned.

They had the whole night ahead of them.

Before dinner, they'd taken turns showering, and now Lucy wore a soft pale green cotton sundress. She'd also combed her hair at some point, and it hung in a silky fall to her shoulders. He loved her hair and didn't give a rat's ass if she colored her silver streaks or not. Either way, her hair still felt the same, and it was still a part of Lucy.

He'd agreed to grill the steaks while Lucy prepared the potatoes, after she'd informed him that she was, at last, famished. It was damn tough not to touch her, not to be as familiar as he now felt he could be. But even though Lucy kept smiling and looking secretly happy, she had DO NOT TOUCH signs plastered all over herself, warning him from pushing too fast.

Lucy glanced up and shook her head at him. "Stop that."

He smiled. He'd been smiling nonstop since she'd had her orgasm in the kitchen. He couldn't recall ever being so happy before.

He took a leisurely drink of his soda before asking, "What?"

"Staring at me. You're making me feel . . ." She hesitated, licked her lips, then shrugged. "Nervous."

"You were going to say 'naked,' weren't you?" He loved teasing her. He loved loving her. "I make you feel naked, when I watch you. Isn't that right?"

Primly she replied, "I don't want to put any ideas into your head." A bird flew close, then landed on the railing to watch them. Lucy tossed a piece of bread to it, and the blue jay snatched it up and again took flight.

Laughing out loud, Bram told her, "Too late, sweetheart. I've had ideas about you for a long, long time!"

"You did not." It was too absurd to be true.

"Did, too. You're beautiful and I can't help myself."

Carefully, with emphasized precision, she laid her fork beside her plate. "Do you mean that, Bram?"

"Cross my heart. You, sweetheart, replaced all my adolescent fantasies, which I gotta tell you were pretty goddamned vivid."

"Even while David and I were married?"

Realizing the seriousness of her tone, Bram, too, pushed aside his food. He felt mellow and semisated after his release and was more than willing to do some of the talking he knew needed to be done. "You're gorgeous, Lucy. Sexy. Smart and caring. Of course I had ideas about you. I'm just a man, susceptible to the same lusty thoughts as any other guy. I tried real hard not to let them show, though."

She seemed to be considering that, then said, "I'm almost forty."

"I know." He shrugged one shoulder. "I'm already forty-one. So?"

"I'm not a gorgeous forty. I'm . . . lumpy."

Bobbing his eyebrows at her breasts, he said, "Nice lumps."

"That's not what I meant."

Bram sighed. "You're talking normal wear and tear, honey. Trust me, I like your body just fine. More than fine. Hell, I *lust* for your body in a big way. Any man who looks at you would feel the same."

Lucy shook her head. "I used to be attractive, I know. It's what drew David in the first place. But now . . . I'm tired-looking and my waistline is shot and I'm . . . average at best."

Bram left his seat from across the patio table to settle at her side. He reached for her hands and ignored her reserved attempts to pull away. "Do you know what I feel when I look at you?"

Blue eyes crystal clear and wide with curiosity, she shook her head.

Bram kissed her quickly, softly. "Whenever you're around me, my stomach gets all jumpy, just like it used to when I was fifteen and getting laid seemed about the most important goal in the world. A girl would give me that certain look and I'd get the inside jitters just thinking about what I was going to do. *You* give me the jitters still."

He touched his open palm over her head, delighting in the feel of her baby fine hair heated by the sun and teased by the hot breeze. "You toss back your hair and I feel it like a punch in the gut. You laugh and I get hard. When it's cold outside and your nipples get puckered, I shake like a nervous virgin."

She laughed at him, shyly.

"And babe, there's no two ways about it. You have always had a world-class ass. When you walk down the street, it doesn't matter if you're wearing a skirt or jeans or baggy slacks, male heads turn."

Her mouth struggled with a smile and lost. "Bram," she said in admonishment.

"Lucy," he teased right back. "You might not think you're beautiful, but my gonads strongly disagree."

Lucy stared at their clasped hands rather than at his face. "I look a lot different without my clothes than I do with them on. Clothes hide a lot of flaws, you know."

He curled his hand around the nape of her neck. "When I have you laid out naked before me, you can bet it won't be flaws I'm looking at."

The smile changed to an outright laugh. "Maybe. But you'll see them all the same."

"Lucy, no man in his right mind expects a woman to be perfect, because men aren't perfect, either."

She thrilled him when she said, "You are."

Bram bit back a grin of sheer joy and remarked teasingly, "Want me to get naked and you can check to see for sure? It'd probably take a real close examination, but I'm sure you could locate a few imperfections."

"Yes. I'd like that."

"Dirty pool, Lucy!" He could feel her words stirring him, making his muscles tighten anew. "And I'll tell you right now, if you give me another boner you're going to have to take care of it."

She trailed one fingertip over his jaw. "I wouldn't mind."

He groaned at the husky way she said it. "Now stop that, woman. The next time we get something going— which if you have any mercy at all will be real soon— it'll be the full mile, and we'll both be naked."

Lucy looked out over the lake, at the way the slowly setting sun turned the water different colors. She said abruptly, "I thought about getting a boob job."

Startled, Bram stared at her. "Good God! Whatever for?"

She looked down at her chest with a wry expression. "Pregnancy and nursing is hard on a woman."

Bram cupped both breasts in his hands. Leaning down to see her face, not letting her shy away from him, he said, "You're soft and sexy, just the way a woman should be. You sure as hell don't need anything plastic added."

"I'm not . . . pert, anymore."

Holding her gaze, Bram reached around her and with casual ease lowered the straps of her sundress. Moving slowly so that she could protest if she chose to, he let the material drop to her elbows, then pulled it away from her breasts and down to her waist.

Dappled sunshine danced across her pale skin, moved by the slight breeze rustling through the tree leaves and stirring the humid air. Sitting there, stiff and uncertain, her backbone straight, Lucy was the most breathtaking sight he'd ever encountered. Bram couldn't take his eyes off her.

"Oh, babe. Anything you don't have you don't need. I swear."

Her breasts rested softly against her body, still full but, as she'd said, no longer so firm. There were a few faint lines, stretch marks from when she had filled with milk to nurse the kids. Bram traced one faded line with his pinkie fingertip, all the way to her nipple. Her nipples had been plump and soft, but now they beaded, drawing into points.

Bram swallowed hard, nearly strangling on emotion, and lowered his head to close his mouth very softly around her. Her nipple was sweet, and he stroked her with his tongue, tugged gently with his lips.

Lucy caught her breath. Her hands settled in his hair, petting him, pulling him closer as her head tipped back. With a low moan she said, "Bram, that feels so good."

"Mmm. I'm enjoying it just as much."

Lucy shook her head, breathless, heated. "No way."

Bram looked at her wet nipple, then blew gently on it and watched her shiver. She was so responsive. Touching her was an incredible pleasure. "When you were kissing me on the couch," he said, "did you enjoy it?"

Her breasts shimmered with her uneven breaths. "Oh yes."

"Because it made you feel good, too?"

She blushed a little but admitted, "Just seeing you like that . . . It made me hot to see you getting so hot." She swallowed hard. "It was incredible."

"Yes." Her words burned into him. "Exciting you excites me. And you are excited, aren't you, Lucy?"

She nodded.

"And wet?"

Lucy squirmed just a little, then shrugged.

"Don't ever lie to me, sweetheart. I know you're wet." He stroked her nipple, squeezed a tiny bit. "Admit it to me."

Her lips parted. *"Yes."*

"You want my fingers on you again? In you this time? Nice and tight?" When she nodded, he ordered abruptly, shaking with his own lust, "Straddle the bench."

He helped her, lifting her right leg up and over so it rested on the other side of the bench. Teasing her and himself, Bram lightly dragged both hands up her legs, from her knees to her groin. The skirt of her sundress rose with the movement of his hands. Bram watched her breasts as he slowly, so very slowly, brought his fingers to the juncture of her thighs, to the wet, swollen lips he could feel even through her underwear.

She jerked, her eyes nearly closing.

Bram pressed a warm kiss to her open mouth. "Your panties are soaked," he whispered.

She reached for him, but he caught her arms and brought them behind her back. "Brace your hands behind you, babe. C'mon, trust me."

Tentatively she did as he asked. The position thrust her breasts out and made her legs sprawl more widely. Bram wanted to get the damn dress all the way off her, but her expression was a mix of anticipation, excitement, uncertainty.

He slipped his fingers beneath the leg band of her panties and encountered slick flesh, swollen and ripe. His voice a rasp, he said, "I want to see how tight you are." And he pushed his middle finger into her all the way, not thrusting hard, but not slowing down until he was as deep as he could be. Her inner muscles clamped down hard on him; Lucy's hips lifted on a gasp.

"Shhh. Easy now." She was snug on his finger and Bram broke out in a fresh sweat just thinking of how she'd feel on his thick cock, how she'd squeeze him, how damn tight she'd hold him.

He couldn't stand it. "Lucy, honey." He removed his hand and lowered her skirt. Her eyes shot open, alarmed, but Bram stood and lifted her. "I can't wait. I need you now. Tell me," he insisted, holding her to his chest with trembling arms. *"Tell me you're ready."*

"Yes."

Bram nearly went through the patio doors, he was in such a rush. His earlier release might not have happened, his control was so shaky.

And then he was finally in the bedroom. He dropped onto the bed with Lucy and her hands started exploring him and Bram decided it didn't matter. It would be OK.

It had to be OK—because he couldn't bear to be without her anymore.

Lucy felt the tight grip of Bram's fingers around her wrists and then she was on her back with him over her. He kissed her naked breasts, her midriff. His mouth was open, biting gently, consuming. "Let me see you, Lucy, all of you," he groaned.

At that moment, modesty had no place. She felt only a slight prickling of unease as she lay docile, allowing him to reach beneath her dress and tug off her panties. Bram came up to his knees, kneeling between her legs, and lifted the damp fabric to his face, rubbing her panties over his cheek, inhaling her scent, while he stared down at her body. His voice was so low and deep it wasn't recognizable.

"I can't believe this," he growled. "I have you beneath me, on a bed, hot and wet, and it's reality, not just fodder for dreams."

"Bram." She'd never been wanted like this, not even when she and David had been young and overflowing with sexual energy.

"Lift your hips."

She did, and the dress was whisked upward. They each struggled until it was over her head and thrown across the room with her underwear.

Bram froze, his eyes hot on her body, his hands hovering just over her thighs. He swallowed hard, his nostrils flaring. *"Christ."*

Very gently, almost with awe, he pressed her legs open. She'd never been exposed in such a way, literally put on display, but it was wonderful and she didn't worry about how soft or fleshy her thighs had become or that her stomach was no longer concave. The look on Bram's face more than reassured her.

His hands drifted over her pelvic bones, his fingers spread until they were tangling in her pubic hair. His lips parted on a deep breath. Using his thumbs, he spread her open, and she groaned, then cried out as he bent and covered her with his mouth.

Voracious, ruthless, he tasted her, delved and lapped and tormented with his tongue, taunted with his teeth. Lucy screamed as he drew her clitoris into his mouth and suckled. She couldn't hold still, couldn't hold back the orgasm that raged through her.

The pleasure was so intense, so startling, she nearly blacked out from the throbbing waves of sensation.

When she finally got her heavy eyes to open again, Bram was standing beside the bed, breathtakingly naked and rolling on a condom. His body was sculpted of hard muscle and thick bones, his legs braced apart, his wide shoulders gleaming with sweat. There was a tightness to his expression, a stormy glitter to his eyes, that told her his control was a thing of the past.

Lucy moaned, seeing his long fingers roll the rubber up the length of his rigid erection. It was long and thick and throbbing, and something insidious expanded inside her; she didn't know if it was anticipation or fear. Staring at him, she said, "I don't know about this, Bram."

Evidently done with wooing her, he didn't give her a chance for second thoughts. He lifted her under her arms and straightened her out on the bed, moving her limp, nearly lifeless body just like he would a doll. Almost the second he laid her flat, he had two fingers pushed deep inside her, stroking. Her sensitized tissues jolted at the invasion, causing her body to shudder and flinch.

"Don't fight me, Lucy. Relax. You can take me." He

ground out the words from between his teeth, sweat dotting his forehead, his temples. "It'll be so goddamned tight I'm liable to die, but I won't hurt you."

She had no reply to that and couldn't have spoken anyway, because Bram kissed her. His body covered hers and his mouth stole her breath and then she felt him at her opening and the burning pressure began.

Wriggling, she tried to adjust to his entrance. Bram caught her legs under her knees and lifted, opening her wide, alarming her to the point that she stiffened.

"No, Lucy. Relax, baby. Don't tense up on me." He panted out the words, every muscle on his body straining. And still he pressed on, coming into her by agonizingly slow degrees, continually driving forward, deeper and deeper. True to his word, for her there was no real pain, only the acute pleasure of being filled once again by a man.

But it was even more than that, because he wasn't just any man. He was Bram, so very special, so male, so overwhelming in every way.

He paused, his eyes squeezed shut. Lucy tentatively stroked his chest and neck, down to his nipples, where she flicked and teased them. His back arched and he pushed deeper still, causing her to gasp.

"That's enough, Bram." Her heart pounded so hard it rocked the mattress. If Bram heard her, he showed no sign of it. He didn't move, but he didn't pull out, either.

Lucy couldn't get a deep-enough breath. He really was too huge, she thought, almost panicked. "Bram . . ."

"Just a little more, baby." He opened his eyes and locked his heated gaze with her wary one. "A little more."

Gently, inexorably, he pressed. Their strenuous breathing filled the otherwise silent room. His chest heaved, his arms trembled. Dark color slashed his high cheekbones and his mouth looked hard and sensual. In a rumble, he urged, "Take all of me, Lucy. Tell me you want all of me."

She wanted to say yes, but she didn't think she could.

LURING LUCY 67

Fantasizing about a man so large didn't even begin to touch on the reality. She tried to relax, tried to accept him, but she felt impaled, ready to break.

Moving her legs over his shoulders, Bram came down to one elbow, balancing himself. With his other hand, he smoothed her hair away from her face. He looked at her mouth and kissed her while he trailed his fingers to her breast and began tormenting her nipple with rough fingertips. Her muscles clamped around him in reaction, making them both moan.

She didn't think she could take any more, but he proved her wrong. Her body was burning, on fire, her breasts throbbing, her nipples painfully tight. And Bram kissed her gently as he reached between their bodies and stroked her swollen sex where she held him. Lucy caught her breath.

"That's it," he murmured, continuing to tease sensitive tissues before readjusting his hand and smoothing his thumb over her turgid clitoris. She jerked hard, crying out.

"No, Bram." Her voice was a whimper, a plea. She was too sensitive, and it felt like too much.

He continued the light touch, growling, *"Yes,"* and there was no way she could stop him. All she could do was accept him and try not to scream as sensation once again built within her.

The pleasure was too sharp, too much, making her squirm and inadvertently helping him to sink into her. Every place on her body was affected by him, her nipples rasped by his chest hair, her mouth caught under his, his erection more than filling her, his thumb driving her insane, and then, to her amazement, Lucy began to climax again. It wasn't your average, run-of-the-mill orgasm. Her body burned with feelings, her muscles all clenching hard so that she ached at the same time the pleasure overcame her.

Bram took swift advantage, pushing himself the rest of the way in so that she screamed after all, but with incredible enjoyment, not pain. He drove into her, his movement rhythmic, slick, deep and deeper. He threw his head back and arched hard into her as he groaned and Lucy managed to get her eyes open enough to watch him. It was wonderful. It was beautiful.

All because it was Bram.

The week went by in a blur. They made love in the lake, late at night, torturing each other with the necessity for quiet. Bram didn't make it easy on her. He seemed to take delight in making her scream, in driving her past the brink of a mere climax.

They made love on the deck in the hot sunshine, hurriedly because of the risk of being caught, which added to the thrill. Though at first she'd honestly believed he was too large, Bram showed her how to accept him in a dozen different ways—in the bed and on the kitchen counter. And on the couch.

He filled her up, indulging her every need, pampering her every desire. He seemed to know her fantasies without her having to ask. And he never hesitated to share his own.

He convinced her to spend one entire day naked, and they never left the cabin. They barely left the bed. She felt drowned in sensual pleasure, but in emotion, too. It had been a lush, indulgent, sultry week.

Lucy felt a little sick with foreboding when the last day of the vacation rolled around.

Bram was sprawled on the deck in the sun, dozing after having just made love to her. He wore only a pair of dark cotton shorts and looked so beautiful, tears blurred her eyes. She'd slipped away from him, promising to return with drinks.

Holding one glass over his chest so that the icy sweat of the glass dripped on him, Lucy decided to face her demons. Bram jerked awake with a curse, saw her, and laughed. He took the glass, but his gaze was wicked as he said, "Paybacks are hell, sweetheart. You can't imagine the things I can do with an ice cube."

No, she thought, but she wanted to find out. "This is the last day of the vacation. When will you pay me back?"

Bram went still, causing her heart to do the same. Then he shrugged, deliberately negligent, though his eyes burned with intensity. "If I tell you," he asked quietly, "how can I take you by surprise?"

Lucy pulled up a patio chair beside him. Looking at her glass rather than at him, she said, "I think I've decided not to sell the summer house after all."

Bram watched her closely. "Oh?"

She wished he'd say more than that. He could have been a little more helpful with the situation, maybe given some clue to his thoughts. He was so damned open about everything else. "I . . . I thought, seeing as how we got along so well here—"

"Got along how?"

She couldn't read his expression, and it made her nervous. Lifting her chin, she said, "I didn't know sex like this even existed."

"And you want more?"

Her heart pounded hard, making it difficult to think. "Yes."

"We're in agreement on one thing, anyway."

"I'm serious here, Bram!" Deciding to just blurt it out and get it over with, Lucy said, "If I keep the house, we can make it a special getaway. No one back home would ever have to know what we're doing."

Bram came out of his lounge chair so fast it nearly tipped over. She could read his expression just fine and dandy now—and wished that she couldn't. He was furious.

"So you want to carry on some illicit little affair, is that it?"

Slowly Lucy stood. "Bram . . . You know how much gossip I had to put up with. All of our friends—"

"David's friends. They were never yours to begin with or they'd have understood."

That was an unvarnished truth. Her true friends, like

Marcy, had stood behind her all the way. She cleared her throat. "The kids were hurt by all of it."

Bram's muscles bunched, from his shoulders down to his fists. "I had nothing to do with that, Lucy, and you know it."

"I know," she rushed to assure him, "but I don't want to even guess at what the neighbors will start saying if they see us together now."

"Fuck the neighbors."

She reeled back, appalled by his anger.

Bram stalked her. "What I want doesn't matter? Is that what you're telling me?"

Half afraid to ask, Lucy said, "What is it you want?"

"You. The kids. Happy ever after. The whole shebang. *Everything*." He caught her face to still her retreat. "I want to marry you. I want us to be a family. I want the right to touch you every damn night and all through the day, not just when we can slip away."

"Bram." Her heart thundered, with emotion not fear. "I . . . I can't. Try to understand."

He let her go so fast, she nearly stumbled. Rubbing his hand over his face, he turned toward the lake. With his voice sounding cold and remote, he said, "You can, Lucy. But you won't."

She wanted to touch him, yet didn't dare. She was afraid he'd push her away. "Bram, why can't we just have this? Why can't we just—"

He didn't look at her. "Because I don't feel like another illicit affair. It's all or nothing, Lucy. You decide."

Appalled, tears prickling her eyes, she whispered, "What does that mean?"

"It means I can't be a casual friend. Not anymore. I can't sit back and pretend I don't love you."

He waited, but she had no idea what to say to that. Bram loved her? Then her own anger ignited and she heard herself shout, "Since when?"

Bram looked at her over his shoulder. His hair was gilded by the sun, and his back looked like polished bronze. She felt snared in his gaze as he muttered very quietly, "I've loved you ever since I've known you."

Lucy's mouth fell open. "But—"

"But you were married to someone else?" He turned and leaned on the railing, his arms crossed over his chest, his eyes hard. "It's a fact I choked on every goddamned day. When you carried the kids was the worst. You were pregnant by David, and I couldn't bear it."

"He . . . he was your friend."

"Until the day he died. I'd never have done anything to hurt either of you. But that sure as hell didn't change the way I felt."

Lucy stumbled back into a seat, dropping hard. "But . . . you sleep with young, beautiful women. You're a . . . a stud."

"Yeah? *Big deal.* I'm a forty-one-year-old man who wants more in his life than a string of one-night stands with women looking for a father figure or a guy who's settled enough that he can buy them a good time. They see me as responsible, mature, when they're anything but. The sex is great, but is that supposed to make my life worthwhile?"

"I don't know." At the moment she didn't feel like she knew anything. Everything had changed so suddenly she couldn't get her bearings.

"Well, let me tell you," he shouted, "it doesn't."

Lucy flinched, and Bram instantly lowered his tone, drawing a deep breath in an effort to calm down.

"Being with you, that's what matters." Bram knelt down in front of her and caught her hands. "This week has been the best of my life. Not just the sex, though God knows you send me through the roof. But it's you, sweetheart. Talking with you, laughing with you. Loving you."

Hearing him say it again made tears roll down her cheeks. She sniffed and then smiled because she couldn't *not* smile. Bram loved her, and according to him, his feelings weren't new.

He smoothed her cheeks, brushed her mouth with his

thumb. "You can't begin to imagine all the times I've fantasized about you, about having a moment like this, being able to tell you how I feel. You're my life, Lucy. You're all I want, not some young female just out for kicks."

Lucy touched his mouth, almost laughing now. He made a "young female just out for kicks" sound like a bad thing, when most men would have done anything to be in his position.

He kissed her fingers. "I want a woman who matches me in maturity, who's intelligent and settled and honorable—and still so sexy that even when she's sitting here crying and telling me she might walk away, I still get hard."

Lucy threw her arms around him, chuckling and sniffling at the same time.

Bram held her, his big hands moving up and down her back. His touch was so gentle, so uncertain, it broke her heart.

And then he asked, so quietly she could barely hear, "Do you love me, Lucy?"

"I always have." That was one truth she could easily admit to.

"No, not like a friend." He pushed her back and held her there, his gaze boring into hers, into her soul. "Did you ever fantasize about me while you were married?"

Such a thing seemed sinful, by thought if not by deed; she couldn't get the words to come.

"Lucy?" His voice was hard, bordering on impatient. "Admit it—you did dream about me, didn't you? I can't be that wrong."

"I . . . I was married to David," she hedged, feeling breathless and guilty and confused, "and even though things weren't great, we—"

Bram shook her. "Damn you, tell me the truth! Tell me you dreamed about me."

"Bram . . ."

"Tell me you wanted me even then!"

"Yes!" Lucy saw his vulnerability, his fear, and everything else ceased to matter. Gently, love consuming her, she cupped his face in her hands. "Yes, Bram. In the beginning of my marriage, I only noticed you as an extremely attractive man. I was so curious, but your girlfriends were always around, always bragging, so I knew, without having to ask much, that you were a good lover. And of course that made me . . . wonder."

Bram turned his head and kissed her palm. His eyes were closed in relief, some of the tension leaving his shoulders.

"When things started to go wrong between me and David," she continued, willing to tell him everything now that she knew he needed to hear it, "I . . . I pretended sometimes that he was you."

Bram jerked around to stare at her. Lucy kissed him, giving him the words without making him ask. "That wasn't any good, because David had stopped caring about what I wanted or needed and sex was . . . Well, I still loved him as a father to my children, as a man I'd known for so long, but I didn't desire him anymore. And pretending didn't help. I knew, intuitively, that being with you would be incredible."

She drew a shuddering breath, guilt melting away with the heat of the summer day and the warmth in Bram's gaze. "So yes," she said, smiling just a little, "when I was in bed at night, alone and lonely, I thought of you." Lucy laughed, then wiped her teary eyes. "You're even better in reality than in my dreams."

Bram stood, caught her arms, and pulled her up, too. "I love you." He kissed her, long and hard. "I love the kids. Let's be a family, Lucy."

Lucy toyed with the hair on his chest. She felt like she was floating, then realized Bram had lifted her completely off her feet. "I love you, too. I think I've been in love with you for a long time, but I just never imagined . . ."

"Your self-esteem was low," he explained gently, rocking her back and forth. "It was a nasty separation and you took it to heart." Then he grinned. "Marcy knew all along how I felt. When I told her I had something to do this week, she knew that I was coming after you. And given how quick she agreed to fill in for me, I'd say she approves."

"Others won't be so generous," Lucy warned. "They'll say that we were fooling around all along, even when I was married. They'll make up stories that you had something to do with the separation—"

Bram released her and turned away. "And you don't want to take the risk of more scandal, is that it?"

Lucy caught him before he'd taken a complete step and hugged him from behind. "No, I just want you to be prepared, that's all."

Bram twisted around to her, his eyes darkened to near black. "Then you'll marry me?"

She smiled and threw herself into his arms. "On one condition."

Bram squeezed her so tight she could barely breathe. "Name it."

"Promise we'll come back here at least once a year, just the two of us."

Bram held her face and kissed her hungrily. Lucy took that kiss as wholehearted agreement. Seconds later Bram lifted her over his shoulder and started for the house.

Lucy squealed from her upside-down position, "Bram! What are you doing?"

"Getting some ice."

"Ice?" She started to giggle until Bram smacked her on the bottom.

"Damn right, woman. I told you I'd get even." He kissed her hip and brought her around to hold her gently in his arms. "And I always keep my word."

Lucy started to feel weepy again, she was so full-to-bursting with love.

Then Bram opened the freezer and pulled out the ice tray, and she took off running, laughing, loving—having the time of her life.

TRUTH OR DARE

•

Laura Bradley

CHAPTER 1

His dark, wild eyes transfixed her.

They blazed, so bold, so angry, so passionate.

He stretched his muscular neck to bring his head up, a loud lungful of air escaping his open mouth to be carried away by West Texas's dry, hot summer wind. The muscles beneath his skin rippled and flexed in a beautiful, almost graceful dance that seemed so at odds with the power of him. The early-morning sun bounced off his sleek black coat, blinding her for a split second. She shut her eyes, the afterimage of his silhouette burning into her retina.

"Hey, girl, watch out!"

A viselike arm circled her waist before she could open her eyes, flinging her off the six-foot-high metal fence just as the bull crashed into the spot where she'd perched. Through the settling dust, Shay McIntyre saw a large pair of scuffed, dusty black roper boots. She lifted her embarrassed gaze to follow a pair of faded blue jeans to where they hugged thighs so sculpted they bulged against the cotton that was worn white in places. At his zipper her imagination was inspired even though the way his Wranglers fit—tight in just the right places—didn't leave much to the imagination. Tomboy Shay actually blushed and hoped it would be written off as an adrenaline rush from her brush with danger. He wore a circuit championship silver belt buckle with a demonic bucking bovine on it.

A bullrider.

A cowboy with a death wish.

The last thing she needed to distract her right now.

With a great deal of mental discipline, Shay halted her perusal of his body parts and dropped her gaze just as his hand reached down in front of her nose.

"Let me get you out of that puddle," he said.

Puddle? Sure enough, she felt dampness seeping through the front of her T-shirt. Until then Shay hadn't even realized she landed on her side elbow-deep in a puddle, or small mud hole to be exact. It rained no more than fifteen inches a year in Sonora. She didn't want to wonder what had created this particular puddle.

"I'm Luke Wilder," her rescuer said in a whiskey-rich baritone.

"Shay McIntyre." She put her hand in his—a hand that had withstood punishment, its wide palm callused. He closed his long fingers over hers. Shay smiled. "Thanks for getting me out of the way of that bull."

"They don't call him Hell on Hooves for nothing," Luke explained in a rough-edged baritone as he pulled her to her feet. Her journey upright brought her eyes even with a flat abdomen and broad, sculpted forearms that stretched the rolled-up sleeves of his black western shirt. Her boots slid in the slippery mud, and he caught her upper arms in his hands, picked her up, and set her back down on dry ground. She doubted it was a mistake when his thumbs brushed the outside swell of her breasts as he released her, but she couldn't stop the small shiver that slithered through her at the intoxicating contact. He was a Texan; his smooth accent, indolent attitude, and chauvinistic smirk left no doubt about that.

Luke continued, "He'd love nothing more than to send everyone within his reach straight to hell. Including you."

"What makes you think I'd go to hell and not heaven?" Shay challenged, planting her muddy hands on her hips, meeting his gaze. His eyes in a deeply tanned face were a shocking changeling gray, stormy one instant and full of silvery mischief the next. They left her feeling off-balance.

Crossing his arms across his broad chest, Luke took her challenge and gave her a long, slow, thorough look from head to toe and back. He cocked his hip, tapped his fingertips against the muscle that roped his forearm, and tapped the toes of his boots against the ground. She wished her T-shirt wasn't wet, but she supposed it gave her a good excuse to give in to a slight shiver, which didn't have anything to do with being wet and had everything to do with his electric charisma. Shay's attention had been drawn to him several times in the few hours she'd been on the rodeo grounds, perhaps because of his confident swagger or his irresistible grin. Still, she wasn't prepared for his magnetism that, in close proximity, was nearly overwhelming. With conscious effort she withstood his scrutiny without succumbing to her urge to fidget. Finally, he brought his gaze back to hers, and he grinned.

"You've got that look about you, girl. Tempting and decadent. A little like I imagine Eve seemed to Adam in the Garden of Eden after that sneaky snake got to her."

While she should've been infuriated by his insinuations, the rascally little boy in the rugged grown-up man made her laugh instead. Shay looked down at the smelly mud streaked across her white T-shirt and Levi's. She wrinkled her nose. "Tempting? You have one helluva imagination."

"That I do, ma'am," he said. A dimple in his right cheek deepened.

Every nerve ending in her body felt the sensual promise in his voice, and her awareness of him, already sharp, became squirmingly uncomfortable. Shay knew that was this cowboy's intention, to turn her into a simpering mass of feminine desire. She'd resisted more than her fair share of macho men, but Luke was especially good at it. Shay had to work hard to hide that his sensual charm was working on her even though the damp heat building behind the zipper of her Levi's was beginning to distract her with an alarming power.

Shay hated nothing more than men who tried to compromise her independence.

Few tried, but this one in front of her now was doing it with a dimple.

Telling herself he was a flirt who needed to be put in his place, she met his gaze and held it.

His left eyebrow rose slowly, and he opened his mouth to push his luck.

And was saved by the bull.

The black bull bellowed, and they both turned to look at the commotion on the other side of the fence. Shay wondered how she could have ignored the chaos for long enough to have a conversation, much less a sexual fantasy. The hulking Brangus had rammed his horns through the slats in the metal fence and couldn't get them loose. The furious animal stomped and snorted in frustration. A dozen cowboys were gathered around—one flapped a red flannel shirt to try to scare him loose; another tried to shove the horns through but gave up when the bull jabbed them farther through and nicked his arm.

"Somebody go get one of the bullfighters!" one of them hollered. "I saw Darby Oakes over by Barn One. He doesn't have his gear, but I guess he'd go into the ring."

"No!" Luke called. "Leave Darby be. I'll do it."

The cowboys went quiet for a moment, the sudden silence accentuating the bull's labored breathing. Luke turned back to Shay. "Excuse me, Miz McIntyre."

Looking from the ton of sweaty, struggling bull to Luke and back, Shay said, "You're crazy."

His dimple just deepened, and his silvery eyes danced. "Beware of a crazy man with a great imagination."

Then he touched the brim of his dusty black Stetson and sauntered toward the melee. The cowboys were either shaking their heads in knowing resignation or laughing disbelievingly, but to a man all bellied up to the fence for the show.

Luke hitched a leg up onto the first slat in the fence, his Wranglers drawing across his tight, muscular butt. His shoulders bunched as he pulled himself up. Shay bit the inside of her mouth to keep from smiling at how well seeing him from the rear competed with seeing him from the front. She couldn't decide which view was better. Then the bull pawed the ground, sending a cloud of dust to turn him into nothing but a dark silhouette.

Debating whether she could bear to watch such a handsome specimen be annihilated, Shay didn't hear someone walk up next to her.

"You're right, you know. Luke Wilder *is* crazy."

Shay turned to the man standing next to her and recognized Monty Shrader, an official with the World Bullriding Professionals Tour. She'd known this friend of her father her whole life, and he was the reason she was there. "Hey, Monty."

"Good to see you, Shay. I'm sorry I wasn't here when you arrived." He stuck his hand out for a formal shake instead of the hug they would normally share if they weren't performing for any onlookers who didn't have their eyes glued to the drama in the arena. He cocked his head back toward the barn, and they retreated a couple of yards from the melee. He spoke to her quietly: "We've already put the word out around here that you're a writer doing a magazine story about the rodeo tour; that's your cover. Whether you want to use it or not is up to you. I think it would be safer, and you'll get more out of the guys if you do. Now as for the case, I told you there's been some suspicious accidents, including two that have resulted in deaths. For the first time this year, WBP is alternating between holding our events in the big cities, then little towns to build our fan base. All the accidents occurred in our small-town events, where the facilities are less than ideal. That's how we explained it away at first, but now we think we may have something sinister going on. We've sent the last busted rigging off to a lab for tests. I'll have all the other details sent in a package to your motel room."

Shay nodded.

"I want to be honest with you, Shay. The WBP Tour chose you for a reason. They think a woman—especially one with your background—is going to get more out of these cowboys than a man would. Feminine wiles and all that. I'm not sold on the idea, probably because your wiles are practically family—your daddy and I being best friends and all. Bottom line is I have the final say, and I'll keep quiet as long as you keep out of trouble."

"If you thought I'd get into trouble, why'd you hire me?" Shay returned, feeling herself tense defensively.

"You're the only investigator I know who won't go running to the media. But I'll hire another in a heartbeat if I think you're mixed up in trouble."

She didn't like his threat to pull the plug on one of the most challenging, high-profile jobs she'd had in her two years as a private investigator. She gauged Monty with a sidelong look while keeping one eye on Luke, who'd just leaped off the fence and into the arena. "And what do you consider 'trouble'?"

He nodded his straw Stetson to where Luke stalked closer to the bull. "Right there."

"The bull or the cowboy?"

"Both, but if I had to put them in order of danger, I'd have to put the cowboy first."

Surprised, Shay raised her eyebrows. "Why?"

"Luke Wilder easily has the potential to be a top-five world rider, but his talent is almost always canceled out by his recklessness. He's been an amateur circuit champion three years in a row, now he's on the pro tour, and he's changed. His daddy's made millions in the computer world, but Luke acts like a dirt-poor cowboy with nothing to lose. Something's driving that boy, driving him blind hard, and if he doesn't watch out, it's going to kill him one way or the other."

"So, how could his private demon—given he has one—hurt me?"

"A fence can keep that bull away from you, but no fence is going to stop Luke Wilder. I saw him looking at you. And here you are, can't hardly keep track of our conversation because you've got your eye on him."

"I'm certainly not the only one," Shay pointed out.

The crowd was growing, with the men and women who'd been in the barns or riding in the other arena drifting over to watch. As Luke neared the frantic bull, he waved off one of the cowboys who tried to hand him a protection vest and lunge whip through the fence. The Brangus began swinging his hindquarters back and forth. Luke slapped his open palm on the bull's rump and stepped away. The animal planted his front hooves, yanking back, muscles straining, his coat drenched in sweat that had begun to froth on his flank. Still his horns remained wedged in between the iron bars. Luke cocked his head and narrowed his eyes. The silent tension built thick as the limestone dust. Suddenly he strode forward, lightning quick, flicked one of the bull's horns loose with a powerful twist of his hand as he reached up with the other hand to grab the top rail of the fence. The bull pulled loose and propelled himself toward Luke, his pointed horn slashing just as a cloud of dust rose to cloak the pair. All the crowd could see were two dark forms merging.

No one breathed.

Then the bull galloped through the dust to the opposite side of the arena, trying to shake his head free of a black Stetson pierced through the rim by a horn.

A half-beat later, Luke leaped over the fence, his short brown hair plastered to his bare head by sweat, a cut on his cheek just beginning to leak a drop of blood. He turned to watch the bull stomping his Stetson into the dust.

"Hell. And that was my best hat."

A smattering of laughter and applause broke the tension, and the cowboys approached him with slaps on the back. A gaggle of female rodeo groupies gathered around him to coo over him and his superficial wound. Luke moved one hourglass blonde over with an arm, scanned the crowd, and grinned at Shay.

Fighting back a smile, Shay held a poker face and lifted both her eyebrows instead. He drew his eyebrows together, his eyes turned down like a puppy dog, his gaze abashed. Then she couldn't stop the laugh that escaped. He was just too irresistible. A naughty daredevil in a package so sexy any woman would be ready for him without even a touch.

Shay hoped she was hiding the intensity of Luke's effect on her as she turned to Monty. "I don't think you have anything to worry about. I'm not going to let a cowboy distract me from my job."

"What if they are one and the same?"

She looked at him questioningly. Monty's warm brown eyes clouded with worry.

"What do you mean?" she asked finally.

"The man you're looking at right now could be the man behind it all."

Luke hadn't wanted to go to the Justin sports medicine station, but he let himself be talked into it. The bull had barely nicked him. Luke had hurt himself more shaving, but his buddy Cody insisted.

"You let the Justin guys look you over. Maybe that old bull jiggled up more of your brain than your rock-hard noggin would show on the outside."

Another bullrider, Joe Zappora, called out from his place at the fence, "We're just hoping Hell's horn let some of the hot air out of Wilder's big head!"

"Not likely. With him surviving that stunt, his head's only gonna blow up bigger," Tim Auerbach put in.

"You're just embarrassed you weren't brave enough to get in there," Luke said with a lighthearted wink.

"No, we're proud that we were *smart* enough not to get in there. And you ought to be grateful you weren't hurt," Tim threw back, eyes narrowed, tone bitter. "Some of us who weren't born with a silver spoon in our mouths have to stay healthy in order to earn a living. Some of us gotta stay healthy to earn *two* livings."

Luke felt the tightening in his chest and began stalking toward Tim. The bullrider frowned at Luke, not afraid of his menacing approach. "You hotdoggers are ruining the sport for us all," Tim grumbled.

Turning Luke away with a powerful shove, Cody said

quietly, "Luke, remember what he's been through. He's not thinking straight."

Luke nodded stiffly and walked away, following Cody to the area designated as the infirmary, where the WBP kept doctors on staff to treat injuries on-site.

The truth was that Luke had an ulterior motive for going to the sports medicine tent. During the hoopla following his bull rescue, Luke had watched Seriously Sexy Shay walking with one of the tour honchos just this direction. He still couldn't believe she'd stood way back talking to the old rodeo official instead of watching him. In fact, it had been her fault he got nicked by the bull, his attention having strayed in her direction just as the bull came loose. Luke had caught her gaze there at the end and she'd laughed, but she hadn't come running breathless to congratulate him. She hadn't come running at all. She'd turned around and left.

And she'd called him crazy.

It made him crazy. No woman had ever told him that until after he'd dumped her.

It had been a long time since he'd met a woman so quick-witted, so strong-willed. It had been a long time since he'd met a woman who didn't want to want him.

Shay McIntyre might want him, but she didn't *want* to want him.

Big difference.

And one Luke wasn't quite sure how to reconcile.

"You know, Luke," Cody put in, "Tim's not all wrong. You do take too many stupid chances—"

"This is an old song and dance, Cody."

"I know, and I'm gonna keep singing it and dancing it until it's good enough to convince you. The fact is, Luke, we've been riding together a long time. You've always been a daredevil, but since you got kicked off your daddy's ranch you've been a maniac."

"Enough," Luke warned, grinding his jaw hard.

"I'm not going to watch my best friend kill himself without at least having a say. So listen up. It's time you started dealing with your emotions instead of asking a bull to deal with them for you."

Luke waved his hand in the air and avoided his friend's eyes. "You married men just envy my freedom—no ties, no responsibilities, just doing a job I love and loving a lot of women."

"I doubt you know what love is," Cody said, shaking his head sadly at Luke as he ducked into the tent.

One of the docs ushered him to a table. "We ought to just put your name on this one, Wilder, since you're our best customer. What'd you do to yourself this time?"

"Why do you automatically assume it's me who's hurt?"

The doctor just laughed.

As Cody went through a blow-by-blow account of Luke's latest escapade, Luke tried to find something to think about besides Cody's comments. A sexy woman would do for distraction, Shay McIntyre being at the top of the list. She was a contradictory combination of spitfire tomboy and composed beauty. Her straight hair that just brushed the tops of her breasts was the color of dark chocolate and looked as thick and rich. Her almond-shaped eyes and dusky skin hinted of some exotic ancestry. The carriage of her curvy bombshell body was confident yet so sophisticated it made him think she was more suited to silk and satin than cotton and denim, although she fit both of those better than fine.

She hadn't flinched at the smelly mud spread across her shirt. He'd caught sight of her earlier, wrestling in the dirt with a scroungy barn dog. Shay seemed comfortable around cow dung and horse slobber yet too good for it at the same time.

"So who is this Shay McIntyre?" he asked aloud.

Luke's surprising non sequitur stopped the conversation between Cody and the doctor. They stared at him and then at each other.

"Maybe he does have a concussion, after all," the doctor said, moving his penlight back to Luke's right eye.

Luke knocked his hand away. "I don't have a concussion. I want to know what brings a classy woman like Shay McIntyre to the prerodeo doings in the middle of West Texas Nowhere."

The doctor looked thoughtful, then put his penlight down and began dabbing antiseptic on Luke's cut. "You must be talking about the reporter. She's here working on a story about bullriders for some magazine."

"Is that the poor woman you subjected to your Superman impression back at the arena?"

"Hey, did you want her to be gored?" Luke grinned.

"You could've plucked her off and set her on the ground instead of soaring her into the puddle of piss just because you wanted a one-woman wet-T-shirt contest," Cody argued. He was happily married, with a wife who was afraid the wild man would rub off on her faithful husband.

"It was tough to manage, but it was worth it," Luke laughed, unrepentant.

"You did that on *purpose*?"

The steel edge beneath the velvet voice told Luke he just might have a setback in his seduction plan. Still he turned around to see the woman in question standing in the doorway, dark eyes flashing and hands fisted on those luscious hips. Her shirt was still damp, clinging to her curves that rose and fell so provocatively that Luke still wasn't sorry he'd been the one to get her wet.

"Ma'am," the doctor intervened, "you can't be in here right now while we're treating a patient."

"Why not?" Shay demanded, striding forward. "He's fully dressed, which incidentally is too bad. If he'd have to strip for the examination, it would be a lot easier for me to neuter him."

"Ha!" Cody chuckled. "Usually they don't get this mad until after they've known you at least twenty-four hours. But then this lady here looks a lot smarter than most."

Shay approached Luke, and the two other men gave her room. She stopped in front of the examining table and was tall enough to be eye-to-eye with him. "I don't appreciate being made to look like a fool, Mr. Wilder."

"And I don't appreciate seeing a fool get hurt," Luke answered.

Surprise flickered in her eyes for an instant before being replaced by cool anger. She flashed a controlled smile. "Then I'd suggest you watch your step, *sir*." Shay turned away then and held her hand out to Cody, who was whistling under his breath in appreciation. "I don't think we've met. I'm Shay McIntyre, in town to do a story about the bullriders on the pro tour."

"Cody Presley, pleased to make your acquaintance, ma'am. I happen to be a bullrider."

"I wonder if you might spare me a few minutes for an interview sometime in the next few days?" she asked.

"Sure, love to," Cody replied, grinning.

"Thank you." Shay nodded at the doctor and walked toward the exit.

Luke watched the sophisticated sway of her hips beneath Levi's that were loose enough to let him see some jiggle while hugging just the right curves. Damn, he was getting hard. And he couldn't resist calling out to her, even though he knew he was stepping into a trap. "Hey, girl, don't you want to interview me?"

She paused. "First of all, I'm not a girl, in case you didn't notice."

"Oh, I noticed all right," he said appreciatively as she reached up to move the flap of the tent, stretching her damp T-shirt to cup the swell of her breasts.

"Second, no, I don't want to interview you." Shay threw that chocolate hair over her shoulder to give him a cursory glance. "I'm just talking to the men who are making this a serious career."

Luke went still. "This *is* my career."

Standing there, with her silhouette against the bright light, she was a man's wet dream. Shay shook her head, shooting him a disdainful look before heading out the exit. "From what I've heard and from what I've seen, you take too many risks to be too serious about bullriding, or about life for that matter."

Frowning, Luke stared as she disappeared around the corner. In the ten years he'd ridden bulls, he hadn't found one woman who didn't consider the extra risks he took in an already risky sport to be the ultimate aphrodisiac. But Seriously Sexy Shay apparently considered his Superman show to be as arousing as a douse of ice water. And she was looking through his head as if it were as clear as ice water. Hell.

"Whoa." Cody let loose with a peal of laughter and slapped his knee. "There's no way you're getting the last word with that one. Never thought I'd see the day Luke Wilder met a woman he couldn't top."

Luke looked from the empty doorway to his friend and let a smile spread slowly across his face.

"The day's not over yet."

CHAPTER 2

After talking to a half-dozen bullriders, Shay needed to burn some restless energy, and nothing helped her do that better than a good ride. So she bummed a retired cutting horse from one of the tour officials, with a warning not to be gone too long, as the mercury was expected to hit a hundred degrees by midafternoon. Not that the heat would bother Shay, who'd been born and raised in it. She'd grown up in Midland, 150 miles northwest of Sonora, where it was just as hot and desert-dry in the summer. Her family had spent eight generations raising premium cattle and acquiring land, so it shouldn't have surprised Shay when a magazine recently named the McIntyres the most powerful ranching dynasty in West Texas. Still it did, mostly because they lived so simply that such an exotic word as *dynasty* shouldn't apply to them. Reading the article, Shay felt a twinge of guilt that she no longer lived the ranching life—she'd loved it for a lot of years but loved mysteries more, which was why out of college she'd apprenticed with a private investigator instead of taking over as the ranch's public relations director.

Shoving her left foot in the stirrup, she flung her right leg over the horse's back and slid into the saddle just as she squeezed the chestnut mare into a trot and headed past the rodeo arena. Several of the cowboys Shay had met waved and tipped their hats as she passed. She forced herself not to wonder where one cowboy in particular was at that moment.

Riding across the land, so like that of her home, brought back memories. She had been raised with the tacit understanding that a girl did certain things, like get A's in home ec, be on the cheerleading squad, and maybe barrel race if she had a wild streak. Shay didn't go out

with the intention of being rebellious; she just preferred
to take wood shop, play on the softball team, and learn
how to fly an airplane. It took some doing to profess her
independence, but now her parents and brothers respected
it and the experience of working for it came in handy.
Becoming a woman in the man's world of private investigators was a daily challenge in proving herself. No bullriding cowboy was going to get in her way.

Especially not one as chauvinistic, presumptuous, reckless, and cocky as Luke Wilder.

No matter how much his silvery eyes, daredevil dimple, and powerful swagger tempted her.

She'd gotten the last word with Luke, and she expected
he'd steer clear of her from now on. Men like him used
their sex to knock their conquests over with a feather.
Men like him didn't like to chase; they liked to be chased.
Men like him didn't like women probing their psyches,
and that is exactly what Shay had done to Luke Wilder
in the Justin tent.

And she'd grazed a truth he didn't want to face.

Was it the demon that drove him to be a daredevil and
maybe worse? Her intutition told her he wasn't responsible for the accidents, but that alone wasn't enough.
She'd find out, but not by talking to him. When she got
too close to Luke Wilder she couldn't trust herself to act
professionally—the first time she'd been nearly panting;
the second she'd nearly clobbered him.

Frustrated, Shay spurred her horse into a gallop; the
mare's hooves bit into the hard ground. The bullriding
tour T-shirt Shay had bought at a concession stand to
replace her filthy one was too big and flapped in the
breeze behind her. Her lust was definitely warping her
perspective; he was a prime suspect. Luke was up for
Bullrider Rookie of the Year; he was in line to qualify
for the national WBP finals. His well-known disrespect
for his own life could translate over into disrespect for
the lives of others. Why not knock off the competition?

It wasn't much to go on at this point; in her investigations Shay always followed evidence to the motive. But since the evidence in this case was lacking, Shay had to move backward, zeroing in on motive first.

She slowed the mare to a walk as she neared a copse of hackberry and mesquite trees, and that's when Shay heard the pounding of the ground behind her. Reining her horse around, Shay nearly collided with a big black gelding. Her mare reared and, catching Shay by surprise, dumped her on the ground. Between the dust and hooves, Shay saw the other rider's hand shoot out and grab her horse's reins before she could struggle to her feet.

She'd recognize that damned hand anywhere. She'd fantasized it touching every erogenous zone on her body since she'd met its owner.

Fury propelling her to her feet, Shay planted her hands on her hips and blew her hair out of her eyes. "I've been thrown off a fence and now a horse. Mr. Wilder, are you making it your mission to see me flat on my back today?"

The moment she'd said it, the implication hit, and the flush spread across her face at the same rate the smile spread on his. "Yes, ma'am. How did you guess?"

As she caught her breath to deliver a rejoinder, he'd leaped to the ground and, holding the reins of both horses, advanced toward her methodically. "Problem is, though, you seem to get up too quick. Are you trying to tell me you like doing *it* standing up?"

Shay backed up with each step he took toward her until her rump hit the trunk of a mesquite tree. He was close enough to touch, to kiss, to taste, to smell. That sharp, moist scent of him reminded her of rain and oak. Desire spiraled through her, making her feel incredibly vulnerable and achingly feminine. She fought it with words: "Like doing *what* standing up? Interview you? I could do that in any position."

Luke grinned. "Want to bet?"

Narrowing her eyes in warning at him, she tried to skirt around the trunk, but a low branch at her waist stopped her. His left hand wrapped one set of reins around the low branch while his right hand rose to wrap the other set around the branch on the opposite side of her head. Stopping just inches from her, he didn't touch her, but his powerful heat was overwhelming. She hadn't noticed how physically large he was before, but before she hadn't been trapped between him and a tree. Luke stood six feet, tall for a bullrider, and strapped with solid muscle.

He tipped his wounded black Stetson back with a thumb.

A trickle of sweat ran down her backbone. "Bet what?"

"You said it yourself—that you can interview me in any position. You pick the question. I pick the position. The first one to crack under the pressure wins."

Shay swallowed. "And the stakes?"

"You win, and I apologize for plopping you in the puddle." Luke paused, his head dipping until his mouth hovered next to her ear. He whispered, "I win, and you dance with me tonight at the tour shindig."

Every nerve ending craved him. The scent of his sweat, limestone-laced earth, and his unique male musk enveloped her. She closed her eyes. Her body begged for her to throw her head back and welcome his lips and tongue on her neck, to take his hands and guide them where she throbbed with need. Instead, she opened her eyes and put just her fingertips on his chest, pushing him back.

He was hot and wet under his shirt. Her fingertips turned hungry. She jerked her hands away and dropped them hard against her thighs. "No, it's not fair. I'd be winning what I ought to have anyway."

"That's because the bet's handicapped, of course. I'm sure you interview people for a living under all sorts of difficult conditions and therefore have an automatic advantage and are destined to win. I have to have some sort of incentive to compete against such odds."

His eyes twinkled and his dimple dug into the side of his face. He looked like such an innocent rascal, Shay had no doubts he talked a lot of women into doing a lot of things. She wouldn't be one of them. She'd play his game and win.

"But you make your living competing—giving you one advantage. You make your living in a sport, which gives you a second advantage when it comes to all-important position."

"Ah." Luke grinned, running his gaze the length of her, the possibilities shimmering in his eyes that suddenly no longer looked innocent at all. "You have a point. I am quite good at position."

His sexual implication hung in the air between them. Shay squirmed against the tree, hoping to dispel the sensations spiraling through her, but it only magnified them. The game was threatening her independence, compromising her case. Maybe she wasn't so good at this after all. She'd try again to throw him off-balance.

"So what position is your best?"

"The most difficult."

His ability to make her visualize with three simple words astounded her. Right now the possibilities filled her mind with amazing reality. Her blush deepened.

"I do have to point out," Luke continued, "you've already cheated because you've already questioned me and I haven't yet picked a position. So, you'll have to be *penalized* for that."

He grinned wickedly.

Visions of bull riggings tied to bedposts made her fidget. "No, no. How about we make the bet double or nothing? You apologize in public if I win."

"And I get a dance and a date if I win."

Shaking her head, she laughed at the eager presumption in his rugged face. "No, no. You get two dances."

"Well, hell. Slow dances, then."

"Deal."

"Deal."

"We have to seal the deal," Luke said. His hand eased down the tree branch toward her head as he leaned into her. "I'd say a deal like this can only be sealed with a kiss."

"I agree," Shay said, surprising him and giving her the advantage for only a moment. She used it, flattening her palm over the zipper of his jeans and sliding her hand upward. The silver in Luke's eyes darkened to gunmetal. His lips parted. Shay slid her hand higher, over his corrugated abdomen, over the swell of his pectorals. Her fingers teased the chest hair at the vee of his shirt. His breathing was coming faster now, as was hers, but she refused to think about his effect on her, or she wouldn't have the willpower to do what she was about to do.

"A deal like this should be sealed with a kiss," she whispered as she drew her hand away from his chest and held it out in front of his lips. "A kiss on the hand, of course."

Vexation, disappointment, and then finally grudging respect reflected in his eyes before Luke took his hands away from the tree and grasped her fingers, draping her hand over his.

"Of course," he said, before flashing that rascal grin. He was up to something.

He brought her hand to his lips and then, with his left hand, turned it around, cradling it palm up just as his mouth descended. The contact of his moist lips on the sensitive center of her palm was more erotic than anything she'd ever experienced before, and Shay was incapable of doing anything but simply *feel*. Closing her eyes, she leaned her head back against the tree for support as his tongue, stiffened to a point, excruciatingly slowly traced the lines on her palm. She swallowed a moan and shifted, swollen and needy, against the scam of her jeans. His hot breath blew on her wet skin, sending lightning sensation rocketing to her breasts, already aching, their nipples pebbling tighter. His lips nipped a trail to her wrist, where with tongue and teeth and in ten seconds he removed the leather band of her wristwatch. Her eyes flew open as the watch fell. Luke pressed his lower body against Shay's to catch it between them.

"Is that supposed to impress me with your prowess? A fancy form of the cherry stem trick from high school?" Shay had meant it to sound mocking—to lighten the atmosphere so heavy with arousal she could hardly breathe—instead it thickened it.

"Hell, you think *that* was fancy?" he whispered, dipping his head to her ear. His voice was rough and thick. "I'd like to show you what fancy is."

They fit well against each other, too well. His iron-hard thighs pressed against hers. His erection, so hot she could feel it searing her through the thick blue jean cotton, filled the hollow between her hipbones. It was all she could do not to run her hands down his back to that tight rear end and press him deeper into her. His hooded eyes drank her in. She knew he felt everything she felt. Suddenly for an instant there were no secrets.

It scared her more than she'd ever been scared in her life.

Shay pulled her hands loose from his and pushed herself free. Luke gave way more easily than she'd suspected he would. She squeezed between him and his horse and then walked away as fast as she could around the left side of her horse and began untying the mare from the low tree limb. Her hands were shaking, but she didn't want him to notice, so she put the horse's head between them, pretending to adjust a piece of bridle.

"Where are you going?" Luke asked, leaning over to scoop her watch up from the ground.

Keeping her eyes carefully trained away from him, she drew in a deep breath and went back to fumbling with the reins. "I have to get back to do some interviews for my article."

"Did you forget about the bet?" He idly swung her watch from his thumb and forefinger.

"Bet?" Shay blinked, her blood pounding everywhere but her head. "Oh, the bet."

"You back out now, I'd win by default. And you'd be giving up without ever trying to win that rare apology."

Luke took a big step toward her, reached under the tree and the horse's neck to slip her watch into her pocket. His fingers lingered, caught there. She was grateful the horse hid her face from him because she had to bite her lower lip hard to keep from moaning. She grabbed the saddle tightly to stop the urge to lean into those warm, mobile fingers. After a moment he withdrew them, but slowly.

"Well, what do you say?" he asked lazily, as he stepped back.

Drawing in a deep shuddering breath, Shay debated. She knew she couldn't trust her body to be around him for much longer; his sexiness anesthetized her brain. She needed to do her job, but the siren in her begged to let their sexual chemistry combust while the rebel in her longed to compromise his arrogance. Could she do it all? But how? Even when she put her defenses up and parried him with words, he skillfully turned it around to her disadvantage.

And took advantage.

Still, to have him apologize . . . that would be a coup. She'd love to take him out in the middle of the rodeo arena so every pro cowboy in Sonora could see it and she could show Monty and her father that little Shay could handle the dangerous bullriders just fine.

"All right." Shay replaced the reins and put her hands on her hips, praying for moral strength. "I've got my question."

His dimple danced. He must've expected her to turn tail and run. She'd surprised Luke Wilder; that obviously didn't happen too often.

"What's the question, then?"

Shay spread her arms out. "Is this your postion? Maybe you're the one who likes it standing up."

"I do, actually." He winked at her, then added, "But

this isn't my position for the question. I want my position to complement the question."

"OK." Shay looked him in the eye. "Can you tell me what it's like to ride a bull?"

She'd surprised him a second time.

Seconds ticked by. The cicadas perched in the trees filled the silence with their scratchy thrum. Shay saw him consider calling her bluff, and that's exactly what it was, but it was also a test. If he suggested she ride *him,* like she guessed the overly arrogant cowboy would, then she'd be gone, damn the bet. But if he didn't, well, she might actually enjoy those two dances.

Suddenly Luke turned around and unwound the leather that attached the saddle to the girth and swung the saddle off the horse's back and onto the tree. Then he untied the chestnut, jumped on, and held his left hand out.

Her gaze flew to his in surprise.

"Come on. Unless you're reneging."

Shay put her hand in his and he pulled her up in front of him on the gelding's bare back. Hands around her waist, Luke eased her bottom between his lap and the horse's withers.

He rested his head against hers and spoke so his words drifted past her ear: "The bull is in the chute, muscles quivering with excitement, with the intense need to break free, all his power just barely leashed. It's tangible—you feel it, and you become it.

"When you slide onto his back, it's all there, between your legs, so tight, near to bursting. All you need is for the gate to open for it to explode underneath you, and then you'll be out of control and able to ride with it.

"But for a minute, this minute, you're in control."

Luke took Shay's right hand and turned it palm up, pressing it down against the horse's withers, shoving it tight between her own legs. He ran the forefinger of his other hand hard across her palm. Erotic sensation shot up her arm. "This is when you wrap your hand in the rigging." He took her other hand in his and fisted it, pounding it against her "rigged" hand. "You try to get into your own head even though you know it's your heart that's gotta get you through the next eight seconds. Time warps in those eight seconds. They seem like a lifetime and no time at all. You know all this as you straddle the bull. You feel yourself letting go. Then you give the nod."

He paused. The cicadas sang. The brutal summer sun beat down on them through the trees. The horse shifted beneath her hand, between her thighs.

"The gate opens and the power underneath you explodes."

Shay had lost herself in his description, part of her hearing his double entendres and being aroused, the other part of her hearing the truth and understanding a little of the madness that drove a man to ride a ton of angry bull.

"You have to throw your free hand up, away, and you're left vulnerable."

Holding her left arm up in the air, Luke undulated his body against hers, mimicking a bull ride. His hand worked hers up and down, rubbing between her legs following the imaginary bucking, twisting, and lunging. His breathing quickened, fanning her cheek and, she realized, matching her own. Shay could feel his heart pounding against her back. The arm holding her right arm brushed her breast. Her thighs tightened against the horse's barrel, but Luke's thighs pushed hers up, letting them fall back and pushing them up again in a rhythmic motion.

"What do you feel?" he whispered in her ear, the heat from his body surrounding her.

"Vulnerable and out of control, riding an explosion of power with only my heart to guide me . . . " Shay murmured. "But most of all I feel alive."

His whiskey baritone thickened with an undertone of surprise. "That's right. You got it.

"Then," he dropped her arm, let go of her hand, and wrapped his arms across her chest and around her torso and gave it a rough shake. His voice hardened to all business. "You land on your ass or your face, bounce back up, and get the hell out of the way.

"You make the eight seconds, and you feel like a king.

"You don't, and you feel like the dirt you landed in."

Shay rested her head on his shoulder and closed her eyes, trying to imagine the letdown, the disappointment. It wasn't difficult; she felt that way now. They'd felt so close, more intimate than she'd ever felt with a man before. Somehow, she'd brushed that secret part of him and he'd closed it off. She opened her eyes and turned her head to look at him. "What makes you try it again?"

Luke paused, thinking hard. When he spoke he sounded like he'd made a revelation of his own. "I guess we do it again to experience those split seconds of feeling really alive, no matter what happens in the end."

His mouth was on hers then. Warm, mobile lips and the rough scrape of his razor stubble made the rest of her swollen aching parts beg to feel the erotic contrast. First, he gently tasted and tempted. She opened her mouth to him, tongues dancing and daring. With his hands, he pivoted her shoulders to face him; then he ran his hands along her sides, eliciting shivers of thrill. Luke slid his hands under her knee and guided it over the horse's neck. Shay didn't wait; she drew both legs up and pivoted until her body faced him. She threw her legs over his thighs. He pulled her into his lap where his hot, hard length pushed up against her. Shay moaned and shifted. Luke groaned and held her hips still against him. He'd never stopped kissing her, hard and soft, playfully, then passionately.

The desire was spiraling through her faster and faster. The horse fidgeted and whinnied. Her mare answered. Shay drew away from Luke to reach at the mane behind her for balance and realized the craziness of what she was doing.

The horses had more sense than she did.

Shay was in the place she promised herself she

wouldn't be; she let the cowboy get to her. She should've known better than to play his game.

"My interview is over."

She brought her left boot up and drew it over his lap. She slid to the ground, running her hands over her face, pausing at her swollen lips, wishing she could make them forget the feel of Luke Wilder.

Escape was what she needed. She willed some steel into her noodle-strong legs and strode unevenly to the tree, freeing her reins.

"So you lose," his voice mocked her from above.

"What?" Shay looked over her saddle at him, glad for the thousand pounds of animal between them.

"I was still answering your question. You abdicated the position. Couldn't take the heat. So I win." Luke grinned and, except for the damp sheen on his lower lip and the mound in the crotch of his Wranglers, he looked totally unfazed. Damn him.

"You play dirty," Shay muttered.

He shrugged. "Whatever it takes to win."

Shay suppressed a shiver of foreboding. Did his casual philosophy include killing to win?

CHAPTER 3

"You're not only talking about winning bets, are you?" Shay asked, her gaze probing. The relentless wind whipped her hair around her suddenly sober face.

Luke sensed a subtle change in the atmosphere between them. He answered carefully, "I'm talking about doing whatever it takes in everything. Career." He paused, deciding to shake her up. "Love."

"So, let's take love," Shay said, not shaken at all. "What have you done that would impress me for love?"

"I've never been in love," Luke said, surprising himself with his frankness, "but I'm prepared to do whatever it takes to keep it once I find it."

"Including sacrificing part of yourself? Including compromising your independence?" Shay asked disbelievingly.

"Including those."

"She'll be a lucky woman then." Was it envy he heard in her honey-rich alto?

"She won't be lucky; she'll be working for it." Luke grinned.

"She will?" Shay looked at him, suspicious. "How?"

"By sacrificing *herself* and compromising *her* independence."

As she shook her head, Shay's face softened for a moment, and she chuckled. "Sounds painful."

He laughed with her. "I imagine it is."

"What makes you think you're worth it?" Shay asked, only half-teasing. Her amber gaze caught his and held it for a beat. Her grin faded with his.

Luke clenched his jaw and looked away, past the trees to the small rocky hills beyond.

"I'm not."

He might want in Shay McIntyre's blue jeans, but it

wasn't worth her irritating psychoanalysis. Without a backward glance, Luke threw the saddle back on his horse, cinched it tight, jumped on, and reined away from the tree. Once free, he kicked the gelding into a jog and weaved in between the low-hanging oak branches until he was out in the open prairie again.

There were dozens of eager, available, uncomplicated women at each rodeo stop. Why did he pick a woman who stirred him up mentally as well as physically? Why did her questions remind him of how empty he felt beneath his brave facade? Why did her probing looks have to remind him why he'd joined the pro tour in the first place, why he couldn't ever go home until he'd made himself famous? He didn't need this. Luke urged his horse into a lope. He had three rounds of bulls to ride tonight. He couldn't afford a wandering mind.

"Why aren't you worth a woman's sacrifice, Luke Wilder?" she called from behind him.

Glancing back, Luke saw she'd caught up with him. He felt his throat constricting with emotion. No one since his mother died had really asked him that question. His father despised him. His brothers harangued and lectured him. Cody dished out advice. But nobody had ever pushed when he pushed back. Nobody but this woman. He shook his head. "You don't want to know."

"Don't tell me what I want," she returned, jamming her hands onto her hips.

"Fine, then don't ask me any more about things that aren't any of your business."

"It's my business if I'm invested in you."

"Invested?"

"The bet. I haven't paid my debt yet."

Luke smiled despite his turmoil. "One day you're going to paint yourself into a corner with that quick mouth of yours."

"I think I already have," she admitted in a rueful tone.

The way this fiercely independent woman could admit she was wrong surprised him.

Shay drew her mount next to his. Luke didn't look at her, but his peripheral vision caught the comfortable way she sat a horse. A woman only got that way by growing up on one. The knowledge made him insatiably curious for more about her childhood.

Hell, he was losing it. He never wanted to know anything about a woman except the location of her G-spot. If that wasn't enough for a woman, well, too bad. It clearly wasn't enough for Shay. But unlike most tiresome women who demanded he get to know what was in *their* heads, Shay kept trying to know what was in *his* head. Why?

"You didn't talk about your career," she picked up where she'd left off earlier. "You say you do whatever it takes to win; what does that include?"

She'd been after something all right, and it was more than his philosophy on love. Her eyes were sharp, her body language tight. She got way too nosy and way too serious for a little article about bullriders. Her probing his emotions was only a diversionary tactic; for some crazy reason, Luke felt a pang of disappointment.

Wait a minute. He hadn't liked the thought of her doing a psychoanalysis to snare him.

Then why did he feel so let down when he figured out she could care less who he loved or how he loved?

Hell, she'd turned his head around worse than the meanest bull.

Angry with himself, he ticked his list off by slapping the ends of the reins hard against his thigh. "I've ridden hurt. Concussions, broken hands, they don't stop me. I've gone to twice the number of rodeos this year my twenty-seven-year-old body probably is built to manage. I don't have a real home, just live out of a duffel bag, in motel after motel."

"I hear you're rich. Surely that makes the travel a little easer to take."

"You heard wrong. The only money I have and ever want to have is the money I earn myself." Luke tensed defensively. "And I don't know what the hell that has to do with an article on bullriders."

"Where you come from has a lot to do with where you are and where you're going." Shay paused, watching him closely before continuing, "Back to winning, then. You ride hurt, ride a lot, and take big chances. That's the stuff you have direct control over. What about the competition? Isn't there anything to give you a leg up there?"

"Not above getting lucky by drawing at the top of the bull pen, lifting weights and running to stay in shape, and keeping healthy by the grace of God and the face of Fate."

"That's it?"

"Mostly." He glanced at her, drawing his eyebrows together. What *was* she after? He added, "Unless I decided to start knocking off the other guys."

When he heard his flippant remark, he knew what she'd been after all along. Reining his horse to an abrupt halt that forced her to backtrack, Luke narrowed his eyes and watched her return. "Is that what this is all about? You heard about the accidents."

"I heard about the bad luck following the tour. You think it's more than coincidence?"

Shay sat in the saddle still and guarded—a muckraker getting her answers at any cost. He liked her a helluva lot better aroused and flustered or even spitting mad at him.

Luke looked hard at her. "You *know* they are more than coincidence, don't you?"

"What if I do?"

Easing his horse over into hers with his leg, Luke reached over and grabbed the front tail of her shirt in his right hand. Slowly, he pulled her toward him as he leaned toward her. "And you think I had something to do with these intentional accidents?"

He held his breath as they stared into each other's eyes.

"I don't know," she said clearly.

She doubted him. For some stupid reason, it hurt more than anything had hurt in his life. Her honesty should've counted for something, but all he felt was the hurt. And fear. Fear for her, crazily enough. Fear that she was messing around with danger.

"You're right; you don't know. And you shouldn't know. You're a writer, not a cop. Let the WBP honchos figure it out; that's their job, not yours. Write about it all you want, but don't get involved."

"Since when do you tell me what to do?"

Since when, indeed. Luke thought of a thousand ways to answer the question. Nine hundred and ninety-nine of them too much like a pure emotion to come out of his cavalier mouth.

"Since you come into my world and act like a fool," he threw back with all the disdain he could muster.

The amber in her brown eyes sparked. "The only foolish thing I've done since I came into the bullriding world is get within ten feet of you."

"Guess you better go find a cowboy who cares, then."

"I don't want any cowboy, period, unless he happens to be a killer," Shay said, glaring right back at him.

"You're a terrible liar." He knotted her shirt up tight between her breasts, revealing the expanse of her smooth midriff. Luke couldn't resist running his forefinger down the center of her abdomen, then along the skin at the waistband of her jeans. He hadn't been wrong about her being suited to silk. Her skin *was* silk.

Shay sucked in a breath. "I'm not the only one," she said on the exhale. "It looks to me like you've been lying to yourself so long you wouldn't know a truth if it was standing next to you."

"Run along, girl." He slapped her mare's rump and she took off at a jog. "You'll have more luck luring a cowboy who cares this way—showing off your best assets instead of your wicked mouth."

Reining her horse to a halt, Shay looked back at him, sad now instead of defiant. "Do you always push people away when they get too close?"

"No, sometimes I just kill them," Luke answered with dead calm as she rode away.

———

Wandering past the bull pens, Shay wondered which would be carrying Luke for the third and last round of bullriding that night. The buzz among the bullriders was that he had drawn at the top of the pen—Undertaker, one of the best bulls, which also meant one of the hardest to ride. Everyone wanted to draw high because the bull was half a rider's score. The rider's performance made up the other half.

Shay felt like she was made up of two halves, too: one-half that wanted Luke to win and the other that wanted Undertaker to deliver him some pain. Bullriders were notorious for having chips on their shoulders they hoped a good ride would buck off. Luke's chip was hidden underneath layers of emotional calluses. Shay wasn't being paid to find out whether unearthing that chip would make him into a man worth loving or whether he really was as charmingly shallow as he tried to seem.

But she *was* being paid to find out whether he was desperate enough to kill.

After a long cold shower in her motel room to freeze her wayward mind into submission, Shay had spent the afternoon poring over the papers Monty had sent over from the WBP. There seemed to be no pattern at first glance. The injuries had all been serious: two bullriders had died, three were still in critical condition, and one was recovering at home. Two had been top contenders, four and six on the money list, one had been in the middle of the list, and two had been near rock bottom. Three had their riggings unravel, initially blamed on the manufacturer or age or circumstance. Three had gotten pummeled by the bulls. It took one of the TV commentators' offhand remarks for the bullriding tour officials to notice they might be more than accidents. Shay had noticed some patterns of her own. The accidents had been going on for six months, since Luke Wilder had started the tour. All the accidents of the daredevils had occurred at events he'd appeared in. It didn't indict him, for there were dozens of other cowboys who had been there, too.

But he'd said he'd do whatever it took to win.

He'd said he wasn't worth loving.

Shay knew she needed to find out Luke's background. So she called in a favor from an Austin PI who owed her. She expected to have all the information he could ferret out by tomorrow morning.

The announcer's West Texas accent, dry as the rocky, scrubby terrain around Sonora, rang out over the loud-speaker announcing the last round of bullriding for the evening. Shay walked past bullriders slipping their hands into leather gloves, using their teeth to hold the leather strap while their other hand wound it around like a tourniquet to hold the glove in place. Their focus was unmistakable and—she'd noticed—unparalleled among rodeo cowboys. While they all took their jobs seriously, the bullriders cranked it up a notch. The same men who whooped and hollered and joked with her earlier in the day wore hard faces along with their protective hoof-and-horn–proof vests and stared at the bulls in the holding pens, discussing in low tones the tendencies of each one.

It wasn't a good time to talk to the men, but she watched closely, noticing the two off-duty sheriff's deputies the tour officials had hired just to patrol the bull pen area were watching, too. Cody limped up to her, smiling wanly. He'd been thrown after only three seconds in the second round, landing caught up in the bull's hind legs. Cody had gotten stomped on a couple of times before the bullfighters in clown clothing could lure the bull away.

"What's the damage?" Shay asked.

Cody shrugged, then winced. "Bruises here and there. No big deal, but I've got an industrial-size bandage on my left thigh over a stitched-up gash a half-foot long. I'd like to cowboy up and go into the third round anyway."

"Cowboy up?"

"Rodeo term," Cody explained. "It means to tough it out as only cowboys can, usually involving some level of stupidity and macho pride."

"I see." Shay nodded in appreciation of his honesty.

"So I'd normally be riding my draw, but my wife's talked me out of it. This has scared her, and she's already spooked about all the rash of accidents anyway. It's hit us all hard, to tell you the truth, like losing a member of our family. It's not worth it to me to worry her anymore, although I'm losing out on a lot of money. Unlike those fancy ballplayers who get paid even if they sit out hurt, if we don't ride, no matter what the circumstance, we don't get paid."

Shay's throat thickened with emotion at the obvious sacrifice Cody was making to spare his wife's feelings. "It sounds like your heart's in the right place."

"Unlike us black-hearted types who'll do *anything* to win," Luke put in harshly as he walked past.

Cody gave Shay a questioning look, but she was too busy watching Luke saunter away to acknowledge it. Luke wore a black-and-silver–striped western shirt, its cuff rolled up on his right arm. His Wranglers only showed through at the crotch seat and calves, covered everywhere else by black leather fringed show chaps decorated with silver conchos. He stopped to talk to another bullrider, flexing his right hand in its suede glove, the muscles of his exposed forearm rippling. He stamped his black ropers twice, leaning over to adjust his roweled silver spurs before he straightened and moved on. The shadow cast by his black felt Stetson hid his face as he turned the corner toward the bullriding chutes.

"That's not like Luke," Cody said, shaking his head. "He's usually at his most charming when charged with adrenaline before his ride."

"Maybe he's spent his charm on someone else."

"Nah, he always has plenty to go around for the ladies."

"Maybe he doesn't consider me a lady," Shay offered dryly.

"Then he's crazy," Cody said with an eyebrow-raised look at her.

"That's my line," Shay laughed. "Do you have a few minutes for a question or two?"

Cody nodded toward the main building. "Sure, if you don't mind we talk over by the bull chutes so I can watch the rides. I have to help Luke get settled on his draw, too."

As she walked with Cody, Shay's heart pounded at the thought of being near Luke as he rode. She didn't want to admit—even to herself—that she'd felt like throwing up both times she'd watched him ride before. How could she care about what happened to a callous, crazy cowboy she half suspected of being a killer?

The rodeo officials all knew to give her free access behind the scenes, so they just nodded as she crowded in with the bullriders waiting for their rides. The first rider was let out of the chute on a bull named Homewrecker.

"Great names these bulls have," Shay remarked sarcastically as they watched Homewrecker spin his rider off after four seconds.

Cody looked at her as he climbed up the metal fence for a better view. "Aw, it all adds to the show time. We're just entertainers, pure and simple, like most sports stars nowadays. Ours just has a little extra testosterone thrown into the mix."

Which was exactly why she had to keep her emotional distance from this crew, Shay reminded herself as she joined him on the fence. She might have grown up in a world that supported the little-woman theory of marriage, but she was living her life independently despite it.

"You might not want to get up on the fence in that skirt," Cody warned with a wink. "The boys will be trying to sneak a peek."

Shay looked down at the denim broomstick skirt she wore cinched at the waist by a concho belt. She wore a sleeveless, scoop-necked bodysuit on top; brown pointed-toe alligator boots covered her feet. "I'll risk it."

"Don't underestimate the low-down, dirty mind of a rodeo cowboy," Cody said with a chuckle.

"I'll try to remember that." Shay couldn't resist a glance at Luke, who was talking with a trio of other bull-riders.

Tim Auerbach was up next on Straightjacket.

"He's going to spin away from your hand!" Cody called to Tim.

"No, he's not; he's going to jump right," Tim answered as he hunkered down on the Brahma, left hand white-knuckled on the top of the chute. The bull pawed and snorted and heaved under him.

Shay's body suddenly flushed in memory of the inti-mate bullriding lesson Luke had given her that afternoon. Closing her eyes, she imagined herself in the rider's place, the hot muscles of the bull tight between her thighs, the power just barely leashed. As she heard the gate open, she opened her eyes and looked straight into Luke's. He stood ten yards away, but the gleam in his silvery eyes told her that he knew what she'd been thinking, felt what she'd been feeling. She hated it but couldn't look away.

While she watched, he put the thin leather glove strap in between his straight white teeth and began winding it around the glove at his wrist, slowly, his eyes never leav-ing hers. Shay fidgeted against the rail, despising herself for letting him control her desire so skillfully from long-distance.

In her peripheral vision, Shay saw Tim hit the ground hard on his shoulder. Luke's eyes never left hers as he slipped his mouthpiece in. Meanwhile, Cody was shaking his head as he watched Tim clamber out of the arena, white-faced with anger. "That boy hasn't been right since Hugh got hurt last year. Hugh's his brother. He's para-lyzed now, neck down."

Nodding absently, Shay made a sympathetic noise. She felt a flush moving up her chest from the obvious sug-gestions in Luke's gaze, so she finally turned back to Cody: "Do you think someone is behind these accidents?"

"You heard about those? Well, I don't know for sure that anyone really is behind anything, or maybe it's just coincidence We all have an uneasy feeling about it, but it could just be the WBP folks being paranoid. Riggings go bad. Bullriders have bad nights. Bulls go crazy. We're not high-tech around here. It's an old-fashioned sport, so it's tough to imagine anyone having enough control over bullriding to sabotage it."

"But if you were to try, how would you wreck a rigging that no one would notice until too late?"

"I guess you could treat it with something to deteriorate the rope. Those that failed literally unraveled in two. Too late to check now, though. I think they all got pitched at the arenas and are long gone."

"It could happen, right? You guys aren't especially vigilant with your things, are you?"

"No, although some of us are more so now, but not by much. We're bullriders. We're risk takers. Most of us also think we're invincible."

"You don't think your injury was anything more than an accident?"

"No, ma'am. My rigging is still in good shape. I felt good out there until he twisted right. It wasn't the bull's fault I fell right in between his legs. He just wanted me off so he could run back into the pen."

The announcer listed the placings; Luke was in second after two rounds with no one yet riding to the eight-second buzzer in the third round. Shay watched him talk with the other bullriders as he made his way down his chute.

"How long have you known Luke?"

"Ten years. We met at the high school rodeo championship, which Luke won hands down. Then we both did the weekend amateur circuit for years while we were both working, always finishing at the top there together. Finally my wife told me I ought to give the pro tour a try; she'd work while I made a go of it. My wins and some corporate sponsorships are paying the bills, so I'm still at it. Luke joined up with the pro tour at the beginning of the year."

"Why now?"

"I don't know really. Truth be told, he should've joined the pro tour out of high school; he's better than I am, always was. But instead he went to college, then went back to work with the family business. His dad owns a computer empire, and Luke absolutely hated the work. But to his family their work is the only work. He tried working as foreman of the family ranch, but it didn't last. Now he's here, and with his focus all screwed up, acting like the devil himself is after him. If you get him to tell you why, you're a magician. Luke's a big talker, just not about himself." Cody paused and looked toward the chutes. "Luke's up."

As they clambered off the rail and walked toward the chutes, Cody looked at her curiously. "You putting all this in your article?"

"No, this is just personal curiosity."

"I like you a lot, Miz McIntyre. I respect the way you can talk back to that redneck fool. But I gotta tell you something else about Luke: he's never dated the same girl more than once."

"I'm not looking to date him."

"Uh-huh, what are you looking for then?"

"Answers, that's all."

"Be careful," he said with a long look at her. "I'd hate to see you hurt."

Shay wasn't sure whether he meant with the investigation or with Luke or with both. Cody put his hand on the brim of his straw Stetson to excuse himself before he elbowed his way to Luke's chute. The Undertaker was making a racket, leaping up, clanging his horns against the rails, bellowing and fighting as the rodeo officials tied his flank rope. When Luke slid on his back, the bull nearly crushed Luke's leg against the gate before he leaped back up on the rail. Shay's heart pounded as she drew closer, trying to make note of the people around the chute for her investigation but finding her gaze returning repeatedly to Luke. He perched on the top of the gate, his tan face stony, his narrowed eyes fixed on the thrashing bull.

Monty shouldered his way in next to the chute. "Wilder. We're letting you do a re-ride. Take another draw. This bull's off."

"No, thank you, sir. I'll take him."

"Don't be a damned idiot, Wilder. We don't want you to be a statistic."

Luke looked past Monty for an instant to lock gazes with Shay. She saw in his storm cloud eyes he was doing this to prove to her he wasn't the killer. Suddenly she couldn't breathe; she was drowning in a thousand different emotions. She shook her head. Luke looked back at Monty.

"Yes, sir, I understand, but I'll still take Undertaker."

Monty opened his mouth to say something else, then shook his head and threw up his hands.

The bull had settled down for a second, sweat frothing on his neck, his sides heaving with exertion. Luke jumped on and wound the rigging rope around his right hand. His left pounded on the tight binding. One. Two. Three. Shay's concentration was so deep, she felt like she was on the bull with him. His left hand grabbed the chute's top rail as he settled his seat. Then, the bull began thrashing again, and Luke nodded fast and hard.

"OK, boys, OK."

The gate swung open. The Undertaker plunged into the open arena, and Shay understood for the first time in her life how time could slow, even stop. Each tenth of a second took a lifetime. Each twisting, roiling buck. Each vicious lunge.

Shay didn't know she'd held her breath until she began to feel faint. She sucked in some air, not sure whether the eight-second buzzer had sounded or not. Then she heard the roar of applause from the thrilled crowd and knew he must have made it. Still he rode as the bull began spinning wildly.

"Damned if he isn't just doing it for show now," one of the bullriders commented. "Someone needs to tell the boy they start marking you off for stupidity every second you stay on after the buzzer."

A few of the cowboys laughed at that.

"Well, show's over, so one of you on the rail pluck his stupid hide off the next time he gets close enough!" Monty shouted.

Just then, with a yank of his free hand, Luke released his rigging and went airborne with the bull's last buck. Luke landed on hands and knees, then jumped up and took his Stetson off to wave it in victory at the crowd. Undertaker spun around, lowered his head, and charged. If Shay had been scared while Luke was on the bull, it was nothing compared to what she felt now. The last bull-rider to die on the tour had been gored in the liver by a bull's horn.

Luke reached the fence just ahead of the bull, who'd been distracted by one of the bullfighter's colorful bandannas. The bull rammed into a wooden section of the fence, reducing it to splinters and catching part of Luke's chaps with his horn. Luke leaped over the fence to thunderous applause and the congratulations of his fellow bull-riders. He looked at Shay through the crowd and held his hands palms up.

Shay shook her head as they announced Luke's score of 92, putting him in first place and untouchable. Suddenly a possibility flashed through Shay's mind; quickly she turned around in search of Monty. She found him high on the fence, yelling at the bullfighters to get the bull out of the arena. The Undertaker was still pummeling what was left of the wood piece with his horns.

"That's not normal," she observed.

"No, it's not. Most riders would've accepted the re-ride."

"I'm talking about the bull," Shay said. "I think you ought to have the vet pull some blood."

Monty turned to her in shock. "Why?"

"I think the saboteur could be screwing with the live-stock as well as the riggings."

Monty's face hardened; the thought that the livestock were being manipulated would mean bigger trouble for the WBP. "Bulls do unpredictable things, but if it'll make you happy, I'll have it tested. I'll let you know at the dance tonight."

"I'm not going to the dance."

"I would if I were you," Monty warned. "When the beer's flowing, tongues get mighty loose."

CHAPTER 4

Sonora's Dance Slab was perfect for a night of honky-tonking: lots of loud live country music, lots of blinding neon, lots of fresh sawdust on the dance floor. And, of course, lots of smiling women in push-up bras, tight shirts, and second-skin blue jeans.

For the first time in his life, Luke didn't take note of the individual assets of any of those women because he was looking for the face of one woman in particular.

That fact alone made him angry. Shay McIntyre had messed with his head, and he couldn't shake it. Add to that the snub she'd given him after his ride at the rodeo that night and he knew he ought to snub her worse, find the curviest cowgirl in the place and dance as close to her as Wranglers would allow all night long. There were two reasons he knew he wouldn't do that, one being he didn't want to, the other being he wasn't entirely sure Shay would care.

He might fluster her temporarily, but it seemed she always kept an upper hand and her distance, unless she was throwing potshots at his emotional armor. Luke hated to be controlled by anyone, but for some reason he couldn't seem to keep his mind off the one person who was controlling him right now.

Night brought a cooler breeze carrying the pungent scent of approaching rain through the covered open-air area, refreshing the group after a day of relentless dry heat.

"You're as much fun as a June bug in December," Cody informed him, doing a three-finger grab on his long-neck and draining it. "I don't know why you insisted Karen and I come with you. Since when do you need a chaperone?"

"I just thought your wife deserved a dance or two for

hanging out with your gimpy hide all day," Luke said, eyes still scanning the crowd.

"Right. Since when did you think I deserved anything but heartache?" Cody's petite blond wife asked with a good-natured laugh.

"You've got me all wrong, Karen," Luke said, swinging her out into a two-step.

" 'Fess up," Karen said as they danced. "What's going on?"

"I want to dance but don't want to do it with one of them." He nodded to an assembled group of women on the prowl. He recognized one of them as Tim's sister, a groupie who followed the tour and had been one of the first to stroke Luke's machismo after his stunt in the arena that morning. She wiggled her fingers at him. He smiled vaguely.

"This is a first, destined for the history books." Karen teasingly put a hand to his forehead. "Are you sick? Did the bull injure some vital parts when he threw you?"

Luke just shook his head and missed a step as he caught sight of Shay talking earnestly with a bunch of bullriders. They broke up laughing, and one of them, Tim, led her out on the dance floor. Cody ground his jaw when the cowboy put his arm around Shay's waist.

"Oh, I get it," Karen said, seeing the look in his eyes. "It's that woman, that reporter Cody told me about. She's gotten to you, hasn't she? Good for her. Maybe she'll dump you to pay you back for all those hearts you've broken."

"She can't dump me if she hasn't picked me up yet," Luke said under his breath, his gaze following Shay as she glided across the floor. She smiled up at Tim. Luke's stomach knotted.

Karen laughed. "Smart woman."

Luke maneuvered them through the couples dancing on the floor to get near Shay and her partner. Just as the band's lead singer belted out the last note of a Wynonna hit, Luke leaned over between Shay and Tim. "I'm cutting in."

Shay turned her head in surprise and drew them too close. Her amber eyes revealed her sexual awareness of him in the instant their gazes met and held; then she stepped back. "I don't think so."

"There's a matter of paying a debt," Luke said.

Her eyes flashed with stubborn fury, and Tim seemed reluctant to let her go. He glared at Luke.

Luke shrugged. "You know payback, Tim."

"Yeah," Tim said as he stalked away, a proprietary hand on Karen's shoulder. "For you, payback is a bull, Luke."

Dismissing Tim from his mind, Luke looked back at his dance partner, who was watching him with narrowed eyes and hands on her hips in that way of hers meant to be intimidating. "Why did you ride that bull tonight?" Shay demanded.

"He was the top of the pen, a guaranteed forty-five- to fifty-pointer."

"He was also acting like he was possessed by the devil himself."

"What better way to prove I'm not a killer than to be killed?"

"You don't need to prove anything to me."

"Forget need. What if I just *want* to?" he asked quietly, leaning into her.

Her gaze softened long enough for him to see the fear behind the anger. She'd been afraid for him. Just like he'd been afraid for her.

It was too psychologically intimate for him, so Luke pushed the thought away and concentrated on shaking her up physically instead.

Sliding his hand into hers, Luke pulled Shay to him, claiming the small of her back with a possessive hand, and tried not to sigh, she felt so good. As soon as their bodies drew together, Shay pulled back, putting a foot between them just as the band began to play Garth

Brooks's "Standing Outside the Fire." Luke chuckled at
the irony; Shay glared. Their sexual electricity had
sparked the moment their gazes had met, and already a
fire was smoldering. Shay might not like him, but she
wanted him, and she hated that.

Good; that made two of them, Luke thought.

Shay cautiously hooked her left thumb into his back
belt loop, keeping the rest of her hand well clear of him.
Luke felt like he was wrestling instead of dancing as she
struggled to keep a ruler's length between them during
the two-step. Her feet followed the music with a natural
dancer's intuition, but her stiff body and his own need to
feel her against him frustrated him. Her long-fingered,
silky hands began to relax in his by the end of the song,
so that when the band started a new song he'd gotten her
close enough to feel her heat and smell that rich honey
scent of her. *Maybe this wasn't such a good idea,* Luke
reflected as he forced his escalating libido from being displayed clearly in his Wranglers.

The song was fast and fun, and Luke spun her out a
few times, watching her dark hair fan out behind her. She
was a sensual dancer, fluid and expressive, following easily as Luke tried more and more complicated steps. Their
bodies and feet communicated without words. Halfway
through the song she couldn't keep from flashing a reluctant smile. By the end of the song, she was breathless,
and he spun her out one last time, drawing her back into
his arms. Only then did Luke notice that the couples
around them had stopped to watch their fancy footwork.
When they clapped appreciatively, Shay looked up at him,
surprise in her eyes. They hadn't noticed anything but
each other.

As the other couples found their places on the dance
floor again, Luke savored the feel of her back, deliciously
rounded backside, and long, strong legs plastered against
the front of his body. He held her hands in his, their arms
crossed over her rapidly rising and falling breasts. Luke

dropped his face down to take a deep breath of her hair—honey and ginger.

Sweet and spicy.

Suddenly realizing the position she was in, Shay wrenched herself out of his arms just as the next song began. She spun to face him, blowing her wild-child hair out of her eyes. She went from wanton to composed so fast it made his head spin. "That settles the bet then," she stated.

"I'm afraid it doesn't," Luke said, stepping closer.

"You got your two dances," she countered, turning to go back to the sidelines through the couples already dancing on the floor.

Luke walked up behind her, catching hold of her hands. He whispered in her ear, relishing the slight shiver that ran through her, "The deal was slow dances. Those weren't slow."

Shay shot him a look of frustrated fury and not a little fear. "*Slow* is a relative term, cowboy. You're used to a ton of bull going a thousand miles an hour. A two-step with the opposite sex is slow compared to that."

"I can do a lot of things slowly with the opposite sex, girl," Luke said into her ear.

"And I bet you can do them standing up, too," she returned.

"That, and ways you've never imagined." Luke turned her around and drew her against the length of his body, expecting her to be stiff and unyielding, but sometime in the last thirty seconds she'd given up the physical fight. Shay was supple, warm, and undulating in his arms. He ran his hands down her shapely back. It would be too much to hope she'd stopped fighting him altogether, he warned himself, as he enjoyed the sensation of the perfect fit of her body against his.

As they moved together to the music, Luke wondered how a man so wound up and hot for release could feel so peaceful and whole at the same time.

———

"One more dance," Luke said in her ear at the end of the second slow dance.

Shay shook her head against his shoulder. "No, cowboy, I'm not so far gone that I can't count."

"I can fix that."

Shay stepped out of his arms and looked at him with a rueful, honest smile. "You're trying your damnedest to."

He gave her his best earnest look. "You owe me one more song. You argued for the first half of the first dance, so it didn't count."

"You only play by the rules when it works to your advantage."

"Is there any other way?"

Shay knew she was playing with fire. He was a suspect and that should be enough to stop her. But Luke was just too damned sexy to resist, even with his idiot recklessness, his emotional calluses, his macho mouth. As soon as she got mad enough to stomp off without a backward glance, he'd give her a tender touch, flash that rascally grin, or deliver a smart rejoinder that would draw her back. Something about the way he held her was hypnotic, beyond their sexual attraction that was now so hot it likely glowed brighter than the Dance Slab's neon.

But Shay had never backed down from a challenge, and she'd never seen one as bold as this one. She could admit her attraction to him and still refuse it, couldn't she?

As the strains of Faith Hill's "Breathe" began filling the room, Luke held his arms out. She stepped into them and felt the thrill of desire sharper than before. She'd thought her body would get used to being exposed to him, kind of like developing a higher tolerance for alcohol. But no, he was more intoxicating with each touch, each look.

She felt drunk, and she hadn't even had a sip of beer.

Shay put her hands around his neck, her hips echoing the movement of his.

Luke let his hands leave her back, trailing down her sides, grazing the swell of her breasts, easing in at her waist, flaring out at her hips, guiding them closer until she could feel his hard length again filling the hollow between her hipbones like he was laying claim there. The slow burn that had been building since their first dance took flame, and she felt herself meeting his pressure with her own. He cupped her buttocks. Shay bit her bottom lip to keep from moaning against the hollow at his throat and sucked in a breath full of the rainy oak scent of him now thick with the promise of sex. Then his fingers danced back up the sides of her hips, his thumbs edging between their bodies as he retraced his path back up. His thumbs grazed her suddenly tender abdomen, up her ribs, just barely teasing the edges of her hard nipples, throbbing for his touch. His hands cupped the underside of her arms, tickling her until she wriggled. He moaned then and rested his lips on the shell of her ear. Shay almost didn't hear him for the way desire was deafening her.

"Shay, stop moving or I'm about to embarrass us both."

It was the first time Luke had called her by her name. She looked up into a face that was naked with need, eyes that had darkened to a gunmetal gray. It was a glimpse into his soul. Shay wondered how long she'd get to know this part of Luke before it went back into hiding behind that reckless cowboy facade.

Her decision was made then.

She brought her hands to cup his jaw, and his mouth met hers. He drew her against him, kissing her deeply. It was a hungry kiss, but not frantic. It was hungry for something beyond sex.

It was hungry for making love.

When they drew apart, Shay realized the other couples were two-stepping to a new song that had begun no telling how long before. Without speaking they both moved to the edge of the dance floor, his hand at the small of her back but not touching her anywhere else. Shay looked up at him as they found a table. Apprehension showed in a tightness around his eyes; their kiss had moved him as much as it did her.

The only difference was it had moved her to acceptance and him to trepidation.

"I'll go get us something to drink," Luke said quickly, pulling out her chair for her. The emotional armor was up; she knew he wouldn't be coming back. But then he turned suddenly to leave and collided with a drunk trying to weave around the table. The old man's whole sixteen-ounce cup of beer cascaded down Shay's back and shoulders.

She jumped up to keep the beer from soaking into her skirt.

Luke looked like he might like to escape anyway for a moment, then went to the neighboring table and grabbed a handful of napkins and began wiping the liquid from the skin at her neck and chest. His eyes met hers and flashed with the passion he couldn't run away from.

"Why is it I always end up *wet* around you?" she said in a low voice, this time fully intending her double entendre.

"Maybe you're just in the wrong place at the wrong time," Luke said, his face guarded, the sensual hurricane raging in his eyes belying her effect on him.

"Or maybe it's just the opposite," she said and waited a beat as that hung in the air between them. "Regardless, I'm going to need help getting out of these clothes."

He raised his eyebrows but didn't respond. He handed her the rest of the napkins, using the other half to clean the table.

She could sleep with him and still ask her questions, couldn't she?

The trouble was, now she wasn't sure she wanted all the answers.

Walking her hands across the soggy napkin-littered table, she leaned across, pinning him with a look of raw sexual promise. Shay lowered her alto: "Time to cowboy up, Luke."

CHAPTER 5

As Shay slid her key into the lock of her motel room, Luke covered her hand with his, turned her around with her back to the door, putting his other hand behind her head. He kissed her again, long and deep. A serious kiss that held desire in check. Shay's heart swelled. He could've ravaged her mouth and she would've relished it, but instead he tested another kiss that promised her a night of making love.

Rainwater ran down the side of her cheek and dripped onto his back from the brim of his Stetson. The thunderstorm had caught them as they ran to her Mustang and, as summer storms do in West Texas, was blowing through with violent speed. Lightning ripped through the night sky now, followed by a bone-shaking clap of thunder. The air around them was thick with steam from the pavement and their own arousal.

"Why did you decide to do this?" he asked.

"You called me Shay instead of 'girl.' "

"Is that all it took? I would've called you Shay in that mud puddle this morning and spared myself all this hard work."

She laughed. "Why did it take you so long to say my name?"

Luke tightened his jaw and watched another jagged bolt of electricity light the sky. "I never say a woman's name," he finally said. "It's always 'darlin',' 'girl,' 'sweetheart.' "

"Why?"

"Because it makes them easier to forget."

"So I guess you'll have to remember me at least until tomorrow."

"Shay, with the way you dance, I've got enough to remember 'til next week at least," Luke said with a teasing grin. "How about working on building my memory for a little longer?"

His mouth closed over hers as she worked her fingers to open the door. This kiss was raw and opened all the barriers to their desire. Thunder rumbled as the door swung open. Once they were in, still kissing her, Luke pushed her with his body against the wall and kicked the door shut. Shay was squirming with a seemingly insatiable need. She threw off his Stetson and watched it fall on a manila folder that hadn't been on the floor when she'd left. Ignoring it, she buried her hands in his thick dark hair as his hips kept her pinned to the wall. Luke ran his lips down her neck as he inched her skirt up.

"I taste like beer," she warned, surprised by the huskiness in her voice.

"Honey and ginger beer," he answered, his tongue wetting a path down to her cleavage. "An exotic taste for an exotic woman."

His mouth met hers again, his tongue plundering and hers plundering back. Her thighs trembled to have him between her, his erection grinding into her but not hard enough. Shay yanked his shirttail out of his Wranglers and threw the snaps open, claiming his broad chest with her hands, then pulling her mouth from his to taste his salty chest.

"And you taste like oak and rain and raw earth."

"A rank, water-logged tree, how appealing. Maybe I should start wearing a scent besides me and bull," he chuckled as he brought her skirt up to her waist and tried to dive his hand into her panties. "What *is* this?" he asked with a frustrated look at her torso-encompassing top.

"A bodysuit; it snaps between my legs."

Pulling his eyebrows together, he looked like a frustrated little boy. "Why'd you wear such a silly thing?"

"To protect myself from you, I guess," Shay said, surprised by the sudden realization.

"Too late." He grinned, the crow's-feet around his eyes crinkling sexily. He pulled her elastic skirt down to the floor, then bent down on one knee. He drew her right booted leg onto his shoulder, nibbling kisses and bites as he went. Shay moaned and writhed against the wall as he kissed her inner thigh and closed in on the mound of her sex that was so hot and throbbing and ready for him she didn't know how much longer she could stand to wait.

His mouth opened wide, closing gently over her, sending his hot breath through the two layers of fabric. Shay braced her hands against his shoulders as a wave of sensation rippled up through her. Then, his teeth settled on one snap, pulling it free. His mouth moved away, nibbling her other thigh, before Shay cried out and directed his head back to where she needed him most. He grinned up at her, then teased around the second snap until she kicked him in the back with her booted heel before he finally pulled the last snap free with his teeth.

"Satin and silk," he said as he saw her pink satin panties. "I knew it."

Through the satin Luke ran his tongue along the cleft, stopping at her swollen clitoris to tease it through the damp fabric. As his callused hands slid her panties down, his lips and mouth found her center hot and wet for him. Shay moved against his lips, feeling the waves of color building behind her closed eyelids. She'd never had someone drive her to this so fast, with such wild abandon, and by doing so little. But it just made her want more.

"I want you inside me, all of you."

"I want to make you happy," he breathed between her thighs, palming her buttocks as he brought her to him again.

"You will," she moaned, pulling at his hair to draw him up. "I want to feel you. Up here *and* down there."

Slowly, reluctantly, he rose, biting a trail over the swell above her triangle of hair, his hand drawing her leg around his waist, his other hand working up under her bodysuit, drawing it over her head as she willingly shook it off. His fingers replaced his tongue, gliding slickly around her swollen center and into where she ached for him, diving repeatedly. Fumbling with his belt and zipper, anxious to free him, she moved against his hand. His mouth dropped to her breasts, licking at her nipples through the satin and lace of her bra as he released the clasp from the back. When the clasp was free, he pushed the cups out of the way and allowed a strap to slip off one shoulder. Luke's tongue teased each nipple of her swollen breasts, until she was begging him to take them into his mouth. He began gently sucking, then drawing the nipple into his mouth hard, echoing the way she wanted to draw him into her.

Finally she had his zipper down, but not free. He was too hard and big, filling the vee space tightly with his thick length. She shivered in anticipation.

"Please, Luke, I want you now."

He withdrew everything from her, his mouth, his fingers. She felt desperately vulnerable, left hanging on the brink. Luke stared into her eyes. "Are you sure, Shay?"

The way he said her name, all whiskey and leather, would've been enough to put her over the edge; she was that close. But she held herself together, waiting for him. "Yes, yes."

With a rough shove, he had his jeans down around his knees, followed by his Jockeys. She stared in awe at the raw masculine beauty of him for a moment. "It's my turn," she murmured.

"No, we have plenty of time for that later," he said in a thick voice, drawing her other leg around his waist as he handed her a packet he'd slid out of his jeans pocket. "You can do this for me."

Shay opened the condom and slid it down ever so slowly, watching with a feminine thrill at the power she had over him as Luke held himself unnaturally still, muscles steel tight. He threw his head back, closing his eyes and flexing his jaw at the pleasurable pain.

"Did that have to take you so long?" he asked.

"I can take longer," she offered.

"Later," he promised.

"We're going to be very busy later," she quipped.

"Yes, we are," he said roughly, cupping her breasts possessively as he brought his mouth down on hers with a brutal urgency. Shay loved it, answering each slash of his tongue with her own, drawing him with her hand to her center until he hovered just at the entrance. She moved into him, but he stilled her hips, staring into her eyes.

The time was there, between them without a word, and he entered with a long, deep, slow stab. Time stood still for an instant as all the pent-up desire and passion rushed up to consume them. He plunged into her as hard. She rose to meet him, her hands gripping his shoulders, her legs wrapped around his hips.

"Deeper, Luke." He swallowed her cry as she flew over the brink. He drove her again and then again; before the waves of one orgasm could subside she was overwhelmed by the next until finally he plunged his deepest and shouted her name. As she felt him shudder in between her legs, she dived with him in a free fall that obliterated anything before in her life as meaningless.

They'd melted into each other.

The beating of their hearts was all Shay could feel for the longest time. She didn't know how long he held her up, for she'd ceased to have the power to do it herself. Finally, he eased her to the floor and looked her up and down, the smile growing on his face with each inch of skin he perused.

"You," he said softly, "look absolutely incredible."

Shay looked down at the boots she still wore with her concho belt. Her bra dangled from one shoulder. "Hmm. It seems you haven't done your job."

"I haven't?" Luke looked hurt.

"Certainly not," she said in her primmest voice, or as prim as she could be standing naked yet accessorized. "You came here to help me get undressed. You haven't quite finished."

"Well, come here and let me finish," he said, pulling her to him by the tail of her bra.

She slapped his hand away. "No, me first."

Shay ran her hand over his shoulders and pushed his shirt off, down sculpted shoulders and biceps and the sexiest forearms she'd ever seen. Then she moved down his abdomen, kissing a path and watching with a grin as his erection jumped in response. Her hands slid his Jockeys and jeans down until his boots stopped them. With her hip, she bumped him onto the bed, where he lay, propped on his elbows, grinning at her. She straddled his leg and yanked on his boot, pulling it free.

He groaned and reached for her. "We're not going to finish undressing you if you don't get out of that extremely tempting position."

She knocked him gently on the head with his boot as she eased his clothing and sock off his long, sexy foot. Then, slowly, teasing him, she straddled his other leg and pulled the other boot off.

"OK, now I have enough to remember you for a month," Luke quipped, pulling her by her waist onto his thighs.

"Only a month?" Shay looked over her shoulder at him with a cocked eyebrow.

"I've got to keep you on an incentive plan." Luke flashed a dimple. "There's lots more hard work to do."

Hooking a forefinger beneath her bra strap, he slid it down her arm and over her hand, drawing the lace and satin over his nose. "Can I keep it?"

"To add to your bra collection?" Shay turned back around, surprised to feel a jolt of jealousy.

"Bra collection of one," Luke said, sitting up to kiss her on her neck. He ran his hands down her neck, chest, over her breasts that leaped into his hands, nipples aching again for his attention, down her abdomen that quivered at his touch. His hands spanned her hips and turned her to face him, settling her in his lap.

"How is that possible, considering all the girls and sweethearts and darlin's before?"

"Because they don't get the chance to take theirs off," he said, kissing her hairline as his hands worked magic on her every erogenous zone, many she hadn't known were so sensitive.

"I can see you're into deep relationships," Shay returned, reminding herself to take this night as a night of sexual fulfillment and nothing more.

She was afraid it was already too late for that.

"I'll show you my kind of deep relationship, Shay," Luke said, huskily, pulling her on top of him as he lay back.

He filled her so deeply that she nearly cried out in release immediately, but he held her still until he felt her regain control. Then he claimed her breasts with his large hands, teasing them until she was back on the edge. He waited again, his gunmetal eyes holding her in place until he moved his hands down to her hips, slowly moving her, his hips undulating beneath, drawing himself in and out, rubbing her in just the right places, withdrawing and filling at just the right times to bring her to a pinnacle she'd never reached before. Finally, she could feel the colors building behind her eyelids and she speeded the rhythm, defying his quelling hands, moving her breasts against his naked chest. Then, she straightened, throwing her head back to feel the desire spiraling through them both until it changed into something else, something deeper, something shared. With cries of passion they turned into a kiss, Luke and Shay flew free together.

As she fell asleep, nestled next to him, Shay wished she could make that moment last forever, and later she dreamed she had.

Hours later, Luke awoke from the deepest sleep he'd ever known. Slowly he became aware of a feeling he could only define as wholeness. He felt Shay's heartbeat against his chest, her body curving perfectly to his. He had one arm cradling her midriff, his leg thrown over one of hers. Her mahogany hair felt like rich silk against his cheek. Her honey-ginger scent mixed with the musky smell of their night of lovemaking. Each breath drove him to want to wake her and spend the day finding new ways to make her as fulfilled as he felt right now.

Gently he ran his fingertips where the predawn light began to play along the satiny skin of her arm. He'd been sated, over and over again, last night.

And, yet, he wanted more.

Shay McIntyre had the incredible ability to read his body like she'd known it forever; more than her touch, even her words had been right—whether they were serious or teasing or begging or grateful. He'd been with more beautiful women, more experienced women, but none were as sexy as Shay.

She stirred in his arms, murmuring in her sleep, her luscious lips opening to show him the cute, and extremely talented, pink tongue of hers. Luke forced himself to lie still when all he wanted was to see her amber eyes, eyelids heavy with sleep and satisfaction, waking up to him.

Luke wasn't sure how long he held her, savoring and thinking. The dawn light through the curtains grew brighter, and finally she awoke, stretching and wiggling against him. Luke groaned in her ear at the force of his arousal. "Good morning."

"It's not morning yet, is it?" she yawned.

Drawing her earlobe into his mouth, he tickled it with his tongue until she moaned and turned to face him. She looked down between them and back at him with a raised eyebrow. "You're insatiable."

"You make me that way." Luke cupped her face in his hands and gave her a deep kiss.

Drawing away, Shay gave him a playful push in the center of his chest. "No matter how much I might want to, I'm not doing anything before I take a shower."

Luke tweaked a nipple. She glared. He grinned.

"Haven't you heard of doing more than one thing at a time?"

"I thought that only applied to chewing gum and jumping rope." She slid out of bed.

"I'll show you what else it refers to." Luke followed her into the bathroom, reaching to cup her bare buttocks. Laughing, she slapped his hand away.

He put a hand on hers to stop her from turning the faucet. "Tell me how you like it, ma'am. Cold or hot or lukewarm?"

"I thought you'd know after last night," she scolded mockingly. "I like it hot as you can make it."

Luke leaned over to test the water for her. "This is as hot as the water gets, but I can make it hotter."

"Is that right?" Shay arched a brow as she stepped into the running water. "I guess you'd better get in and show me how."

"I thought you'd never ask." Luke followed her into the small space, reaching down for the soap. Watching her throw her head back into the stream, her long neck stretching, he marveled that an act as simple as that could make him want to abandon his slow plan of seduction and bury himself into her right then.

But Shay was worth the wait.

He lathered his palms and knelt down, running his fingers between her toes, over her feet, up her shins, over her calves and knees to her water-slick thighs. He stopped to lather up and heard her whimper of need over the rushing water. Luke moved back to where he'd left off, running his hands over her buttocks, between her legs, and up over her triangle of pubic hair to her abdomen with that sexy swell just below her navel. He circled his finger in her navel and she grabbed his head in her hands to draw him into a lusty kiss.

Luke drew back. "I'm afraid you're not completely clean, ma'am."

"Around you, I'm never going to be completely clean," she observed wryly as he went back to ministering to her midriff, back, and each breast in excruciating detail. Washing her armpits made her giggle, and he did it again just to hear the sweet sound.

He kissed the hollow at her throat as he reached for the shampoo, working it into her gorgeous hair, massaging her scalp, rinsing it clean. Luke didn't think he could wait any longer. He was harder for her now than he'd been after a day and night of foreplay. But she opened her eyes and pinned him with a quelling look. "My turn," she said in that silky alto.

She went slower, though Luke admitted it might have been his lust-altered perception, as she worked from his head down, her long, graceful fingers massaging his muscles, slippery on his skin. When she got to his erection she washed it with just the most torturous mix of gentleness and roughness. Luke pulled her back up to him, barely able to talk. "I think I'm clean enough," he said, unable to keep his kiss from being rough. But she loved it, tugging at his hair, tangling with his tongue. He pushed her against the cold shower tile and drew back, then buried himself into her. And paused. She sighed his name. She felt so good, so right.

There, in a shower in a no-name hotel in the middle of West Texas Nowhere, Luke Wilder felt like he'd come home.

The water had long since gone cold. Luke looked into her passion-filled eyes. "Are you OK?"

"No," she said, her eyes heavy-lidded with lust. "I need you to hurry."

"Hurry?" he teased, pulling out ever so slowly and easing slowly in again, enjoying the myriad of sensual sensations reflected in her eyes. "How about that?"

"No, that's not it at all." Shay shook her head almost desperately. "Faster."

Luke moved slower and dived deeper, again and again, until she was nearly panting. "How's that?"

"Like that, but faster."

"I aim to please."

"You do; you do," she breathed, drawing his head to hers in a deep kiss that drove him to the edge. He felt her ready but drew back to look into her eyes as they both careened into that place that was new to him—not just exhilarating release, but bone-shaking in its ascension and incomparable in its spiraling peace. A few minutes later, after Luke had filled every inch of her face with feathery kisses, she protested the cold tile.

He put her gently down. "I'm going to feed you."

"You've fed me about a half-dozen times, now."

"Real food, Shay. I want to keep your energy level high." He winked.

"I'm just going to stand here in the ice water for a minute and get my body temperature back from stratospheric to normal."

Kissing the single freckle on back of her left knee, Luke got out of the shower and, toweling off, stepped into the room to collect his clothes. He slipped into his underwear, jeans, and boots. He began to whistle, surprising himself at how light and joyful he felt. He might just break into a skip; he grinned at himself in the mirror at the silliness of it. Even as a boy he hadn't ever felt like this, always dragging around the weight of expectation from his big brothers, the business, his father. Luke was labeled a carefree rascal, but the truth was it was a hard-earned reputation he was driven to uphold. The way he felt now—like jumping onto a passing cloud—might be ridiculous except he was beginning to realize this condition was something to take seriously.

He was in love.

Luke reached down to retrieve his hat off the floor and saw the manila envelope with an Austin return address.

Luke's stomach clutched.

It was addressed to Shay McIntyre.

Underneath it said: PRIVATE INVESTIGATOR.

She'd lied.

He peeled open the envelope and pulled out the papers.

They detailed the life history of one Luke Mason Wilder.

She'd pried.

And that was much, much worse.

CHAPTER 6

Shay finally felt closer to normal, or as close to normal as she was going to get and still be this near Luke Wilder. Shay's body felt like it belonged to someone else, and in many ways it did. She wasn't the same woman she had been twenty-four hours ago.

The realization stopped her for a moment. It scared her and thrilled her. She turned off the faucet and toweled off, hearing Luke whistling in the other room. She smiled, even as she ran the rough motel cotton over sensitive skin.

The whistling abruptly stopped. Shay ran the brush quickly through her hair, wrapped the towel around her, and peeked out into the room.

Luke stood damp and bare-chested, his Wranglers only half-zipped, reading a handful of papers. It took Shay a moment to peruse his body first before being curious about the papers, but once she got his face—dangerously empty—she knew she was in trouble. He held the envelope she should've kicked under the bed when they'd come into the room last night. It had to be the envelope from her colleague in Austin.

Shay was mad at herself—for being careless at her job, for letting her heart believe Luke was innocent when her head shouldn't have accepted it without proof. She'd never been so angry.

But she wasn't as mad at herself as he was.

When Luke looked up at her in the doorway, his face tightened with barely contained fury. "So you're lying *and* spying."

"What have I lied about?" Shay asked.

"You're not a reporter working for a magazine. You're a private eye working for the WBP."

"You ought to understand," Shay threw back, hating

the hard bite of her own words. "Aren't you the one who said you'd do whatever it takes to win?"

"I did, and as I recall, you didn't like it very much."

"No, because it makes you a more viable suspect. And I didn't want that."

"Oh, sure, you didn't want that; that's why you ordered the gory details of my life. That's why you spent the night getting to know me inside and out," he snapped with a narrow-eyed look at the rumpled bed, her clothes strewn around the room. A flash of betrayal showed through his armor of anger for an instant before he lashed out again. "You certainly are a *thorough* investigator; you must get a lot of practice."

His barb hurt, but she refused to let it show. She held her voice calm. "I asked for that information to clear you of suspicion."

"Well, it certainly won't do that. While I don't have a criminal record of sabotaging rodeos with wild abandon, I do come off here as a poor-little-rich-boy-gone-poor-again, a sullen, good-for-nothing son who was disowned by his family. That might be enough for a motive."

"I haven't read it yet," Shay said softly, hurting for him now more than for herself. The pain of his childhood was etched on his strained face and in the miserable tension in his body. She knew instinctively he'd never said those words to anyone before, but he'd carried them in his heart always.

"Don't bother, unless you like a good tragedy of a wasted life."

"Luke, the only time you waste your life is when you live it for someone else instead of yourself."

"Oh?" Luke raised his eyebrow. "I didn't see PSY-CHOLOGIST written after PRIVATE INVESTIGATOR on your envelope."

"It's not," Shay said. "Here is who I am. I grew up in Midland; I have three big brothers. I went to college at TCU. I got out and apprenticed with a private investigator with my parents' reluctant support. I started out on my own two years ago. I live in a small house with a cat named Richie. I've collected enough information about this bullriding to think it is sabotage, and I know you didn't do it. And that's the truth."

"I can't trust that's the truth."

Shay could see he'd closed himself off again. She'd lost him not by the private eye business so much as poking into his past. She dropped her towel and began to dress in fresh panties, bra, T-shirt, and jeans, noting his jaw flexing. She knew that despite his anger, he wanted her body again, but it wasn't enough for Shay. She wanted him to want her heart, her soul. Yet she knew it was a long shot with a man with such emotional scars. A man she'd betrayed.

"How can I prove it to you?" She could see she'd driven him to be even more reckless, more willing to risk his life on the next bull just to prove he hadn't lost control of his life.

"Why do you need to?"

"Because I care about you."

"That makes one of us."

He'd said more than he'd intended with the flippant remark. Shay decided to play life his way and see if she could win back another chance for them both.

"How about a high-stakes competition to find out the truth?"

He narrowed his eyes and stalked closer to her, step-by-step, finally circling her slowly with his hypnotic words. "While I can attest to skills that might make you a good bullrider—wicked wraparound legs, a body with just the right combination of tight muscle and exquisite rhythm, and a perfect stroke with your free hand—I really think the bullring is not the place for you."

Shay steeled herself against the shiver he'd expertly orchestrated. How could she want him when he was being intentionally cruel to her? How could desire course through her at his words that were only meant to push her away? "That's not the kind of competition I'm talking about. I want us on equal footing—how about Truth or Dare?"

"I haven't played that since high school," he scoffed, walking back across the room, away from her.

"That certainly surprises me," Shay said acidly, "considering your level of emotional maturity."

He aimed a narrow look at her. "Very funny."

"It wasn't meant to be. How about the game?"

"I don't care enough to go to the trouble of a game," Luke said, his face hard, baritone cruel.

Shay thought she'd probably already been relegated to the graveyard of his one-night stands, no matter what they'd said or felt last night. Still, she had to try. She cared about this stubborn, hardheaded cowboy. She wanted him to care about himself. Fighting the tears that pressed against her eyelids, Shay turned away from him to slip her sunglasses on. "It's your choice. I have to go now to check up with the WBP on the investigation."

"Of course, since sleeping with the prime suspect didn't turn up anything enlightening on your end."

Knowing what he was trying to do, yet barely able to contain her fury regardless, Shay stalked up to him. "I didn't *make love* with you for the case. And you know it."

"All I know is you're the one who talked me into bed."

"Yes, because you got scared. Big, tough bullrider almost ran away from a little 'girl.' You hate to lose control. You always want to make the moves so you can protect your precious heart and soul. Careful; if someone got to what's inside you, you might have to admit you're worth loving after all. You're pushing me away because I managed to get too close again."

Luke turned away from her. "I'm pushing you away because you lied to me and spied on me."

Throwing her bag over her shoulder and leaving the envelope in his hands, she opened the door to the motel room and walked out. "If you want to know if I've lied about the things that matter and spied because I care, meet me at the Devil's Crook off the Llano River at noon."

Luke stomped down the road after leaving Shay's motel room, having had to walk back to his because he'd ridden to the dance with Cody and Karen. It wasn't a long walk, and it probably did him good to blow off some steam. His emotions had never soared so high or dropped so far so fast as they had in the last twenty-four hours. And never would again if he had anything to do with it.

"That's what happens to you, Luke, when you leave your heart open," he muttered to himself as he kicked a rock on the shoulder of the road. "I told you so, stupid redneck."

Yeah, he knew better than to let a woman get to him and still he let Shay sashay right in, sweet-talk him, and steal it away. Well, not really sweet-talk—she was more of a sharp talker; the only thing sweet about her was the way she tasted.

And smelled.

And sighed.

And lied.

"Hey, cowboy, you get bucked off already this morning?"

Luke turned to see Tim Auerbach's sister. She pulled her pickup truck onto the shoulder and leaned out, revealing plenty of cleavage and a toothy grin. Her name was Bunny or Berry or Cherry or something like that, and she was attractive in a pouty-lipped, overly made-up, dyed blond, super-teased sort of way that Luke was afraid would never appeal to him again after his night with a woman whose idea of makeup was a single swish of mascara and whose hairstyle involved ten swipes with a hairbrush. Still, he slowed his walk to a stop. He was desperate to find a distraction. Luke never dallied with the groupies, since they didn't fit into his never-see-again requirement, but this morning it was tempting to bury himself into another woman just to see if he could empty his memory of Shay.

Bunny-Berry-Cherry opened her passenger door, leaning over farther to give him a better view inside her shirt. "Hop in, Luke. I'll give you a ride."

He just bet she would. He slid onto the vinyl seat and realized how wrong it felt to be there with her.

"Where to?"

"You can just drop me at the lobby of my motel."

"Sugar, I know you bullriders like an audience, but that may be pushing it." She giggled, gave him a sidelong look, and realized he was serious. "OK, sugar, just a drive then. It'll be enough of a charge just to have those awesome buns sharing my seat for five minutes. Just remember, my offer is always open." She slid her short-shorts-clad legs wider just to emphasize her point.

Luke suddenly hoped someone else's offer was still open.

They rode in silence until she stopped in front of the motel. Thanking her, Luke got out, went to the lobby, and asked for directions to the Devil's Crook.

"The bull had been injected with methamphetamine—speed. Enough, the vet says, to make a ton of animal temporarily crazy. It can take thirty minutes to an hour to take effect, and its effects can last from four to twenty-four hours. The bull got here yesterday around noon." Monty sat down across from Shay in his trailer that served as his traveling office on the tour. "So, it could've been injected anytime in its trailer or while it was penned. If it was before the draw, no particular cowboy was the target. If it was after, then the target was Luke." Shay's heart pounded; her throat grew dry.

"Right. We've informed the authorities here. They've put some investigators on it, but right now with no damage done it's just ranked as criminal mischief and is pretty low-priority for them. The fact is they just want the WBP to get out of Sutton County without getting hurt; then it's not their problem anymore. We've hired some more off-duty cops to watch the bulls tonight in addition to the riders and the riggings. But you're still our ace in the hole, Shay. You can still be the eyes and ears, since nobody knows you're working for us."

"Except Luke."

"Shay, I told you he was trouble."

Shay couldn't deny that. "Don't worry for the WBP's sake. He's not going to tell anyone. You think it would look good for his macho image to have been duped by a female PI?"

"What if he's the suspect?"

"He's not."

"How do you know?"

How could she tell Monty that she'd made love to Luke, she'd felt his soul, and it was tortured but not guilty? That's why she knew he was innocent. The bull's blood test proved it. "Come on; you gave him the option for a re-ride. If he'd injected the bull, he could've easily taken it and no one would've been the wiser."

"I guess you're right. You think he's the one the suspect will be gunning for?"

"Depends on the motive. Luke is only in the middle of the WBP standings, still ten places away from qualifying for the finals, so it just makes him among a host of suspects if the motive is to knock off the competition."

"What other motive would there be?"

Shay flipped quickly through the papers in front of her. "I've been looking at the list and I think it has something to do with the recklessness. All these bullriders were risky riders, showboats."

Monty nodded. "Those showboats, like Luke, are crowd favorites, and I have to admit that more and more the crowd reaction is starting to affect the judging like never before. A lot of times a little flash will overcome an inconsistent ride and get a better score than a simple, solid ride."

"Maybe it's a dull but solid rider with a point to prove," Shay mulled.

"Most of the guys are decent, fair competitors; I just can't see any of them doing it, taking the chance at getting caught." Monty shook his head, his brow furrowed with concern. "But of course with bullriding growing so much, there's more money to be won than ever before. Maybe greed *is* a factor."

Only half-listening to Monty, she nodded. Shay knew she didn't quite have it but was getting close. Knowledge floated in her subconscious that she couldn't quite bring to the surface. She looked back down at the sheaf of papers Monty had given her with every WBP cowboy's background. An edginess, her investigator's sixth sense, buzzed stronger than ever, telling her she could solve the mystery with just a single right question.

"Can I get the list of injuries from last year?" Shay asked, still thoughtfully paging through the papers.

"You think they started last year?" Monty asked incredulously. "I told you we checked—"

"I don't know what I think," Shay interrupted. "Just get them for me if you can."

Monty nodded and phoned the WBP headquarters. A few moments later, the fax machine began to hum and spit out the information.

Looking at her watch, Shay grabbed the fax and walked to the door.

"Where are you going?" Monty asked.

"I have an appointment."

Monty shot her a skeptical look. "For what?"

"To get some answers," Shay said, shutting the door on his warning.

CHAPTER 7

The crisp smell of the morning air after a cleansing thunderstorm was being burned away by the merciless Texas sun as Shay turned her Mustang convertible onto what was little more than a dirt path off a gravel road. A craggy limestone hill dotted with cactus, mesquite, mountain cedar, and hackberry trees rose up to the right, separating the path she bounced along from the road. She estimated she was at least five miles from Interstate 10 now and three miles from the farm-to-market road that led her to the gravel drive. In a part of West Texas where you could go for hundreds of miles without seeing any sign of civilization she felt isolated and alone. For the hundredth time she wondered if Luke would come.

For the ninety-ninth time she told herself not to bet on it.

She had found out about the Devil's Crook by eavesdropping on some teenagers who'd been eating breakfast at the Dairy Queen where she stopped when she first came into town. It apparently was a branch of the Llano River, fifteen miles northeast of Sonora, where teenagers slipped away to skinny-dip at midnight. Shay asked for directions that morning from another teenager behind the counter at the convenience store.

Rounding the next outcropping of white rock, she nearly drove into the river. Throwing the car into park, Shay stepped out and took in the view. The Llano River, like most rivers in West Texas and the Hill Country, was small but beautiful. Crystal-clear spring water ran across the limestone rock, making the river a gorgeous aquamarine color. The water was running faster after last night's rain. Tall cypress trees and taller-than-usual live oaks grew up next to the bank, always a giveaway to where the water was in the near-desert. She walked along the bank, listening to a mockingbird's call and its mate's answer.

Shay was afraid she wouldn't know the place, but then she saw it. A stubby creek coming out of the river was in the shape of a crook of a cane, curling back on itself, and appeared lovely more than menacing. It was testimony to the dramatic bent of most Texans that it would be named after the devil instead of some somnolent old man.

Slipping out of her boots, she walked barefoot to the bank, dipping her toes in the surprisingly cool water, closing her eyes, and feeling herself relax. A soft swish of cotton settled over her eyes just as a knot tightened around her head. Adrenaline rushing, Shay tried to spin around, tried to reach up to grab at her face, but a vise grip and big body held her still. She screamed even as she began to recognize the rainy oak scent that suddenly surrounded her.

"There's no one to hear you for miles, Shay," the baritone she knew too well said in her ear.

The adrenaline-fueling fear quickly transformed into fury. She jerked against his restraining muscles, and he loosened his grip. She yanked off the bandanna and spun to face him. "What are you doing, Luke?"

"I'm showing you how easy it would be for anyone to sneak up on you." His eyes bored into hers with no apology.

"So you're teaching me a lesson?" she demanded, planting her hands on her hips.

"I'm teaching you you're going to have to sharpen your mental defenses in order to survive if you're after a killer."

"Why?"

"Why what?"

"Why do you care if I survive?"

Luke paused, taken aback. "Is that your first Truth or Dare question?"

"Yes."

He grinned just enough to show the hint of his dimple. "Then I take the dare."

Shay frowned in frustration and his dimple deepened. She'd been foolish to suggest this game. The daredevil would take every dare; she wouldn't learn anything about him, but maybe she could arrange it so *he* would.

Reflecting on the look on his face when she'd asked the question, Shay decided maybe he already had learned at least one thing about himself.

"The dare is," Shay said, looking from him to the tall oak tree next to them, "for you to climb the tree, hang upside down from that limb."

"OK." Luke took his Stetson off, placed it tipped back on her head, slipped off his boots and socks, and scaled the trunk. Sitting down, he grinned down at her from the branch, showing her a glimpse of the little rascal he once was and still was in so many ways. Too many. He flipped upside down, hanging on with his iron-strong thighs. He crooked his finger.

"Come here to check."

Shay came hesitantly, knowing there was a trap in this somewhere. She reached out, cupped her head in his hands, and pulled her lips to his. Her first kiss with an upside-down man. Shay would've laughed, but just then he deepened the kiss, and she was too breathless to do anything but draw away before she lost her focus.

"That wasn't part of the dare," she admonished, backing up.

Luke reached up to grab the branch, released his knees, and jumped to the ground. "Maybe it was just preparing you for *my* dare."

A sensual awareness shimmied through her at his intonation. She braced herself against it. "Who says I'm not going to offer the truth?"

Luke hooked his fingers into her belt loops and dragged her to him. "OK, when did you last see your favorite color?"

His question so surprised her, Shay began, speaking

too quickly, "My favorite color is a red, with a gold-orange, and a little magenta mixed in." She paused, realizing as she spoke she'd dug herself into a hole, or perhaps, with intuitive skill, he'd put her there. "It's really a persimmon color, I suppose. Red, orange, a passion fruit pink . . ."

His eyebrow arched, dragging her a little closer, until their body heat mingled. With a knuckle under her chin, he tipped her face up. The hat fell off. "I didn't ask you what color, Shay; I asked you *when* you last saw it."

Shay felt breathless. Her mind's eye had filled with an explosion of persimmon the last time they'd made love. How had he known?

"I'll take the dare," she breathed as a blush heated her face.

"The dare is"—he paused, caressing her with his gaze—"to show me the most sensitive spot on your body. The most secret one. The one I never would know unless you show me."

Shay shivered, not from the desire but with the reality his questions, his dares, were showing her. He cared about her. Did he realize it?

"Well?" he asked, walking around her, twirling a forefinger around a hank of her hair, pulling it back to kiss her behind her ear. "Would it be there?"

"No."

His hands cupped her breasts and breathed feathery kisses on each nipple that upturned immediately at his touch and poked through the thin fabric of her T-shirt. "There?" He palmed below her zipper that warmed in his hand. "Or here?"

"Those aren't very secret, are they?"

He looked at each, eyebrows raised, gaze appreciative. "No, I guess not. They are tattletales."

Shay's blush deepened.

"Still no answer?" Luke continued. "Then I will continue torturing you until you tell me the truth, or do the dare."

"Here," she said finally, afraid that if he tried any more tactile guessing she would be lost and the game over before it really began. She unfastened the top two buttons of her Levi's, rolling down her waistband, turning slowly, lifting her shirt to point at the dip in the small of her back. She looked over her shoulder at his eyes darkening to gunmetal. "Here," she said.

He knelt on one knee, his hands spanning her hips as he kissed her back. "Here?"

Biting back a moan, Shay nodded.

"I didn't hear you," he said, breathing the words on her skin. He tickled the spot with his tongue. "Is this your secret erogenous zone?"

"Yes," she sighed, squirming as his hands slid up to her bare waist, his tongue tracing a trail up her backbone as he stood.

Luke dropped his hands and stepped back, leaving her body bereft. "Now it's your turn again."

His hot-and-cold treatment was driving her crazy, even though she knew that was precisely his intention. Shay watched him wiggle his bare toes in the water. For some reason his bare feet made him look so vulnerable and that much sexier because of it. She sucked in a breath and took a gamble that could send him back to Sonora. "Tell me about the biggest disappointment in your life."

First Luke's look turned introspective; then he glowered, not at her so much as at a memory. "What if I told you it was falling off the rankest bull on the tour and ruining a perfect one-hundred score?"

"I wouldn't believe you."

"I didn't think so." He blew out a breath. "I'll take the dare."

"I'm going to put the blindfold on you and lead you."

Luke shook his head.

"You have to decide if you'd rather trust me with the truth or trust me not to lead you into a pile of fire ants or a snake hole."

He grinned, but only with a hint of humor. "You're treading in dangerous territory now."

"It's worth it; I get to find out which you value most—your secrecy or your control."

Luke flexed his jaw, his eyes guarded. "Put the blindfold on."

"Ah, secrecy wins," Shay said, plucking the bandanna off the ground and slipping it around his eyes, tying it behind his head. Luke tensed.

Shay slipped her hand into his and began to walk along the riverbank. The simple sensation of her small hand comfortable in his large one touched her the way nothing else they'd shared had. She smiled, watching his bare feet feel around rocks, knowing instinctively that he'd never before in his life trusted anyone enough to give up this much control.

She led him up and over a small rise that jutted over a deep pool in a curve in the river. They walked to the very edge, where Shay finally stopped him with a hand on his chest. She looked down at the twenty-foot drop to the water and judged the pool deep enough to absorb six feet of two-hundred-pound man.

"I want you to jump."

His jaw flexed.

"That is, if you know how to swim," she said.

"I guess you'll just have to find out," he said, pulling his shirt out of his jeans, yanking the snaps apart, and discarding the shirt behind him.

For a second, Shay's heart went to her throat. He wasn't daring enough to jump without knowing how to swim, was he? She put her hand on his bare biceps. "Wait."

He shook his head and used his feet to feel his way to the edge of the limestone shelf. "No. A dare is a dare."

Without warning, Luke jumped out, landing in the water with a loud splash. Shay was on the verge of jumping in after him when he bounced back to the top, the bandanna in his hand. Grinning up at her, he shook his wet head, the spray flying. "It looks like that scared you more than it did me."

Realizing she'd been holding her breath and her fists tight at her sides, Shay let both go and sat on the edge of the precipice, drawing her knees to her chest. She watched him tread water easily, the clear water giving her a magnified view of his muscles flexing with each stroke. "OK, your turn."

"I want to know if you've ever been in love before," he said.

Before what? Shay wanted to ask. *Before now?*

Maybe she was reading too much into his words that he could be using carelessly.

"I was, once, or so I thought."

"What do you mean?"

"I was twenty-one. He was an attorney I met when I was working my first PI job, a simple background check on a witness. He asked me to marry him but wanted me to give up my work. I decided I loved my independence more than I loved him. I guess I wasn't willing to do that compromising we talked about yesterday. Now it's my turn."

Luke was looking up at her with a mixture of raw jealousy and curiosity on his face. She bit back a smile at how unwittingly transparent he could be at times and so emotionally opaque at others.

"Why do you ride bulls for a living?"

She knew the moment she asked that it was too broad a question, one he could shimmy out from under without giving her the insight into him she craved.

"Because I'm good at it, and I love it."

"Why?"

Still treading water, he held up a hand and shook his head. "You can use that for your next Truth or Dare. Now it's my turn."

Knowing a dangerous question was coming, Shay tensed as he floated on his back and closed his eyes and said, "I want you to tell me what it would take for you to compromise your independence for a man you love."

Shay was grateful he kept his eyes closed as she felt her heartbeat accelerate and her face flush. The answer sprang immediately into her head.

For you to tell me you love me.

She couldn't risk it.

"I'll take the dare."

"Jump in," he said, dimple digging into his cheek.

Shaking her head, Shay stood.

"The truth then." Luke's gaze tried to read hers. To avoid it, she leaped over the edge without thinking anymore.

The water was cool and seductive, turning her clothes that floated around her into a thousand stitches of erogenous stimuli. He'd gone under the water to pull her up in his arms, kissing her as they kicked to the surface. They each drew in a breath before his lips closed over hers again, tongues exploring the hot recesses of her mouth made exotic by the coolness of the water around them.

Luke gazed at her thoughtfully. She felt like he could see inside her soul. She tried to see into his to ask the right question, remembering what Monty had said about Luke being driven and what Cody had said about him being reckless since being kicked off his father's ranch. She wanted to ask him about what he'd do for love, but knew he had to first come to terms with the demon that drove him. "It's my turn and I want to know what's the first thing you will do after you win the championship trophy at the World Bullriding Pro championships."

She'd hit close to the bull's-eye. She could see it in the intensity in his silvery eyes. Neither one spoke for a full minute. Their legs kicked; his arms still held her, her arms wrapped around his water-slick back. She would've bet he would take the dare, but then he said quietly but harshly, "I will drive all night to get home and march into my father's office and put that trophy on the mantel so that every day he and my brothers can see it and know I wasn't the loser coward they told me I was."

Then, overwhelmed by the hate and revenge, he released her and swam toward the riverbank. She grabbed his arm and stopped him. "Luke, tell me why they said that."

"If you'd read the background check on me, you'd see why. You shouldn't have walked out without it this morning. I brought it with me; you should read it when I'm gone."

"I don't want to read it, I want you to tell me."

They both stood on the riverbed, the water swirling around them, Shay's hand on his arm, Luke tense and withdrawn. His storm cloud eyes looked past her. "My father owns the fastest-growing computer company in the nation. My brothers will make it the biggest before they die. We were all raised for the business, but I've always hated it. My father talks every day about his 'dynasty.' I hate being forced into anything. I tried, though, for years, then ran the ranch, and got into bullriding more and more. Finally my father told me never to come back until I could prove I was ready to take responsibility and be a man instead of a lazy good-for-nothing."

"And you think showing him you're the best bullrider in the world is going to change his mind?"

Luke tensed his jaw. "Maybe."

"Luke," she said gently, touched that he'd confided in her finally, but not wanting to give up this opportunity to make him understand himself. "You're going to discover that the empty feeling inside you won't be filled when you march into your father's office with your trophy. You need to ride the bulls for yourself. Win for yourself. And you have to stop agreeing with your father."

"I've never agreed with my father!"

"You share a low opinion of you."

"You don't know what you're talking about," he said, yanking his arm out of her hand.

Shay pursued him. "You're living life for the wrong reason. You can't live life for revenge, to prove something to your family. If you do, you're running away from things instead of running to things."

"What if I've been running to you?" he said roughly, pulling her into his arms and kissing her deeply. His honesty made her weak, and she let him pull her soggy shirt over her head, let his hands float over her skin, let him draw her jeans off, carry her to a patch of soft grass on the bank, and love her body.

Shay wished he could love her soul as well, even though in her heart she knew he couldn't until he loved himself.

Luke woke to a raucous squawk and looked up in the cypress branch above them to see a black grackle mocking the human couple in a tangle of damp arms and legs and clothes. The river water had dried on the skin, but sweat was taking its place as the hundred-degree afternoon heat steamed the ground under them, even in the shade. Luke guessed they'd slept a few hours and knew he had to get up, the bullriding would begin in a couple of hours, but he hated to let loose of the woman in his arms just yet.

The idyllic times they'd spent together had been stolen—first by staving off suspicion, then by distracting her from her psychological probing. It would all end with the ultimatum that he knew would come by the end of the afternoon.

He just didn't know who would be making it.

They were both too strong, too independent, to be together for long, especially in the middle of someone else's game with deadly stakes.

Shay stirred, moaning softly in a way that tweaked Luke's heart. He relished the feeling for a few minutes; then those incredible amber eyes opened and blinked in consciousness. She smiled. "Why do you always wake up first?"

"I like to watch you sleep. You look actually tamable when you are unconscious."

"What an odd thing to say."

"You're a little like the broncs and bulls in the rodeo. You can waltz right over and stroke their noses, their necks, but the moment you try to master them by hopping on their backs they don't want anything to do with you."

"But didn't you say when you get on the rough stock the idea is to hang on for the thrill ride—let loose of the idea of controlling it?"

Luke laughed, surprised she was sharp enough to turn his bullriding philosophy back onto a human relationship. "I did."

They shared a look that left Luke fidgeting. He wasn't ready for this. It was time to push her away, make her want to leave and never look back at him again. He drew his arm out from under her and handed her her damp shirt. "It's been fun, but it's time I got back to the motel and dressed for tonight."

Hurt flashed in her eyes for just an instant before it was replaced by her businesswoman look. She adjusted her bra, slipped her shirt over her head, and handed him his jeans. "We have to talk about that, Luke. You can't ride. It's not safe. The bull you rode last night was drugged. You are the killer's target."

"How do you know that?" He frowned, disbelieving. "Anybody could have drawn that bull."

"Yes, and when you did he was injected with a substance that made him deadly crazy." Shay watched Luke as he jumped rocks across the river and hiked back up the ridge to get his shirt, then his boots. She followed him across to get her own boots. "There's a pattern, Luke; the guys killed or put out of commission under suspicious circumstances have all been the most reckless riders on the tour. There aren't that many coincidences. The last rigging that went back came back from the crime lab as having an acid injected into the center, which disintegrated from inside out. How do you see something like that until it's unraveled from the pressure of a twisting buck and your head is crashing into a metal gate?"

Luke shook his head, sauntering up to her as he slipped

his arms into his open shirt. "You still don't have a good motive. All this could be just stuff the WBP is cooking up to beef up the TV ratings. Couch potato rubberneckers will be tuning in all over the country because of the better odds of seeing one of us die on camera."

Shay shivered and shook her head at the deadly image. "I have come up with a motive. All of the reckless riders are getting bonus points from the judges. I thought that maybe a conservative rider would be resentful enough to try to teach you all a lesson or—"

Luke paused, her words striking a memory that left him cold. All Tim's sly lectures on having to be careful because of having not one, but two, families to support could've been grim rationalizations instead of mere complaints. "Or it could be someone teaching us a lesson for a different reason."

Shay put her hand on his forearm. "What do you mean?"

"Tim Auerbach's brother was number one on the tour last year and got there by being a flashy risk taker. He'd stay on the bull longer to get the audience wound up, would throw his free arm wilder, spur the bull harder even when keeping him close would've kept him on for eight seconds, He'd ride with a broken arm, a concussion, without a vest. He was paralyzed the week before the finals practicing on a bull that the tour refused to take on because he was too crazy rank."

Shay looked at him. "And those of you carrying on his brother's legacy are higher up in the rankings."

Luke thought for a moment. "Yeah, most of us."

Cupping his jaw in her hands, Shay brought Luke's eyes to hers. "Don't ride tonight. If it's Tim, he'll try again. If he's injecting bulls he's taking a huge risk and won't stop until he's caught. He might already have found out your draw and gotten to it. He might have broken into your motel room and have sabotaged your gear; he might have come up with some entirely new strategy. I'll alert Monty and the WBP officials, but they won't cancel the event and it might be too late to find out exactly what he's done. Don't take the chance."

The fear in her voice scared him—not for his life but for his heart. He refused to lose control because of some emotional vulnerability. "I won't be a coward."

Shay's eyes misted with tears, but she stood tall and planted her hands on her hips. "It's not cowardly to be smart. It's cowardly to hide from yourself and who you are and why you're doing what you're doing. You're taking the biggest chance of your life for a man who doesn't care about you and won't care if you survive this. Gamblers are cowards—rolling the dice and letting Fate decide. They say it's not their fault if they lose just like you'll say it's not your fault if you die. You are going to gamble out there and lose everything whether you live or die."

Her "everything" meant what they'd shared together. She was telling him something he wasn't ready to hear. Shay was trying to control him by caring about him. Luke refused to let her, so he pushed her away where she knew she couldn't push back. "OK, I'll not ride tonight if you give up the investigation. Get in your car, drive back home, and sleep in your own safe bed tonight. Quit messing around with killers and bulls and crazy bullriders."

Shay was unnaturally still for a full minute, her gaze both tempted and regretful. Luke felt his heart twist painfully in his chest when she said, "I can't do that. I have a job, a responsibility."

"And so do I."

Luke turned and walked away, over the rise where he'd parked his truck out of sight. She called to him at the top of the rise. Luke turned to see a tear burning a path down her cheek. He didn't move.

"What if I give you a better reason not to ride tonight?"

"What's the reason?"

"I love you."

Even the summer breeze seemed to halt waiting for Luke's answer. He could see she wasn't breathing, and almost waited so she'd pass out and not see him walk away. But if he did that he wouldn't be able to leave her lying there. He cared too much. Far too much. He'd already hurt her enough, and now because of him her perspective was skewed and she might be in more danger, from a killer. He had to end it now.

"Get over it," he said down to her as he disappeared over the ridge.

CHAPTER 8

"I want you to cancel the event," Shay told Monty after she'd explained her theory on why Tim Auerbach was the best suspect for the sabotage.

Monty shook his head as they walked toward the bull pens. "I can't do it on suspicion alone, Shay. You'd see it, too, if you were talking from your head instead of your heart."

Shay stopped, facing Monty. "What do you mean?"

"If you thought tonight's victim were anyone but Luke Wilder, you would be talking me into a way to set a trap and catch the suspect instead of squelching the whole event. Look at it clearly, Shay. Whoever is behind this is desperate enough to be killing people and won't stop just because one event is canceled. He'll be back at it when we head to Houston next week and up in Oklahoma the next. We'll put our heads together this week and figure out a strategy to catch him.

"For tonight, we'll put a deputy on Tim and one on the bull Luke draws. We'll make sure Luke has fresh gear from our trailer, though knowing him, he won't take it anyway."

Shay shook her head, not because Monty was refusing her—she'd expected he would—but because something seemed wrong and she couldn't say what it was. Leaning her arms on the bars of the metal bull pen, she looked out over the bulls and tried to pinpoint the source of her disquiet.

Was her emotional turmoil muddling her mind or was there a point she'd overlooked in the case?

Monty patted her shoulder before walking back to his trailer. "Don't do anything stupid."

I already have, she wanted to say, *I've fallen in love with a man who can't love me back.*

After a few minutes, Joe Zappora joined Shay at the fence. "How's the article going?"

"It's hit a snag," Shay said morosely, watching across the pens as Luke sauntered into the contestants' entrance, his gear bag thrown over his shoulder. Her heart fell as she saw he intended to ride. Some part of her must have held out hope he'd reconsider once he thought about what she'd said. But he'd said to hell with her love, he'd ride anyway. Luke threw a charming smile at the busty red-headed gate guard and stopped to ask a WBP official a question. The man shook his head and walked on.

"Hey, that's too bad it's not going good," Joe continued, unaware of her heartache. "Maybe you're just tired of talking to us boring bullriders. Go find someone else to get another perspective on it, like the bullfighters, a bull breeder, or better yet one of the groupies who follow the tour."

Shay turned to Joe. "A groupie."

"Sure." Joe shrugged. "They certainly see things others don't, and we get so used to them around they get a lot more access behind the scenes than most folks."

"A groupie," Shay repeated thoughtfully, her heartbeat accelerating.

"There's one now." Joe pointed out a bleached blonde in jeans too tight and a shirt a size too small swiveling her hips over to where Luke stood, laying his gear out. "A'course she's a little different because she's a family member, too, though Tim doesn't like to claim her."

"Tim?" It took all of Shay's willpower not to go racing over and tell the bimbo to get away from her man. The woman ran her fingernails along Luke's hairline. Luke grinned and shook his head. Now Shay wasn't sure whether her sixth sense was warning her about the woman or it was just old-fashioned jealousy.

"That's Berry. She's Tim Auerbach's sister. Been hanging around the tour since the season started. She's a hot property, but I wouldn't get near her, and not only because Tim's my friend. Just between you and me, I've noticed the guys she's hung around with the past couple of weeks have been the ones ended up hurt." Joe shrugged apologetically. "I guess I'm superstitious."

Or smart. "There's nothing wrong with that. A bull-rider ought to have a rabbits' foot or two."

Sheepishly Joe reached into his pocket and flashed three rabbits' feet, purple, pink, and green. "One for each round."

Shay laughed. "So you don't need me to wish you luck."

"I'll take whatever I get."

"You've got it then," she said. She thanked him, then moved to follow Berry, who'd left Luke and was now headed back toward the front of the bull pens. Shay debated stopping at Monty's trailer to tell him to ask the deputies to keep an eye on Berry as well but talked herself out of it. Monty would probably scoff at the thought of her suspecting a woman and likely accuse her of being jealous, which Shay hated to admit was probably true.

Shay didn't know exactly what she thought. But even if Berry only gave Shay some insight into her brother, she knew she ought to talk to her. Shay caught up with Berry as she stood flirting with a young, blushing bullrider named Chad at the main entrance. Chad nodded at Shay.

"Berry?" Shay held out her hand. "I'm Shay Mc-Intyre."

"I know who you are." Berry looked down at Shay's hand, ignored it, and resumed admiring the teenager's belt buckle. His blush deepened.

Shay dropped her hand. "I'd like to talk to you if you have a few minutes."

"Why?"

"To get a different perspective on my article. Why you like to follow the tour—"

"Because bullriders do it best." She winked at Chad before turning back to Shay. "But then, you know that, don't you? You drew at the top of the pen last night."

Narrowing her eyes, Shay wondered why Berry had

noticed she and Luke had left the dance together. Was she envious? It didn't feel like it; it felt like Berry was frustrated but not jealous. Shay tried to get a read on the woman, but Berry had so many angles and was using all at once; she was a cipher. Shay forced herself to stay rational.

"So, can you spare a few minutes for me?"

Berry gauged her for a moment with eyes that were surprisingly sharp with intelligence. "OK. There's a bull pen around the back end of the arena, behind all those sponsorship signs. I'll meet you there in five minutes and we can talk with some privacy."

Winking at Chad, Berry added: "I might have all sorts of secrets you boys won't see 'til they're in print."

Luke finally found Monty going over the list of bulls with his crew chiefs, responsible for the logistical nightmare of getting them from pens to chutes in the right order. "I'm not going to ride."

Monty looked up, stunned. "I don't believe it. If anything would make me accept that the bullriders are being injected with mind-altering drugs, this is it."

"My mind is clearer than it's ever been. Where's Shay?"

Monty shook his head. "You're both crazy as March hares. You know she was just after me to cancel the event. Can you believe it? To hell with the investigation; she was only interested in saving your sorry hide. I should've fired her on the spot for losing her objectivity, but, hell, if she's turned you into a real human being, maybe it was worth it after all."

Luke felt his heart swell. She'd been willing to jeopardize her job for him. A sudden sense of urgency pushed him to hurry. His eyes scanned the grounds, pausing at each female figure, moving on quickly. She wasn't anywhere in sight. "So, where's Shay?"

Monty held his hands palms up. "I don't know. She was going to look for Tim."

Luke felt his mind go into sharp focus. "Has he checked in yet?"

"No, and you know that's part of what doesn't add up with this. Tim is always the last one on the grounds at every event. How is he getting all this done, if it's really him?"

"That's bothered me, too. The only way I can figure it is he's working with someone else."

"What a mess." Monty shook his head. "We've got to get this cleared up before anyone else gets hurt."

"Listen; don't announce my withdrawal until the last minute. Meantime, I'll make a big show of setting my gear out and leaving it. Keep an eye on it while I go look for Shay."

Nodding, Monty stuck out his hand, and Luke took it. "I'm sorry I misjudged you, Luke. I always thought you were a helluva bullrider and not much of a man. You're proving me wrong."

"You weren't far wrong," Luke said, thinking it took the love of a good woman to turn him into a man.

"Good luck with Shay; you're going to need more of it with her than in riding a bull. She's an independent cuss. But maybe you can settle her down and get into the family business. Her daddy would like nothing more than to have another branch to his dynasty."

Luke felt himself go cold at the word. "Dynasty?"

"You didn't know? Mac McIntyre heads up the Reid Ranch, second in power only to the King Ranch. You may have fallen not only into love but into the clover, too, my boy."

Luke wandered away, the dread tightening like a vise around his chest. He'd escaped his own family hell only to fall in love with a woman attached to another one. Luke didn't want to be a corporate anything—not of a computer empire, not of a ranching dynasty. As he ran his hands over his bullriding gear near the chutes, Luke knew—no matter what trouble she was in—he ought to run as far and as fast as he could away from Shay McIntyre.

And never look back.

CHAPTER 9

Shay wasn't sure where amid the labyrinth of empty pens to wait for Berry Auerbach. A single black Brangus bull she recognized as the infamous Hell on Hooves stood in the pen at the rear, so Shay chose the pen farthest from him and closest to the arena. The land sloped down from the arena fence and was completely covered with sponsorship boards, making the pens invisible to all but the top row of stands, which were empty. After a few minutes, she leaned against the metal bars and tried to peer at the action across the arena through a space in the boards. The rest of the stands were beginning to fill up with spectators. At the chutes, a bullrider was laying out his gear. Even at this distance, Shay knew Luke. The way he cocked his head to the right when he was concentrating, the way he tipped his Stetson back with his thumb.

He was going to ride.

She was going to solve this case.

And they'd both go their separate ways, each carrying intact independence, free from compromise.

And full of loneliness.

"Nobody can see us over here; that's for sure."

Startled, Shay turned to see Berry beside her. She wondered how a woman who looked so loud could move so quietly. Uneasy, Shay wanted the conversation over before it started. "It is certainly private. What secrets did you have to tell me?"

"I think you've guessed some of them, or we wouldn't be here. Why would a reporter want to talk to a rodeo groupie? No, you don't care about my stories from the road. You want to know why I'm killing cowboys."

Shay gasped—at Berry's audacity, at her own accurate instincts, and at how blatantly she disregarded them. If she'd respected her instinct that Berry was dangerous, she wouldn't have planned to meet her in a place no one in the county could see.

"You're doing it for your brother?"

"Not quite, but close. You do good research," Berry said with genuine appreciation as she walked away. Shay watched her for a moment, before turning back around to look for a means of escape. "But you know smarts is a double-edged sword; that's why you're in this position now."

Shay felt a loop drop over her, tightening around her arms and torso. She spun around, falling to the ground and having the wind knocked out of her as another loop came up over her feet and tightened around her ankles. Helpless as a bulldogged calf, Shay watched as Berry dropped her last rope in the dirt and picked up her two loose ends and brought them to where she lay. Writhing, Shay fought, but Berry dragged her to the fence, gagged her, and tied her face-out. Before Berry got her legs secured, though, Shay kicked out and sent Berry flying. She landed in a heap in the mud.

Berry looked at Shay with a glimmer of respect. "I think I'd really like you if you weren't getting in the way. But I have a lesson to teach these bullriders, and it's not over yet."

Berry rose and dusted off her jeans. She reached into her back pocket and withdrew a huge syringe. For a horrible moment, Shay thought Berry meant to inject her, but then she saw it was empty. That's when she heard Hell on Hooves pawing and snorting in the neighboring pen. His mouth had begun to foam in drug-induced fury. Berry smiled.

And Shay saw she wasn't crazy; she was lucid as they come.

Perhaps that was the thing that scared Shay the most.

"You see, the most flashy, reckless cowboy who could stay on for eight seconds was going to win the finals last year. My baby brother Hugh wanted to be the one to do it, and now he's half a man—can't move anything but his mouth and might as well be dead. Now poor Tim, who was always careful, is being penalized and is having to feed two families. And still the daredevils are winning, even though they're hurting and dying. I have to keep showing them and the WBP officials what's wrong and what's right. Until they figure that out, I can't stop."

Berry laughed, humorlessly, walking toward the pen where the bull was becoming more overwrought. "It's too easy for me—sleep with a cowboy, ruin his rigging. Compliment the sexual prowess of an official, inject a bull behind his back. I thought I had the perfect cover. And I still do. In this male chauvinist world, only a woman would think another woman capable of getting away with murder."

She opened the gate and leaped over the fence. "So I get rid of you, and I'm back in the business of making my point."

Shay was so angry she didn't have room for fear. With adrenaline pumping, she struggled against the heavy roping twine that wouldn't give, the bandanna that absorbed her screams. Berry turned around one last time. "If it makes you feel any better, hon, your lover will be joining you shortly. I'm trying something new, injecting the cowboy. Could be easiest of all." She pulled a smaller syringe out from her cleavage along with a dead wasp, slipping both up her sleeve.

Suddenly ice cold with the fear she wouldn't allow for her own plight, Shay went still as she watched Berry round the corner, slapping Hell on Hooves as she departed. "Hey, that jugular injection works fast. I'll have to remember that."

The bull heaved his tonnage against the metal, which shook with the impact. Keeping one eye on him as he knocked his way through the maze of gates, Shay craned her neck to see through the crack in the boards. Luke stood along with a half-dozen other bullriders at the chutes. He seemed to be talking to each one in turn, getting to Tim and gesturing frantically. She noticed Tim shaking his head sadly. Then she saw Berry approach the men who were smiling and giving her appreciative pats on the rump. Her eyes were focused on Luke, who was now talking to Chad. The teenage bullrider pointed toward where Shay was hidden. Berry was only an arm's length away from Luke.

Shay struggled against her bindings and screamed fruitlessly through the cotton in her mouth. She'd never felt so helpless in her life.

Then the loudspeaker above Shay's head vibrated to life. "We'll be beginning our evening of the World Bull-riding Pro Tour in fifteen minutes, so get in your seats and get ready to watch our bulls try to unseat the world's top bullriders! We do have one announcement. Our leader after last night has withdrawn; Luke Wilder won't be riding tonight. Sorry, folks." Shay watched as Berry, glowering, changed direction and headed down the stairs, away from the chutes.

Tears ran down Shay's cheeks; she'd never felt so happy. Luke would be safe. He'd compromised. Did that mean he loved her, too?

Hell on Hooves had reached Shay's pen, crashing through the half-open gate. The rest of the metal fence shuddered and Shay tried to topple it by pushing against the ground with her feet, but although it swayed, it didn't fall. The delirious bull focused on the red bandanna wrapped around her face and lowered his head, hooves digging into the muddy ground. He slipped just as his horn gave a bruising brush to her ribs, crashing full force into the fence instead of her torso. With an angry snort, he backed up and aimed again, just as Luke came leaping over the sponsor boards from the arena.

Distracted, the bull paused only for an instant before adjusting his direction to charge at Luke.

"Get her loose, boys. Get her loose. Hang on, Shay."

Terrified more for him than she'd been for herself, Shay shook her head. The bull caught Luke with a horn and sent him flying into the metal fence, which collapsed

around him. Still the bull chose fighting instead of freedom, lowering his horns and stabbing at Luke's prone
form on the ground. Shay couldn't see through the tears
and didn't feel when Joe and Chad released her. "Come
on out, fast!" they shouted.

She pulled the bandanna off as police officers and sheriff's deputies and WBP officials swarmed from all directions but kept their distance because of the bull. Luke was
throwing the fence off his legs as the bull rammed him
again. A bullfighter flapped his arms. The bull ignored
him and stamped in the middle of Luke's chest. Shay ran
to him, but Monty's long arm grabbed around her torso.
She strained to get to the man she loved, motionless and
bloody on the ground.

"I'm not ordering up two coffins today, Shay," he said.

Then, he squeezed her injured ribs so tight the world
went black.

CHAPTER 10

The antiseptic smell assailed her first. Shay wrinkled her nose against it even in her half-conscious state. The tinny voice of a doctor's page confirmed what she suspected: She was in a hospital. Alone. Then she thought she caught a whiff of rain and oak but shoved it aside as a memory. A cruel one.

She remembered Luke's inert body and lots of blood and talk of coffins.

He hadn't ridden. He'd saved her. He'd loved her.

Now he was gone.

Fighting back bitterness and the tears that came with it, she looked to her right and saw a white curtain dividing the room in two and keeping her from seeing out the window.

Shay scooted to a sitting position, trying to swallow a moan but failing.

"You awake now, girl?"

Coming from the bed on the other side of the curtain, the gravelly voice of an elderly woman who'd downed one too many bottles of liquor in her life startled Shay. "Uh, yes, ma'am."

"Good. I was getting a little lonely over here. Lord knows I like to be independent, but sometimes I wonder where independence leaves off and loneliness begins."

"I know what you mean." Shay's heartbeat accelerated as she began to recognize the familiar whiskey tone.

"Good. A well-chosen compromise, now that can make independence stronger instead of weaker."

"I had to learn that the hard way," Shay said, carefully, pulling the thin blanket gingerly off her legs and pulling them to the side of the bed.

"Oooo. And what other things have you learned the *hard* way, girl?" the now obviously falsetto voice on the other side of the curtain chuckled lasciviously.

Smiling, Shay crept on shaky legs to the curtain, ribs cringing with each step. "How to love a hard-headed, hard-bodied handsome heartbreaker."

"Any love left over for a noodle-headed, broken-bodied, butt-ugly cowboy who just found his heart?"

Shay felt like her own heart had swelled enough to burst. She threw back the curtain, ignoring the shot of pain that ran down her side. He lay swathed in bandages and casts, his silvery eyes twinkling, dimple digging into a face crisscrossed with bruises and cuts. "I just might consider it, *if* all the cowboy's important parts are in working order."

"Just what do you consider *important*?" Luke's eyebrow went up, and he winced.

Shay laughed, and she winced. Lifting up the sheet, he patted the bed next to him. "Better come check it out."

She slid into the bed beside him and kissed each and every scratch and bruise she could find; then she stopped, putting her head on his chest to listen to the delicious pounding of his heart. Whole and happy, Shay knew she could do nothing but listen to this beautiful music forever. "This is the only thing that matters to me."

"Well, there's something else that matters to me." He took her hand in his and guided it under his hospital gown to his erection, the only part of him not wearing a bandage. "I was a little worried after the bull got through with me, but I see now that it just needed just the right motivation."

"Like most things in life," Shay said.

"Like most things in *love*," Luke corrected, covering her mouth with his and drawing her on top of him for a kiss that lasted a lot longer than eight seconds.

COMPROMISED

·

Gayle Callen

*To Maggie Shayne, dear friend and writing buddy,
who answers my questions, commiserates
with my problems, and is always there
when I need her.*

CHAPTER 1

"Whom shall I flirt with?" Lady Elizabeth Stanwood murmured to herself as she stood on tiptoes and searched the large gilt-ceilinged room, crowded with dancing couples. She was through waiting for Lord Wyndham to ask for her hand in marriage—she was one and twenty, and it was time to do something to make it happen.

She needed the perfect man to make him jealous. She wasn't certain whom she was looking for; an acquaintance would surely play along with her scheme, but a stranger might make the evening all the more interesting for her, and unnerving for Wyndham. And wouldn't that be enough to make his lordship squirm?

She caught a glimpse of Sir Ralph Cobham and quickly looked away. She had had to repeatedly dissuade him from asking her father for her hand in marriage. There was an underhandedness about the man that made her dislike him, so she certainly couldn't use *him* to make Lord Wyndham jealous.

Then she saw a newcomer step into the room, and her eyes narrowed as she examined him. He was tall, taller than most of the men in attendance, with a breadth of shoulders that needed no padding. His clothing was years out of fashion, only a simple short tunic, belted at the waist, with a cloak thrown back over those impressive shoulders—as if it were not the hottest summer of her memory. His legs were thick and sturdy under his plain hose, and he wore a flat cap over close-cropped brown hair. His strong-jawed face was clean shaven, appearing stark amid the hall's plenitude of curled and colored beards.

Though woefully out of place, he didn't appear ill at

ease. Could he be someone's idea of entertainment, a joke to enliven the party?

Whatever he was, the man was perfect for Elizabeth's plan. She gulped the last of her wine, then smiled as she slowly made her way through the crowd, dropping small, perfect curtsies to the noblemen, dipping her head modestly to the ladies, but all the while keeping her gaze on the newcomer.

It wasn't long before he saw her. He glanced away; then his gaze returned to her with satisfying swiftness. She allowed her smile to deepen, to grow mysterious in that way that her suitors had long admired. As his gaze dropped down her body, she took a deep breath, amused when he seemed in a hurry to return to her face. He was perhaps . . . embarrassed.

How unusual.

No one came up to greet the stranger; no one arrived to join him. It was as if he were put directly in Elizabeth's path for her purpose.

She walked ever nearer, aware of the faintest thrill as his height towered ever higher above her, making her feel delicate and feminine.

Surely it was her overindulgence in wine that was inspiring her imagination.

When she finally stopped before him, the stranger's eyes widened for a moment.

"Good evening, my lord," she murmured, and when he didn't deny the noble title, she relaxed ever so slightly.

"My lady," he responded, in a deep, gruff voice that sent a shiver through her.

She had always loved the rich tones of a man's voice.

Once again his appreciative gaze dropped to her amply revealed bosom, and she surprised herself by blushing, surely due to the warmth in the great hall.

She suddenly remembered Lord Wyndham and turned to see if he had noticed her. But he was deep in conversation with their host, the Marquess of Worcester. Elizabeth frowned.

"Are you waiting for someone, my lady?" the man asked softly.

"No." She glanced back up as he leaned toward her. She felt the faintest touch of his breath on her cheek, and it was strangely pleasant. He was close enough now for her to smell the outdoors about him, to feel the heat of his presence. For a moment, she was slightly over-whelmed.

But no, he was plain, with ordinary brown hair and ordinary brown eyes. He was only a man, and never had a man been born who could resist her charms—or her control. She had to find a way to attract Lord Wyndham's notice.

"Kind sir," she began softly, "the dancing is about to begin. Would you partner with me?"

"Regretfully no, my lady," he said. "I do not dance—at least not this sort of dancing."

"What other kind is there?"

"The country dances of my home," he answered, "but they are performed much . . . closer together."

His voice had dropped, become almost husky. This time she noticed a faint accent. She thought she should ask him where he came from, but once again his gaze drifted down her body, and she had the uncanny feeling that her skin heated wherever his gaze touched.

"Perhaps someday you can show me these country dances," she found herself saying with a sudden breath-lessness.

What was wrong with her? He was only a simple man from the country. So what if his presence loomed large and rugged before her? She had to remind herself of her purpose. She glanced once more at Lord Wyndham, who finally sent her the smallest frown.

Elizabeth smiled up at the stranger. "Would you care to accompany me to the refreshment table? The wine this evening is excellent."

She waited for him to hold his arm out to her, and when he didn't, she wet her lips and bravely slid her arm through his, feeling deliciously warmed by the heat of his body. She was suddenly very glad her parents were not in attendance this evening.

Now she felt Lord Wyndham—and others—watching her. She had not done anything truly scandalous, just enough to make her feel an unusual thrill of excitement.

Soon, she and the stranger both held goblets of wine, and they studied each other as they drank.

John Malory was doing his best to conceal his surprise. He'd never been to London, though he'd been told the nobility here lived a different kind of life than he did in the north. He was used to women waiting for his attention, with the deference they always felt was due him. Perhaps they'd even felt a sort of fear. He'd grown larger than his parents, larger than his older brother, and it bothered him that he intimidated so many.

So he'd come to London to make a fresh start at finding a wife.

Oh, he had doubts that this comely woman before him had marriage on her mind. He was just the newest face, the newest amusement.

But if this was how London women greeted strangers, he would be going to more parties.

She was not the kind of woman he was seeking, with her rare beauty, of which she seemed very aware. Her wheat blond hair hung in maidenly curls down her back, tumbling over her shoulders past her impressive breasts. Jewels clung to her hair, shimmering with candlelight when she but inclined her head. Her breasts were full and rounded, and he imagined their heavy weight would fill his hands with pleasure. She obviously wanted them looked at, because she showed them so readily.

But it was her secretive green eyes that held him enthralled. There was mischief in her gaze, leaving him feeling pleasantly off-guard. He might enjoy these strange London customs.

He watched her mouth as she sipped the wine, let his glance linger on the curve of her throat as she swallowed.

Her skin would be so soft to touch. She was a pretty thing, and he was certain some man would find her useful as a wife.

But not him.

He gave another regretful glance at her breasts. Ah, he could think of other uses for her, though. Then he chastised himself for such base thoughts.

She leaned closer to smile up at him, and he felt the first heady taste of forbidden passion.

She was dangerous, this one, and he should move on to women more suitable to be his wife. But still he stood at her side and looked his fill and imagined her warming his bed. He was suddenly glad for the tunic that fell to his thighs and hid the obvious.

"How is it that I have never seen you before, my lord?"

"I am new to London, my lady."

"New? In all of your life, you have never been here before?"

She seemed shocked and disbelieving at such a notion, and he hid a smile.

"It is at least five days' journey from my home, my lady. I have not found it necessary to travel to London before now."

He waited for her to ask why, imagined scaring her away by telling of his quest. But again she looked past him at someone else.

He felt a sudden stab of unease—surely it was not jealousy. He hardly expected his simple conversation to hold the attention of a sophisticated woman, whose name he didn't even know.

But this evening it seemed important to prove to himself that he hadn't made a mistake by coming to London. He smiled at her and was rewarded by her full attention again. In fact, she seemed to be looking him over as much as he was looking at her.

He took her free hand in his, and when she stiffened, he rubbed his thumb over her knuckles.

The woman stared at their joined hands, then raised

her wide, luminous eyes to his. He felt his breath catch in his throat, then heard the most ridiculous words leave his mouth.

"This room has become overly warm, my lady. There is a full moon tonight—perhaps we could look upon it together?" He took her trembling hand and laid it upon his chest over his racing heart.

John kept expecting her to pull away, to alert everyone with her screaming. But she only stared at her hand and nodded.

"There is a door to the garden near here," she said in a soft but clear voice. Then she linked her fingers with his to lead him away.

Elizabeth felt excited and warm—and terrified. Could she have consumed too much wine? She had never done anything so wild, and though somewhere in her mind she heard the word, *No!* she was powerless to listen. The need to make Lord Wyndham jealous was fast fading beneath the heated passion in this stranger's eyes.

She pushed open the tall lead-paned doors leading to the garden and drew the man out with her. Immediately it was like breathing in hot, wet steam. The heat of the day had not dissipated and clung in wet droplets to the foliage and rose like a mist from the hot ground. The moon illuminated overgrown paths; stone benches seemed to call from secret hideaways.

Elizabeth let go of the stranger's hand, keeping her back to him. Perspiration broke out on her face and chest, and she felt the strangest need to pluck her garments away from her skin.

Suddenly he rested his hands on her shoulders. She froze, feeling his nearness at her back and the hot heaviness of his large, rough hands, half-afraid and half-excited to find out what he meant to do.

"Would you like to dance?" he asked softly.

"But you said—"

"I could teach you my dancing."

It was his voice, surely it was his voice weaving this

strange languorous spell through her. "You may," she whispered.

"I have your permission, do I?"

Was he laughing at her? She turned around and looked up into his face, shadowed by the night. He wasn't smiling as he slipped an arm around her waist. She gasped as he brought her up against his well-muscled body, then began to turn her about the stone terrace, faster and faster.

The earth tilted away from her as he put his arm beneath her knees and swung her up into the air. With a little cry, she flung her arms around his neck. She was breathing hard, surely from terror, and he was breathing just as heavily.

"Put me down, my lord," she commanded, but it sounded weak even to herself.

He grinned and dropped her legs until she slid down the length of his body. And then she felt what a man's codpiece normally kept hidden.

For an astonished moment, Elizabeth hung suspended against him, her toes only brushing the ground, feeling a strange, tense heat blossom low in her belly. She didn't know where to look, what to do, until finally she raised her gaze to his.

His face was darkly shadowed, his cheekbones high and sharp. His eyes stared at her with a passionate heat that made her forget any other sensation but this. She couldn't stop herself from looking at his mouth.

Suddenly he lifted her higher and touched his lips to hers. The sweet shock of it sent a shudder through her. She'd never been kissed, had never wanted to let a man do such a thing to her.

But it felt wonderful. His lips were expressive, gentle, so soft as they moved against hers. She kissed him back, barely noticing that he was carrying her deeper into the garden, away from the lights of the house. He sat down on a bench with her in his lap, and she caressed his shoulders, his strong neck.

He threaded his hands through her hair, then cupped

her face in warmth. He tilted his head, his kisses growing
more insistent, his mouth opening against hers. She didn't
understand what he wanted until his tongue rasped along
her lips. She was startled as an arrow of heat lanced
through her, and with a soft moan she opened her mouth.
His tongue invaded, met with hers, and danced until she
tentatively responded. The party, her problems, everything
retreated except for the moist heat of him. When her
tongue finally entered his mouth, he groaned and clutched
her tighter to him, pressing her aching breasts to his chest.

Every part of her felt alive and needy and so sensitive
to his touch. He moved his hands down her back, rubbing,
caressing. He pressed kisses along her cheek, blew softly
in her ear until she shivered. She tilted her head back as
he nuzzled at her neck and licked along her collarbone.
Her fluttering hands touched his shoulders, then flattened
along his chest, until he surprised her by shuddering.

When she pulled away, he groaned against her neck.
"No, please touch me," he whispered.

She gladly gave in to her curiosity and explored his
hard, muscular chest as he pressed his mouth ever nearer
to her breasts. She had a single moment of clarity where
she knew she should stop him.

But then he licked between her breasts, and she had to
bite her lip to keep from crying out at the pleasure of it.
He suddenly lifted her until she was straddling him, and
although her skirts were bunched between them, he
cupped her buttocks and pulled her hard toward his hips.
The pressure *there,* between her legs, felt like nothing
she'd ever imagined—hot and throbbing and so forbidden. For a wild moment, she wished there were no garments between them.

Smoothing his hands down over her shoulders, he slid
his fingers beneath her neckline. She held his head to her,
her breath coming in panting gasps as she watched what
he did to her. With only a twist of his hands, her breasts
spilled free.

Neither of them moved for an endless moment. Before

she could feel embarrassed, he cupped her breasts in his hands and looked into her face.

"You're beautiful," he whispered hoarsely.

When he rubbed his thumbs across her nipples, she gasped and clung to his shoulders. He watched her face while he caressed her, and she couldn't look away from him. Every movement of his fingers sent a pulse of desire through her, and it all seemed to be centered between her legs.

Then he bent his head and took her breast in his mouth, and the endless possibilities of passion stretched out before her. He moved back and forth between her breasts; every tug of his mouth made the pressure and wanting build up inside her. She didn't know *what* she wanted, only that he never stop making her feel this alive.

She felt his hands beneath her skirts, sliding up her legs, caressing her skin. How much longer could she bear this wanting, this needing? With a groan, she pressed her hips harder to his. His hands slid up her legs, his thumbs forming little circles on the inside of her thighs. She suddenly felt a rush of warm air and realized he'd pressed her skirts back. She was truly naked to him now, except for her gown bunched at her waist. But the thought only aroused her as she pressed her breasts against his mouth and let his hands explore her.

And then he touched her in a most private place, where she'd never imagined a man *wanting* to touch.

And it was paradise.

He frantically kissed her mouth, her breasts, but his fingers moved at such a slow, taunting pace she wanted to urge him faster. She was mindless with the new and overwhelming sensations. So this was why men and women were drawn together; this was why they risked their very reputations to—

And that thought brought her first sense of unease.

"Please, my lord," she began breathlessly, then groaned as his finger slid inside her. She was actually wet down there, and she tried to tighten her thighs in embarrassment.

His fingers started circling on her flesh, finding a new, secret place that made every part of her body shake.

But her unease was growing, and she knew she had to stop this before the worst happened, and she was compromised. What could she have hoped to accomplish with this insane plan?

"My lord, you must stop!" Her voice was louder now, stronger. She caught his hands and pulled them away from her while scooting back toward his knees. Her body was bereft, aching with the need for something now out of reach, something only he knew how to give her, and she quickly got to her feet. Between her thighs, she felt swollen, aching.

He leaned back on the bench, tilting his head back, and in the moonlight he looked severe with pain. Did he feel it, too, even though she hadn't touched him as he'd done to her?

"You're right," he murmured hoarsely, and his voice was enough to make her want to collapse against him in surrender. "We shouldn't have come out here. I shouldn't have—"

He broke off as he looked at her again. Elizabeth realized her breasts were still bared, white in the moonlight, and she quickly tucked them back into her bodice, suffused by a hot feeling of shame. She desperately wished she could pull the neckline higher, but her attempts only made him wince.

"Tell me your name," he whispered. "Let me come to visit you."

"Oh, no, you mustn't! There's a man—"

"You're married!" he said, too loudly.

"Shh!" She looked back over her shoulder, and her panic only increased at how foolish it was to be out here alone with a man. And now she knew the reason why. "No, I'm not married, but I never should have done this. There's a man inside who wants to marry me."

The open expression on his face suddenly vanished, and he surged to his feet to tower over her. "He is in there now? You deliberately brought me out here, hoping he was watching us?"

"No, I—I forgot about him," she insisted, beginning to back away from this stranger who fascinated her yet frightened her. What could she have been thinking? She knew nothing about him. And though she'd originally wanted Lord Wyndham to notice her, this was not what she'd hoped he'd see.

"You used me to make him jealous, when he damn well could have come out here and found us together!"

"I . . . I never thought—"

"That is very obvious, my lady. You don't think much, do you?"

She stiffened in anger. "There is no need for insults! It was your idea to be alone with me."

"And your quick suggestion where we could go. You even took my hand and *led* me, by God, so don't play the innocent with me." He advanced on her. "Do you do this every evening, pick the most gullible man and taunt him with your beauty, then deny him that which you promised?"

"I promised nothing!" she cried, shaking with her fury—and her rising fright. "I never meant any of this to happen, and I certainly have never done such a thing before!"

"Maybe you'd be married by now, if you'd chosen to arouse that other man you're so anxious to please."

They glared at each other, both breathing hard.

"I have to go," Elizabeth said as she backed away, hoping she could escape the tall, imposing stranger. "I'm sorry that I . . . that this—"

"You're not sorry. I'm only surprised you didn't wait for your own pleasure before you denied me mine."

She shook her head, not understanding what he meant. She turned and ran back through the garden, then slipped into the open doors to the great hall and disappeared into the anonymity of the crowd.

CHAPTER 2

Elizabeth awoke late the next morning and stared blindly up at the canopy over her four-poster bed, feeling damp and overly warm from the oppressing heat. She had had a difficult time falling asleep and even then slept fitfully, with dreams of the stranger haunting her, making her feel somehow unfulfilled.

She rolled over and covered her head with the pillow. How could she have been so foolish? She knew her father believed her less than intelligent, and now she'd proven it. She thought of the words she'd once overheard between her parents, how they'd told each other to emphasize her beauty, because it was all she had besides money to entice a man.

Well, it had worked, she thought bitterly. The stranger had certainly not been enticed by her clever conversation. She felt the tears start again, but she conquered them before they could fall. She would not cry over her stupidity. Her mistake was finished, and luckily no one had seen them out . . . groping in the garden.

When her maid came to help her dress, the girl seemed particularly wary and wouldn't meet Elizabeth's eyes.

Elizabeth finally touched her arm. "Matilda, is something wrong?"

The girl shook her head, her little linen cap dipping to cover her eyes. Then suddenly she twisted her hands together, took a deep breath, and looked Elizabeth in the face.

"Milady, yer father just seems . . . upset. He 'ad a visitor early this mornin', and now the man is back. I brought them ale, and they barely stopped their arguin' 'til I was gone."

Elizabeth felt a cold shiver of dread. "Is the stranger a . . . tall, broad man, dressed plainly?" Even now she could remember the width of his shoulders beneath her exploring hands, and she cursed her good memory—not an asset her parents could brag about.

"Nay, milady, he's rather . . . short, on the puny side, even."

Elizabeth gripped the back of a chair and tried not to sway with relief. She was so worried that the stranger would find her and tell her parents what a sinful woman she was. My God, he could even try to blackmail her into further intimacies. How much more proof was necessary before she realized she truly was a foolish woman?

With Matilda's help, Elizabeth dressed in a sedate blue gown, with a starched ruff clear up to her chin. It was difficult to feel decently covered. She could still vividly remember the stranger's hands on her breasts, his fingers stroking between her thighs.

Her face flushed, Elizabeth said, "Thank you, Matilda. I'll be down to break my fast shortly."

Just as the maid opened the door, they heard the earl's loud voice. "Elizabeth! Come down here please."

She blanched as she realized how her father's voice carried up the marble staircase from the front hall. He had never before shouted at her like that. Her heavy gown clung to her damp skin and choked her neck. Her knees almost buckled, and she held the door frame for support, nodding into Matilda's terrified face.

"You go on about your day, Matilda. 'Tis me he wants to see."

The girl bobbed a curtsy and fled toward the back staircase. Elizabeth gazed after her longingly, wishing she, too, could escape. Even though the stranger had not come for her, she had a horrible, sinking feeling of dread.

When she stepped into her father's withdrawing room, she was startled to see Sir Ralph Cobham sitting in the seat of honor before the hearth. The look he shot her was malevolent, triumphant—had he convinced her father to let her marry him?

She warily looked at her father, only to find his dignified face cold and remote, as if she were a stranger.

"Father, you wanted to see me?" Her voice sounded high-pitched, not like her own.

He didn't invite her to sit down, so she stood with her hands fisted in her skirts, as if waiting for her executioner.

"Earlier this morning, Sir Ralph told me a tale that I could not dismiss easily."

For a moment, she felt confused. This wasn't a marriage proposal?

"What went on at the party last night, the one your mother and I couldn't attend?" Every word grew colder and colder, as if icicles should be dangling from his lips.

She dug her fingernails into her palms, and her stomach quivered with nausea. "I danced, I talked to people, I—"

"Did you go into the garden with a strange man?"

"I—" She shot a wild glance at Sir Ralph, who sat back and folded his arms over his narrow chest, as if waiting for an enjoyable play to commence.

"Did you go into the garden with a strange man!"

Her father barked out the words so furiously that Elizabeth stumbled back a step from his disgust.

"We just walked!" she cried, and the first embarrassing tear slipped down her cheek. The lie almost choked her, but she had no choice. Had Sir Ralph followed them— stood in the shadows and watched? She felt like retching.

"Sir Ralph," her father said, in a calmer voice, "what did you see?"

Some of Sir Ralph's triumph faded. "I was dancing with Mistress Penelope, my lord. I only know that your daughter was gone a long time, and when she returned— alone—her face was flushed and her clothing disheveled."

Before her father could speak, she demanded, "How was my clothing 'disheveled'? The wind could have—"

"There was no wind, Elizabeth," her father said in a low voice.

"Father, do you believe the things he is implying? He holds a grudge against me because I do not return his affections. He would enjoy seeing me humiliated!"

"It is easy to know the truth," her father answered. "I have sent for the man in question."

"How did you find him? He had only just arrived in London." Elizabeth tried to tell herself this was a good thing, that all the stranger had to do was repeat her denial, and there would be no proof.

"Sir Ralph told me that he is a distant cousin to your host of last evening. I sent my men to learn what they could of him." He paused and eyed her almost contemptuously. "Do you even know his name?"

She felt her face flame with embarrassment. "No," she finally said, lifting her chin.

"John Malory." He sat down at his desk and they all remained silent, waiting.

John Malory, she thought to herself, sitting as far away from Sir Ralph as she could. John. A plain name for a plainly dressed man.

John was shown into the palatial home of the Earl of Chelmsford, and he followed the maid through an immense hall lined with marble columns, with floor tiles laid out like vines in a garden. In his mind he was suddenly in the dark, hot garden again, with the passionate stranger in his lap. He could see the woman's sultry green eyes, just at the moment he'd bared her breasts. The frustration of their encounter wouldn't leave him.

He shook his head to clear it. He had no idea why he'd been sent for, what an earl could possibly want of him. John had told his cousin, the Marquess of Worcester, that he didn't need help. Recalling his cousin's worried look, John now wondered if that had been a mistake.

The maid showed him into a withdrawing room, which had tall rows of windows along two walls. He almost had to squint at the two men who'd risen as he entered. But as his sight adjusted, he could see that they were strangers to him.

There was another movement on his right, and he forced himself not to flinch as he saw that it was the woman from the garden. By daylight she still wore her beauty with an immense dignity, even though her face looked strained and pale as she stared at him.

"John Malory?" said one of the men.

John turned to the older man, who could only be the nobleman who'd summoned him. He wore power like his daughter wore beauty.

"Yes, my lord?" he asked, feeling a knot of tension tighten in his stomach.

"I am the Earl of Chelmsford, and this is Sir Ralph Cobham. In worry for my daughter's reputation—"

John thought he heard a strangled sound from the woman behind him.

"—Sir Ralph wished me to know that you and my daughter, Elizabeth, were seen leaving the party last night. Can you defend your actions?"

For a moment John was stunned, then full of anger at his own stupidity. Shouldn't he have known that liberties taken with a noblewoman would return to haunt him? Then he remembered her willingness and wondered if she had deliberately set out to make a fool of him. By the looks of her father's mansion, the woman did not need to marry for wealth, so what was going on here?

John looked at Cobham, saw the cold pleasure he was obviously taking from the woman's humiliation, and knew the kind of man he was. He would spread tales across London, maybe all of England, to appease this obvious hatred he had for her—for Elizabeth.

John turned to look at her again, and if anything her face had grown paler. Had she led Cobham on, too, only to throw his desire back in his face?

John clenched his hands behind his back. His dreams of having a wife like his brother's faded into the ashes of his own foolishness. He could not let the girl suffer alone for what they both had done.

"I went into the garden with your daughter, my lord, that is true."

"And?"

My God, what did the man want from him, details? "We kissed," he said shortly.

The earl slammed his hand down on the desk in anger, Cobham practically burst with the pleasure of his revenge, and Elizabeth gave a startled cry.

"That's not true!" she said.

He suddenly realized she had lied to her father to protect herself. Didn't the foolish woman know it was too late, that even if they both denied it, the rumors would ruin her?

"He must want my dowry, Father; surely you see that!"

John flinched at the insult and turned his cold gaze on her. "I did not seek this meeting out, my lady. I did not force you into the garden, either."

Now it was her turn to draw back as if he'd slapped her. "This isn't fair," she began plaintively, but her father interrupted.

"You and my daughter will be married," the earl said shortly. "I will have a special license procured quickly."

John felt a flush creep up his neck as he saw how disappointed the man obviously was at the thought of his daughter marrying so low.

Elizabeth stepped toward her father, who almost seemed to shrink away. For a brief moment, John felt sympathy for her.

"But Father, we know nothing about him! He could be a—a tradesman for all we know!"

John's sympathy evaporated.

"He is a baron," the earl said shortly, "and for that you should be thankful. Sir Ralph, you may leave us now."

Cobham looked disappointed as he got to his feet. When the earl said nothing else, John made it a point to block the doorway and tower over the wretch.

"Elizabeth is going to be my wife," he said in a low, cold voice. "Should I hear even one unsavory rumor, I will know who started it." He leaned close to Cobham's pale, twitching face. "And I will hunt you down."

Cobham darted around him and fled the room. In the

heavy silence left to them, he saw Elizabeth staring wide-eyed at him. And he suddenly wanted to hurt her.

"I didn't do that for you," he said shortly. "But for the honor of my family."

She flinched, and he suddenly wished he could take back the words. Their situation was not only her fault.

In a quieter, calmer voice, he said, "Leave us now, Elizabeth. Your father and I have much to discuss—and you have to pack."

"Pack?" she whispered in a weak voice. "Where are we going?"

"Yorkshire, my home."

That seemed to shock her more than their marriage. He caught a glimpse of her glistening eyes before she lowered her head and ran from the room.

Elizabeth shook with suppressed tears, but she could not cower in her room. She sat on the stairs in the hall, watching the door behind which her father and *that man*—John Malory—planned her life without even considering her.

Malory had ordered her from the room, and her father had let him! What could they be saying? Was her father ready to ship her off with an impoverished baron into the wilds of Yorkshire? Could he truly be that angry with her?

He was, she thought bleakly, and shivered at the contempt she'd seen on her father's face. She had gotten herself into this mess, all because she'd tried to make Lord Wyndham jealous.

And now he'd never ask to marry her.

When the door opened, she rose quickly to her feet. John Malory closed the door behind him, and he was alone. He walked across the hall, unaware of her presence, his face pensive and distracted. Where was his triumph? Surely he only concealed it well.

He saw her and stopped. She had forgotten how imposing he was, how even in his plain garments he seemed larger than her father's overpowering hall.

"Did you wish to speak with me, Elizabeth?"

"I have nothing to say to you," she said in a low voice, hating the quiver he would certainly hear.

He only inclined his head, as if she wasn't even worth arguing with. Her eyes burned with unshed tears.

He walked past her and out the door.

She quickly wiped her wet lashes, then marched to her father's door and knocked.

There was a long silence before he told her to come in. He was sitting at his desk but staring out the windows to their sprawling garden along the Thames. He didn't look at her; he didn't speak.

Every feeling of unworthiness she'd ever had crowded into her head. When her mother returned from the country, Elizabeth would have to explain it all again. And her mother might ask exactly what she had done in that garden.

She was every bit the stupid girl they thought she was. "Father?"

To her horror, her voice broke, and the tears finally spilled down her cheeks. She wanted her father to hold her, to tell her everything would be all right. But he'd never been that kind of father, and he certainly wouldn't start now.

He cleared his throat but still didn't look at her. "I'll have the license sometime tomorrow. The marriage will take place the next day."

"But Father, surely there is something else we can do. All he wants is my money!"

"Then why did he tell me to keep it for one year, until he'd proven himself?"

She didn't know what to say to that. Finally, she asked, "What about the marriage contract?"

Her father picked up a quill and bent over his desk. "At least he's willing to marry you. Perhaps you should have thought of money before you brazenly kissed him. Now please leave, so I can decide how to tell your mother of your disgrace."

Elizabeth held back her sobs until she was alone in her

own room. My God, not only was she to marry a man who expected her to live far from London, but he was impoverished, too. As if marrying her was supposed to make up for that! How could her father allow this to happen?

How had *she* allowed this to happen? she wondered dully.

CHAPTER 3

At the church, John married Elizabeth, who was pale and red-eyed and wouldn't look at him as she trembled through the whole ceremony.

He didn't like feeling sympathy for her. Every young girl expected to have a wonderful wedding someday, and hers was attended by few people. Her three brothers were away, and her parents stared at the ground, rather than at her. He'd been introduced to her mother earlier that morning, and the woman had looked him up and down and promptly burst into tears. It seemed that Elizabeth had disgraced not only herself but also her entire family.

John was having an increasingly difficult time understanding this. He was marrying her, after all.

He had wanted a strong woman who would work at his side and be able to oversee his castle when he had to travel to his other holdings. But he couldn't imagine Elizabeth Stanwood having those capabilities. He thought of his brother William's wife, Martha, and how capable she was. Everyone admired her and came to her with their problems and illnesses. She made time for her five children and plenty of time for her husband, if William's satisfied smile was any indication.

A feeling of grief hung heavy about John's heart. He had allowed himself to be swayed by a pretty face and comely body, and he'd have to pay the price.

At the end of the ceremony, Elizabeth presented her cheek to be kissed, and he knew with grim certainty that it would be an awkward wedding night.

Elizabeth spent her wedding day in a daze. She barely remembered the ceremony, so confused and heartsick were her thoughts. The wedding feast was small and tense, and as she sat beside her new husband, she could only think how . . . plainly dressed he was. And poor.

She shuddered and looked about the immense dining
chamber of her parents' home. Would she ever see any
of this again? Would his entire home fit in this room?

Whenever she felt like crying, she looked at her
mother, who was doing all her crying for her. That was
all she'd done since she'd arrived the previous night, making Elizabeth feel miserable and guilty.

She had only her maids to lead her up to her bedchamber, since none of her friends had been allowed to attend
the wedding. She knew her father was telling society that
she and Malory were a love match, in such a hurry to
marry that a proper wedding couldn't be planned.

As her maids dressed her in a sheer night rail and
turned down the bed, Elizabeth clutched her stomach and
thought she'd be sick. She knew she was expected to lie
with her husband, but the passion of their evening in the
garden had fled. At least her anger was returning, she
thought, watching as the maids scampered from the chamber and left her alone.

Anger was all she had left to feel, so she fed the flame
by remembering Malory's betrayal to her father. Why
hadn't he lied? The only reason could be money, no matter how her father thought otherwise.

And there was no point asking where they'd be living—or even how—because it would only make her more
miserable. By not knowing, at least she could still hope.

John stood outside the bedchamber and told himself to go
inside. He was holding a pouch with the wedding gift he'd
brought from home, and he wondered if his new wife
would throw it back at him.

With a heavy sigh, he gave a brisk knock and opened
the door. Elizabeth stood at the window looking out at
the last pink of sunset, but she whirled and faced him, her
arms folded tightly across her chest. It only took him a
moment to realize why. The rail she wore was made of
the sheerest silk and lace; it clung to her hips and outlined

even the indentation between her thighs. He stood there stupidly, knowing he was gaping at her yet unable to stop himself.

"They made me wear this," she said.

He heard the mutiny and anger in her voice, and it broke the spell of desire she so easily wove around him.

"Then I'll help you take the garment off if you'd like," he said mildly. For just a moment, he'd somehow let himself believe she could be welcoming him.

Instead she glared at him. "Oh, yes, you've already proven how skillful you are at disrobing a woman. Had lots of practice, have you?"

"Not as much as I would have liked," he said, forcing himself to smile. "But then you seemed quite at ease with letting a man disrobe you. Had lots of practice, have you?"

She advanced on him and pointed her finger at his face. "Never in my life has a man been so crude as to touch me as you did that night in the garden."

"So you've succeeded in convincing all your suitors that you're made of ice?" John's voice was husky, and he'd barely gotten the words out coherently. Her breasts were only hidden behind scraps of silk that outlined her nipples and revealed the shadowed valley in between. His erection became almost painful.

"My suitors were gentlemen," she said, stalking away from him.

He almost choked at the sight of her backside, which he wanted to grab in two handfuls to haul her up against him. "I've brought you a wedding gift," he managed to say.

She made no response, only sat down in a chair before a little table littered with her combs and perfumes. When he sat across from her, she slid back farther in her chair, as if she were afraid to touch him. And a little devil inside him made him lean even closer. He held out the pouch, and she reluctantly took it.

She opened the drawstring and withdrew a small hand

mirror, its handle twined with silver and gold.

"It was my grandmother's," he said, glancing at the dressing table, with its fancier mirror.

Elizabeth set it on the table behind her, then looked up at him with wintry eyes. "Thank you for the gift."

"Ah, good breeding wins out," he said, trying to smile and make the best of their situation. He took one of her soft hands in his, but she pulled away and stood up. Her night rail brushed across his skin, and the scent of her perfume made him once more think of the secrets of her body he'd only begun to explore.

"I just have one question for you," she said.

John turned in his chair, letting his arm dangle over the back, amused at her defiance. She was certainly not afraid of him, and for that he was grateful.

"All you needed to do was tell one small lie," she said, her voice cold and steady. "Why didn't you? What other reason could there be except for my dowry? You were obviously looking to marry, considering that you'd brought all the way from Yorkshire a gift for the lucky, chosen woman."

The last was said with such sarcasm that he barely held back a smile, even though he knew she meant to offend him. "I told you I came to London to find a wife, and regardless of how low you think I am, I did not need to compromise a woman to get one to marry me. What happened between us was . . . unplanned, although certainly enjoyable."

She rolled her eyes.

"I would have said nothing, but once the gallant Sir Ralph came forward—I take it he's another of your spurned suitors—I was not about to lie. I could have easily gone home, my reputation intact, perhaps strengthened, and you would have been ruined."

She stalked back toward him, and again her lovely body made thinking difficult. "Are you saying you told the truth to *protect* me?"

"Yes. For that and honor, of course."

"Honor? Forcing a woman to marry you is honorable?"

"It was your father doing the forcing, and believe me, I was hardly overjoyed. But I could not leave you behind to suffer for what we'd done."

"How noble of you," she said sarcastically, blinking back tears. "But although I went outside with you that night, I had no idea what was involved, what you'd . . . what we'd—"

The tear that slipped down her cheek made him stand up and enfold her in his arms, though she remained unyielding.

"I didn't know that," he whispered into her ear. "And I'm sorry."

Elizabeth stood in his warm embrace and listened to his apology. For just a moment, she almost believed he was sincere, but then against her belly, she felt the hard reminder of his desire.

She stumbled away from him. "Will you say anything to get me into bed?" she cried, dashing away her foolish tears.

"I can't help how my body reacts to you."

"Is that your only excuse for compromising me, marrying me—"

"Elizabeth—"

"No! I won't do it! I don't care what you expect from me, but this is one thing I control."

She watched him come at her, and even though she backed up until her legs hit the bed, she refused to be afraid of him.

"Elizabeth, if you believe that, then you are lucky to be married to me."

"Lucky!"

"Any other man would put you on your back, spread your legs—"

She winced at his crudity.

"—and take your maidenhead, as is a husband's right. But perhaps this is your game. You are flaunting your body—"

"Flaunting!"

"—in hopes that I'll force myself on you and prove myself some kind of monster in your eyes. Then you'd have something to complain to your father about."

"I would scream before I let that happen!"

"Maybe they'll think you're screaming with pleasure."

His voice had dropped into that low range that did something strange to her insides. She could only blink at him. Scream with pleasure? Women did that?

Then she remembered being in his arms, alone in the garden, his hands stroking, caressing—and the embarrassing sounds she'd made. Could she have eventually screamed? She blushed and turned away from him, only to find the bed spread out before her.

She stared at the turned-down coverlet and said very firmly, "The only way I will lie with you tonight is if you force me."

Behind her he said nothing, and she risked looking over her shoulder. He watched her with those unfathomable dark eyes.

"I won't allow this marriage to be annulled," he said softly, dangerously. "I am willing to wait until your . . . sensibilities adjust, but I won't promise not to persuade you."

"Persuade!"

"Very easily, in fact. And I'm going to keep trying until you succumb."

He reached out and although she flinched, she could do nothing else, because the bed was right behind her. He slid his warm fingers down her neck, then along the lace neckline of her night rail. Holding her breath, she prayed he could not tell how rapidly her heat was beating, how much her body was betraying her, melting beneath his caress. She was so weak, she would need little persuasion at all.

His thumb rubbed across her nipple, and she gave an involuntary shudder as a spasm of pleasure rocked her.

"You're easy to gaze upon, Elizabeth, and you certainly look like you'd have no trouble producing my heirs."

She licked her lips and watched his hand cup her breast and gently squeeze. In a weak voice, she tried again to dissuade him. "I have scars—big, ugly ones."

"Well, it certainly was dark in that garden, so I might have missed it. Let me see."

He flicked the night rail off her shoulder, and it bared her breast before she could catch the silk and cover herself.

"You promised not to force me," she whispered, and her gaze caught and held his.

After a moment, he stepped back. "I won't."

"Then where will you sleep?"

He gave her a disbelieving look. "Right here."

He unbelted his tunic and lifted it over his head to reveal a white shirt. As he untied his codpiece, she flung her hand up to her throat and sat back heavily on the bed, but thankfully he was wearing linen braies beneath. He dropped his boots and hose to the floor, and she noticed that his bare legs were hairy.

When he pulled the shirt over his head, she almost stopped breathing. His chest was broad and sculpted with muscle, scattered with brown hair that narrowed down over his stomach. The arms that had lifted her, held her, were even more impressive bare. If all men were made like him, it was a wonder women weren't being compromised all the time.

"I have scars, too," John said, a grin transforming his face. "Want to come and see?"

She shook her head quickly. "I can see just fine from here."

Elizabeth knew she shouldn't even be looking, that he'd lose much of his power if only she'd ignore him.

But . . . how to ignore a man whose presence, whose very maleness, made the room seem smaller around him? Even the few scars across his chest and arms were impressive.

"Did you not bring something to wear?" she asked.

"I don't wear anything to bed, and certainly not on my wedding night."

He dropped the braies to the floor and stood before her naked. She couldn't stop her eyes from widening as she looked at his . . . his large . . . manhood, which seemed to point accusingly at her. She was not so innocent that she didn't know where *that* was supposed to go. But she had thought it would be . . . smaller. He walked toward her, and she couldn't stop staring at it.

"I don't suppose this persuaded you," he said, so close to her she had to lean back on her hands not to touch it.

She looked up his body at his face, to find him no longer smiling.

"Certainly not," she said, quite pleased when her voice didn't shake.

He shook his head and crawled onto the bed beside her. "That's a shame. You don't know what you're missing."

"Is that a boast?"

"I don't need to boast." He stretched out his long body until his feet almost hung over the end. His manhood lay large and flat on his stomach.

"Aren't you going to cover yourself?"

"No. It's rather warm in here, isn't it?"

She could hardly deny that, not when her skin felt moist and clammy. She was flustered and tense—and fascinated enough to want to stare at his body, even touch it. She stood up quickly before she could make a fool of herself.

"Lie down, Elizabeth."

She looked wildly about the room, knowing he wouldn't allow her to escape. He'd promised not to force her—but he hadn't promised not to touch her. She shivered.

"Cold?" he asked, and she heard amusement in his voice. "I wouldn't have thought so in this heat, but I promise I'll keep you warm."

She blew out all the candles, leaving the room in complete darkness. She should feel relieved not to have to stare at his nakedness, but she was left with the worry of what he might be doing.

After perching on the bed, she lay stiffly on her side, keeping as close to the edge as possible. When he didn't move or say anything, she allowed herself to relax the tiniest bit.

His arm suddenly caught her and pulled her closer to him. She gave a little shriek, trying desperately to push him away.

"Elizabeth, I won't have you falling off the bed. Now go to sleep."

He withdrew from her, but now she worried that he'd touch her again. She lay wide awake, even after she heard his soft snore.

CHAPTER 4

John came awake before dawn and lay still in the gray darkness. The air was warm and humid, and he had remained uncovered through the night. Of course he was also kept warm by Elizabeth, who in her sleep persisted in cuddling up against him. Even now, she lay with her back pressed against his side.

He stared at the frilly canopy over the bed and sighed. At first he'd almost been angry. It had taken a long time for her to fall asleep, and her small movements kept him awake—along with the erection that had seemed to grow harder with her every sigh. When she'd finally slept, she'd rolled against him and snuggled in for the duration. Twice he'd pushed her gently away, especially when he could feel her pointed nipples in his back and when she threw her leg right over his groin.

But John was awake now, and she lay against him so provocatively, and hadn't he promised he'd keep trying to seduce her? Carefully, he turned on his side and slid behind her, molding his thighs to hers, her buttocks cradling his erection. He was so hard, even a few thrusts like this would be enough.

But certainly not satisfying. He settled his arm around her waist, feeling the smoothness of the silk as he splayed his hand across her soft stomach. He hesitated, then slid his hand up her rib cage and cupped one generous breast. She stirred in her sleep, squirming her hips. Taking a ragged breath at the delicious assault, he buried his face in her hair.

He told himself to stop, that in the end he would be the frustrated one, but instead he caressed her nipples through her night rail, rubbing them to hard peaks between his fingers. She moaned softly, moving restlessly, and he rubbed his hips against hers from behind.

Pushing her hair out of the way, he nibbled her earlobe and let his fingers trail down her stomach between her closed thighs. As she shuddered and moaned again, he probed as deeply as the silk let him, rubbing against the curls over her woman's mound, tickling at the nub that was the center of her passion.

Elizabeth came awake feeling afire, achy, and almost feverish. What was wrong with her? And then she felt John's body behind her, his arms encircling her, his mouth kissing her ear, her cheek. One arm was beneath her, his fingers tormenting her breast, while he pulled up her night rail. Every inch of her skin felt alive with sensation as the silk slid against her, and she was frightened by how much she wanted his hand between her legs.

She knew she should stop him, but she was held immobile by the mounting flames that seemed to engulf her body. Her breath came in frantic gasps. When her night rail was finally bunched at her waist, he sank his fingers into her curls, rubbing and stroking until she cried out at the wondrous pleasure mounting in her.

Then he suddenly stopped, withdrawing his hands but not his body, leaving her lost, aching. She froze as he whispered in her ear.

"I am too much a gentleman to force you, but not so much as to suffer alone."

He rolled away and got out of bed. Mortified, Elizabeth pulled the night rail down her thighs and sat up.

"You did that on purpose!" she whispered, pushing her hair out of her eyes to glare at him.

He kept his back to her as he pulled on his braies and hose, and she wondered if his codpiece could possibly cover what he now kept hidden from her.

"I told you from the beginning that I would try to seduce you."

John faced her bare-chested and angry, and she was reluctantly impressed by how magnificent he looked.

"Since you spent all night pressing against me," he continued, "I felt free to take some liberties." He hesitated, and his voice became deeper, deadly to her self-control. "I could come back to bed. Are you asking me to?"

For a moment, she almost opened her arms to him, so desperate was she to find out what would end this dreadful ache. His brown eyes burned into her, and when they dropped down her body she could have gladly stripped off her night rail.

She was coming so easily under his control, she thought bitterly. He wasn't the husband for her, and she didn't want this marriage. Though he said he would not allow her to annul it, there might be other ways around him. Raising her chin, she gave him the haughtiest look she could muster.

"Thank you for the invitation, but I have to decline," she said coolly.

His slow grin made her knees shaky as she stood.

"Suit yourself, my lady. I'll be waiting. All you have to do is ask."

She turned her back on him and wanted to cover her ears when he laughed.

After he'd gone, she wrote the letter she'd been composing in her mind since this horrible wedding disaster began. She didn't want Lord Wyndham to think she was suddenly in love with another man, not after his lordship had been pursuing her so sweetly. She begged his forgiveness, writing that she was unhappy with both the marriage and the idea of living so far away in Yorkshire.

She reread it. Would Lord Wyndham understand that she had withheld her favors from John, that there might still be a chance for her and his lordship to be together?

For a moment, she felt guilty—until she remembered John's promise to seduce her, to make her a wife in every way. Wasn't that the same thing as forcing her?

Before she could change her mind, she sealed the letter with wax, then had her maid deliver it.

John was mildly surprised when Elizabeth's parents did not argue with his plans to depart the day after the wedding. It was customary to spend a few days with the bride's parents, and he might have relented had they asked him to stay—but they hadn't. Elizabeth took the news with a pale, composed face.

When he returned to their home at midday after renting horses and a cart, hiring servants, and buying a coach for Elizabeth, he found a multitude of trunks holding her garments. Dismayed but not surprised, he had the servants load the cart as best they could, but the final two trunks would only fit inside the coach with his bride.

After a small dinner that John felt hardly suited a final farewell to the only daughter of the household, he stood outside near the coach and watched Elizabeth and her mother, who was dressed as if in mourning, descend the stairs.

"Did your father already say his good-byes?" John asked, reaching for Elizabeth's hand at the final few steps.

She ignored his help. "He was called away to court," she said, and he could tell she was making every effort to control her voice.

John made no effort at all to hide his angry scowl. Her father was certainly slapping her into place every chance he got. John was beginning to realize that Elizabeth would fare much better with *his* family—if she would let herself.

Elizabeth turned to her mother and hugged her hard, and though she whispered to keep her words from him, he had excellent hearing.

"Mother, don't worry for me. John is not a cruel man. I swear that somehow I will make you proud of me."

Though Lady Chelmsford continued to cry, she did not hold her daughter for long. John helped Elizabeth into the coach, and when she raised her eyes to his, he smiled encouragingly. She only stiffened and looked at the trunks piled on the opposite seat and at her feet.

"How am I supposed to be comfortable like this?" she demanded—not too loudly.

He shook his head, but he wasn't surprised that she felt the need to rebuff his sympathy.

"Leave these trunks home, and you won't have a problem," he answered.

"I cannot do that! I need all these things, especially in the uncivilized north."

"Uncivilized?" he echoed, and flashed her a grin. "We'll see who is uncivilized."

He shut the door before she could say another word.

During the first few days of their journey, John tried to resurrect his sympathy for his new bride. It was dreadfully hot, and she had to wear all those garments and trap herself in the coach. Though he kept asking her to ride her own horse at his side, she continually refused. A hired maidservant kept her company, and he soon pitied the girl.

The farther north they journeyed, the more morose he became. He couldn't imagine introducing his spoiled bride to his family. He was angry at her and angry at himself for even following her into that garden. Though Elizabeth treated the servants decently and soon had the men falling over themselves to do her bidding, to John himself she was cold and remote.

At night when her pavilion was erected, she remained inside with her two maids, rather than sit with him near the fire. He never even got a chance to touch her hand, let alone attempt to seduce her. How was he to endure this marriage when he didn't even get the satisfaction of sexual release?

In the last hour before dawn, something besides the heat woke Elizabeth. She lay still on her lumpy pallet, hoping it was just one of the maids snoring but knowing in a cold, chill way that it was not. She could no longer see the bright shadows of the fire on the walls of the pavilion, though she distinctly remembered John ordering the guards to keep a fire going at all times.

When she heard rustling out in their camp, she wondered if they were being invaded by wild animals—which

John had assured her the fire would keep away. Why was she worrying? For a man who'd never been to the city, never been to court, John had proved himself more than capable of command. The farther from London they traveled, the larger and more expansive he seemed to grow while she felt small and lost.

Yet he was the first one she thought of now that she was frightened—not her father, not Lord Wyndham. The noises outside had grown louder, and she heard flesh striking flesh and a man's moan. As she awoke her maids, she hushed their voices, whispering that they had to dress quickly.

There was a call of warning, and then the sounds of men yelling and fighting. As the maids cried, Elizabeth was trying not to. She was afraid to look outside and afraid to sit here unknowing. With shaking hands, she parted the canvas flap and peered out.

Men she didn't know had invaded the camp—thieves? There were fistfights and swords clashing and men shouting. But soon she realized there were fewer and fewer men, that John's guards were slipping away into the forest. What kind of men were they, to desert the lord who'd paid them with what little money he had?

She turned to look after the maids, only to find them gone, the pavilion torn where they'd taken a knife to it. For a moment she was tempted to join them, but she didn't know anything about forests and wild animals. Her only safety was John, who was fighting for his life—and who'd put her in this terrible situation in the first place, she reminded herself.

But what if he died? What if she was left at the mercy of such barbarians?

When she looked back out, John was running toward the tent, and a feeling of relief brought tears to her eyes. He wasn't dead.

For a strange moment, she noticed everything in the growing light of dawn—the surprised faces of the thieves, the blood that trickled from a cut at John's temple. Then he grabbed her and shoved her behind him, brandishing his sword menacingly.

"Just take whatever goods you want," he said to the thieves. "But hurry, because this is a well-traveled road, and someone is sure to come this way soon."

Elizabeth felt her throat closing up, just when she might need to scream. The men looked at her contemplatively, as if she were a side of beef on market day. My God, did John think they might want *her*?

There was a tense moment of silence, and she was frozen with fear and anxiety, wondering what they would do. Her hands dug into John's waist as she clung to him, pressing her face against his back.

"Leave 'er," said a tall, spare man, who seemed to be the leader. "Take everythin' else."

With a cry, she retreated into the tent, trying to save some of her belongings, desperately pulling on her farthingale to hold up her skirts. John grabbed her as the tent was invaded and thrust her out into the trees.

"Do something!" she pleaded, looking over her shoulder. "They're taking my things!"

"I did do something—I saved you from them. And they're taking my things, too," he added dryly, pulling her deeper into the dense foliage, "including the horses and cart and coach."

"But surely the servants will return for us."

"They're London-bred, Elizabeth, and they didn't fancy Yorkshire, let alone being robbed in the wilderness. I think we've seen the last of them."

Soon they were alone in the dappled sunrise, shaded by the encroaching Sherwood Forest.

"What are we going to do?" she whispered.

"We're going to walk, of course."

"To the next town? Will we find horses there?"

"We've no money to buy them. Unless . . ."

He suddenly leaned toward her and snatched at her hair. She gave a wild cry and batted him away, knowing she was overreacting but unable to stop herself.

"Easy, my lady," he murmured, not even angry, which made her feel worse. "You have a jeweled hairpin which we can trade for supplies."

"Supplies! But it is a gift from my father. Surely it is worth—"

"I'd be grateful if it were worth a pair of horses and enough food."

"But—"

"Elizabeth." His voice lowered in warning.

She studied him in silence, seeing the bruises that had begun to darken his cheekbone and the blood that was drying on his face. He had done his best to protect her—and it had worked. She could have been the prize to a band of thieves.

Suddenly dizzy, she staggered toward the meandering brook they'd followed. She cupped water and brought it to her mouth, then splashed her hot face. She glanced over as John knelt beside her and did the same. When she realized that he was trying to wash away blood, she felt a moment of shame. Should a wife help with such things when there were no physicians about? He *had* been trying to save her, after all.

"You're missing a spot," she said. "Let me."

He sat quietly while she dipped the edge of one of her underskirts in the water and dabbed at the blood on the side of his face.

"This will need sewing by a physician."

He shrugged. "It will heal by itself—and then I'll have another scar to show you."

Elizabeth blushed at the memory of his naked body and the fine mapping of scars he'd displayed so proudly, as if it were an honor to be so disfigured. She suddenly realized how close together they were, that she practically knelt in his lap.

On their four days of journeying, she'd managed to keep people between them. But now they were alone, impoverished, unprotected. She should feel frightened—except that their solitude called to her, that his face, even wounded, was so hard and masculine and . . . exciting. Barely holding back a groan of mortification, she quickly turned away from him.

It didn't take long for John to find a farmer more than willing to accept Elizabeth's bauble in exchange for two plain but sturdy horses and a few days' worth of supplies. Her court finery, seldom seen so far north, drew plenty of stares as they traveled. And beneath her gown, she still wore that ridiculous farthingale to flare her skirts wide at her waist. She clung to it as her only possession left, even though she had to hold down her skirts as she sat side-saddle on the horse. He breathed a sigh of relief that at least she was a decent horsewoman.

That night, he led her off the main road into a clearing in the forest, and she remained on her horse as he dis-mounted. Twilight settled about them in a lush, warm haze as he gazed up into her beautiful face, and for a moment, he thought he was a lucky man.

But then she opened her mouth.

"I cannot stay here," she said firmly, looking down her perfect nose at him. "That village we passed would have been—"

"Stop this, Elizabeth." John sighed as he pulled off the saddle and shared a long-suffering look with the horse. "We have no money to pay for lodging. Asking for shelter in the village would only get us a smelly mound of hay in a dilapidated barn. At least now we're under the stars—and alone."

He touched her knee and she pulled away from him.

He laughed. "Allow me to help you down."

"I can—"

Hauling her off the horse, he set her on her feet. She staggered and would have fallen but for his grip on her arms.

"Elizabeth?"

With a pained expression, she limped away from him. "I am merely stiff."

He watched her hobble about the clearing, wondering when she had last ridden a horse. At least she wasn't complaining—yet.

"I'm going into the forest to look for firewood," he said. "I would appreciate your help."

"Firewood? I wouldn't know what to look for."

He clasped his hands behind his back and watched her. "Pieces of dry wood on the ground."

Even by the setting sun he could see her blush. "I've never . . . done anything like that."

"There's a first time for everything," he murmured, his gaze dropping down her body.

"I'll wait here," she quickly replied.

Feeling vaguely disappointed—but not surprised— John turned and stepped between the trees. He hadn't gone far before he heard her voice.

"Wait! John, wait!"

She caught up with him, her wide skirts scraping between two trees. For a moment, he thought she was trying to be helpful.

"I—I didn't want to be alone," she said, making no pretense of looking for wood.

He tried not to be disappointed in his wife, but it was a feeling that was constantly with him. He forced her to carry half the wood he found, regardless of the fact that it dirtied her sleeves, as she so quickly informed him.

Using the flint and steel he carried in a pouch at his waist, he started a small fire, then spread a blanket for Elizabeth to sit on. She squinted down at it, uncertainly smoothing her skirts, which hung bell-shaped from her waist.

"You should remove that farthingale," John said shortly. "You don't need it on this journey."

"It's the only one I have left, and who knows if I'll ever be able to purchase another one."

She eyed him speculatively, and he suddenly knew her intent.

"Are you worrying that I might not be able to keep clothing on your back?"

"I don't know the status of your wealth, after all."

"Family and home are more important than money."

"People who don't have money say that," she said tartly. "Exactly how much do you have?"

He angrily strung the bow he'd bartered for that afternoon. "Enough to keep any reasonable person happy— but probably not enough for you."

There was a strained silence between them, until Elizabeth said softly, "What are you doing?"

"Seeing to your food."

"But didn't we purchase—"

"There was no meat. Unless you'd like to live on biscuits and dried apples and—" He saw a movement out of the corner of his eye, turned, and shot the arrow.

She gave a little squeak of surprise. "Whatever did you do that for?" she demanded.

"Supper."

Elizabeth's growling stomach suffered a moment of nausea as she watched John pick up the dead rabbit. She was used to seeing her food already prepared, not dead, fuzzy, and . . . bloody. When he tossed it at her feet, she jumped back.

"You skin it while I—"

"No!" She knew her voice had an edge of hysteria to it, and she cursed herself for being a fool. But it was dark, and the wind whistled through the trees, and she was alone with him, and she was so hungry. Suddenly everything seemed overwhelming and miserable.

"Do you mean to say you don't know how to prepare a simple meal?" he asked quietly.

She stiffened. "We had servants for that! Whyever would I have learned such a thing? And if I had married anyone else—" She broke off at the cold gleam in his eye as he advanced toward her.

"Well?" he demanded. "Aren't you going to finish explaining what you're thinking?"

He seemed as tall as the trees as she arched her neck to look up at him. She was alone with him—a stranger she'd known mere days, who now controlled her fate.

CHAPTER 5

Elizabeth took a calming breath and forced her fears away. After all, even if she'd married Lord Wyndham, she would have been at his mercy. And what did she know about him, either? "All I was going to say was that if I had married anyone else, I would still be in London, with servants."

John shook his head and picked up the dead rabbit. "And you never would have known what new and wonderful things you would be learning."

"Skinning a rabbit?"

He gave a half-smile, and again his gaze drifted down her body, lingering on her breasts until she felt naked. "I can think of things you will enjoy learning even more."

She bit her lip and refused to answer—but refused to look away as well. Even his smile made her feel strange inside.

"Come, then, while there's still light. I'll show you how to prepare roasted rabbit."

Elizabeth soon understood why there were servants to do such a messy task. She forced herself to watch while John skinned the rabbit but closed her eyes and winced when he cut off the head. Only when the carcass was mounted on a stick, roasting over the fire, did she relax. Soon, the smell coming from it made her stomach begin a chorus of gurgling.

"You can sit down next to me, you know," he said, pointing to a log he'd rolled from the woods. "But you'll have to get rid of that farthingale."

With a sniff of superiority, she settled gracefully onto the log, her skirts spread around her. She pretended that her gown wasn't dirty and beginning to smell like the horse.

John shook his head. "Well done. So that's what you've been taught, eh?"

She ignored his taunting. When the meal was ready, she was so hungry that even the prospect of eating with her fingers didn't dismay her. The meat tasted so good it could have been prepared in the queen's kitchens. Between them, they devoured the entire rabbit.

In the darkness, she sat drowsily before the fire, watching John finish the last of the meat. "Do you think the thieves have followed us?"

He glanced at her. "No. After all, they took everything we had. Are you still frightened?"

She shook her head quickly, then glanced up as the hoot of an owl echoed through the dark forest. When he put a gentle hand on her arm, she pulled away, troubled by how his consideration made her feel.

"I need to clean up," she mumbled, holding her hands out before her.

"Greasy?" he asked.

The laughter in his voice offended her. How dare he be jovial, when they'd lost everything? She took a deep breath to berate him, but he rose and knelt before her. In the darkness his hair and eyes blended mysteriously into the shadows, and she shivered, too fascinated to move.

He took her hands in his and turned them palms up. He placed a kiss in one palm, and a delicious budding of heat uncurled inside her.

And then he licked her, and she gave a little jump and tried to pull away, but he didn't let go. Somehow her voice had deserted her.

He glanced up at her from beneath the fall of his hair. "You taste good," he rumbled in a low murmur, then sucked one of her fingers right into his mouth.

Elizabeth's jaw dropped in shock, and she couldn't seem to swallow or take a deep-enough breath. He must certainly feel the shaking that began in her hands and spread throughout her whole body. He licked and sucked each of her fingers slowly, completely, until she thought she would dissolve from the pleasure of it. There was a hot ache between her thighs that nothing could appease but his touch.

And then she remembered his promise to seduce her. When he pressed her hands against his cheeks and she felt his warm, stubbled skin, she knew this had to stop. Pulling away, she stood up, forcing him to fall back onto his hands.

He gave her a bemused smile. "Is something wrong?"

"I'm going to wash in the stream," she said, hating the unfamiliar sound of her voice.

"Elizabeth, you shouldn't wander off by yourself!" he called, and laughed as she practically ran from him.

Away from the fire it was dark and cooler. She slowed to let her eyes adjust to the shadows of the uneven ground and the sloping bank of the river. As the sound of gurgling water drew her, she fell to her knees and plunged her aching hands in, as if she could scrub away the memory of his mouth on her skin.

She sat back on her heels and looked out at the rippling water, with the moon reflecting off it and dancing in her eyes. She was afraid of John, afraid of herself—more than she was afraid of the wild forest. Every moment of her life with him was filled with things she didn't know how to do, new ways to disappoint him and herself. If he cared at all for her, wouldn't he be helping her? Wouldn't he stop teasing her?

If only she had the courage to triumph in this intimate battle between them. Maybe she could prove to herself that she had control of at least a small portion of her life.

When she turned back, he was sprawled leisurely on the far side of the fire, propping his head on one arm, watching her.

Elizabeth climbed up the bank of the stream, marched to her side of the fire, and glared at the hard ground.

"It's more comfortable over here," he said softly.

Defiantly holding his gaze, she reached up beneath her

skirt and untied her farthingale, then stepped out and set it aside.

He grinned. "Warmer, too."

"As if I need that," she said stiffly. "I'll be writing a letter home to my father. If you're thinking to prove yourself worthy of my dowry, I'm sure *this* will not help your cause."

Though he still smiled, it no longer reached his eyes. "The fact that I saved your life will be looked on poorly by your father?"

She lay down on her back and looked up at the sky, lit with pinpricks of light. "No, just the fact that you're forcing me to travel under such circumstances. It is beneath me."

John's voice no longer sounded amused. "I find your arrogance pathetic, Elizabeth. 'Tis a shame that no one saw fit before now to teach you to withstand life's problems with more grace."

She bit her lip and felt a rush of tears sting her eyes. Rolling onto her side, she faced away from the fire, away from her husband.

It had taken John a long time to fall asleep, and he had hoped that somehow a new day would make things miraculously better. Instead, at dawn a heavy rain began. He shook Elizabeth awake roughly, unable to shake away his anger at her. She sat up wearily and watched him saddle the horses while water dripped through her hair.

"Is there anything to eat?" she asked coolly.

"Dried apples and cheese in the saddlebag." He didn't look at her.

She heaved a sigh. "When will we be there?"

He patted the horse's neck absently, in his mind seeing not the animal's brown coat, but his estate and the centuries-old castle that dominated the land for miles in every direction. That was still two days distant. He could almost see the two of them arriving miserable with each other, Elizabeth as angry as any fishwife. Just the thought

of his brother's sympathy and his mother's disappointment was enough to set his teeth on edge. How could he
introduce his wife to his family? How could he explain
his foolishness?

But by evening he and Elizabeth would be able to
reach his hunting lodge, and a respite there would give
John a chance to think.

The rain had not let up by nightfall, and if anything,
the humidity seemed worse. When he steered the horses
off the road and onto a small woodland path, Elizabeth
finally broke her day-long sullen silence.

"What is this? Where are we going?"

Though her face was pale and dripped with rain and
her hair tumbled in muddy disarray down her back, he
still could summon no sympathy.

"Our home." Before he could say it was only a hunting
lodge, he watched her face go ashen, and she actually
seemed to brace herself as if preparing for squalor. His
outrage fouled his mood even further and he bit off any
explanations. Let her think what she'd like.

In the gloom of approaching night, the small stone-
and-timber lodge looked forlorn, abandoned. John glanced
at Elizabeth, whose wide eyes stared about her.

"Is there . . . a village?" she asked.

He shook his head.

"Neighbors?" Her voice sounded softer.

"If there were, I'm sure not the kind you're used to."

"But . . . you're a baron. Doesn't living like this bother
you?"

"No." Part of him felt guilty for misleading her, but
here he could have one last chance to know and understand her. It would be a test, a way to be certain she could
really be his wife—in every way—without the prying
eyes of his family and his servants. The lie suddenly felt
a little better.

She bit her lip, then murmured, "Well, shall we get out
of the rain?"

They left the horses to graze while they entered the

lodge. John watched Elizabeth closely as she took in the dust and gloom and shadows. There was a table and benches, two chairs before the hearth, cupboards and trunks, and a bed in the corner near the hearth. He saw her swallow.

"Is this . . . the only chamber?"

He nodded. When she said nothing else, he was relieved enough to smile at her. "Let me open the shutters so you can see it by the last of the day's light."

But although the gloom lifted as he threw back the shutters from four windows, the light only showed how much dust had accumulated since he'd been here last spring. He glanced back at Elizabeth and found her staring at the floor, trembling.

"I'll make a fire before I put the horses in the barn."

"Must you? It's so hot."

"We need to heat water and cook food, don't we?" he asked gently. "Now watch how I do this, because the fire might go out someday while I'm gone."

"But what if I can't do it?"

"Then we'll have to huddle together for warmth."

Elizabeth tried hard to concentrate on what John showed her, but she found her gaze roaming the tiny room, no bigger than her own bedchamber in her father's mansion. She was stunned that he expected the two of them to live forever in close quarters, with only each other for company.

But after a day of his angry silence, she felt relieved that he was smiling at her again. Without his good nature, everything seemed duller, more miserable, and she felt disgusted with herself that she already relied on his even temper and gentle humor.

When John suddenly stood up, she took a quick step backward.

"All right, let's get you out of those wet clothes," he said.

She wanted to protest, but she didn't have the heart for it. He unlaced her gown at the back and pushed it down over her shoulders, where she clutched it against her chest.

"I can finish this myself. Thank you."

He hesitated. "Elizabeth, you have many undergarments. In fact, I see a tie here that you can't possibly reach."

"John—"

But he'd already plucked it, and she took a deep, rib-expanding breath.

"You've been wearing a corset all this time?" He sounded incredulous.

"Of course," she answered, absurdly angry at his ignorance.

"Elizabeth."

His voice deepened, roughened, and she closed her eyes, wondering when she would get used to its effect on her. Her breath caught when he lowered her smock partway down her back.

"Your skin is rubbed raw right here."

He touched the skin below her shoulder, and though there was a tiny sting, that was nothing next to the feel of his hands on her, the way he rubbed her bare shoulders.

"Oh, Elizabeth," he murmured.

She felt his breath on her neck only a moment before he pressed his mouth there. He said her name over and over, parting her garments down her back, kissing everything he laid bare to her waist.

She swayed with numbing weakness, longing to fall into his arms and let him carry her to bed. She would be warm, protected, loved—

Her thoughts came to a reeling halt and she pulled away from him. Over her shoulder, she saw John rest his hand on the floor as if bracing himself, his head bent. Then with a sigh he arose.

"I'll see to the horses. In one of the trunks there should be shirts and hose but, regrettably, no female garments. I'll bring you some water from the well, so you can wash yourself."

As he left, she groaned and covered her face with her hands. What was she thinking? He didn't love her! He loved her money and only tried to seduce her so she wouldn't tell her father all that had befallen her.

And she would never love him. How could she? He'd brought her to this dreary, dank, tiny cottage, where she'd spend the rest of her life without her family or friends.

She had a sudden image of sitting beside John at this table, with laughing children surrounding them.

Elizabeth groaned again. What was happening to her?

After John set water to heat over the fire, he found musty—but dry—linens for Elizabeth to wash with and shook his head ruefully when she asked if there was a tub. He took his time in the barn, giving her the privacy he knew she wanted. But it was physically painful not to be there when she removed her garments, when she stood naked before the fire. He could imagine the wet cloth sliding over her skin, leaving her glistening in the flickering light.

Suddenly it didn't seem so terrible to want to keep her all to himself. Maybe . . . somehow she could come to accept their marriage, to love him.

He shook his head, cursing himself for a fool.

When he returned to the lodge, he found Elizabeth seated before the fire, one of his shirts dwarfing her, his hose drooping down her legs. He thought he might laugh but instead found himself admiring the long hair tumbling down to her waist. Even garbed so, she managed to look incredibly feminine, very appealing.

That night, he cooked their meal out of the dry stores he kept at the hunting lodge. He explained everything as he went, and he thought she tried hard to pay attention, but occasionally he saw her gazing about the room with an overwhelmed expression. He told himself to be patient.

John went outside once more to close the barn. When he returned, he found Elizabeth already in bed, the blankets pulled up to her neck as she faced the wall. Even in this unbearable heat, she felt the need to cover herself from his gaze. He stood over her, watching her breathe slowly, evenly—perfectly.

He heaved a great sigh and murmured, "Well, I hope she thought to shake the bugs out of the bedding."

With a shriek she flung back the blankets and launched herself out of the bed. Laughing, he caught her against him. She was so unpredictable, his Elizabeth, surprising him by trying hard to follow his example with chores, then reacting exactly as he expected about insects. At least he would never be bored with her.

When she sputtered her outrage, he couldn't help kissing her, holding her soft body against his, opening his mouth and slanting it across hers.

CHAPTER 6

When she turned her head away, John groaned with frustration. "What did you do that for?"

"Don't think you can make me jump out of the bed only to lie back on it with you. I told you I won't be forced."

"Elizabeth," he whispered, pressing kisses to her cheek. "How much longer do you think I can wait? I want to caress you, to make you wet for me—"

"Stop!" She shoved at his shoulders. "I—I can't trust you! I don't want"—she flung a hand out—"this!"

He let her go and she stumbled back.

"I don't even know how we'll survive!" she cried. "How can you feed us here in the depths of the forest without fields to plant?"

"I can take care of you!" he insisted, regretting the lies he had told. But he knew if he told her he was wealthy, he could never be certain whether her loyalty was to him—or to his money. "Why *can't* you trust me? Do you think I would let my wife starve, or go about garbed in sackcloth?"

"I'm already garbed in *your* clothing! There's nothing for me here!"

"Except me," he answered, surprised at how hoarse his voice sounded. "I still have hopes that that will be enough."

Elizabeth closed her eyes and turned away, whispering, "You set your sights too high, John."

She began to strip the bed. When the sheets and blankets were draped over her arms, she finally looked up at him with red, swollen eyes.

"Where should I shake these out?"

And he relented and helped her, cursing himself for these foolish emotions that made him ache for her acceptance. Could he be falling in love with her? God help him, for she would crush his heart.

When John awoke with Elizabeth warm and soft in his arms, he told himself the day would go well, that she would adjust to their marriage, that he would be able to take her home to his family soon. But she lifted her head off his chest and looked up through strands of her hair at him. Her eyes suddenly widening with realization, she slipped out of bed. Though her gown was still damp and filthy, she dressed in it, even putting that cursed farthingale back on.

The day only became worse. Everything she tried to do ended in failure—although at least she was trying. When she brought in wood for the fire, she ended up with a face full of ashes. When her wide skirt caught on fire, she was only saved from terrible burns because he saw the smoldering fabric near her heels. While he was out hunting, she pulled the growing vegetables out of the kitchen garden instead of the weeds. Plucking the partridge he'd killed made her teary-eyed, and she scorched her fingers when she overcooked it. But he ate every last bite and tried to keep up a cheerful conversation, while she sat in dejected silence.

"Elizabeth, you've done your best today," he said, wanting to touch her hand, knowing she wouldn't let him. "You can be proud of that."

She closed her eyes and shook her head sadly.

Why couldn't she see that trying to learn was a start, that things would get better? But for some reason every failure made her even more depressed.

That night after closing up the barn, John went inside the lodge and found his wife crying. He stood silently in the doorway, listening to her great sobs, and knew deep in his soul that she hated being married to him, that she would never adjust to the life of a country lady. How could she oversee his many estates and people when she couldn't even handle this simple hunting lodge? He felt a bleak emptiness inside him as he imagined no longer touching Elizabeth, kissing her, trying to seduce her— trying to make her laugh.

Elizabeth covered her face and cried harder when she heard John enter the lodge. She was a complete failure at everything she tried, even this unconventional marriage.

From behind her, he said softly, "We'll never make this work, will we?"

She wiped the tears from her face but couldn't look at him.

"I thought I could find a wife like my brother has," he continued. "Maybe no woman can live up to what I think a marriage should be."

"You're jealous of your brother?" she demanded, turning to face him, feeling nauseous inside that all along he'd been comparing her to another woman.

"No, I just wanted the same kind of life, with lots of children. They have five now."

"Five! Who can live up to this paragon of womanliness and beauty?" Every word he uttered burned her failure deeper inside her.

"I never said she was beautiful. It's about the kind of woman she is."

She wanted to groan her misery. The only thing she had to give—beauty—was the one thing that didn't matter to John. Elizabeth had foolishly hoped that that would be enough. But not for a man like John, a man who needed a different kind of woman.

"What did you expect out of our marriage?" he asked, stepping to her side and resting a hand on her shoulder.

She looked into the fire and sighed. "I don't know. I wanted to make my husband proud, to be admired."

"Like a piece of jewelry, Elizabeth? Is that all you want to be, a pretty object to look upon from afar, never to be a partner and share the joys and the sorrows of life?" He knelt down at her side.

The tears slipped down her cheeks and she didn't bother to dash them away. "You want me to be the one to change, but you're not willing to do the same. I will never be like your sister by marriage, no matter how much you want me to be! My parents told me the truth long ago, that my beauty is all I have. I have always accepted this."

"Elizabeth—"

"My beauty and my dowry. Aren't they what you wanted me for, after all? Don't deny it—you'll never convince me otherwise."

She got shakily to her feet, glancing at John's bewildered expression before she crawled into bed. Though it took awhile, she fell into an exhausted sleep and never knew if he joined her.

In the morning, Elizabeth awoke alone and halfheartedly ate the berries John had left on the table. After an hour of feeling sorry for herself and wondering what to do, she heard the jingle of many horses coming near and the shouts of men.

She opened the door to see at least a score of soldiers and servants, led by Lord Jasper Wyndham, who was dressed in court finery that glittered out of place in the cool green of the forest. His narrow, handsome face and blond hair usually made her sigh with delight. But something lodged in her throat and wouldn't let go as John approached the traveling party. Her eyes began to sting when Lord Wyndham dismounted and the two men talked. She had forgotten all about the letter she had sent Wyndham. As John glanced at her with no expression on his face, she knew he was learning of it.

The two men approached the cottage, and Elizabeth saw Wyndham's surprised gaze sweep down her body. She hadn't bothered with her farthingale, so her dirty skirts trailed on the floor. Her hair and face hadn't been properly washed, and she felt miserable. But worse was John's calm stare. Why wasn't he angry?

"Elizabeth," John said, "Lord Wyndham received a letter from you on our departure from London, which made him decide to follow us. The villagers in these parts know me and it was easy enough for him to do."

His voice seemed only tired to her, and her chest began to hurt. What could she say?

"He seems to think you would rather come with him than remain married to me."

She opened her mouth, but he held up a hand.

"We both know it's true." His voice softened. "I want nothing more than your happiness, and now I know you cannot find it with me."

"Lady Elizabeth," Lord Wyndham began, sweeping into a deep bow, "I wish to marry you."

These were the words she'd always wanted to hear. Why, then, could she barely keep her eyes off John's face?

Lord Wyndham said, "Lord Malory assures me that your marriage has remained in name only. In fact, he has been so kind as to offer witnesses, your hired servants, who can verify such a thing."

John met her gaze for only a moment before looking away. She didn't know what to think; why wasn't she reveling in achieving everything she'd wanted?

"I won't contest an annulment," John said shortly. "Go on, Elizabeth; there's nothing here for you."

She hesitated, then whispered, "Thank you."

When Wyndham took her arm and drew her from the cottage, she felt like a doll being led about. She continued to stare over her shoulder at John until he went inside and shut the door. The sound of it startled her and she shook, but Lord Wyndham was there, helping her onto a horse, putting her into the care of maidservants. She didn't look back at the cottage as they led her away.

John knew that it was time to leave the hunting lodge. He should go home, tell his family that he had failed to find a suitable wife, that he would have to try again.

But he couldn't imagine wanting a wife who wasn't Elizabeth.

He spent the day chopping wood to replace the stores they'd used since they arrived. With every stroke of the ax, he tried to make himself believe that he'd done the right thing letting her go. But he couldn't forget what she'd said about her parents, that they'd told her all she had was her beauty. What kind of parents were they, to so devalue their daughter?

No wonder Elizabeth thought she could succeed at nothing else. And then he'd played the fool and compared her to his sister by marriage. God above, all he'd done was confirm in her eyes that she was only a beautiful woman, with little else to offer a man. It made him sick inside to know that maybe he was like her parents after all. He had wanted a certain kind of woman, and instead of learning to understand Elizabeth, he had tried to mold her into someone else.

As night descended he stood alone before the hearth, hearing only the distant animals in the forest, feeling a loneliness he'd never imagined before. Being with Elizabeth had filled an emptiness inside him. For he hadn't just wanted to lie with her—he realized he'd wanted her love.

He *still* wanted her love. And he'd given up too easily.

John smacked his fist against the mantel. He could still see her face, the look of shock—not happiness—when she'd seen Wyndham. Without giving her a chance to make a choice, John had given her away like a necklace he no longer wanted.

He had to find her. He had to explain that he had done what he thought *she* wanted, not what *he* wanted. He wanted to love her until she finally understood that there were no conditions, that he could change as much as she could.

Morning would be too late. He packed the few supplies he needed—including the farthingale—saddled one of the horses, and set off by moonlight, knowing he had to win Elizabeth back or his life would be meaningless.

———

Elizabeth awoke in luxurious surroundings, in the best chamber at the inn, with maidservants sleeping on pallets at her feet. But although she was clean and comfortable for the first time in days, the sick feeling she'd gone to bed with had not left her.

During their slow journey south yesterday, as a cold rainstorm settled about them, she'd tried to tell herself that leaving John was for the best, that she could never live the kind of life he wanted her to live. But the truth was, she thought she could never make him happy. She'd been afraid to try, afraid to fail like she had failed at everything else.

But traveling at Lord Wyndham's side had been a revelation. Now that she knew John, she felt as if she was seeing Wyndham with clear eyes for the first time. The man she'd so worshipped back in London treated his servants disdainfully, thoughtlessly, and had talked to the innkeeper in an arrogant manner. And the worst of it was wondering if she used to behave just as badly.

John was courteous even when he was angry with her, and he treated everyone down to the stable boys in a fair manner. He didn't care how she looked; he enjoyed her beauty, but it wasn't important to him. Society's notion of fashionable ladies' attire didn't concern him as much as her comfort.

She remembered his sweet words of encouragement when she'd done nothing but fail at every task he'd asked of her.

But the worst punishment was trying to forget this yearning he had awakened inside her, which made even his nearness more exciting than any other man's touch.

Could she have fallen in love with him?

She felt a prick of tears behind her eyelids as she thought of his gentle humor and goodness. If she went back to him, would he allow her to begin their marriage again? Could he grow to love her even if she wasn't like his sister by marriage?

Somewhere deep inside herself, Elizabeth felt a reserve

of strength she'd never called upon. She had to return to John. She had risked everything once, going out to that garden with him; she owed it to both of them to risk it all again.

After the maids helped her dress in the new gown Wyndham had brought for her, Elizabeth joined him in the inn's private dining parlor. He glanced up at her with a nod but concentrated on his food. She couldn't help but compare him to John, who would have risen to his feet with a frank smile and made her feel wanted.

When she didn't sit down immediately, Wyndham looked up again. "We're leaving soon, Lady Elizabeth. Do eat something."

"Lord Wyndham, I need to speak with you."

He nodded and continued eating.

She took a deep breath. "I have made a mistake. In all good conscience, I cannot marry you."

Wyndham slowly set his knife down and sat back. "The annulment will not be a problem, Lady Elizabeth. And I'm certain my family can be persuaded to accept you."

She felt a chill at just the thought. "But my lord, I am married, and I find I do not wish to end it. I—I miss my husband."

He regarded her with narrowed eyes. "You miss that uncivilized country lord?"

"He and I suit one another, Lord Wyndham," she said firmly. "With your permission, I would like an escort back to his cottage."

Giving her a dismissive look, he went back to his food. "I think not, Lady Elizabeth. I went through much time and effort because of that ridiculous letter you wrote me. I cannot spare anyone now. And please give that gown back to the maidservants."

She blinked in amazement, and her anger heated her words. "Are you saying you wish me to travel alone? In that ragged garment? That you begrudge me even one servant?"

"I am." Though he didn't look up, he smiled.

She shook her head regretfully. "I'm sorry you feel the need to punish me for telling the truth. And I'm sorry that I played with your affections when I wrote that letter, but I have learned much about myself since then. I can do anything I set my mind to—even traveling alone. Farewell, my lord."

CHAPTER 7

Elizabeth rode the horse she'd stolen from Lord Wyndham north along the road that would take her to John's cottage. She was almost certain she would be able to find the wooded path once she came upon it.

The trees closed in around her as the village disappeared from view. She knew she had many hours of travel yet to go and she was alone. It was a foolish, dangerous thing to do, but she was beyond caring. She was so afraid John might have left the cottage to go looking for a new wife.

In the distance, she saw another traveler approaching her from the north. She was just entering the forest, and she felt small and vulnerable next to the towering trees—and the approaching stranger.

Surely he would ignore her. She looked like she was wearing a noblewoman's old cast-offs. She bowed her head, tried to slump in the saddle, anything to appear old and tired and worn by work.

When she could hear the muffled sound of the other horse's hooves striking dirt, she risked a glance from under her eyebrows. The man was still far enough away that she had to squint.

"Elizabeth?"

Straightening in stunned surprise, she called, "John?" Relief and gratitude and love swamped her, making her almost giddy.

With a quick tap of his heels, he guided the horse nearer. He seemed almost wide-eyed, uncertain, something she'd never seen in him—and she felt the same way.

"Did you get lost?" he asked as he came nearer.

She shook her head, feeling her happiness fade into apprehension. What if he still wished to end their marriage? How could she bear it?

"Did Wyndham—did he change his mind?"

Again she shook her head.

"Then I don't under—"

"John, just stop speaking and listen to me." She slid down off the horse and approached him. When she stood below him, she rested her hand on his knee, surprised that she wasn't trembling. "I made a terrible mistake."

He sighed. "The annulment—"

"No, not that!" She gripped his knee in desperation, reminding herself that she could make this work. "I made a terrible mistake in leaving you!"

His eyes went wide, and with the dawning of a smile he lifted his leg up over the horse and jumped down in front of her. "Elizabeth? What are you saying?"

He gripped her upper arms, and she rested her hands on the front of his chest. She could feel his heart; how she ached to put her cheek there, to feel safe and loved. And his hopeful smile was like the sun to her.

"I knew from almost the moment I left yesterday that Lord Wyndham wasn't the man for me—he wasn't you." She reached her hand up and touched his stubbled cheek. "I love you, John."

His smile died, and for a moment, a feeling of terrible regret swept through her. It was too late.

He squeezed his eyes shut, then took her hand in both of his, and kissed her palm, cupping it to his mouth. "Elizabeth," he murmured hoarsely.

The low sound of his voice and the feel of his lips on her skin made her shudder.

"Elizabeth, I made mistakes, too. I thought I was doing what was best for you by letting you go. But without you . . . I felt like half a man."

Tears filled her eyes as he frantically kissed both her hands, then cupped her face.

"I love you, too," he whispered. "I was coming to fight for you, to prove to you that we could make this marriage work."

"And I was doing the same thing!" She stood on tiptoes

and pressed her mouth to his. "Can it be true? Oh, John, I promise I will learn everything you think I need to know! I will be such a good wife to you. I want to love you and have your children and share everything."

He threw his head back and laughed, then swung her off the ground in a circle. "Elizabeth, I have so much to tell you, things you do not know." He set her down and held her body close as he looked earnestly into her eyes. "But the most important thing is that I treated you unfairly, comparing you to another woman. That was no better than your parents' behavior, and I regret the heartache I caused you. I wouldn't blame you if you couldn't forgive me."

She felt giddy and free and wonderfully alive as she threw her arms around his neck and just held him, her cheek pressed to his, their hearts beating near each other.

"Forgive you? Oh, my love."

"But Elizabeth, why are you traveling alone?"

She looked up into his face. "When I told Lord Wyndham that I wanted to return to you, he was upset at the time and money he'd wasted, so he wouldn't help me."

John's eyes narrowed. "That fool left you to travel alone on these dangerous highways? Let us return, so that I may show his lordship the error of his ways."

"I don't care about him, John, just you and me. And if you give me this one thing, then I can forgive you anything."

"Just tell me what you want."

"Our wedding night."

He went still, his smile fading, while an odd tension lingered in his brown eyes.

"Which is closer—the hunting lodge or the inn?" he asked swiftly.

She laughed and ran her hands down his chest, feeling the muscles she'd been longing to touch. "I don't need either. Do you?"

He gaped at her.

"I can't wait," she whispered, leaning up to kiss him.

With a groan, John crushed her against him and slanted his open mouth across hers. His tongue was an invasion she welcomed as his hands swept down her sides and hips.

"Elizabeth, are you certain?" he whispered against her mouth. "I don't want to force you—"

"Then I'll force *you*." She took his hand, and he gathered both horses' reins and followed her between the trees. She was nervous and excited and so very grateful that he loved her. Spending the rest of her life with him was all she could want.

"Wait, Elizabeth. I brought you something you left behind."

He let go of her hand, and after a moment's fumbling with straps behind the saddle, he pulled out her crumpled, bent farthingale.

He held it out to her. "You wear anything you want, my love."

With a laugh, she took it and flung it into the trees. "I won't be needing *that* anymore." She grabbed his hand again and pulled him along behind her.

At the first small clearing in the forest, where the sun shone on a soft patch of moss, Elizabeth turned to face him. She unlaced the ties behind her neck, then pulled the gown down her shoulders and let it fall to the ground. She stood clothed in only her smock and underskirts.

"Your turn," she said with a smile.

He was quick to pull off his belt and tunic.

She unfastened each of her underskirts and let them drop.

John untied his hose and codpiece and pulled his shirt over his head. Her breath caught in wonder at how beautifully made he was, how broad and tall and proud. Only the loose linen braies hung low about his hips, barely hiding his enlarged penis.

His smile looked strained. "Your turn."

Wetting her dry lips, she reached for the hem of her smock and slowly lifted it over her head. The sun was hot where it touched her bare skin, and she thought she'd feel embarrassed. But John watched her like she was his every dream come true, which made her feel proud and humble and so thankful all at the same time.

"Your turn," she said, surprised to hear her own voice crack.

As the braies fell to the ground, she barely got to look before he crossed the small clearing in two strides and took her in his arms. The feel of his hot, moist skin and hard muscle pressed to every part of her sent a delicious rush of pleasure through her body. His lips covered hers, and she met his tongue gladly with her own as she explored his mouth. They were finally free to enjoy each other as husband and wife. She caressed his broad shoulders, his neck, his arms, which held her so tightly. She kissed his cheeks and his chin and his ear, wherever she could reach.

"Elizabeth, you're bewitching," he murmured.

She bent to kiss his nipples, as he'd done to her. If anything, his shaft seemed to grow larger against her stomach, and she reached to touch it, amazed at the heat and hardness. It moved in her hand and she glanced up at his intent face.

"Does this hurt you?"

"God, no," he answered with a short laugh. "I'm just longing to be inside you."

She smiled. "Then why don't you?"

He groaned and closed his eyes. "Soon, my dearest."

He cupped her breasts in both hands and held the weight of them while Elizabeth gasped and swayed against him. "My goodness, that feels lovely," she breathed.

When his fingers teased her nipples, she gripped his arms, knowing her knees would buckle if she let go. As her head dropped back, he took her mouth in deep, languorous kisses, then spread kisses down her neck and behind her ear and across her shoulders. He dropped to his knees, and she held his head between her breasts for a moment, while the poignancy of her love for him almost overwhelmed her.

But then his tongue licked along the curve of her breast and swirled about her nipple. She cried out, remembering now why she'd been unable to resist him that night in the garden. He worked magic with his mouth and his hands, until she was suffused in the passion he wove about her.

He suckled her, drawing her nipple deep into his mouth. Every tug was answered in the depths of her belly with a shudder of restlessness and yearning. He'd made her feel it before, and now finally she would understand the mystery of it.

Shaking and weak, she leaned into him, and he swept his hands down her hips and gripped her buttocks. His fingers met and teased the crease between them, and she moaned with the forbidden excitement of it.

She stood dazed in the middle of the forest as her husband trailed kisses down across her belly and into the curls above her thighs.

She tried to pull away. "No, surely . . . you mustn't—"

"I want to taste every part of you," he murmured against her, spreading her legs wider so he could fit between them.

Elizabeth was excruciatingly aware that they were out in the open, beneath the sun, where anyone could see him doing this to her. But then she felt his tongue parting her, exploring her, and every thought in her head vanished except the desperate wish that he never stop. Every thrust of his tongue made her shudder with pleasure that was nigh unto pain. She held onto his shoulders, unable to look away from the sight of him between her thighs. He opened his eyes and they stared at each other until her legs gave way, and she was held up by his hands cupping her buttocks, pressing her against his mouth.

Then suddenly he dropped her back into the pile of her garments, spread her legs even wider, and began to lick her with long, slow strokes that made her shudder and whimper and squirm. She raised her hips and gave herself up to this incredible mounting pleasure. When her legs were shaking and she was rolling her head back and forth with little moans escaping her, he slid both hands up her body and rubbed her nipples.

With a hoarse cry, she plummeted deep into the pleasure he gave her, shuddering and shaking as waves of it engulfed her and swept her under. She lay still, gasping, as her awareness returned. Slowly she opened her eyes and found him on his hands and knees above her, grinning.

She covered her hot face with her hands.

"Elizabeth?"

He peeled her hands away, and when she opened her eyes she saw his concern.

"Are you all right?"

With a groan she threw her arms around his neck. "Compromise me again!"

"Oh, Elizabeth," he murmured, bracing his hands and settling his hips between her thighs. "This might hurt a little, but I promise you—"

"Please, just make me your wife!"

She felt the probing of his shaft against her swollen, sensitive flesh, and then he thrust home. The momentary pain she felt vanished as she watched him shudder and hold himself still.

"Is something wrong?" she asked cautiously.

John opened his eyes and came down on his elbows to kiss her. "There's nothing wrong with finding heaven, my love. It exists only in you, and I want to savor every moment."

She touched him then, caressed him with all the love he inspired in her. He pulled out of her and entered again, and the joining of their flesh together renewed the wonder of her desire. He rocked against her, in and out, and she pressed kisses wherever she could reach his hot skin. She licked his nipples and was rewarded when he held still deep inside her body, trembling, his head thrown back, his face pained with concentration.

With a groan, he suddenly moved again, thrusting over and over inside her, until she knew by his hoarse cry that he had found the same release she had. She held his shuddering body against her and knew a profound satisfaction. This was something she did well without even trying.

But the only person who made her feel this way was John, her husband, her love.

Exhausted and happier than he'd ever thought possible, John braced himself on his elbows and looked down at Elizabeth. He watched a gentle smile transform her and knew he was looking into the face of true love. They would awake every morning in each other's arms, and the love in her eyes would be the last thing he saw each night before sleeping. Through Fate or luck or a higher power, he had found the one woman who could make him feel whole.

EPILOGUE

Bathed in warm summer sunshine, Elizabeth rode her horse at John's side, no longer afraid of what lay before her. She knew he was impatient to introduce her to his family. He'd told her about his true home, his many estates. She couldn't even be angry at his deception when memories of her own behavior in the first few days of their marriage left her wincing with shame. And the way he'd made it all up to her still left her blushing.

Coming to the crest of a hill and seeing the immense size of the sprawling castle before her made her catch her breath with the tiniest bit of apprehension.

John leaned from his horse and reached for her hand. "You can do this, Elizabeth. You can do anything."

"I tamed you, didn't I?" she answered, and he laughed.

When they rode down to the gatehouse now overflowing with people, she could tell by the love on John's face who his family was. His mother, his brother, and his brother's wife came forward, and John introduced Elizabeth with such pride in his voice that she was near tears.

His mother stepped forward when he helped Elizabeth dismount. The woman kissed her son and looked between them wearing a happy smile upon her face.

"We received your missive days ago, John. But what has happened to the two of you?" she asked, laughing and shaking her head as she studied the ruined garments they'd been wearing for days.

John put an arm around Elizabeth and hugged her to his side. "Our wedding trip, Mother. And what an adventure it was."

Elizabeth felt his love wash over her, protect her, and knew she'd come home.

TREADING DANGEROUS WATERS

•

Victoria Marquez

For my husband, Paul, and our beautiful daughters,
Genevieve and Jacqueline, who fill my life
with love and happiness.

Special thanks to my agent, Paige Wheeler,
for her support and savvy expertise.

CHAPTER 1

"Men!" Sofia grunted, adding a strong measure of disgust to her tone. "Who needs them?"

"I need Daniel," Tia Lucita replied softly.

Seeing her aunt's look of despair, Sofia gentled her tone. "The only man who has redeemed himself is your Daniel. He's a gentleman from the old school. The best word I can use to describe him is *gallant*. If he hadn't hired me to do his bookkeeping I'd be penniless and desperate for work."

Lucita made the sign of the cross in mock horror. "God forbid you'll ever be penniless! Don't even joke about it."

Sofia hugged her aunt. "OK, I won't.

"How does a two-week all-expenses-paid cruise sound to you?"

"Great," Sofia said. "When are you going?"

Lucita's pretty, softly wrinkled green eyes sparkled with mischief as she returned Sofia's disbelieving glance with a disarming smile. "When are *we* going?"

Sofia Sandoval abruptly set her *café con leche* on the cloth-covered kitchen table and stared at her favorite aunt. Studying her with a mixture of curiosity and affection, Sofia wondered what the dear old lady was up to now.

Sofia airily waved her hand. "Oh, come on. I can't go on a two-week cruise. I'm supposed to search for a new job, remember?" Dismissing the frivolous, tempting idea, she turned her attention to the Colombian *arepa* on the plate before her, a golden pan-fried cornmeal patty oozing with mozzarella cheese and slathered with butter. Her mouth watered before taking a bite. "Mmmm, delicious," she moaned. "You spoil me terribly."

Lucita nodded indulgently. "Don't change the subject. You know I love having you stay with me, even if it is only temporary."

"Tia Lucita, you've been such a life-saver. I don't know how to thank you." Sofia sipped the creamy *café con leche*. "So what's this about a cruise? Still trying to cheer me up?"

Lucita looked her square in the eye. "I *would* like to see you return to your usual self."

"Oh, Tia, you've done enough for me already." With a wistful sigh, Sofia peered out the bay window of the breakfast nook in Lucita's cheerfully appointed kitchen. Fuchsia bougainvillea cascaded over a stone wall, reminding her of the view she'd had from the apartment she'd recently had to vacate.

"I want to invite you on a cruise to Mexico and the Virgin Islands," Lucita announced happily.

Sofia shook her head. "I can't let you do that; it's a huge expense."

"Actually . . ." Lucita grinned. "Daniel is inviting. We're getting married on board ship and we want you to celebrate with us."

Sofia shot up from the table and hugged Lucita's petite, round frame. "Congratulations! I couldn't be more delighted. You know how much I adore Daniel. He's such a charming gentleman and so perfect for you!"

Lucita blushed and fanned herself daintily. "I know." She smiled. "He certainly is charming."

"So, when is the wedding?"

"Next week," Lucita replied matter-of-factly, as if a wedding ceremony aboard a ship was no big deal.

"Next week! Why so sudden?" Sofia asked, wondering why her aunt hadn't confided in her sooner.

An anxious shadow passed over Lucita's eyes. "It's because of Daniel's son, James. Daniel is worried that James will make trouble for us if he finds out that we're getting married."

"But he hasn't even met you, has he? Why is Daniel keeping him away? Is he that horrible?" What kind of a man could oppose his father getting married to an adorable and unfailingly generous woman like Lucita Sanchez?

Lucita shifted in her seat. "It's not that James is horrible, quite the contrary. He's too handsome for his own good. I've seen his photograph. *Es demasiado guapo!*"

Sofia snorted. She didn't care how handsome her aunt found James; anyone who would willingly make trouble for Lucita and Daniel had to be mean-spirited. "I wasn't referring to his looks. His personality sounds unpleasant, to put it mildly."

Lucita sighed. "He is a bit too cynical for one so young."

"How old is James?"

"Thirty."

"He's not *that* young. He should know better than to come between his father and the woman he loves."

"I wish it were that simple. James is a very successful divorce attorney. Unfortunately, he's seen the worst scenarios of marriage in the breaking-up stages. It doesn't help that after his mother died when he was a little boy, Daniel had two unhappy marriages that ended in divorce. So, now James is determined to make sure that his father doesn't fall into a 'greedy trap' again." Lucita smiled sadly. "Don't frown at me, Sofia. Those were his words, not mine. That's why it's so important that we elope next week."

"Hmph. He doesn't sound like anyone I'd like to meet."

"Oh, but you will eventually. In fact, as soon as we're married, I'd like you to consult him about that vile woman who got you fired last month. James is an excellent attorney. Since James is going to be my stepson, Daniel mentioned that he would like him to help you clear your name."

"Oh, please." Sofia stood and carried her dishes to the sink. She turned to look at Lucita. "Anyway, I'd rather put all that behind me."

"You can't without a fight, Sofia! Mrs. Fernandez has

made very serious allegations against you, all of them untrue. Because of that woman, you're out of a good-paying job and you've lost your apartment. Those are things worth fighting for."

Sofia's chest constricted with a numbing ache at the injustice and humiliation she'd been made to suffer because of one woman's insane jealousy. "I did fight—initially. But by the time Mrs. Fernandez got through telling lies about me, the other doctors' wives believed her and they banded together to have me fired." She took a deep breath and tried to dispel the stinging personal pain that their callousness had caused her. She tried for a bright smile. "Let's talk about your wedding plans instead. I'd rather not rehash those ugly events."

"You're not fooling me one bit, Sofia. Without decent recommendations, you won't be able to find another job in a doctor's office."

"I'm not sure if I want to work in a doctor's office again. I can do bookkeeping elsewhere."

Lucita stiffened her delicate shoulders militantly and rose to join her niece beside the kitchen counter. "Nevertheless, justice must be served so you can resume being the happy person you've always been."

Sofia smiled at her aunt's loyalty. "Perhaps, but seeking help from a bitter divorce attorney is not the solution."

"I wouldn't necessarily say that James is bitter. According to Daniel, his son is a little confused in the ways of love," Lucita said with a wise smile.

Sofia shrugged. "Whatever. All I know is that I'm tired of men interfering in my life and trying to fight my battles for me. I had to deal with Papi as a little girl, and you know how strict he was. Then when I was a teenager, Paco, Sergio, and Roberto became so bossy, I couldn't wait to live on my own."

Lucita laughed. "Your older brothers only wanted what was best for you."

"Well, they went a little too far. First the interrogations about boyfriends, then too many opinions about how I dressed and how much makeup I was wearing. I know I'm the 'baby' of the family, but it still annoys me." She sighed. "When I finally did move away from home, I entered a relationship with Manny, a man who not only cheated on me but also had the nerve to try to bully me into forgiving him when I found out about it!"

Helpless anger welled up inside of Sofia. The two-timing rat! Her temples throbbed just thinking about how she'd cried over her ex-boyfriend's deception and how she had begun to doubt her ability to judge a man's true character.

"I am half-tempted to accept Daniel's generous offer and go with you on this marvelous cruise," Sofia said. "I'd love to get away from Miami and clear my head."

"Oh, but you must come with us! Daniel and I wouldn't have it any other way. We're meeting tonight at his favorite Irish pub in Coral Gables. Will you join us at John Martin's around six for cocktails?"

"I wouldn't miss it. Can't wait to congratulate Daniel personally and let him know how lucky he is. If you pamper him half as much as you do me, he's going to be spoiled rotten before long!"

Lucita's round face reddened suddenly. "It's *my* pleasure. I never thought I'd remarry after Vincente passed on. And it's not because I haven't dated," she said, giggling shamelessly.

Sofia joined in her mirth. "*Ay,* Tia Lucita. You're a regular Scarlett O'Hara."

"Don't be disrespectful to your old auntie," Lucita admonished with gruff fondness.

Change. That's what James liked, the challenge of meeting new women and enjoying their company for enjoyment's sake, nothing else. The moment the women got a little needy, he backed off and severed the relationship. No sense in encouraging something that would never result in what they wanted. *Marriage*—the word gave him the willies. He had enough conscience not to purposely

wound a woman's tender feelings. His father had drilled
this into James from an early age with stern but loving
discipline. Whenever he was about to break up with a
woman, he heard Daniel's blustery warning in the back
of his mind: *Son, you'd better not hurt that girl's feelings
or you'll be answering to me.*

James Connor leaned back on the barstool at John Martin's and drank his scotch and water. Of all the swanky
places in Miami, this cozy, dark, unpretentious pub was
Daniel's favorite spot on a Saturday night. Not only did
Dad enjoy his native Irish food, but he also joined in the
merriment provided by an Irish band, singing and tapping
his feet to the music. So if James wanted to intercept his
errant dad, who hadn't returned his phone calls for the
past week, he figured he could always catch up with him
at John Martin's.

He glanced at his watch. Ten of six; Dad would be
arriving soon. It never failed to amuse James how much
his father was a creature of habit, unlike himself, who
shunned routines and welcomed change. Hell, he'd never
allow himself to sink into a rut like so many men he'd
taken on as divorce clients. He often cited that as one of
the reasons he didn't intend to marry.

Unfortunately, Dad's love choices hadn't been wise
ones. Even though he was larger than life, with a strong,
decent character, Daniel had a weakness for women, especially pretty ones. Younger, greedy women had twice
burned him, and that branded him as a "fool for love" in
James's opinion. Which was precisely why he found himself at John Martin's on a Saturday night, instead of in
South Beach enjoying delicious cuisine with a hot date.
Maybe he could still make it; this wouldn't take long.
He'd been through this type of thing before.

He suspected that his dad was up to one of his hopeless
romantic trysts again. The clues were all there. First Dad
had announced a month ago that he didn't need James's
help anymore with his finances since he'd hired a book-
keeper. Now a retired orthopedic surgeon, Daniel had

known squat about finances then and hadn't had an inkling of desire to pursue it. He was a healer and scientist, first and foremost, so he'd heavily relied on James to invest his money. And thankfully, the investments had been lucrative, affording Daniel a privileged lifestyle.

And now Dad seemed to be avoiding him, not even returning his phone calls. When James had finally been able to locate him last weekend, Dad had sounded almost too cheerful, a sure sign that he'd fallen in love again. If that was the case, it had to stop before dear old Dad ended up married again.

Lord knew Daniel's previous wives had done their best to deplete his bank account. If it hadn't been for James's expertise in the courtroom, they would have taken Daniel to the cleaners. No way was James going to let some greedy little gold digger ruin his father's retirement and break his heart in the process.

James was interrupted from his musings as he watched a middle-aged red-haired woman enter the bar on wobbly feet. He immediately rose from the barstool when he realized she was heading his way. Doreen D'Angelis. And from the way she was swaying, he wondered if she'd been on a drinking binge.

"Oh, James, what am I going to do?" she wailed as she tottered over to his side.

James held out a steadying hand, but instead of taking it, she collapsed against the front of his shirt, wetting it with copious tears.

"What's wrong?" he asked, stunned by her emotional outburst. He'd never seen Doreen out of control. She was a private woman, always immaculately groomed and in control of the travel agency she owned.

He pulled away from her stiffly lacquered hairdo that was always styled in a perfect flip, to hear her muffled words. "It's Daniel. I think he's getting married again!"

Instead of swearing a mean streak, which would have given James a measure of release, he regarded her with a mixture of pity and frustration. None other than the woman who had been pining after his father for years had just confirmed his suspicions.

"How do you know that for sure?" he asked gently, peering into the poor woman's mascara-streaked, reddened eyes.

She emitted a long, shuddering sigh before she could control her breathing enough to continue. "When he booked a cruise a few weeks ago for two, I presumed that it was a birthday surprise for you, because he warned me not to mention a word to you."

"Oh, really?" the lawyer in him asked nonchalantly. James braced himself for what was to come as he retrieved a white handkerchief from his sports jacket and handed it to her.

Doreen accepted it and loudly blew her nose before continuing. "I was going to finally make my move this week and invite him over for a home-cooked Italian meal before he left on the cruise. But I never got to." She paused dramatically.

"Why not?"

"Because he casually mentioned that he wouldn't be a single man when he returned to Miami. Then he bought another ticket for a family member who would be accompanying him and his lady guest. Probably his fiancée," she groaned.

"When are they leaving?" James asked quickly before she gave in to a fresh bout of tears.

"Next week. And they're taking a two-week cruise, one I've always dreamed of taking for *my* honeymoon!" she wailed, starting to get worked up again.

With a flash of irritation, James wondered if his dad had ever realized that the businesslike spinster had been hopelessly in love with him for years. Unfortunately, her starched demeanor and conservative dress were not what the roguish Daniel found attractive in a woman. He had a penchant for overtly feminine, sensual women, the more flirtatious the better.

A tall, shapely brunette wearing a turquoise jersey

dress that skimmed over sinful curves sauntered through the front door, instantly capturing James's attention. The young woman appeared foreign, perhaps Latina. Shoulders thrust back, she exuded self-confidence in the sleek dress that flattered her high, round breasts, small waist, and curvy hips. The hem ended in a slight swirl around pretty knees just above nicely toned calves. He could hear her high-heeled sandals click against the tile as she headed toward the dining room.

When she turned her back, a potent surge of lust shot through James's groin as his gaze fastened on the most perfect, heart-shaped backside he'd ever seen. Lush and round, it swayed with just a tad of jiggle to tempt any hot-blooded male into stroking or squeezing it, anything just to get his palms on those sweet curves and feel the soft flesh beneath the thin fabric of her dress. With keen eyes, he watched her speak briefly to the hostess before returning to the entrance.

Daniel arrived at that same moment, escorting an elderly woman with curly blond hair wearing an orchid wrap-style dress. James was floored as he watched the striking young Latin woman affectionately squeeze Daniel's other arm and sidle up to him. Arms linked, the threesome entered the dining room.

Damn. He should have known that she was his father's latest chickie-babe. *The brazen little fortune hunter.* James stared at her tantalizing derriere with a malevolent urge to swat it instead of offering the caresses he'd fantasized about earlier. He forced his gaze away, at the same time shifting his stance to accommodate an uncomfortable state of arousal that only served to make him angrier. He wondered who the older lady was . . . probably her mother.

Doreen's violent tug on his sleeve snagged his attention. "Hey, you're not listening to me," she whined.

James was thankful that Doreen's back was turned to the arriving party, but he didn't want to take any chances. He tossed down the rest of his drink and banged the glass on the counter.

"Let's go." He clasped Doreen's upper arm and ushered her to the other side of the bar, far enough out of sight where he could observe his father without her noticing them, and vice versa. Careful to keep her back turned to the entering party, James pulled out a barstool and gently pushed her down on it. "Sit down, Doreen; you're about to topple over."

"Oof, that feels better," she conceded, burying her head in her hands. "I *am* a little dizzy."

"Just keep your head down for a while," he said absently, patting the top of Doreen's helmet hairdo as he zeroed in on his father's new love interest.

His thoughts were still haunted by the young lady's seductiveness. Many women in Miami dressed provocatively and had great figures, but there was something about this one that had made him catch his breath when she entered the restaurant. Sultry and exotic, her mere presence had been an intense magnet luring his undivided attention. The resulting turn-on had been so sudden and intense, it floored him.

It also irked the hell out of him that the luscious beauty had been clinging to her sugar daddy—*his father.* She couldn't be a day over twenty-five, he surmised. So that made his seventy-year-old father almost three times her age! It was disgraceful. The mere thought of the young woman's greedy, underhanded motives made James see red.

"Jaaames," Doreen whined in a singsong voice. "You're not paying attention to me again."

"What now?" he snapped.

She sniffled into the handkerchief. "You're mad because I spoiled your surprise. I'm sorry."

"No, of course not. I'm sorry I barked at you. I'm just mad at my father for planning another wedding," he said, wearily patting her back in consolation. If Doreen continued to drink in the sad state she was in, she'd end up a sloppy mess. Deciding that he had to get her out of here fast, James gently pulled her up into a standing position.

"Hold onto my arm, Doreen. I'm taking you home. You're in no condition to drive."

"But my car's in the parking lot. I walked over here from the agency."

"Doesn't matter. You can get it tomorrow."

She nodded glumly. "You're right; I can't drive when I'm feeling so brokenhearted."

"Please don't waste your energy and tears on my father. Dad's a great guy, but he hasn't had a good track record in romance. You know he's already been divorced twice and from much younger women who were up to no good. You're better off without him," James said, trying to soothe her bruised feelings. Once they reached the exit, he walked her to his car and carefully put the seat belt around her before he got in on his side.

One thought droned in his mind as he drove Doreen home. He was determined to stop the damned wedding, come hell or high water. In this case it would be high water, because come next week he planned to be on that cruise aborting their wedding.

CHAPTER 2

Daniel handed the dessert menu back to the cruise ship waiter. "I'll have the *crème bru*—hell and damnation!" he muttered, his blue eyes squinting as he scowled at the dining hall entrance.

"What's wrong, Daniel?" Lucita asked. "You look as if you've seen a ghost."

"He's no ghost." He shot a quick glance at the vacant chair between Lucita and Sofia. "So this must be why there's an empty fourth setting. Now he's going to ruin everything."

"Who is? What are you talking about?" Sofia asked, swiveling her head around to catch a glimpse of what had Daniel so rattled.

"My son, James. Doreen must have told him about the cruise. Damn!"

Awestruck, Sofia sat in breathless silence as she took in every detail of James Connor's arrival. Tall and muscular, James's intensely masculine physique commanded attention as he approached their table with grim, purposeful strides. The determined set of his broad shoulders coupled with the arrogant tilt of his dark head gave him an intimidating air.

Sweet Jesus! Tia Lucita hadn't been kidding. James *was* too handsome for his own good. But a better description might have been too *brutally* handsome. Thick, close-cropped black hair framed a chiseled, masculine face. His midnight blue eyes lit on the trio with ruthless severity. Impeccably dressed in a dark blue sports jacket, starched white shirt, and tan slacks, James' elegant attire fit in with the other passengers, except for one detail—his large, square hand gripped the handle of a black leather briefcase. She took in the stern set of his sensual mouth and she swallowed hard.

He looked downright confrontational!

James Connor was one person she wouldn't want to cross, in a courtroom or elsewhere.

Daniel rose from the table. "James, what are you doing here?" He raised a cynical eyebrow at his son. "Do I dare hope that you're on vacation?"

"What a greeting," James said in a flat tone. "Aren't you going to introduce me?"

"Of course." Daniel gestured toward the women. "This is Lucita Sanchez and her niece, Sofia Sandoval."

With a curt nod, James shook Lucita's hand. His lips scarcely bared strong white teeth in a perfunctory smile. "Pleased to meet you, Mrs. Sanchez."

Sofia wasn't so lucky. Piercing blue eyes studied her for several moments before he extended his hand and clasped hers in a hard handshake. "James Connor." His clipped tone warned her that he wasn't pleased to meet *her*. She tried to look away from his arresting eyes, but they held her riveted, glittering like blue crystals against a tanned visage. He stood before her in unmistakable battle stance with wide shoulders squared and long legs slightly braced apart. His expression was so forbidding, she found herself dumbstruck, a rare occurrence since she was seldom at a loss for words.

When he cleared his throat, Sofia quickly snatched her hand out of his firm grip and gave her aunt a furtive glance. Maybe Lucita's gift for diplomacy could diffuse the tension from the air.

"What a pleasant surprise," Lucita murmured on cue. Her nervous giggle sounded like bells tinkling. "Daniel never mentioned you'd be joining us."

James didn't respond. Instead, he remained standing as he snapped open the briefcase and retrieved a large manila envelope. He placed it on the table and turned his attention to Sofia. His blatant male gaze rested on her décolletage, then returned to her eyes, pinning her with an *awful* look.

She was painfully aware that James towered over her,

affording him a choice view of her bosom. Scorched by the sexual implication of his raised eyebrows, Sofia glanced down, mortified to note how her breasts strained against the rose silk fabric and peaked above the dipping neckline, forming a noticeable cleavage. It hadn't looked like that when she had glanced in the mirror earlier. But then she'd been standing, not sitting as she was now with the crepe fabric pulling downward.

If she hadn't indulged in so much of her aunt's fine cooking these past weeks, Sofia's dress would have fit comfortably, as it had before. Since there was nothing she could do about it now, she straightened her shoulders and glared back at him. She wasn't about to let his insult slide.

Arching a cool eyebrow, she allowed her gaze to travel the length of his body in an insolent once-over inspection, starting at his polished wing tips and working its way up to lock gazes with him.

"Do you have a problem, Mr. Connor?" she inquired.

"Yes, you," he said bluntly.

"Me?" His answer momentarily stunned her. Was the man psycho or something? Other than the recent introduction, he had no idea who she was, yet his antagonism was palpable. "You must be kidding," Sofia said, frowning at him.

"I'm dead serious," he replied.

"James," Daniel growled warningly.

Heavy awkwardness settled around them when James didn't respond. Surely there was a misunderstanding. Could it be that he was hurt because Daniel had excluded him from the wedding invitation but had included Sofia? But this was silly! They were all adults.

Her heart went out to Tia Lucita and Daniel when she saw the dire expressions on their faces. Rooted to their chairs, the wary couple eyed each other with growing apprehension. She had to do something to make peace between everyone. Perhaps if she invited James to join them, he'd be amenable to a friendly discussion. She was sure that he'd adore Tia Lucita once he got to know her.

Before she changed her mind and gave into her gut instinct to tell him to go away, Sofia blurted, "Won't you join us? We've finished the main course, but we—"

"This won't take long," James snapped, cutting her off in midsentence. "Just long enough to boot your greedy little rear end off this ship."

Sofia's eyebrows practically hit the ceiling as her mouth fell open in shock. She could deal with a disparaging glance at her attire from him, but a threat was something else! She didn't actually believe he would attempt to "boot" her behind, but the dangerous gleam in his eyes left no doubt that he would have relished doing it.

"James, what is the meaning of this?" his father boomed, slapping his hand on the table.

"How dare you!" Sofia fumed at the same time, stung by his cutting remark.

"Be quiet," James commanded softly before turning his attention to Daniel. "Everything is in this report, Dad. Read it and you'll see the real reason Miss Sandoval no longer has a job and is latching on for a free ride." His steely gaze anchored hers with chilling contempt. "She was recently fired for being unprofessional. The current office manager called her a home-wrecker and a tease. All of this was substantiated by the other doctors' wives."

Sofia's eyes burned with furious tears as she sucked her breath in sharply. This was her worst nightmare come true. A stranger, no, not a stranger but *Daniel's son,* accusing her of misdeeds she had never committed! His cruel remarks dredged up the raw pain of humiliation she had harbored since being unfairly fired. Mindlessly she groped for the right words to defend herself, but Daniel beat her to it.

"You've shamed me, James. Stop it immediately!" Daniel demanded in a low roar, his voice surprisingly strong and authoritative for a man in his seventies.

James planted his hands on the table and leaned forward to face his dad squarely. "I won't let you make another mistake getting married again, Dad."

"Aaagh!" Daniel suddenly cried out, clutching his stomach.

"Dad?" James rushed to his father's side. "Are you all right?" For a brief moment, his harsh face softened with something akin to tenderness.

"I'm not supposed to get upset like this, son. Must be my ulcer acting up again."

"Have you seen a doctor?" James demanded, blue eyes ablaze with concern.

"Yes, I'm on medication. Dr. Maxwell has me following a special diet and has instructed me to avoid any *stress,*" he said pointedly.

When James gave his father an assessing look, Daniel added, "I've had a bleeding ulcer before. It's like a burning dagger in my gut! The purpose of this cruise was for medicinal reasons. Sofia and Lucita graciously came along to keep me company. If you can't behave like a gentleman, I suggest you leave at once."

"We'll discuss this tomorrow morning at breakfast. Make sure to take your medicine, Dad. Good night." James turned on his heel and stalked out of the dining room, leaving them flabbergasted by his sudden retreat.

"The ulcer always does it," Daniel muttered wryly. "Beneath the tough surface is a boy worried about his father's health." His tone held an air of triumph.

"That doesn't erase what he said about me," Sofia said, burning with anger. "He has no reason to dislike me so much. Until tonight, I never laid eyes on him."

"He was repeating the lies they told him at the doctor's office, Sofia. You really must take legal action against them," Lucita urged, glancing at her with maternal concern.

"That still doesn't explain his open antagonism," she muttered. But she decided not to belabor the issue so Daniel wouldn't know how much James's uncalled-for attack had hurt and humiliated her. It would only make him feel worse.

Just when she was going to say something to smooth

things over, Daniel threw his head back and gave a shout of laughter.

"What is so funny?" Lucita demanded. "You should take your son in hand for hurting Sofia's feelings!"

"I'm sorry, dear," Daniel said, trying to contain his mirth. "But I just realized why James is acting like he has a hornet on his tail."

"Please enlighten us, Daniel," Lucita chided, a smile tugging at her lips.

Daniel sobered enough to say, "Somehow James must have found out about my trip and began to investigate whom I was going with. He must have jumped to the conclusion that Sofia is my fiancée."

"That's ridiculous!" Sofia said, appalled by James's mistaken conclusion.

Daniel's fair complexion turned bright red. "I'm afraid that my past wives have been considerably younger than me." He took Lucita's small hand in his and held it tenderly. "Little does James know how much I love your aunt."

Tia Lucita giggled softly. "Oh, Daniel. It's so absurd, it's almost comical!"

"I don't think it's the least bit comical. He was horribly rude to me," Sofia said, seething at the injustice of his inappropiate attack.

"I'm so sorry, Sofia," Daniel said. "James was reacting on misguided intentions. He usually has better manners. Once I set him straight, he will apologize to you."

"No. Don't deny me the pleasure of giving him a piece of my mind. *I'll* take care of James." Sofia spoke with much more bravado than she felt since she was not a confrontational person by nature. Having grown up as the youngest of four children and the only girl, she had always been the peacemaker, unless it involved her personally. Only then did she become aggressive. With three bossy older brothers, she had learned there was no other way or they'd walk all over her.

"You won't gain anything by fighting with him," Daniel warned gently. "James is a ruthless tiger in the court-room."

And a bully outside of the courtroom, Sofia felt like adding. But she couldn't bring herself to ruin the couple's romantic evening, especially with their hopes of marriage and a new life together. She owed both of them so much. If Lucita and Daniel hadn't come to her rescue at the lowest point in her life, Sofia would have been forced to move in with her mother, who now lived with Sofia's eldest brother, Paco, and his wife. The mere thought filled her with dismay.

"I don't care how ruthless he is. By the time I'm fin-ished with James, he won't be attacking like a tiger; he'll be mewling like a pussycat," Sofia predicted. As soon as the words were out, she realized that she might have over-stated her ability to handle someone as imposing as James Connor. She'd have to do some pretty quick thinking to keep him out of the way long enough so Daniel and Lucita could get married.

Lucita's eyebrows lifted with curious amusement. "What are you going to do?"

Sofia straightened her spine, drawing inner strength from the desire to help them in their predicament. "I'll pretend that I really am Daniel's intended. If I tell him that I'm not Daniel's fiancée and he believes me, then he'll turn against you, Tia. You heard what he said about not wanting his father to get married again. You must continue with your plans to get married and enjoy this honeymoon cruise!"

All eyes were on her as she drummed her fingers on the table and mulled over the best way to deal with him. "I've got it!" she said suddenly, her mind hatching a great scheme.

"What?" Daniel and Lucita asked in unison.

"You'll have to work with me on this. Just hear me out before you protest."

Lucita gave Daniel a searching glance. He winked at his bride-to-be and squeezed her dainty hand, the hand that sported his four-carat engagement ring. "Of course, Sofia. Do go on," he urged with a congenial smile.

"While I'm pretending to be Daniel's fiancée, I'll do my best to monopolize James's time so you two can continue with your wedding plans."

"How will you do that?" Daniel asked, his brow furrowing with doubt.

Sofia smiled. "I'll tell him that it is his father's fondest wish that his son get to know me. I'll say that you asked me to spend a lot of time with him so that he would approve of me and give us his blessing."

"He's a lawyer. He'll find out eventually," Lucita pointed out.

"By then you will be married and he'll have to leave you alone," Sofia said.

"That *is* true," Lucita conceded.

"Anyway, why should we let James ruin the wedding? It isn't his life, so he should butt out. As soon as you're married, I'm going to tell him so."

Daniel had been quiet during Sofia's reasoning, but her last comment stirred a strong reaction from him. "My son is a formidable adversary, Sofia. I won't stand by and watch him hurt your feelings."

Daniel had no idea how deeply James had already wounded her feelings, but she'd never distress him by admitting it. "Leave your son to me. I've had to deal with overbearing men before. James might be tougher to handle than most, but there's no way I'll let him ruin your lovely cruise."

"This time I really did get a sharp pang in my stomach." Daniel's hand lightly rubbed the area just below his ribs. "*I* should be the one handling my son, not you."

"Sofia won't change her mind, Daniel. You don't know how stubborn she can be," Lucita said, shaking her head with feigned patience.

Sofia took pity on Daniel's distress and gave him her most reassuring smile. The older man looked beside himself, and she knew he dearly wanted to make amends for his son's horrid behavior. But this was one battle she'd fight for herself. Lucita was right: if she didn't start fighting back, people would begin to believe the lies about her. The thought was so distressing that she was eager to take James on as her first battle.

"Don't worry about me. It's better this way. I'm actually looking forward to making his life a misery for the next two weeks." Sofia smiled with the malice she felt toward James. "Have you ever read *The Taming of the Shrew*?"

"Who hasn't?" Daniel chuckled wryly. "It's one of my favorite Shakespearean comedies."

"We'll call this 'The Taming of the Tyrant'!" She downed the contents of her wine goblet in several unladylike gulps before rising from the table. "You two stay and enjoy yourselves. Have a lovely time at the show tonight. I'll see you tomorrow morning."

"Don't you want to stay and have dessert?" Daniel asked.

"Nope, I'm not hungry anymore."

For a brief moment, Sofia's stomach felt a bit queasy, but thankfully it subsided. Must have been the way she gulped the wine. She sweetly kissed Tia Lucita and Daniel on the cheek. "Good-bye, dears."

Lucita's soft hand detained her arm for a moment. "Where are you going?"

"To make sure that James gets *his* just desserts," Sofia said, clutching her handbag as if it were a weapon. She left quickly, before they tried to change her mind.

CHAPTER 3

It didn't take Sofia long to find the insufferable man. James stood at the ship's railing, facing the ocean. From the rigid set of his broad shoulders, she surmised that he wasn't too pleased with the outcome of the evening. She had started to walk toward him when a wave of seasickness assailed her, making her stop in her tracks. There was no use in confronting him when she didn't feel well. Better to get a good night's sleep before tussling with the tiger.

Just as she began to retreat, James turned around. His abrupt action held her immobilized. "Miss Sandoval. Where are you going?"

"I was planning to take a walk on the deck, but I changed my mind."

He quirked an eyebrow. "Oh? Because you saw me?"

"Of course not."

"Then?"

"I was feeling a little dizzy. Must have been the wine," she said airily.

He smirked. "Not used to alcohol? You *are* rather young."

There was no doubt in her mind that his aim was to point out the vast difference in age between her and Daniel.

"Not at all. I drink all the time," she lied. The truth was that she was only a social drinker at best. A glass of wine could make her woozy on an empty stomach. Good thing she'd had a full dinner.

"Ah, an experienced drinker."

"Yes," she said, narrowing her eyes at him. Was that a patronizing smile he was trying to hide? Who cared? She wasn't going to stick around long enough to find out.

"How is my father feeling?"

"Fine, why?"

"A little while ago, he was complaining of severe stomach pain."

She waved her hand. "Oh, that. Your rude arrival upset him and annoyed all of us. He's perfectly fine and content when he's with me." When she noted how quickly James's handsome features sharpened and his face darkened with disapproval, she decided to make a hasty retreat. "Well, if you'll excuse me."

"Don't leave." He issued the command with the blunt arrogance of a man accustomed to being obeyed.

"Why not?" She couldn't pull her gaze away from his. Intelligent blue eyes scrutinized her in a way meant to make her squirm.

"I have some papers I'd like you to look at. Could you join me in my cabin?"

If he had told her to jump into the water she couldn't have been more surprised.

"Not tonight," she said, backing away. "Maybe tomorrow."

"No. It has to be tonight." His inflexible tone left no doubt that he wouldn't back down.

"Why is this so urgent?" she asked, annoyed that he was determined to make her agree.

"I have important matters to discuss with you."

"Oh, by all means," she drawled. "Once you get to know me, you're bound to like me." She gave him an impish look just to annoy him.

"I sincerely doubt that, Miss Sandoval," he said, his tone smooth yet final.

"Sofia, please. We're practically family now." She grinned with evil relish. "Don't worry; I won't expect you to call me Mommy."

His square jaw clenched rhythmically. "I don't find that particularly cute or amusing. I'm giving you forty-eight hours to convince me that you're worthy of marrying my father."

"I don't need forty-eight hours to convince you," she

said, her mouth forming a smug smile. "A couple of hours will do."

James's dark brows furrowed over a hard stare. "I don't have time for your banter." He advanced toward her and took her arm just beneath her elbow. "Do it for your *beloved's* sake."

The mocking way he emphasized *beloved* made her want to grind her teeth. "Do what?" she muttered, shaking her arm out of his grip.

"Come to my room. We have important matters to discuss," he said again.

There was no getting around his pigheaded persistence. Sofia gave in, only because she was curious to see what he was planning. But she wasn't feeling particularly well. She couldn't ignore the queasiness any longer now that it was accompanied by intermittent bouts of dizziness.

They walked inside the ship and rode the elevator in silence, without partaking in conversation until they were safely inside James's cabin.

"Please sit down," he said, his voice civil as he motioned to one of the two upholstered chairs beside a small, round mahogany table. He retrieved his briefcase from the closet and joined her at the table. With a brisk snap, he opened the lock and pulled out a folder labeled: MISS SANDOVAL. *Dear God in Heaven, not another background check.* She breathed a sigh of relief when she saw that it wasn't. But her relief was short-lived when she realized the legal document was a prenuptial agreement! No wonder the bully had never been married.

"Once you've read over the terms, you'll need to sign three copies. One for Daniel, one for me, and one for you," he said briskly.

She shouldn't have been as stunned as she was, but the cool authority in his tone set her teeth on edge. It was almost as if he were trying to set boundaries with her before all hell broke loose. Ungraciously taking the document from his hands, she gave him a surreptitious glance. She was sure that his merciless stare was meant to intimidate her into signing. She almost laughed out loud at his tactics. Little did he know that it was a futile effort on his part, since she wasn't *really* Daniel's fiancée.

Ensconced as the unrelenting lawyer, James demanded, "Read it and sign. Let's not waste time."

What nerve. "I'm not going to sign without having my attorney read it first."

He shrugged. "Either you sign it soon, or I'll sit down with Dad and demand that he read the whole unsavory report on your background. Either way, this will be settled before the cruise is over."

"Don't try to blackmail me! I won't be rushed," she argued stubbornly. "I'll need time to read it carefully before I even *consider* signing such a ridiculous document." This could be a great negotiating tool that she could use to monopolize his time. But she was put off, nevertheless. The thought that her dear Tia Lucita would soon be inheriting this tyrant as a stepson was too distressing.

Suddenly the fine print began to swim on the page before her as she strove to tamp down a dizzying wave of nausea. Losing the battle, she rose from the chair but had to grasp the table's edge to brace against the onslaught of bile rising in her throat. "Where's the bathroom?" she choked out.

"Over there," James said, pointing to his left at a closed door. "What the . . ."

On wobbly legs, Sofia bolted into the bathroom just in time to throw herself on her knees and vomit into the toilet bowl. James followed closely behind her. She pushed her hair away from her face with one hand and clutched her heaving stomach with the other.

"Please get out!" she wailed when the vomiting subsided. She flushed the toilet before slumping back on her heels, furious that he'd followed her into the bathroom and seen her lose her dinner. It was just too much to bear. "Leave me alone!"

"Don't get hysterical; I've seen worse," he said bluntly.

She didn't care if she sounded like a hysterical banshee. She desperately needed privacy.

But the obtuse man left her side only long enough to wet a washcloth and wring it out. Returning beside her, his large body hunkered down as he lifted her heavy hair, holding it securely in his hand. He pressed the cool washcloth on her nape. "This should help."

"I don't need your help," she uttered through clenched teeth. Of course she needed his help, but he didn't have to know that right now.

"I'm not going anywhere. So settle down," he said, stroking her back with a firm hand. "It's just a little seasickness. You'll be OK in a few minutes."

"I know what it is! Leave me alone." Another bout of nausea seized her as her stomach heaved again. Luckily nothing came out this time, only dry heaves, but the awful sound mortified her. She was dying of embarrassment and James wouldn't budge from her side. Suddenly everything started to go black before her eyes. She was dimly aware of being lifted up in strong arms and carried to the bed.

After placing her on the bedcover, James gently tapped her face a few times. "Hey, don't pass out on me."

"Wha . . . what do you want?" Sofia moaned between panting breaths as she gained consciousness. Her chest felt squashed, compressed beneath the binding fabric of her dress and the restrictive strapless bra.

As if guessing her dilemma, he quietly turned her over.

"Stop it! What do you think you're doing?" she asked when he unzipped her dress all the way down to just below her panty line. *Grreat.* Now the hateful man knew that she wasn't wearing panty hose and that she'd been wearing pink thong underwear to avoid ugly panty lines beneath the silky fabric. This would only augment his image of her as a hussy. With a practiced flick of his fingers, he unsnapped the tight bra, giving her instant relief, even though her face was squashed into the pillow.

"There, now you can breathe," he said, his gruff voice sounding strangled.

"Get your hands off me!" She struggled up on her elbows in hopes of turning over but noted with disgust that she had the strength of an infant.

James's strong hands casually flipped her over again face upward. Incensed, Sofia's hands flew to her chest to make sure the front of her dress wasn't gaping open.

"How dare you manhandle me," she fumed.

"I was gentle and you know it," he said through taut teeth. "You shouldn't wear such tight clothes."

She wanted to retort, *They're tight because I over-indulged in my aunt's delicious food, you cad!* But she felt too weak to argue. She couldn't bear to spend another moment with him, especially after what he had just witnessed in the bathroom.

It was time to regain her dignity. "I just need a few moments to settle my stomach; then I'll leave," she said.

"Sure, lie still until it settles. We don't want you puking again."

Sofia closed her eyes against the rude indelicacy of his remark. Even though he *had* been decent enough to tend to her, he was no gentleman beneath the sophisticated facade of evening wear. Through half-closed eyes, she watched him cross over to the table. He poured bottled water into a goblet and returned to her side.

Taking a seat beside her on the bed, he nudged her hand. "Drink a little of this."

She pursed her lips and shook her head. "No. I won't be able to hold it down."

"I'll get a wastebasket just in case."

"Forget it." She really *was* worried that she'd be sick again if she took a sip of water. She pressed her lips tighter lest he think he could force a drink on her. "Please leave me alone," she demanded, pushing his hand away so vigorously that water sloshed over the rim and drenched his pants leg.

Leaning forward to drive home his point, he growled low, "Stop being childish. You're confirming my belief that Dad is getting saddled with yet another brat."

That did it! Why should she cooperate when he was flinging insults? When she mutinously didn't budge, he lifted her upper body by the shoulders and plumped up the pillows behind her head. She purposely went limp in his arms. No need to make things easy for him. Undeterred, he held her up easily with one hand as he used his other to place the goblet in her hand.

"Open your mouth and take a tiny sip," he ordered, his forceful look daring her to argue. His rough tone softened a notch when he spoke next, catching her by surprise. "You'll feel better. I promise."

She thrust her chin out belligerently, knowing that would irk him something fierce. "You're just in a hurry for me to sign the prenuptial."

"Damn right I am," he growled again.

Sofia squelched a small triumphant smile that kept threatening to surface. There was only one useful thing coming from this debacle. James was being forced to spend unpleasant time with her while her aunt and Daniel enjoyed the Broadway revue on board. Served him right for coming to the wrong conclusions about her and his father!

"Quit stalling." His calm command drew her attention back to the moment. "The sooner you take some water, the sooner you'll be able to swallow some of this medicine and be out of my hair." Even though he struggled to keep his tone level, she noted the strained look on his face. He was clearly out of patience, but she had no intention of drinking anything just yet. Not if it meant throwing up again.

When she didn't take the glass from him, he warned, "Don't confuse me with my father. I have no inclination to put up with your stubbornness. You just threw up in my bathroom and now you're taking up space in my bed."

She lifted her chin at a haughty angle. "You are nothing like your father. *He's* a gentleman."

"Yes, he is, and you'll do well to respect that."

"I do," she said wearily. They were getting nowhere

fast. It was obvious he meant for her to take that sip of water and he'd sit there all night if he had to. "Give me the damned glass. If I get sick, it will be all over your nice suit," she said with a nasty grin.

"I'll take my chances."

Now that her nausea seemed to be subsiding a bit, she took a sip of water and waited. When nothing vile happened, she sighed with relief. Handing the glass back to him, she sank against the pillows. "Satisfied?"

"Not yet." He walked into the bathroom and returned with a small bottle in his hand. He quirked one dark eyebrow and gave her a penetrating look. "You're not pregnant, are you?"

"Of course not, you idiot!" There was no end to the man's rudeness.

"God forbid," he muttered darkly. "Take one of these."

She eyed the pill with distrust. "What is it? Poison?"

"A motion sickness pill," he replied, ignoring her smart remark.

"My, my. The barracuda lawyer is prepared for everything, isn't he?"

A flicker in his hard-eyed stare was the only reaction she got to her taunt. "Swallow one; then close your eyes and relax," he said evenly.

If she remained nauseated, she wouldn't gain a thing, being the weaker party. Anxious to feel better soon, she dutifully obliged. He didn't have to urge her to close her eyes; they did so of their own accord. But relaxing was going to be impossible, just knowing that he sat there, scrutinizing her every move.

"I'll rest until I feel a bit stronger. But only if you give me some privacy," she said, slyly peeking at him beneath lowered lids.

To her surprise, he rose from the bed. "As soon as you feel stronger, I'll walk you back to your cabin. Dad is probably worried and searching for you everywhere."

"I doubt it. Daniel urged me to spend this evening getting to know you."

"Any other man wouldn't be so generous with his fiancée on a pleasure trip."

"*He's* self-confident and he trusts me," she retorted, her eyelids feeling heavier by the moment. "Besides, you're his son. Why should he have anything to worry about?"

"Humph."

Her eyes shot open at the extreme displeasure in his tone, and she found herself spellbound by the blue fire blazing in his eyes.

"Rest now," he said, not taking his fiery gaze from hers. "I'll be back in a little while. If you need anything, ring for the valet."

James left the room in a hurry and stepped outside to pace the deck. If he had to sit there one more moment arguing with a half-dressed, tousled temptress he was liable to go crazy. All evening long when she had lifted her chin to defy him, he'd been tempted to kiss the sass from her rosy mouth. Most people backed down from an argument with him, especially women.

But not Sofia. The little nuisance had done her damnedest to provoke him, and she had succeeded too well. In one short evening, her brazen manner, sultry dark eyes, and sinfully curvaceous body had sexually frustrated him more than he'd ever been.

Against his will, he remembered how her full breasts had taunted him, straining against the confining bodice of her dress. Once he had unzipped her, he'd caught a glimpse of a tantalizing cleavage rising above the loosened neckline. Forehead beading, he swallowed hard, trying to block out a mental image of pale, round breasts peaked by tightened, dusky rose nipples.

Damn her sexy little hide! She was his father's fiancée and he had no business fantasizing about what her naked bosom would look like. It was wrong to be lusting after her. His hands fisted at his sides, trying to deny the potent arousal she'd stirred in him.

James's necktie suddenly felt tight around his neck, not to mention how snug and confining his pants felt. He had seen Sofia at her vulnerable worst, bent over a toilet, spilling out her guts. But somehow that hadn't diminished her appeal. Just moments later, he had felt poleaxed by lust when he'd pulled down her zipper and gazed at the bewitching indentation of her utterly feminine spine.

His palms grew sweaty just remembering the velvety softness of her skin when his fingers inadvertently brushed against her bare back. She'd been wearing a lacy strapless bra. *And that pink thong.* His eyes nearly misted with the arduous effort not to picture it. It had barely encircled a curvy bottom that lay bare beneath the thin fabric of her dress.

Groaning out loud, he suddenly smacked his palm against his forehead. Damn! How could he have been so blind? It was the perfect solution. Why hadn't it occurred to him sooner? If he succeeded in seducing the little temptress, his father would be convinced that she had only been after his money. There was no time to waste. It had to be done swiftly, before the old softie fell harder for Sofia and before she made further plans for his money.

Sofia's obstinate behavior earlier had convinced James that she wasn't planning to sign the prenuptial agreement he'd drawn up. Even weakened by seasickness, she'd been feisty as hell.

It wasn't the money or his future inheritance that James was most worried about. He had a lot more money and investments than his dad had at his age. He just didn't want to see his old man made a fool of over a little hussy young enough to be his granddaughter! *Someone* had to look after him; he was seventy years old. James could only hope that his father would someday forgive him and understand that he had acted in his parent's best interest.

He returned to the room at once. Stalking toward the cabin, he flung open the door once he reached it. In mounting disbelief, his gaze zeroed in on the bed before searching the darkened room.

The little witch was gone!

CHAPTER 4

James rushed out of his room the following morning intent on intercepting his dad before he entered the dining hall. If he knew Dad, he'd be having breakfast at 8:00 A.M. sharp. Despite his haste, James didn't arrive until 8:05. He found Daniel already inside, having an animated conversation with the older woman, Mrs. Sanchez.

"Morning, Dad. Mrs. Sanchez," James said, nodding in her direction when he approached the table.

Mrs. Sanchez smiled. "No need for formality, James. You may call me Lucita. Everyone does."

"OK, Lucita." James couldn't help noticing how pleasant the older lady was, with her sparkling green eyes and friendly expression. So unlike her unruly niece, he thought with a flash of irritation. "Where is your niece? Has she gotten over the seasickness?"

"Sofia?" she said absently. "Oh, yes. She's feeling chipper this morning. So much so that she's taking her morning jog."

He should have known she wouldn't stay down for long. James turned his attention to his dad. "How are you feeling, Dad? No more stomach pain?"

"Not yet," Daniel said, giving James a meaningful look. "I plan on taking it easy today. I'm sticking to a light breakfast and then I think I'll play some bridge. What are your plans for today?"

James shrugged. "I haven't planned anything yet."

"Good. Sofia has her heart set on the eleven o'clock swing dance class that I had promised to join her in. I don't want to disappoint her, but since my ulcer acted up last night, I don't dare indulge in dancing until I feel *much* better." His wise blue eyes zeroed in on James as he gave him a persuasive smile. "I was wondering if you'd step in for me."

"Me?" James asked, making an effort to sound civil.

"Yes. I'd like you to be Sofia's dance partner," Daniel announced.

That was what James had been afraid of. "Can't she find something else to do?" He was well aware his tone had turned sharp, but wasn't that just like Dad, to want to please his young fiancée at all costs? "After all, she is your guest and you have to take care of your health."

"That's not the point." Daniel shook his head at James as if he thought his son was dense. "This is the first cruise the little one has ever been on and I want her to be happy. You don't know how much she loves to dance. And she's good at it, too," he said, chuckling indulgently.

That was precisely the problem, James thought bitterly. His dad would always have a penchant for putting the royal "little one" first and catering to her every whim— until she wiped his bank account clean. If he'd had his doubts late last night about his plan to seduce Sofia, they were wiped out by his dad's naive statement. Too bad James had lost sleep over his new venture. The sooner Dad was rid of the pampered *little one,* the better.

"Fine. I'll do it," he said abruptly before turning his attention to Lucita. "Do you play bridge, too?"

"Oh, yes. I've played bridge for years at the country club," she said.

"Great," James said. "Then you won't mind being Dad's bridge partner?"

"Since when have you become my social secretary, James?" demanded Daniel before Lucita could respond.

Lucita smiled at Daniel with the warmth and self-confidence of a mature woman. "I'd be delighted if you'll have me as your partner."

"I'd be honored," Daniel graciously replied.

Good; that would keep Dad and the nice old lady out of his hair so he could concentrate on wooing Sofia. "Then it's settled," James said in vast relief. "You and Lucita will play bridge while I play dancing partner to 'the little one.' "

"James . . ." Daniel's tone held a note of admonition.

James turned to the approaching waiter, intent on feeding the sudden wolfish appetite inside his gut. "I'll have orange juice, black coffee, a mushroom-and-cheddar omelet, skillet potatoes, and whole-wheat toast. Oh, and bring me a small fruit plate as well. I'm going to need all my strength to dance with the little . . ." He paused when he caught Daniel's raised-eyebrow look. "Chita Rivera," he finished, opting not to rile his dad unnecessarily.

"You'd better be nice to her, James," Daniel warned.

"I will, Dad. You can count on it," he said with wicked relish.

From a distance, Sofia watched James stroll into the ballroom in khakis and a short-sleeved cotton print shirt. His penetrating gaze surveyed the room until he found her. Daniel had already warned her that James was to be her dance partner, but she was startled when her pulse quickened at the mere sight of his imposing good looks. Suddenly she wasn't sure she was up to dancing with him, but it was too late to change her mind, since he was heading straight at her.

When he approached her side, he leaned over and kissed her cheek, surprising her with the casual gesture. "Hey, good morning. You look good, considering what you went through last night."

Heat crept up from her neck to redden her cheeks as she blushed against her will. "Don't remind me of last night. I'd rather forget about it," she muttered, taken aback by the affable way he regarded her. It was a dramatic change from his earlier bulldog demeanor.

The corners of his firm mouth kicked up slowly and revealed strong white teeth. She stared in awe at the transformation of his face. He had a charming, almost boyish grin. Never in her wildest dreams would she have imagined that James's stern face could metamorphose into something so . . . so *utterly appealing*. But it had, and she could only stare at him, mouth agape in astonishment.

There was no denying the *nice* way he was looking at her, as if he was anxious to make amends for last night. Maybe he had a Dr. Jekyll/Mr. Hyde personality, she thought nervously. Or maybe Daniel had read his son the riot act this morning about being rude to her.

Coming to her senses as she thought of Daniel and Lucita, Sofia snapped her gawking mouth shut and reminded herself that James was the killjoy standing between the older couple's happiness. He had to be using his courtroom tactics on her, she decided wryly. James thought he could conquer her by grinning at her with such aplomb that she'd forget what he was about when all he really wanted was for her to sign the prenuptial agreement. That wasn't going to happen anytime soon.

She would string him along and not sign until Lucita and Daniel were safely married. From what Lucita had said, the captain planned on marrying them at the end of the week. Even though it wasn't really a long time, it seemed like an eternity to have to fib just to keep James from ruining their plans.

There was one little problem, though. His disarming grin had wiped out her short-term memory and she couldn't seem to remember what he'd just said, or what *she* had, for that matter!

"Um, what did you say?" she asked, her gaze inexorably drawn to his.

"I didn't. You were saying how awful last night was for you."

"Oh. Well, I feel much better now. The motion sickness pill you gave me helped a lot. I took another one this morning. I hope you don't mind that I kept the bottle. You didn't need it, did you?" She flashed a bright smile.

"You can wipe the sassy grin off your face." His mouth curled up at one corner in dry amusement. "Sorry to disappoint you, but I don't get seasick. My secretary bought it for me and stuck it in my briefcase before I left."

She arched her eyebrows daintily. "Must be nice to

have people clamoring to please you," she murmured. "Why are you here?"

"Dad asked me to fill in for him."

Sofia's gaze leisurely slid over the length of his body until it reached his boat shoes. "I hope you like to dance, because after this I might want to take in a country line-dancing class."

He looked as if he was amused by the thought of her line-dancing. "Oh? You're that much of a country-western enthusiast? I would have thought you'd be more into salsa."

"That's where you're wrong. Salsa isn't native to Colombians. It has gained in popularity there recently, but I still prefer to dance *cumbia* and *merengue*."

He smiled. "I stand corrected. Anyway, I'm willing to dance anything you want."

"Really?" Her tone held a hint of incredulity. "I'm having a hard time believing that the new you is authentic," she remarked.

"And what is the new me?"

She shrugged. "Pleasant, agreeable . . ."

Nonplussed by her sarcastic tone, he said, "Don't worry, honey. I wasn't forced to be here. I came of my own accord."

Was she supposed to stand there and pretend that he hadn't called his father's supposed fiancée *honey*? After pausing a moment, she decided to let it go. No use in making a big deal out of what was probably a slip of the tongue for a man who was capable of calling all women "honey."

"You'll find that I'm a fast learner," he said.

"I'll bet you are. Although I wouldn't be surprised if you stomped all over my toes on purpose."

He glanced at her bare toes peeking out of the sandals' open straps. "Cute toes. I'd never hurt them."

Did she detect a teasing twinkle in his eyes?

"I'm here to form a truce with you, so I can get to know you better." He paused, his eyes searching her face for a reaction. "I'm willing to put the hostility aside and give you a chance, even though I still think it's odd that someone as young as you would be devoted to a man old enough to be your grandfather."

"How nice of you to point that out," she said, stiffening beside him. Maybe *she'd* be the one to stomp on *his* toes.

"Don't take it the wrong way. For some reason, it's important to Dad that we get along. I'm willing to make the effort, if you are." His blue eyes exuded such forthright openness that she had to look away. Boy, he was a smooth one!

"OK, then." She held out her arms in a flippant manner. "Shall we dance?"

"By all means," James replied, only to be intercepted by a chubby young woman heading toward him with a purposeful gleam in her round green eyes.

When she reached James and Sofia, the young woman reached out and clasped James's hand. "Hi, I'm Betina. You're just the partner I was looking for," she said, linking her arm through James's unsuspecting one. "I need someone big enough to twirl me around. And I think I just found him. Just look at those strong arms!" she cried gleefully.

James took a step backward. "I'd be happy to oblige any other time," he said diplomatically. "But . . ." He indicated Sofia. "This young lady is already my dancing partner."

Betina glared at Sofia with menace. "No way. I've been waiting here longer than you have. We're supposed to share partners in this class. That's what the teacher just said." Betina softened her attitude long enough to ask Sofia, "You don't really mind, do you, ma'am?"

Sofia stifled the wild urge to giggle at the sudden turn of events. Out of the corner of her eye, she caught James frantically signaling her to say that she did indeed mind. "Oh, I don't mind at all. Be my guest," she said with wicked enjoyment.

Broad shoulders stiffly bent in surrender, James followed his rotund partner, but not before wagging a finger at Sofia that seemed to say, "You'll pay for this."

Sofia watched James maneuver Betina on the dance floor while he conversed with her. She was amazed at his good-natured mood and impressed that he'd been willing to dance with the pushy girl. She almost wished that she could believe this civilized side of his personality was genuine. If it wasn't an act, then Daniel had raised his son well. Perhaps beneath the tough, arrogant lawyer exterior beat the heart of a gentleman.

She still felt thrown for a loop when it came to James. She could handle his open antagonism; in fact, she relished dishing it right back to him and putting him in his place. But now that he was being pleasant, she didn't feel on such equal ground. And when she thought about last night, she had to admit that even though his style had been high-handed, he'd been decent enough to care for her and allow her to rest in his bed until she felt better.

Be that as it may, she couldn't afford to let her guard down and be pleasant back. She feared that if she did, she'd like this side of him and find it hard to continue living the lie long enough for her aunt and Daniel to get married without James's intervention. Her recent betrayal by Manny had made her vow that she'd take her sweet time before blindly trusting in any man's good character.

Lost in her musings, Sofia wasn't able to enjoy the delightful swing music as she danced with her assigned partner. He was a short middle-aged man who danced well but was too intent on chatting. Nodding politely to his comments, she was acutely aware that James hadn't let her out of his sight the whole time he was dancing with Betina.

An hour later, Sofia watched Betina kiss James on the cheek and leave the salon. He practically limped over to Sofia's side. The other dancers had already cleared out and the music had ended.

She clapped softly. "Bravo, nice job."

"My feet certainly paid for it," he mumbled, wincing as he looked down at them.

Sofia suppressed a smile. "I thought you did admirably well, considering that Betina was on a mission to keep you as her partner."

"True," he agreed ruefully.

"I'm surprised you gave in so easily. When you picked her up, I thought you were going to topple over," she remarked with an unrepentant grin. She shrugged. "I didn't fare any better. My dancing partner was what we Latins refer to as *un inspector de ombligo*."

Dark brows drew together to form a straight line over quizzical eyes. "What is *un inspector de ombligo*?"

Sofia couldn't help giggling at James's pronounced gringo accent. "It means belly-button inspector. My partner was so much shorter than me that his eyes were practically resting on my navel," she quipped.

James threw his handsome head back and laughed. It was a robust, very masculine sound that filled the room with mirth—and grabbed Sofia in the pit of her stomach.

"You have a nice laugh. Too bad you don't do it more often," she blurted out before she could stop herself.

"That was pretty damn funny about the belly-button inspector. It's a good thing his eyes were resting on your navel and not anywhere higher." James's heat-charged gaze descended to her breasts, then back to fuse with her eyes.

Despite an inner voice urging her not to let him bait her, Sofia's nipples tightened in response. James's eyes turned a deep indigo, inexorably luring her into their sensual depths. She forced her gaze away from his, lowering it briefly to the floor. She hadn't meant to sound like she was flirting, but the air had suddenly grown heavy and she could hear her pulse racing at his proximity. Sofia stood before him, transfixed by the intense sexual heat emanating from his powerful body, bemused by a sudden craving to feel his strong arms pull her in for a passionate kiss.

She didn't have long to wait for her wish to come true. James tilted her chin up and lowered his head to kiss her upturned mouth. His lips felt warm and soft and firm against hers. Trying to negate the hot coil of desire curling inside her womb, Sofia opened her mouth to protest. But James took the opportunity to slide his tongue inside. Sighing against the delicious invasion, Sofia allowed him to draw her tremulous body closer to his. Weak with desire, she inhaled deeply of his delectable, manly scent, nearly swooning from the sheer pleasure of being held in his solid embrace.

One large hand rested firmly on her waist and the other wound in her hair as he deepened the kiss, compressing her breasts against the muscled planes of his hard chest. His thick erection nudged her soft pelvis, yanking Sofia back to reality. With a jerk of her head, she pulled back and stared at him, woefully unprepared for the steam heat of desire in his eyes.

Without a backward glance, she fled the room, deaf to his calls.

The following afternoon, James headed toward the line-dancing class in hopes of finding Sofia. If it hadn't been that Daniel had mentioned at lunchtime that she would be there for the five P.M. class, James would have had to search the huge ship for her *again*.

When Sofia hadn't joined them at dinner the previous evening, Lucita and Daniel had seemed as surprised as James was. Daniel had questioned James's behavior toward Sofia, wondering aloud if the reason she wasn't there was because he'd been rude to her. After explaining that they'd had a pleasant time at the swing lesson, James was finally able to allay his dad's fears. But try as he might, he hadn't been able to find her all evening.

James's frustration mushroomed when he futilely searched the deck in hopes of finding Sofia jogging the next morning. There was no question that she was avoiding him after the hot kiss they'd shared the day before.

More than likely she was probably trying to get out of signing the prenuptial, too.

Arriving at the lounge at ten minutes past five o'clock, James stood at the back of the room and searched for Sofia among the dancers. It wasn't until he located her that he realized just how anxious he had been to see her. He remained there, hoping he wouldn't be noticed while his gaze was inexorably drawn to the way she shook her hips to the "Boot Scootin' Boogie." She put extra oomph into every movement, smiling and chatting with other passengers while giving the dance a Latin twist that might have been cute on anyone else. But with Sofia it was damn provocative, given the way the snug jeans cupped her curvy tush.

He spent the next half hour watching her succulent body move with such abandon that a fan club formed around her comprised mostly of fawning males. She looked too sexy for her own good! James couldn't take his eyes off her as he noticed everything about how she tossed her dark, lustrous hair over her shoulder and inclined her head to one side, peeking through long dark lashes as she chatted with several men. Her almond-shaped eyes sparkled with fun and a touch of mischief.

A few seconds later, one of the men, a good deal older than she, was leading her in a Texas two-step, his weathered hand firmly clasping her slender waist. With a lively smile, she interacted with the man until the dance was over. When the next song began, the same man returned to her side, seeking her attention.

James felt his blood pressure rise dangerously as his jaw clamped down. Why did she have to come on to older men like that? She was behaving shamelessly, flirting and giggling while she attempted to master line-dancing techniques with a seductive wiggle of her shapely little ass. Was she looking to add to her collection of sugar daddies? James wondered in growing disgust. Poor Dad.

For a brief moment, Sofia looked straight at James and smiled in recognition. He stared at her warm, inviting smile but didn't return it. Instead, he left the room before he gave into the temptation to haul the brazen hussy aside for an explanation. Shaking his head to clear it of the wrath she'd provoked with her saucy flirting, he reminded himself to get a grip. He needed to remain on friendly territory with Sofia if he was going to accomplish what he'd set out to do—thoroughly seduce her, then confront his father with the sorry outcome.

CHAPTER 5

Shortly after midnight, Sofia waded through the crowd of people dressed in tunics for Toga Night. Earlier that afternoon, white sheets had been delivered to each cabin to encourage the guests to design their own togas for the party on the top deck. After the line-dancing lessons that afternoon, she and Daniel and Lucita had ordered dinner from room service to catch up on the events of the day. Later, while Daniel napped, Lucita helped Sofia create a toga out of the white sheet. She wrapped it around Sofia's body in a strapless fashion, leaving her tanned shoulders bare. Using a wreath of ivy she'd brought from Miami, her aunt had adorned Sofia's loose hair for the party.

Amid a lot of conspiratorial giggling, they had sent a message to James via the headwaiter for him to join Sofia at the toga party at midnight. Happily freed for the evening, Lucita and Daniel had accepted an invitation from Daniel's childhood friend Capt. Sven Landergaard to join him in his quarters for champagne and caviar.

Shifting her thoughts to the present, Sofia surveyed the multitude of people, hoping to find James and put an end to the awkwardness she'd begun by avoiding him. Truth was, after that knee-buckling kiss yesterday she *had* been reluctant to see him again. She couldn't stop thinking about the way her body had betrayed her in helpless surrender to his touch.

Earlier, when James had found her at the country line-dancing class, she had initially panicked. He had stubbornly remained at the back of the lounge instead of joining her, trying to remain inconspicuous as he spied on her through hooded eyes. That's when she had decided to deliberately annoy him. But the plan backfired when he made eye contact with her briefly, his expression dangerous as he stalked out of the room before she could speak to him.

In hindsight, she regretted that her overt friendliness with the men had only succeeded in validating the unfavorable background report James had received on her. She tried not to let it bother her too much, but deep inside she was distressed that she had only intensified his negative image of her.

"Sofia," a deep male voice intoned behind her.

Sofia whirled around and was robbed of speech when she caught sight of James dressed as a Roman. Darkly handsome, the arrogant man had fashioned a one-shouldered toga from the sheet that left his broad shoulders and muscular arms exposed.

"Caligula, if I'm not mistaken," she said, pleased that she'd remembered the name of the despicable Roman emperor.

James's sensual mouth tightened imperceptibly, the only indication that he'd understood the slur. "You have an odd sense of humor, honey." To her surprise, his gaze leisurely traveled the length of her body until his darkened blue eyes captured hers with a look of pure male prowess. "You're looking beautiful tonight."

Caught off-guard by his uncharacteristic compliment, Sofia felt her whole being flush, transfixed by his potent aura. Her body shivered deliciously in a deeply feminine way, responding to the appreciative gleam in his hot gaze.

As she stared at him, her resistance grew weak and she found herself floating in heady sensations. She mentally shook herself to dispel the trance. She couldn't give in; it wasn't right. They were treading dangerous waters. Even though she wasn't *really* Daniel's intended, James thought she was. She couldn't let things get out of hand, no matter how much she was dying for him to kiss her again.

His lips lifted into a slow, sexy grin. "I'm glad you set up this clandestine meeting. I've missed you."

Narrowing her eyes, she leveled a firm look at him. "It is not clandestine. Daniel knows all about it. It was his

idea. He's been very distressed that you've made it a point
to complain about my absence at mealtimes."

"You have been a little inconsiderate," he chided
mildly. "Aren't you supposed to be keeping Dad company?"

"I've given him a lot of quality time."

He shook his head. "You sound as if he's some sort
of responsibility, not the man you love."

"That's not how I meant it. Daniel has encouraged me
to participate in as many activities as I want, even if he
isn't up to joining me. It pleases him to see me happy."

James's jaw tightened. "I would have thought that
you'd be more worried about Dad's health than having a
good time."

Insufferable man. "You're the one who upsets his
health by standing in the way of his happiness," she countered.

Just when she thought James was going to turn into an
aggressive prosecutor volleying pointed questions, he
chuckled. It was a dry sound, devoid of mirth, but a
chuckle nonetheless, masking the strong accusation of his
words. "I'll bet he has spent more time with your Aunt
Lucita than with you!"

"Not true," she refuted immediately, lest he catch on
to the real nature of their relationship. "I've spent plenty
of time with Daniel. I only agreed to set up this meeting
tonight because it's important to your dad that we get
along. Contrary to what you choose to believe, his peace
of mind and happiness are very important to me." She
accompanied her sincere words with a warm smile to
show that she meant it. "I guess I have to work a little
harder at making *you* happy."

"Goood," he drawled. "I'm looking forward to making
you happy, too. Let's dance."

That was a switch. Before she could decline, James
placed his big hands on her hips. With palms resting on
her hipbones and fingers curved toward the small of her
back, he drew her toward him, his strong body coming

into contact with hers just as the music slowed to a sensual *bossa nova*. Sofia closed her eyes and let the exotic melody infuse her whole being. The heat of James's hands branded her skin beneath the tunic's thin fabric. His clean, masculine scent lured her to move in closer. Their bodies undulated to the slow beat, her soft breasts pressed against the rigid, muscled planes of his broad chest.

When the music ended, James stepped back from her and gazed at her with an unfathomable gleam in his eyes. "Shall we get a bite to eat?" he asked, his smile warm and inviting.

Before Sofia could collect herself and come down to earth, he strolled toward long tables showcasing a lavish spread of seafood amid dolphin and kingfish ice sculptures. Even though she had no appetite for food, she followed him and served herself a small plate.

"Let's sit over there, away from the loud music," he said, motioning toward a darkened corner of the deck.

"OK." She would have preferred to stay in the well-lit buffet area with the crowd, but James seemed intent on having a conversation with her in private. Sofia looked around nervously. They were several feet away from the action where the full moon illuminated a night so full of stars that the sky seemed like a black sheet dotted with silver sparkles. She sat down on a double chaise lounge and looked up at the sky. "Just look at the moon and all those stars. They're glorious!"

Instead of sitting across from her, James sat beside her on the double lounge chair, a little too close for comfort. They ate in companionable silence until Sofia placed her half-empty plate on the small table. Finishing his last bite, James set the plate down. He took hold of her hand and studied her with keen eyes. "Why have you been avoiding me, Sofia?"

"I've been busy," she said, trying not to enjoy his warm, firm grasp. But the way he held her hand nestled in his larger one was too inviting. "Anyway, *you're* the one who's been avoiding me."

James slowly slid one finger down the length of her cheek and squeezed her chin between his thumb and fore-finger. "Come on, honey. We both know that you've been hiding out since I kissed you."

He released her chin, but her skin still felt electrified by his impromptu caress. She had to get a grip on her reactions to him; he was so bluntly sensual that it bordered on outrageous.

She refused to acknowledge what her reaction had been to his bewitching kiss. "I might have missed a few meals in the dining hall, but Daniel mentioned that you might be joining me today in the line-dancing class. When I tried to get your attention, you totally ignored me and left before we could speak."

Despite the dim lighting, she noticed the blue fire crackling in his eyes. "You had enough men keeping you busy. That type of flirting will only upset Dad and tick me off."

Taken aback by his possessive tone, Sofia gaped at him. "Daniel knows that I love to dance. He . . . he en-couraged me to take as many classes as I like," she stam-mered. "I was just having fun."

James's mouth tightened as his sharp gaze pierced her composure. "Doesn't it bother you that you were fired from your job for the same type of 'fun'?"

Stung by his accusation, she didn't reply right away.

He commanded softly, "Answer me."

"Of course it bothers me!" To her dismay, her eyes welled up with hot tears. "You don't know how betrayed and humiliated I felt when the doctors' wives conspired to fire me unfairly."

James's harsh expression gentled as he handed her a paper napkin to dry her eyes. "Suppose you tell me about it."

Sniffling, she quickly wiped away her tears. "It's a lit-tle involved."

"I'm not going anywhere."

"OK. Just give me a minute to calm down." She took

a deep, slow breath, then proceeded. It felt cathartic to finally have her day in court with James. "I worked at a sports medical facility for three years. During the last year there, a new orthopedic doctor joined the other two partners. Dr. Fernandez was overly friendly at first; then later he started paying way too much attention to my clothes, making unprofessional comments about my figure and my looks in general."

"Why didn't you report it to the other doctors?"

"Because it wouldn't have done any good. They're childhood friends. Initially, Dr. Fernandez only went as far as complimenting me about my appearance. Although I always got an uncomfortable feeling around him, I was naive enough not to imagine that he would go as far as he did," she said, her stomach twisting with regret at not having left the job sooner. The harsh memories came back vividly and Sofia's body began to tremble with rage.

"Hey, take it easy." James rubbed her back in soothing circles. "How far did he go?"

Sofia shuddered and James placed his arm around her shoulder, his large, warm hand stroking the length of her bare arm. "It's OK, honey. Just tell me."

Swallowing hard, she nodded. "One evening, I was working late in the office because we had recently added a new network provider. While I was standing at the file cabinet, Dr. Fernandez came up behind me and caught me by surprise." She almost choked on the next words as the disturbing memory rushed back to torture her. "The vile man put his hands on my breasts and squeezed while he pressed himself against me."

James's jaw clenched. "What did you do?"

"I was so shocked, I froze. I was horrified by what he had dared to do to me. When I came to my senses, I put my hands on his and tried to pry them off me." Her voice cracked. "It was at that precise moment that his wife flung open the door and caught us in the compromising position. Mrs. Fernandez wouldn't listen to any of my explanations, no matter how much I pleaded with her. She

started to scream and called me all kinds of filthy names.
I tried to defend myself, but she wouldn't listen. Dr. Fernandez tried to calm her down with lame excuses, but
when she wouldn't stop ranting, he forcefully pulled her
out of the office." Her eyes stung with fresh tears. "The
following morning, I received a phone call from another
partner in the medical group, telling me that I was fired."

Blue eyes hardening with ire, James shook his head.
"Why didn't you sue for sexual harassment?"

"How could I? There were no other witnesses, other
than Mrs. Fernandez. She believed her husband's lies instead of the truth. In one night, she managed to turn the
other two doctors' wives against me with her phone calls
telling them that she had caught me holding her husband's
hands over my breasts." Sofia squeezed her eyes shut to
block out the degrading memory as two fat tears slid down
her cheeks.

James gently wiped the wetness away from her face
with his hands, warming her heart with the tender gesture.
"Don't let them make you cry anymore, Sofia. The other
wives were jealous and feeling threatened by you."

"I'm not the type of woman who cries over everything." She blew her nose into the napkin. "But I haven't
been able to get a decent job since being fired. That doctor's office was the only place I've worked since gradu-
ating from college."

"You have to fight this. I'll help you."

"Why would you want to help me?" she asked, between hiccups. She peeked at him through wet, spiky
lashes. "Did Daniel ask you to?"

"No. I haven't discussed this with anyone. When we
get back to Miami, I'm going to sue Dr. Fernandez's ass.
Don't worry. When I get finished with him, your name
will be cleared." James tilted up her chin and held her
face still as he wiped the mascara under her eyes with a
napkin.

She looked down from his penetrating gaze, embarrassed to be enthralled by his tender ministrations. She

felt his chest expand, then contract beside her as he drew in a deep breath and exhaled sharply.

"As for Dad . . . I don't want him to remarry," he said implacably. "His heart has been broken too many times already. I don't think he could handle another disappointment. Dad is the best there is. He's a generous, decent human being and I won't stand for him to be ridiculed."

Cut to the quick, she pulled away from him. "I would never ridicule him! What makes you think I'm capable of that type of cruelty? Bring me the prenuptial agreement. I'll sign the stupid paper right now!" She poked his chest angrily. "You don't have to worry about your inheritance. I don't want a dime."

James grasped her shoulders. "I don't care about that, Sofia! I have a lot more money than Dad ever had at my age, or has now, for that matter."

They stared at each other for several tense moments before Sofia sighed deeply. "All right. I believe you," she said, noting how desperately he wanted her to understand his concerns. "I promise you I'll never hurt Daniel. On the contrary, I will always honor him for being the kindest man I know."

"I'm glad to hear that." After a long pause, he visibly composed himself. "Tell me what you did today."

Taken aback by the sudden shift in conversation, Sofia reflected on James's concern for his dad. It was obvious he felt relieved that he'd said his piece, but she had a feeling that the subject wasn't closed.

"Well?" he prompted. "What did you do today?"

"I took an early-morning tour of Cozumel with Tia Lucita."

"Did you enjoy yourself?"

"I liked the tour. But it was sad to watch the other tourists haggling over souvenir prices with little children who were so poor, they weren't even wearing shoes."

He nodded sympathetically. "I know what you mean. Seeing a poor child makes me rage inside."

Sofia's heart warmed when she heard his compassionate words. So there was a generous heart beating beneath the tough lawyer's veneer, after all.

James scooted over for her to stretch out beside him on the double chaise lounge. "Lie back and get comfy while you tell me about yourself."

"OK, but only if you talk about yourself, too."

"Sure," he said casually. "How about if I start with one question and you follow up with another one?"

"Fair enough. Fire away, counselor." Settling back against the cushion, Sofia kicked off her sandals and wiggled her toes. She couldn't believe that she was getting cozy with James, but he was being so open and friendly she felt obliged to chat with him a little just to be sociable.

Who was she kidding anyway? His proximity made her want to curl up to his strong body and press her nose into the crook of his warm neck, inhaling his appealing masculine scent.

"How did you meet Dad?"

"I don't want to talk about Daniel anymore. It will only lead to arguments."

"Fine," he agreed right away. Evidently, he didn't want to approach the sore spot, either. "Would you like to go rock climbing with me tomorrow morning?"

His impulsive invitation bewildered her. It sounded like he was asking her for a date. "Sure, sounds like fun. I'm looking forward to climbing the waterfalls at Ocho Rios soon, so I guess I'd better tackle rock climbing first. I love trying new adventures."

Sitting up, James handed Sofia a glass of wine and drank deeply from his.

She took a few sips as she glanced at his empty plate. "I noticed you didn't take any sushi. Don't you like it?"

He grimaced. "Nah, I think sushi's overrated."

"Really? Me, too," she said, surprised that his comment mirrored her opinion exactly. "I prefer my fish cooked."

"Yeah, I'll drink to that." He finished the wine and set it down before leaning back again. "Do you have any brothers and sisters?" he asked, apparently intent on asking random questions.

"Yes." She took several more sips of the mellow wine, then eased back on the chair, empty glass in hand. "I'm the 'baby' of the family, the youngest of four, with three older brothers."

He grinned and squeezed her knee. "Aha, so you're the spoiled baby of the family."

"I didn't say I was *spoiled,*" she protested, even though it was true her parents had indulged her far more than her brothers.

He patted her knee, then removed his hand. "You didn't have to." She peeked at James and watched him fold his arms behind his neck as he lay beside her with his eyes closed, a playful grin teasing the corners of his mouth.

Sofia gave his ribs a quick jab with her elbow. "What's so funny?" When he yelped in response, she said, "As an only child, you must have been spoiled rotten yourself."

He opened one eye and peered at her with a look of mock affront. "Me? Never."

"Ha! I find that hard to believe. I'll bet you always have to get your way in everything. It goes with being a successful lawyer."

"Yeah, well who doesn't like getting their way?" he asked, turning his full attention on her.

"You have a point. Now it's my turn to ask a question. What's your favorite book?" she asked on impulse.

Without pausing, he answered, "*The Fountainhead.* Best book I ever read."

"I *loved* that book, too. Roark is a character I'll never forget. I'm amazed that you and I have so much in common," she marveled.

"Yeah." He took the empty glass from her hand and set it down. "Hold on; I'm going to get us some more wine."

With newfound eyes Sofia watched him walk away. Just knowing that he shared her love of *The Fountainhead* pleased her immeasurably. She was beginning to see that James shared many of Roark's noble qualities. He was strong and decent and cared deeply for his father, all character traits that she admired. She only hoped he didn't see her as Dominique in the book, the cruel temptress whose selfish love nearly destroyed Roark.

James returned and handed Sofia a glass of wine; he drank from his, then placed it on the table. She took a few sips before setting her glass down, shivering when a cool ocean breeze washed over them. James put his arm around her and nudged her closer to his warmth. Sighing blissfully, she reclined her head on his shoulder and closed her eyes.

For the next hour they talked about books, movies, and music. They learned about each other's tastes and values, their life triumphs and downfalls, their dreams for the future.

"Ever been in love so bad she made you cry?" Sofia asked after a stretch of silence. She felt his body stiffen at her nosy question.

"Only once when I was a freshman in college," he admitted gruffly. "She was my first love. But it'll never happen again," he said, his tone turning hard. "How about you?"

She sighed in remembrance of that painful time in her life. "Yes, I shed too many tears over my ex-boyfriend. It wasn't so much that I cried over breaking up with Manny. It was his betrayal that devastated my trust in men."

"All men?" he asked, turning to gaze at her with a hard glint in his eyes.

"Not Daniel," she said quickly. "I trust him implicitly."

"Oh." The mere mention of his father seemed to rankle James again. She saw his jaw tighten with annoyance.

"What happened with your first love?" she asked, anxious to steer away from talking about her fake relationship with his father.

"I had been dating Jenny steadily since my junior year

in high school. But when I confessed that I never planned to get married, she broke up with me. After that, she avoided me like the plague." He gazed at the moon with a disgusted expression. "The following year, she got pregnant by someone else and had to get married."

"Sounds like a pretty bad letdown. But what did you expect, James? Most young women want to get married."

He shrugged. "I guess. Anyway, that letdown was the best thing that ever happened to me."

"Why?"

"It made me toughen up inside. In my line of work, I've realized that most marriages don't stand a chance of lasting a lifetime."

"God, that's pretty cynical. I totally disagree with you. There's a soul mate out there for everyone. It's just a matter of finding the right person."

"I've seen too many ugly divorces to believe that," he stated bluntly. "The only thing I regret about my aversion to marriage is not having children. I really love being around them, but I've seen how much they suffer when their parents divorce." For a brief moment, a shadow of longing passed over his eyes.

She felt a sharp little hitch in her chest when he revealed that tender side of his personality. "I adore babies, too," she said quietly. She couldn't elaborate and tell him how she'd always planned on having a big family. Not when he thought she was his father's girlfriend. His views on marriage disturbed her. "But James, every marriage doesn't end in divorce," she said, her hand lifting to touch his lean cheek.

"I know, honey. I don't mean to sound bitter." James brushed his lips against her temple. His mouth tantalized her skin with warm kisses along her cheek. Her breathing quickened into shallow pants as intense desire coursed through her body. Try as she might, she couldn't ignore the strong effect his touch had on her. It was so powerful, so overwhelming, she was oblivious to anything else.

Her stomach tightened into a knot of panic as she retrieved her hand from his face. It was killing her to continue the charade as Daniel's fiancée, but she had to honor her promise. She couldn't ruin everything because of her uncontrollable desire.

"God, you're beautiful," he murmured before tilting her head up to gaze in her eyes. His face was dark with lust so intense it pained her to look at him. "I can't get enough of you. It's madness. I've wanted you from the moment I laid eyes on you," he whispered in a low, grating voice.

"No," she moaned weakly, looking away from the raw desire in his eyes. "Don't say that."

"Hush," he said, rubbing her lower lip with his thumb. "For the past two days, I haven't been able to get you out of my mind. Something wild and exciting happens when you're close to me. Your sweet, passionate response tells me that you feel the same way."

Her heart wrenching, she turned her head away when he attempted to kiss her. Undeterred, he whispered roughly against her hair, "Don't deny it, honey. I felt your nipples harden against my chest while we were dancing. Yesterday, you were wildfire in my arms after just one kiss."

Just one kiss, Sofia repeated to herself, dying inside with desire. There was no escaping his keen scrutiny; he'd even noticed how her breasts had pebbled in response to his nearness. How foolish of her to think that by running away from him she could hide how much his kiss had turned her insides to jelly and her knees to mush.

She had thought about him constantly since that moment, remembering how strong his arms had been around her and how wildly erotic his deep kiss had felt. She had wanted to surrender and enjoy his caresses, but he'd been a man in deep lust and the intensity of his kiss had scared her, especially when she'd felt his rock-hard arousal. Just reliving the moment made her whole body ache with unfulfilled desire.

"I can't let you kiss me again, James," she said, meeting his hot gaze evenly. "We both know why."

The harsh tension on his face showed every last ounce of self-control he was exerting. "You belong with me, damn it, not Dad. Can't you see that, Sofia?" he asked between clenched teeth. "Admit it!"

She placed her hand over his mouth to silence him, but he kissed the center of her palm, ending with a flick of his tongue. Singed, she snatched her hand away quickly, shocked by his carnal intimacy. The feeling of his slick tongue jolted every nerve ending in her body and electrified her with unbearable craving.

"Stop. We can't let this happen. Not now." She was frantic to hold onto her willpower, but his wicked, provocative caresses held her spellbound.

His hand cupped her chin, holding her face still as his eyes bored into hers with blatant intent. "Look at me."

"No, I can't." She squeezed her eyes shut to block out the naked desire in his eyes, the savage tension brutally etched on his mouth. "Just hold me and let me enjoy your closeness . . . just for one night." Her body ached and it was difficult to breathe, but if she allowed him just one kiss, she wouldn't be able to hold back the emotions she'd been fighting to keep in tight check. The sheer intensity of her need for him rocked her equilibrium, shocking her profoundly.

He didn't answer her plea but honored her request by holding her securely against his powerful body without attempting to kiss her. Her head lay pressed against his solid chest as she heard the loud thump of his heart matching her own.

Silence enveloped them as the night air bathed their heated bodies in dew. Much later, they fell asleep with Sofia's head cradled on James's chest and his large hand possessively resting on her hip.

CHAPTER 6

James opened his eyes and squinted at a glaring yellow sun. He felt inordinately warm as he kicked at a sheet covering his legs. Peering down at his prone body, he realized with a start that he'd fallen asleep on the chaise lounge wearing the toga. He glanced at his watch. Six-thirty A.M.

Where was Sofia? Erotic thoughts of the sultry Latin beauty helped him shake off the remaining sleepiness. Last night, every time he'd gazed into her exotic dark eyes he had burned with a primitive need to make love to her. He had wanted to bare her delectable curves and kiss her naked flesh in the moonlight, to make love to her until she was clinging to him, writhing against his body in ecstasy.

His hands clenched into frustrated fists. Lately he had felt like a hormone-crazed teenager, lusting after Sofia in a loaded constant state of arousal. He had never been so violently attracted to a woman he'd known for such a short time. How was he going to get through another day playing the gentleman when all he wanted to do was bring her to peak after unbridled peak of excitement until she screamed with the pleasure of her release?

It had been pure torture when she'd fallen asleep beside him. He hadn't even gotten a chance to kiss her sumptuous mouth, to feel the softness of her full lips and savor her delicious taste. Yet he'd been stone hard most of the evening, ready to go off like a rocket. He had held her velvety body in his arms, dangerously close to orgasm, yet unable to slake his lust. His sex stirred and thickened just imagining how her baby-soft skin would feel to his lips. Last night, he'd had to honor her request by simply holding her when his raw frustration grew more volatile by the moment. Like a rigid statue, he'd forced himself to lie there with her sweet-smelling body in his arms, his self-control nearly annihilated.

Sofia had been so sincere and tender in the way she had talked about his dad that James no longer saw her as a gold digger. She was at a vulnerable low point in her life and was probably looking for some sort of security, but it couldn't be with Dad. James no longer worried that she was only after Dad's money. Her wide brown eyes had been so earnest; he'd been hard pressed not to believe her.

It was glaringly obvious that she shouldn't marry Dad. James's original intent had been to seduce her with swift, ruthless purpose, providing the evidence of her moral weakness so Dad would change his mind about her. But after hearing her soul-baring confession about being fired, he had believed every word. A fierce need to protect her from further hurt had blinded him to the initial reason he'd planned to seduce her. Hell, he'd been so incensed over what Dr. Fernandez had done to her that he would have relished beating up the loser.

They had talked volumes about so many subjects and shared so much of their inner selves last night that he felt he knew her well. Sofia must have realized that she had much more in common with him than Dad. It wasn't just the age difference; it was a generation thing. She was young and into experiencing new adventures; Dad had already experienced enough. Dad was a helluva lot more interested in bridge and golf than rock climbing and climbing the Ocho Rios waterfalls. James was damned sure about it!

He stretched, amazed at how revived he felt after sleeping on the plastic chair. Normally he was a bit of an insomniac, and he didn't usually sleep more than four or five hours at night. He couldn't believe how deep his slumber had been once he'd finally fallen asleep. It must have been the hypnotic effect of holding Sofia's warm, luscious body in his arms. *Intoxicating.*

Prompted by a rampant need to drive some sense into

her thick little skull, he rose from the chair. With decisive intent, he hurried inside to get to his room quickly, before the other passengers saw him dressed in the toga. Once he showered, he would look for Sofia on the deck during her morning jog and they would have that talk.

When he got off the elevator on his floor, a steward intercepted him.

"Excuse me, Mr. Connor," the smiling young man said.

"Yes," James replied, noting that the steward seemed amused that he was still dressed in the ridiculous toga.

"The flowers you ordered for your wedding have already been set up in the captain's quarters."

"Did you just say wed—" James stopped himself just in time. "Ah, yes. The wedding flowers," he said, recovering immediately. "Very good. What time will the ceremony be? The captain said he'd confirm it to me today."

"Four o'clock this afternoon," the steward replied, giving James an odd look.

"Yes, that's what he mentioned. Thanks." James hurried toward his cabin before the steward realized he'd given the wrong Mr. Connor a choice bit of information.

There was only one thing James could do now if he ever hoped to hold his head up. He had to come clean with Dad and confess his feelings for Sofia. He couldn't live with himself knowing that every time he looked at his father's new bride, he'd be lusting after her. It wasn't just her lush body he coveted; it was all of her. He loved her honesty and kindness, her big heart and toughness of spirit, the way her dark, luminous eyes twinkled with mischief, and the way her radiant smile illuminated her lively face. He was drawn to her uninhibited dancing and how she relished experiencing new adventures. All of this had shone through last night when she had dropped her defenses and shared her innermost feelings.

James had never admitted to anyone just how much he regretted the fact that he would never have children. Yet he'd shared this weakness with Sofia and she had simply gazed at him with a haunted look in those big brown eyes.

Her eyes had turned sad as she'd held his cheek with her soft hand and assured him that not all marriages ended in divorce.

Surely she wasn't planning on a family with a seventy-year-old man. The thought was disturbing. It wouldn't be fair to a baby to have a father who was a senior citizen. Didn't she realize that by agreeing to marry Dad she had denied herself the joy of having children? And, damn it, hadn't she told him that she *adored* babies? The only baby James wanted her to have was his. *Period.*

In a stunning revelation, he realized that he wouldn't breathe a calm breath until he made Sofia his woman, and that meant only one thing. God, the staggering realization nearly sent him to his knees! Not once in his thirty years had he been tempted by the thought of marriage. But now all he could think about was not letting Sofia slip through his fingers. His need for her was so pressing, so violent, that he wouldn't rest until he made her his wife. He had to find her and tell her before it was too late.

But first he had to go to Dad and put his heart on the line. He had originally set out to seduce Sofia, but instead, he'd fallen in love. He'd have to confess all of it to Dad, then ask for his forgiveness. He could only pray that one day his father would find it in his heart to understand and forgive him. The thought of hurting Dad made James feel like the worst heel on earth and he would have done *anything* in his power to avoid it, but there was no other way.

Deep in his gut, James knew what he had to do. He only hoped he could stop Dad and Sofia before they made a huge mistake.

CHAPTER 7

Seated in a chair in Daniel's cabin, Sofia faced the dear couple with sad news. "I can't go on living this lie. I have to own up to the truth with James. I'm so sorry."

"We know it's been hard on you, Sofia," Daniel said with gruff fondness. "But it will be over very soon."

"I never intended for this to happen, but it was beyond my power." Sofia's voice rose in anguish. "Don't you see that I've fallen in love with your son?"

Daniel squeezed her hand. "Yes, and I couldn't be more delighted. I think that James feels the same way about you."

Sofia's stomach twisted. "He won't when he finds out the truth. If I don't go to him right away and confess, he'll never forgive me."

"Of course he will, dear. James is a lawyer; he'll listen to your explanations before making judgments." Daniel smiled. "Besides, this is a good thing for him. It leaves you available for him to pursue."

"I can't help but be worried about his reaction," Sophia fretted.

"Can't you hold off just a little longer, until this afternoon?" Daniel asked.

"*Sí, mijita.* Please wait until the captain marries us," Lucita pleaded. "Then you can tell James the whole truth and we'll be happy to explain that we were behind the scheme all the time."

Sofia shook her head. James's pride would be wounded and he'd never believe another word she said. "He's going to hate me for the deception, the lies . . . He'll feel like I made a fool out of him!" she cried.

"No, I won't!" James boomed, entering the room, to Sofia's profound shock.

"Good God, have you been lurking behind the door,

eavesdropping?" Daniel demanded, his face reddening with outrage.

"These walls are like paper. I heard every word," James said, grinning with unrepentant male arrogance.

In speechless shock, Sofia's mouth dropped open. How could he be cheerful after hearing everything?

"Well, I'll be damned, Dad," James said, shaking his head with amused merriment. "You and Lucita . . . I couldn't be happier."

"I thought you never wanted your father to remarry," Sofia muttered, narrowing her eyes at him with mounting suspicion.

"Yes, but that's because I thought he was going to marry a sweet young thing like you, honey." He nodded at Daniel. "I heartily approve of you marrying Lucita. She's mature and lovely and shares your interests. I can't imagine a woman more suited to be your wife, Dad."

"Well, that's a relief," Tia Lucita chortled, giving James's hand an affectionate squeeze. "I'm looking forward to being your father's wife."

James chuckled wryly when he next spoke, although he made a deeply disturbing confession. "It looks like we were operating on our own agendas independently." Sofia heard a low rumble of mirth in his chest. He turned to Lucita and smacked his forehead as if he'd just figured something out. "To think I set out to romance your niece just to show Dad that she was all wrong for him! At least Sofia showed me she has an iron core beneath the softness. Much as I tried to tempt her, she didn't allow me to seduce her."

Sofia felt as if James had just given her face an openhanded slap. Feeling vulnerable and terribly exposed, she burned with humiliation. In paralyzed horror, she stared at the three people before her, her pride shattered.

Daniel's face reddened in outrage. Lucita patted Daniel's arm as if to say, "Let them work it out." And James, damn his arrogant hide, grinned at her, entirely too pleased with himself.

"How dare you!" Sofia shrieked at James before dashing out of the room in a frenzy of shame.

James ran after her and caught up with her in a heartbeat. Pulling her against his strong chest, he kissed her long and hard, his mouth crushing hers with unrelenting passion. She struggled to get away from him, but he picked her up and carried her toward his cabin. Flinging the door open, he carried her inside and set her on her feet.

She reached up to slap him, but he caught her hand and turned it over, palm upward. His hot, hungry eyes never left her face as he kissed the center of her sensitive palm, sending a current of lust shooting through her quaking body. "What are you trying to do to me?" she cried, pulling her hand away from his moist, warm lips.

James's firm mouth softened sensually and she watched the savage passion in his eyes become tempered with a look of tenderness. "I'm showing you how much I love you, Sofia. Give me a chance."

"You're hateful!" How could he stand there and profess to love her when he had just confessed his hidden agenda in front of his dad and Tia Lucita? "You're no better than my ex-boyfriend Manny who cheated on me, then tried to force me into forgiving him."

"I'm nothing like your ex-boyfriend and I'd never cheat on you, Sofia. I love you," he repeated, this time more forcefully.

She put her hands over her ears in a futile gesture of denial. "You only say that because I was the forbidden object of your desire, something unattainable . . . a challenge. Well, now you know the truth about Lucita and Daniel, so you don't have to seduce me to prove what a money-grabbing floozy I am!" She grabbed the door handle and twisted it. "I'm leaving. I never want to see you again!"

"Stop it," he ordered quietly, removing her hand from the handle. With firm gentleness he held it prisoner in his strong grip. "Hear me out."

Her mind told her to walk out on him and show him just how despicable she thought he was, but her heart won out. Deep inside she wanted to give him a chance to redeem himself so she could resume respecting him as much as she had before he revealed his cruel motives for seduction.

She tugged at her hand, but he wouldn't let go. Fuming, she looked at her watch. "You have five minutes to convince me that you're not the lowest rat on earth," she said, thrusting her chin out in a deliberate challenge.

Not taking his eyes from hers, he clasped her other hand and joined it with the one in his hands. His eyes turned the bluest shade she'd seen, their depths so filled with longing that she was almost moved to tears.

"I want to marry you." It was said simply, implacably, as if he'd wanted it all his life.

"Marry you?" Sofia froze before him, her body rigid with disbelief. This coming from a cynical man who disdained marriage, a man who would do anything to stop his father from committing the mistake of getting wed! She collected her wits and pulled her hands out of his grasp. "I'd sooner marry a skunk; at least his stripe would warn me of the stink."

"Sofia," he warned, his tone deepening with impatience. "You forget that the three of you have been playing me for a fool this past week. I should be furious with you."

She felt her heart thud against her chest with a loud thump. "I know." She lowered her gaze to the floor, to hide the nagging guilt that plagued her.

He tilted her chin up and met her gaze evenly as his sharp tone gentled to a tantalizing drawl. "But guess what, honey? I don't really give a damn in this instance. I've already forgiven you."

"You have?" She had been so busy being incensed that she hadn't stopped to realize that James would feel betrayed, too. At the very least, she owed it to him to listen.

"I realize that my callous admission hurt your feelings.

It was damned stupid of me to say it in front of your aunt and Dad. I never meant to hurt you. But I blurted it out because I was so relieved that you weren't marrying Dad and that I wasn't going to betray him by going after you."

She could already feel herself caving into his sincere blue eyes, but she needed a better understanding. "You're a lawyer. I can hardly believe that you just blurted something out that wasn't true."

He put his hands on her shoulders and held her anchored with his gaze. "I never say anything without deliberation in the courtroom. But this is different. Unfortunately, what I said *was* true and I'm ashamed I ever thought of using you that way. Last night I desperately wanted to make love to you, but not because I wanted to expose your base nature to Dad. By then I was torn up inside with wanting you because you revealed a beautiful side of yourself. I love your big heart, Sofia, and your tender soul."

Tears welled up in her eyes as she stared at him, her heart swelling with love.

"I lose control around you. Hell, I'm turned inside out right now just trying to tell you how much I need you." His earnest blue eyes searched her face as his hands tightened on her shoulders. "I can't live without you, Sofia."

In helpless surrender, she swallowed against a lump in her throat. "Really?"

"Yes, damn it," he growled. He pulled her against him, his large hands holding her buttocks as he pressed her against his swollen erection. "Look what you do to me. I'm about to burst. I'm on fire. God, I've never felt this crazy for any woman. Ever!"

He kissed her thoroughly, nibbling her lips, rubbing his tongue against hers with a carnal hunger that made her legs buckle and her body hum with pleasure. She slumped against him and held his shoulders for support as he raised the back of her dress and slid his hands into her panties. He palmed her bottom where her buttocks met her thighs, then maddeningly parted her feminine folds and stroked the delicate pearl within. She moistened against his fingers until she was moaning, begging for release with soft, plaintive cries.

Cupping her cheeks in his hands, he lifted her off the floor as his fingers played havoc with her, mercilessly teasing her tender flesh. Just when she thought she would climax against his hands, he set her on the edge of the bed and tore off his clothes.

With breathless anticipation, she watched him walk toward her in naked splendor, his muscular body tanned and fully erect. In seconds he joined her on the bed, flinging the covers aside before he pulled off her dress, panties, and bra. Gathering her full breasts in his hands, he reverently kissed each one, then took the sensitive tips into his mouth, feasting on them until they pebbled and she thought she'd go mad.

"Oh, that's too exquisite!" she cried.

He kissed her belly and alternated warm, damp kisses with gentle love bites along her thighs. His fingers stroked her pulsating wetness until the mounting sensations became excruciatingly pleasurable and her pelvis crashed against his relentless hand, lifting higher with each caress. Thrashing her head from side to side, she cried out, her primed body convulsing in the throes of a shuddering climax.

"Oh," she moaned, her womb contracting with tiny pulses.

"Easy, honey." James pushed her damp hair away from her face and kissed her brow. "You're so gorgeous," he murmured hoarsely, soothing her quivering body with slow, lingering strokes, bringing her to a new level of arousal as his hot breath tickled her ear with earthy descriptions of how he intended to please her.

His ardent mouth covered hers, rubbing his tongue across her lips, then sliding inside with an in-and-out motion that promised erotic delights. He nibbled her earlobes and gave her luscious little love bites along her neck as he cupped her breasts and gently tweaked her tender nipples. A flood of pleasure washed over her again. She bent her head and kissed his flat nipple before laving it with her tongue. She moved over to kiss the other one as her hands slid down to caress him.

His jaw clenched in his passion-darkened face. "Don't," he muttered through his teeth, his voice clogged. "I won't be able to hold back."

"Then come inside me," she urged, her breaths coming fast and shallow, her blood rushing through her veins like flames of fire.

James covered her trembling form with his large body, bracing his weight on his elbows as he loomed above her, strong and fierce. She felt the engorged tip of his erection nudge her soft cleft as she parted her thighs to receive him.

He held her face and kissed her again. "Do you want me?" he taunted, the veins on his neck corded with the sheer effort of holding back.

"More than you'll ever know," she said, meeting his hot gaze hungrily.

"Will you marry me?" he demanded, his gruff voice low and urgent as he slid his hands under her buttocks and lifted her pelvis, penetrating her damp sheath with maddening slowness.

Arching into his thrust, she gasped, "Yes, yes, I'll marry you. Oh!" she cried, when the last inch of him was deeply embedded inside her. He drove in repeatedly, slowly at first, with a thoroughness that sent her spiraling higher and higher. Her sex pulsed and tightened around him each time he plunged inside, pulling him closer to her throbbing ache. Delicious, unbearable, too intense . . . too *exquisite*. Straining toward release, she hovered on the brink, her body desperately arcing to meet each thrust. When she thought she couldn't take any more, James drove harder and deeper until she lost it, bucking wildly beneath his solid weight, her nails digging into his wide shoulders. She screamed in release, her body shuddering violently beneath his.

He came with savage abandon, his body slick with sweat, his groaning release loud and harsh. She reveled in the sound of his thundering shout. Her heart brimmed with so much love she couldn't contain it.

James rolled over, bringing her with him until her limp body lay sprawled on top of him. He pressed a kiss on her temple. Boneless and breathless, Sofia rested her cheek against his chest and listened to his strong, beating heart. Sighing, she felt deliciously depleted of energy as his hands gentled her body, stroking the length of her spine while murmuring hot endearments. Moments later, his actions stilled and he rested his hands possessively on the curve of her buttocks.

Lifting up on her elbows, she cradled her chin in her hands and gave him a saucy smile. "Still want to marry me, counselor?"

He chuckled and patted her bottom. "You bet. You're not getting away from me again, honey."

She blushed and didn't say a word, too taken by the determined look in his sexy blue eyes.

"I think we should make it a double wedding this afternoon, if Lucita and Dad don't mind. What do you think?"

"I think I love you, James Connor."

"Good," he said, his arms tightening around her.

After a few moments, she moved to cuddle beside him, but his strong hands held her in place. "Stay where you are. Let me savor holding you like this. Soon we'll be married, but I want to remember this moment for the rest of my life."

"Our lovemaking?"

He chuckled and squeezed her. "Not only that, honey, but hearing you say that you love me. I've been to hell and back, yearning for you, despairing that I wouldn't be able to stop your wedding with Dad in time. I feel as if my life has only just begun."

"Mine, too, darling," she said, pressing a kiss on his gorgeous mouth. "From the moment I met you I was lured to you, even when you were fighting me on behalf of your dad. While you were trying to get me out of his life, I was attracted to you beyond my control. Then when you kissed me I went over the edge with needing you, needing more. Your passion thrilled me and scared me at the same time. That's why I avoided you."

"Don't worry, honey. We have a lifetime for loving."

"About that child you mentioned you wanted . . . I think we might have started something already," she said, giggling with delight.

His mouth widened into a potently male, very satiated grin as he hugged her. "Good thing you've agreed to be *my* Mrs. Connor."

"Not yet," she said with a dreamy smile. "But very soon, Mr. Connor. Very soon."